"If you are looking for an exciting romp through space then you came to the right book!"

— Robert Bose, Author

"I've taught literature at several colleges over the last 35 years, and this read is a harbinger of great adventures to come."

— Dr. J.P. Waller, former editor for Vice-President Al Gore

"Take a trip outside our universe with Jack Castle's Europa Journal"

— M. Bonds, CDA Press

This book was the first book in years that I couldn't put down. The gripping story of the characters and the way Jack Castle skillfully weaves between past and present creates a spider web of intrigue and suspense leaving the reader wanting more. I couldn't put this book down. I fell asleep in mid sentence because I didn't want to stop but still needed sleep. Needless to say, when I woke up I pick right back up. I am on my third time reading this book and the more I read, the more I become part of the world that lies within the pages of Europa Journal

— Ryan Chidester, Award winning Actor

EUROPA
JOURNAL
JACK CASTLE

EDGE-Lite

An Imprint of HADES PUBLICATIONS, INC.

CALGARY

Europa Journal

Copyright © 2015 by Chris Tortora

EDGE-Lite

An Imprint of HADES PUBLICATIONS, INC.
P.O. Box 1714, Calgary, Alberta, T2P 2L7, Canada

The EDGE-Lite Team:
Producer: Brian Hades
Editor: Ella Beaumont
Cover Artist: Enrico Agostoni
Cover Design: Janice Blaine
Book Design: Mark Steele
Publicist: Janice Shoults

ISBN: 978-1-77053-104-8

EDGE Science Fiction and Fantasy Publishing and Hades Publications, Inc. acknowledges the ongoing support of the Alberta Foundation for the Arts and the Canada Council for the Arts for our publishing programme.

Library and Archives Canada Cataloguing in Publication
CIP Data on file with the National Library of Canada
ISBN: 978-1-77053-104-8
(e-Book ISBN: 978-1-77053-091-1)

FIRST EDITION
(20150919)
Printed in USA
www.edgewebsite.com

Dedications

Dedicated To Those Who Kept the Dream Alive...

My wife, muse, and soul mate, Tracy Tortora
My first and biggest fan, (and best friend), Chad Bryant
My mentor who helped me hone my craft, Dr. J.P. Waller
My other best friend, Greg Wahlman
My sister, Margie, who typed up my very first script
Our Lord and Savior

I would also like to acknowledge these folks for transporting Europa Journal from my nightstand drawer to your fingertips. Ella Beaumont, editor supreme and literary archeologist who unearthed my novel from her gargantuan slush pile. Photographer Jordan Carter, Janice Shoults for all her marketing and promotional efforts, Janice Blaine for cover design elements, Mark Steele for his book and eBook designs and of course, Mr. Brian Hades, the Mad Hatter in charge, who allowed all of this insanity to happen.

"Those who from heaven to earth came eventually tired of their toils, so they created a primitive worker."

— Sumerian tablet, *c.* 2000 B.C.

"Faith is the substance of things hoped for, the evidence of things not seen."

— Hebrews 11:1

Prologue

On 5 December 1945, five TBM Avenger bombers embarked on a training mission off the coast of Florida and mysteriously vanished without a trace in the Bermuda Triangle.

A PBY search and rescue plane with thirteen crewmen aboard set out to find the Avengers ... and never returned.

Chapter 1

Final Descent

TWINKLING STARS PINPRICKED the stark lavender sky and watched like spectators as one of their own arced gracefully across the darkening hemisphere and fell from the heavens.

The U.C.P. deep space transport plummeted from the upper atmosphere on its own decaying path; it slowly and delicately began to glow, its color changing from off-white to rich gold. The glorious blaze expanded into a burning sphere that resembled a shooting star.

Flames and sparks trailed from every engine and wing. Heat-shielding plates flew off the underbelly by the dozens as the space transport began breaking up, a thousand-mile-long jet stream of clouds and debris in its wake. The nosecone began to crumple under the onslaught of the burning winds. Unbelievably, the occupants in the cockpit still fought for their survival.

—— o ——

"MWAAP … MWAAP … MWAAP … Crashing! Crashing! Switch to manual!" the crash program's computer voice announced. After a moment's pause, it repeated the warning, as if the shuddering cockpit, bleating Klaxon, and flames shooting past the forward windshield weren't enough.

"Really, no kidding," Mission Commander MacKenzie O'Bryant, 'Mac' for short, replied to no one in particular. Behind the navigation console, she struggled to keep the quivering *Explorer II* from nosing over and pinning her crew beneath the flaming wreckage.

Out of the corner of her eye, Mac saw the young pilot on her right examining the gauges that screamed for his attention, 'Lt. L. Dalton' stenciled over the right breast pocket of his uniform, a Canadian flag patch sewn onto the left shoulder. His expression betrayed his growing disgust as highly unacceptable readings came back on the console before him. "Vertical descent — one hundred and twenty-five thousand. No, wait: one hundred and sixty-five thousand — no, twenty-four thousand."

"Which is it, Leo? Twenty or sixty?" Mac asked. *It was a pretty big difference.* Mac wore an American flag on the shoulder of her jumpsuit, as if her Southern accent itself weren't indicative of her roots.

While she waited the few seconds, which seemed like hours, for Leo's reply, Mac cast a quick glance on the monitor displaying their three payload passengers, who were located one deck below.

Not much to her surprise, the three battle-hardened commandos' stolid faces were the epitome of calm. Sure, as their bodies were crushed by g-forces, their fists were clenched to their seats, and their eyes fluttered and rolled back in their heads, but if they had any idea how bad the situation was, as she suspected they did, they should have been screaming. These men were professionals, the best of the best; they knew that they could do nothing to help, so they resigned themselves to their fate and placed their lives in her hands.

Mac wasn't about to let them down.

"I don't know. It keeps jumping back and forth between the two; I can't get a proper altitude reading. First it's in the twenties and then the sixties," Leo replied. Banging on the side of the console, he added, "Wait a minute. There it goes: one hundred and twenty thousand."

But Mac didn't need an altitude reading to know that the ground was coming up much too fast. Passing through the atmosphere the ship had been engulfed in flames, blocking their view, but now that they had finished dropping through a thin layer of clouds, she saw a landmass, one that looked like a big island or a small continent. It came into view a mere 100,000 feet below them.

Mac frowned at her monitor, touched a button, and pulled back on the control column with even more fervor. If she didn't get the nose up, the ship would go into a spin, and if that happened at this speed, they would be finished.

Displayed on a monitor was a visual image of a Korean man sitting at the flight engineer's station. He announced, "Number two and four anti-gravity generators are still off line." To Leo, he added, "I told you. I told you not to touch it, but you wouldn't listen." Mocking Leo's voice, he said, "Why, what's the worst that could happen?" In his own voice, nearly hysterical, he replied, "Well, we found out didn't we?"

Mac wasn't quite sure what had led up to this latest predicament, but it was pretty clear that her flight engineer felt Leo was somehow responsible.

"Hey," Leo shot back, "I didn't see you doing anything to help."

"Give me an EC pressure reading," Mac shouted to the flight engineer, cutting their argument short.

"EC's in the pike, five-by-five," Tae called forward. It was the first good news she'd heard in the last six minutes.

Of course, Commander O'Bryant had trained for landing a ship after engines failed following shuttle launch. She had even trained to land a malfunctioning transport in Jupiter's infamous gravity well. But no training simulation in the known galaxy could have prepared her for landing a crippled space shuttle on a planet that had never been seen before by human eyes. Deep space travel was a breeze; it was atmospheric landings that caused the majority of shuttle pilot fatalities. As if the situation weren't bad enough, the *Explorer II* hadn't been designed to land under Earth-type gravity conditions.

Still miles above the planet, Mac saw a panorama of mountains coming into view below them. The range of white, snowy peaks was cast in pitch-black shadows and graced by a glint of the departing sun. In a way, it was kind of pretty. *A nice little spot for their final resting place.* No, she couldn't think like that. She had to remain focused, stay positive.

"I have a visual line of sight," Leo announced.

"I can see that," Mac spat back, her tone tense. She didn't dare look away from the landmass filling the cockpit windows, as if her will to keep the vessel aloft might waver the moment she looked away.

"Correct course ten degrees up, four minutes right," Leo offered, monitoring the gauges.

Mac complied with his directions and was rewarded with a reduction in the maelstrom of bouncing winds and heavily quivering bulkhead. The ship, her ship, was finally beginning to ease.

"There, that's a bit better. Try and hold it there if you can," Leo added.

Impossibly, she and her flight crew were pulling it off. She felt her descending ship finally leveling out. There was actually a chance they were going to make it. Barring an extraterrestrial downdraft or some other unpredictable off-world catastrophe, by God, if there was an Order to the universe, they were going to make it.

But just then, the opposite balance of the universe, the part that some call Chaos, dealt his nasty hand. A panel of circuitry in the molded helm console before Mac sparked several times in quick succession and exploded, enveloping her hands and face in a blazing inferno.

—— o ——

"Oh, geez!" Lt. Leo Dalton didn't miss a beat and grasped his own set of controls the moment the panel erupted in his mission commander's face. He risked a glimpse at her. She was slumped in her harness, burn marks on her cheeks and hands. He was unsure whether she was dead or unconscious, but one thing was for sure: it was up to him to land the spacecraft and up to him alone. *Oh yeah, and Tae.*

The ship suddenly jumped upward, as though in a reverse air pocket, and then resumed its hair-raising descent.

"Did a thruster just fall off?" Leo asked incredulously.

"Yup," Tae replied matter-of-factly. "That's okay. That one wasn't working anyway."

"I'm losing hydraulics," Leo yelled back over his shoulder. He saw a yellow tongue of flame burst from the avionics bay and light up the nosecone like the end of a sparkler on Canada Day.

"That's because everything is on fire," Tae shouted up to him. "That last explosion knocked out another one of the anti-gravity generators."

"Well, put the fires out," Leo ordered through clenched teeth.

Tae flicked a switch and the WHOOSH of the interior cabin fire extinguishers, which were embedded in the fuselage, doused everything and everyone in thick chemical foam.

"Fires' out," Tae said dryly.

No hydraulic system meant no flaps and no brakes, but Leo doubted the ship would hold together long enough to reach the surface, let alone land in a manner that required brakes. *One problem at a time, Leo, one problem at a time.*

"Aww, geez. Terrain's crap," Leo said, but then he spotted a flat, open area just beyond a wide range of mountains. He maneuvered the crippled ship with what little controls he still had and aimed for the large plateau. "I'm going to try and spiral us in as best I can toward that mesa."

The ship entered its final approach and Leo guided the *Explorer II* through a crest of mountains, fighting crosswinds and protesting gusts the entire way. Only a miracle prevented a rock wall from ending their glide path in an abrupt and squishy stop.

Sixty seconds before impact, Leo and Tae could just make out trees peppering the snow-coated peaks.

Ten seconds before impact, the trees and mountains parted like the Red Sea before Moses and revealed the large, flat mesa that Leo had seen from over a mile away.

"Flat land, five degrees right!" Tae shouted.

"I see it; I see it," Leo replied grimly. He was so focused on coaxing the helm controls and maneuvering the falling ship in a do-or-die, wheels-up approach that his voice was nearly inaudible.

The last of the trees vanished, and the snow-covered mesa quickly rose up in greeting. "Wheels unresponsive. I'm going to have to put her down on her belly."

"Six hundred feet and dropping," Tae announced as he focused on the altimeter. "Five, four, three, two, here we go!" The hull vibrated and there was a deafening crash as the ship's metal frame and the planet's unyielding, jagged surface clapped together in unison: one, two, three times. The windows shattered on impact and blasted the exposed skin of the cockpit's occupants with frigid air and thousands of tiny shards of glass.

The ship settled down in a heavy power slide through the snow. "Deploy shoots!" Leo shouted.

"Deploying emergency drag shoots," Tae replied. The deployment of the quadruple chutes threw both men forward in their harnesses.

Leo strangled the flight controls, feeling helpless as the ship slid for what seemed like an eternity. In actuality, it was little more than a half mile until the *Explorer II* finally came to a clumsy, unceremonious stop.

Aside from the sound of Tae purging the last of the fire extinguishers onto the numerous sparking and burning consoles, the only audible sound was the arctic wind rushing through the broken cockpit windshield. *At least we're on the surface.*

Leo was the first to say anything, and as it was, he meant it only for himself. "I did it." It was all his trembling lips could manage.

He stared blank-faced out the windshield. A pile of snow was gathering around the windows and spilling inside, but he no longer saw mountains or trees, only open sky. *That's strange,* Leo thought. *The ship feels level, so I should see something besides open air.* Before he could investigate further, a slight groan from Commander O'Bryant drew his attention. He leaned over in his chair and felt the mission commander's pulse. It was good and strong. She was a little beat up and had some first-degree burns on her face and hands, but it wasn't anything that bandages and burn cream couldn't fix.

Despite everything they had just been through, Leo's thoughts gave way to fancy. Maybe, just maybe, after the commander found out what a spectacular job he did landing this wounded bird and after they got rescued, maybe, just maybe, she'd finally give him the chance he wanted above all else …

But that was as far as Leo's fantasy went, for Chaos still had an ace up his sleeve, and he decided to play it. Leo's heart rose to his throat as he felt the ship tilt. He watched helplessly as the ruined nosecone of the shuttle slowly teetered forward. The view was both breathtaking and horrific.

It was now clear to Leo that the *Explorer II* had not landed on an entirely stable area. The view of open-air nothingness was slowly replaced by a view of a vast ocean far below: the *Explorer II* balanced on a cliff that had to be at least ten thousand feet high.

That's why we couldn't get a proper reading coming in, Leo thought. *We were reading this plateau and the ocean's surface below it.*

Leo heard the sounds of rock giving way beneath the busted cockpit as the view tipped back to sky. The young lieutenant knew that they didn't have much time. The thrusters and anti-gravity generators were totally stalled. If the ship were to fall now, they'd never survive. From this height, the watery surface might just as well have been concrete.

"Tae, you back there?" Leo whispered into the intercom while holding perfectly still, as if his mere one-hundred-and-eighty-pound frame might keep the enormous transport ship from slipping the rest of the way over the ledge.

"Yeah, but why are you whispering?" Tae's voice came back over the cockpit speakers. Leo could hear the commandos in the payload area speaking amongst themselves near the engineer, congratulating themselves on being alive.

"Tae, listen to me. I need you to get the anti-gravity generators back on line. Do you hear me? I need everything you can give me in as little amount of time as possible."

"Why? What's going on?" Tae asked. The revelry in his voice turned to concern.

"Just do it, Tae," Leo said harshly. The nosecone teetered once more toward the ocean.

"Are we moving? Maybe we should abandon ship."

"Trust me; there's no time." Leo shook his head, biting his lip. With as much calm as he could muster, he said, "Tae, listen to me. If you don't get those A.G. generators back on line, we … are going … to die."

"Okay, okay, just give me about ten seconds."

But they didn't have ten seconds. With Leo shouting, "no, no, no," the shuttle teetered on the edge, and then, gaining momentum, slipped from the rock face and plunged into the gaping void.

Chapter 2

The Bort Report

48 **HOURS PRIOR**

—— o ——

EXPLORER II, **UNITED COALITION OF PLANETS
SPACECRAFT
PRESENTLY IN ORBIT OF EUROPA MOON
MISSION DATE: AUG. 15, 2168**

—— o ——

I don't know; it still looks like a dirty cue ball to me, Commander 'Mac' O'Bryant thought. She glanced at Jupiter's smallest moon, which spun lazily outside the cockpit windows, and focused on the brownish-orange blot that marked the moon's relatively crater-free covering of solid ice.

Mac slipped her slender frame behind the navigation console and began her morning ritual. As she sipped a cup of 'mud' — coffee so thick that it held the little wooden stirring stick upright — she looked over the various readouts that monitored every integral component of the ship. At present, she examined navigational readouts that confirmed what she already knew: the deep space cargo transport *Explorer II* was in a perfect geo-synchronized orbit of Jupiter's moon Europa.

Mac knew that Jupiter's smallest moon, which was only slightly smaller than Earth's moon, was one of four satellites discovered by Galileo in 1610. First, scientists had thought vast oceans covered Europa; next, they had thought it was covered by ice. In reality, the small moon turned out to be a little of both: an ice planet with pockets of water. Gravitational tides from the other three Galilean satellites heated Europa's interior, enabling it to support an ocean. The ocean's thermal vents, in turn, supported life — not mere microbes or tiny fish, but orca-sized creatures. The discovery of life thriving in Europa's dark ocean had resulted in everything from plushy toys to speculations of human-level intelligence just waiting to make contact and people, especially members of the press, couldn't get enough.

The lucrative toy market wasn't the only reason for the space program's keen interest in Jupiter's littlest moon — no, not by a long shot. According to Mac's sources in the field of xeno-archeology, the space program hadn't really kicked into overdrive on Europa until orbiting satellites had captured thermal images of what appeared to be a five-sided pyramid resting on the moon's ocean floor. After this discovery, it had taken the space agency less than five decades to get a base set up on the icy surface, drill through the 10 kilometers of ice, and build an undersea base conveniently near the pyramid. Of course, the government had never told the public about the pyramid, and this information remained highly classified.

The surface base had become a budding colony that rivaled those on the moons of Mars and Saturn. Naturally, construction workers and scientists had been the first to arrive, but it wasn't long before their families followed. The last time Mac had visited the Jupiter moon, it had boasted a population of nearly one thousand.

Thanks to the invention of the Powell fusion drive, her current voyage to Jupiter's Europa moon base had taken only six months, as opposed to six years.

Commander O'Bryant blew a practiced cooling breath on her cup of 'mud' before taking a tentative sip. She relished every caffeine-stimulated neuron, particularly as she had recently cut back from six cups a day to one. It had been tough at first, but she had kept that resolution ever since space dock. It was just part of her makeup; when she decided to do something, she did it, and that was that.

Nearby, loud music in the form of an epic battle soundtrack, emanated from the muffled earphones of a virtual-reality helmet worn by a young officer sitting to her right in the pilot's station. Lieutenant Leo Dalton was playing his full-emersion video games again. Normally, the VR helmets were reserved for training-module simulations, but the young pilot had rigged it to play video games instead.

Boys will be boys, Mac thought as she watched his head bob and weave to the music. *And this is the guy who wants to marry my daughter.*

The thought of her only offspring back on Earth made Mac's heart ache. Emma O'Bryant had followed in her mom's footsteps after college and had recently made first classman at the U.S. Space Academy. Just like Mom, Emma was top of her class.

Emma had met Leo when he was training under Mac's supervision for the Europa missions. A year-and-a-half later, he had proposed. According to both sides, it had been love at first sight. Initially, Mac had disapproved of the cocky young man, who was five years older than her daughter and whose reputation as a 'player' had preceded him. Not only that, Mac hadn't wanted Emma to go through the heartbreak of having a doomed long-distance relationship with a deep-space shuttle pilot — the kind of relationship Emma's father and Mac had had. But over time, Leo's charms had whittled away at Mac's trepidation. More importantly, the young man treated her daughter like a queen, which was far more than her spunky, stubborn, thickheaded (yet brilliant) offspring deserved. She was a regular chip off the old block.

Of course, their engagement had to be kept secret. The reasons were twofold: first, it was forbidden for anyone in the space program to date an underclassman, and second, she didn't want Leo to lose his spot in the Europa transport rotation.

But Leo hadn't received the highly coveted pilot position just because he was dating her daughter. He was a gifted pilot, just short of brilliant. Most importantly, Mac knew that he wouldn't drive her crazy, even if they were cooped up together in a tin-can-like shuttle transport for sixth months. Nonetheless, he got no special treatment from her. If anything, she was even harder on him than on the others.

"Leo," Mac said, trying to gain his attention. Officially, she disapproved of him playing his games while on duty, but she knew that he had rigged all of the ship's sensors to alert him the moment anything was even the slightest bit out of sync. Realistically, she knew that there was little for either of them to do on such a long journey, and she'd rather have him alert and occupied then asleep at the wheel. By their own admission, the two international space agency pilots considered themselves little more than glorified truck drivers.

"Leo," she said, louder this time. Still no response. Judging by the way his head was bobbing up and down and side-to-side, he was deeply involved in some sort of deadly virtual combat.

"Leo!" She gave him a swift kick with the ball of her deck shoe. Although it was her third deep space mission to Europa, it was only Leo's first. Even so, they had long ago dropped official pleasantries between them, at least when they weren't in front of any ground crew. If they were, then it was back to the commander-and-lieutenant relationship.

"Damn it!" Leo reached up, pressed the pause button, and quickly removed his helmet and gloves. Pushing a hand through his spiked, dirty-blondish hair, he said, "Ah, good morning, Commander." He attempted to hide his frustration with his patented shark-eating smile. "You do realize that you just cost me the Mars Colony all-time high score on *Gateway Chronicles?*"

Simply put, Leo was a twelve-year-old boy in a good-looking twenty-six-year-old's body with a genius I.Q., especially where computers were concerned.

She could see why her daughter had been won by the young buck from Canada, but Mac considered herself an old romantic and preferred a man's man — the kind of guy who could build the frickin' Swiss Family Robinson tree house, with a two-car garage and Jacuzzi out back, after being dropped in the woods with only a pocketknife.

"Time to pack it in and let the skipper take a turn at the wheel."

"Aw, Mom," he said and again flashed the charismatic grin that had won her daughter's heart.

"Call me 'Mom' one more time, and you'll find yourself floating the rest of the way to Europa," she warned. In truth, at 38, she only had him by thirteen years.

"Well, yeah, but ..." Leo trailed off as he suddenly got lost in the hypnotic visage of Jupiter's moon, which spun slowly below them. "It's beautiful."

"You mean the dirty cue ball?" Mac asked. When he didn't laugh at the appropriate time, she explained, "It looks like a giant mud-splattered cue ball to me."

"Yeah," Leo breathed, his eyes still glued to the window, "I can't believe you got to see this three times."

"Yep. I must be the luckiest girl alive," she retorted, purposely thickening her South Carolina drawl. Although she did not find it difficult to beat down Leo's enthusiasm, she could hardly blame him. This was Leo's first run, and he still had the 'pixie dust' sprinkled all over him. It was Mac's third, and to her, it was just another milk run that brought her one step closer to a space station command, a command that would enable Mac and her daughter to live together on base. The best of both worlds. Mac hoped they would be able to get back some of the time they had lost during her career with the space agency. That was her goal, and she was focused on it. Everything else was just minor details.

Her tone grew serious. "Got anything to pass on to the day shift, Lieutenant?"

Leo got the hint and concentrated on the official business at hand. "Not really. The right stabilizer for the internal dampener went 0.005% out of phase variance for about six minutes last night, but by the time I went to wake up Tae, he was already there. I swear that guy is wired right into the internal sensors."

Mac smiled at the thought of the third and final member of their intrepid crew, Tae Yung, a Korean tech-head, who, it seemed, would rather spend time with the *Explorer II*'s fusion engines and his scientific journals than with the ship's crew. He mostly kept to himself; so much so, it often seemed as if he'd found some way off the ship. When Mac did happen to stumble across Tae (and, in one case, Mac had nearly broken her neck doing so), he was usually buried in some technical schematic of just about everything and anything: the *Explorer II*'s fusion drive; the orbiting space stations around Europa, Saturn, or Mars; or the findings of the latest deep-space probes.

Originally, they had started off with thirteen additional passengers who were rotating out to the icy moon, but just before launch, the passengers were pulled off to make room in the payload area for two soilmovers that were needed on Europa.

"Other than that, you got a package," Leo said.

"Who's it from?" Her eyebrows perked up and betrayed her excitement. She wasn't expecting any mail. Only her daughter wrote her anymore, and she had just received a letter from her two days ago.

"Dunno. It was marked for your eyes only."

Mac cocked an eyebrow at her future son-in-law as if to say, "Who are you trying to kid?" They had been together long enough for her to know that he had already hacked into her mail.

"No, really," Leo replied. He tried to look hurt, failed miserably, and accepted defeat. "It's encoded and a damn hard one to crack at that."

Mac knew Leo prided himself on his hacking skills. His pride wasn't exactly unfounded, either. In addition to being one of NASA's best pilots, he was one of the best computer engineers NASA had to offer.

Leo sighed and then admitted, "I did manage to break all the barriers but one, and you'll need your password for that. A 'Dr. Bort' wrote that you would know what it is."

Intrigued, Mac glanced down at the blinking file with her name on it.

Leo got up and stood over her, waiting impatiently for her to open the file. She realized that the unbreakable encoding must have been a real bur under his saddle, bugging him all night long.

"Do you mind?" she chided.

Ignoring her, Leo asked, "Well, aren't you going to read it?"

"Not just yet," she replied, reveling in his annoyance. It was a little game they often played. She was usually the winner. No, she was always the winner. After all, rank had its privileges.

"Fine," he said as he grabbed his jacket off the back of the co-pilot's seat. "I'm gonna go grab a shower before final descent."

He exited the cockpit with feigned annoyance but returned seconds later to retrieve his game gear from the helm console. Mac suspected that this was merely a second ploy to gain access to the encoded document. After seeing that she still hadn't opened the file, he shot her another pouty look, grabbed his gear, and disappeared in a huff.

Mac did a quick mental tally of the score: Mac 671, Leo 0.

Normally, she would never tend to personal matters while on duty. However, her friend's communiqué was marked 'urgent', and this ship, her ship, had already cost her a marriage and nearly eighteen years with her daughter. After three two-year tours as a pilot, she had finally made mission commander. She had earned the right to indulge herself and take the time to read a letter from an old friend. Damn, she really needed another cup of 'mud'. She started reading the communiqué instead.

She typed in the correct user name and then her password, 'Emma-1'. A letter, complete with enclosed photos, flashed onto the screen.

Mac soon realized that the history of humanity was about to be changed forever.

—— o ——

***** TRANSMISSION SECURED *****
Dr. Joan Bort
Alpha Base Headquarters
Europa Moon
c/o Jupiter Station
Commander MacKenzie O'Bryant
Europa Moon Convoy
Band 24-1706
Earth Date: August 15, 2168
SUBJECT: Europa Moon Underwater Pyramid Site

—— o ——

Mac,

I can't contain my excitement any longer. If only you could have been here for the opening of Europa's underwater pyramid!

At the time of your last visit to Europa Moon Base Alpha on the moon's surface, engineers had nearly finished constructing Europa Moon Base Beta on the ocean floor near the five-sided pyramid.

*After the completion of the underwater base and
    the subsequent tunnel leading to the pyramid,
    and after months of trying to find a way into the
    structure, my survey team and I finally entered
    the pyramid. When my hands broke through the
    outer wall, I felt like my childhood idol, Howard
    Carter, on that eventful day in 1922 when he
    first broke though the inner chamber of Pharaoh
    Tutankhamen's tomb in the Valley of the Kings. In
    fact, as you will see, there are striking similarities
    between various Egyptian ruins and the Europa
    pyramid.*

*However, upon entering the pyramid, I was more
    amazed at the similarities between it and the
    ruins on Mars. The physical structures, which are
    composed of rough-hewn blocks, and the sandy,
    white flooring are identical. In addition, the same
    peculiar golden symbols appear at both sites. Mac,
    they're the same symbols as the ones on the Mars
    engraving, the ones that were compared to the
    symbol found on the Dead Sea Scrolls!*

*There was always sufficient proof to support the
    hypothesis that there was intelligent life on Mars,
    although it remained to be determined whether
    indigenous life forms or visitors from another solar
    system inhabited the planet. And now this… I
    think we have solid evidence here.*

*But I'm getting sidetracked… The similarities weren't
    the most surprising discovery at the site… I can't
    even begin to describe our astonishment when
    we found a corpse, wearing what appeared to be
    World War II garb, lying beside a deep circular
    pit in the center of the pyramid's inner room (see
    attached photos).*

—— o ——

Mac stopped reading to examine the series of digital pictures.
Her head buzzed with excitement. She and Joan had been
sharing news of archeological finds and debating origin
theories back and forth like a game of chess since Mac had

stumbled into her strange fascination with Martian relics.

Immediately, she was spellbound by a photo depicting the inner chamber of the pyramid, noting the resemblance between the chamber and the Egyptian pyramids on Earth. She looked closely at the pit, which was encircled by several high-powered light stanchions placed by the dozen extraterrestrial archeologists wearing environmental suits.

Her eyes opened wide in astonishment when she saw the next image, a close-up of the human remains lying on the outer rim of the pit's edge. The corpse wore a bomber-style flight jacket adorned with a captain's insignia, and it was surrounded by various military artifacts. Mac used her zoom key and focused on an antiquated army belt and holster that looked like they belonged in a World War II museum. *If this is fake, someone certainly went to a lot of trouble to stage this scene*, she thought.

Mac returned to Dr. Bort's report.

—— o ——

I looked up the name Reed, which was stenciled on the jacket and dog tags worn by the corpse, and after searching our database and crosschecking it with the library computer on Earth, I learned that a Captain Harry Reed piloted a PBY that disappeared in the Bermuda Triangle during a 1945 rescue mission. Reed's plane simply vanished; as did the planes he and his crew had been sent to rescue.

—— o ——

Mac had been holding her breath unwittingly, and she suddenly exhaled in astonishment. Like any good pilot, she was familiar with nearly every form of aircraft ever made. If memory served her correctly, the PBY was the last word in rescue apparatus at the time and could land like a gull in the roughest of seas.

—— o ——

Subsequent DNA testing proved what I already knew in my heart to be true: Captain Harry Reed's body lies in the center of the Europa pyramid. According to records on Earth, at the time of his disappearance, Captain Reed was thirty-one years old and was survived by his wife and two daughters. His military record shows that he flew 25 bombing missions in his PBY over the Pacific during World War II and received the Navy Cross for Outstanding Acts of Heroism.

As incredible as this discovery might sound, the contents of the book beside him are even more amazing.

Base security and the base commander have ordered me to keep all findings top secret and to turn over all data and alien artifacts to the United Planets after they have been catalogued. I don't know how they plan to keep the findings secret, especially when members of the Undersea Base have already visited, photographed, and seen the relics with their own eyes. But I do know that security has become so tight that it will be a miracle if this communiqué reaches you.

I am sending you this information and trusting your secrecy, Mac, because I fear what the future holds, and this information is far too important to be lost or buried. This is it, Mac, what we have suspected for years. All of our suspicions are true, and now we can prove them.

At the time of writing this report, I have only been able to give the book a cursory glance. Initially, it's a pilot's logbook that contains flight plans, dates, and times, but then it turns into a journal that details how Captain Reed and his crew were abducted from the Bermuda Triangle and transported to another world "with no recognizable stars or constellations." The captain even describes some of the alien inhabitants he encountered and the features of an alien planet. I have only begun transcribing the journal, but what follows is a small portion of the entries I have copied so far:

—— o ——

Pilot logbook (05 Dec 1945)

> *1630 hrs – Having just reported in as "ready crew,"
> my twelve-man crew and I have been ordered to
> search for a patrol of TBM Avengers lost over the
> Atlantic. We bear a fuel load more than sufficient
> to stay aloft for over twenty-four hours.*
>
> *. . .*
>
> *1715 hrs – Approaching last assessed position of the
> lost patrol. Holding course. Faulty compass. No
> sign of the missing craft.*
>
> *. . .*
>
> *1730 hrs – Faulty radio. Lost contact with mainland.
> Lt. Doug Johnson suspects faulty voltage regula-
> tors. Still no sign of lost patrol.*
>
> *. . .*
>
> *(Editorial note: As near as we can figure, this was
> Captain Reed's last day on Earth. Now here's
> where it gets interesting…)*

—— o ——

Before Mac could read any further, a signal from the communications console indicated that the shuttle had an incoming packet from Europa Moon Base Alpha.

She read the incoming communiqué and then flipped the intercom switch. She dialed in the ship's bathroom and heard Leo singing some mid-twentieth-century rock-and-roll song in the shower.

"Leo, get your butt up here," she ordered, cutting his crooning short.

Leo's slightly embarrassed voice came back over the cockpit speakers, "Acknowledged Commander." With concern in his voice, he added, "Everything 10-2?"

"Yeah, everything's okay. We've got final clearance to land. I didn't travel a billion miles just to stare at the damn thing, so get up here so we can start our final checklist and put this pig on the ground," she said, eager to get surface-side.

"Yes, ma'am. Next stop, Mudball Central!" Mac imagined her future son-in-law smiling that big dopey grin of his.

Chapter 3

The Europa Moon Base

EUROPA'S SURFACE BASE, Moon Base Alpha, was hidden deep inside a large crater, whose ice walls provided protection from radiation and errant meteors. The *Explorer II* entered orbit and landed at the base without incident and in record time. As much as Mac hated to admit it, the credit was mostly due to Leo's piloting skills. Her quirky space-jock son-in-law was shaping up to be quite an astronaut. The fact that he seemed to do his job effortlessly made it all the harder to admit.

Safely tucked away in the base's hangar bay, the *Explorer II* was swarmed by colonists anxious to unload badly needed supplies, to mingle with the newest arrivals, and to hear the latest news from Earth.

However, Mac wasn't one to waste time with small talk. The sooner she got the supplies unloaded and the outgoing passengers onloaded, the sooner she would get back home to her daughter.

She was supervising the unloading of the first soilmover when Leo's patience finally wore out. As it turned out, it had taken him a lot longer than she had anticipated.

As he handed her the updated returning payload manifest he asked, "Aren't you even curious about the pyramid?"

"No," she replied curtly. She didn't even bother to ask how or why he had hacked into her files and read the Bort report; they had both known he was going to do it anyway.

"Not even a little curious?" he prodded.

"No, it's restricted." She waited for a passing lift operator to move out of earshot. "It's classified, and we're not even supposed to know about it. That's all I need to know." No, nothing — not even the secret of the universe — was going to cost her that promotion to base commander. She'd already lost too much over it. She waited for another passerby and then whispered harshly to him, "There's no way I'm going down to that pyramid."

Mac had pushed aside her feelings of curiosity regarding Joan's report, but she was still anxious to see her friend. She was surprised that Joan wasn't waiting for her the moment she stepped off the ship.

"Commander MacKenzie O'Bryant," said a gruff and weathered voice.

Mac looked up to see a full-star general and a space commando appear on either side of her. They both looked directly at her, as if Leo weren't even there. She noticed that they wore tactical gear and were armed with standard issue A.P.D.F. (Allied Planet Defense Force) rifles and sidearms. She quickly summed up both men in a glance.

Mac recognized General Zimmerman immediately. She knew him by reputation, and she'd also met him on her last visit. The general was an older man with stark white hair; a tough, lean body; and calloused hands. He was not a physically threatening man, in terms of his size, but his eyes seemed old, as though they had seen far too much for any one man. Mac suspected that this was a result of his extensive service during the Seven-Year War with the Coalition. She knew the general was now in charge of security for the entire base and was probably responsible for keeping Dr. Bort's findings top secret, as well.

"My name is General Zimmerman, and this here is Sergeant Brett Harper."

The commando standing next to the general nodded and tipped his watch cap. "Ma'am," he said with a Midwestern twang that rivaled her own accent from the Carolinas.

Mac didn't know the six-foot-four, two-hundred-and-twenty-pound commando from any of her previous visits, but she could tell from his all-American, boyish good looks, which included a shock of reddish hair sticking out of his cap, that he was probably a country boy from the Midwest. If he weren't in uniform, Mac imagined that he would be wearing a flannel shirt and would have a prairie weed sticking out of his mouth. The wad of chew hidden beneath his lower lip only confirmed her suspicion.

"What's wrong?" Mac asked the general. She was more concerned now than ever that Dr. Bort hadn't been in the hangar bay to greet her.

Brett answered for him. "We have a situation developing. One Professor Joan Bort has commandeered a guard's gun and locked herself in the underwater base. She's threatening to shoot anyone who enters."

Mac wasn't completely surprised. Professor Joan Bort wasn't about to give up the secrets of the universe without a fight. Joan's husband had died nearly twenty years ago, and her kids were all grown and had their own kids, so in Joan's mind, she probably had little to lose. But still, this was crazy, even by Joan's standards. Mac gave the general a questioning look, as if to say, "What does this have to do with me?"

"We think you might be able to help us diffuse the situation," the general explained. "Base Commander Ingram said that she was a friend of yours. We're to escort you down to Beta Base to see if you can talk some sense into her."

When Leo realized that Mac was being invited to enter the secret pyramid, he gave her his best puppy dog look *ever*.

She sighed and turned to the general, "If I'm going, my lieutenant's coming along. I'd rather not find out what kind of trouble he'd get into if I left him here on his own."

"Where we going?" Tae asked.

As usual, Tae had popped up at an inopportune time.

Before the general could say anything, Mac turned to the general and said, "And if she's locked any hatches behind her, Tae's your man."

General Zimmerman shook his head and smiled before walking toward the exit. Mac understood the smile to mean that the general wasn't telling them no.

"No, seriously, where we going?" Tae asked Leo.

Leo quickly looked around to confirm that no one was

listening. "To an ancient five-sided pyramid on the ocean floor," he said, "but don't tell anyone. It's top secret."

Tae still looked confused or amazed — Mac couldn't tell which — so she added, "The Beta Base wasn't chosen at random, like everyone believes. It was built near an underwater pyramid that was discovered by thermal imagers about fifty years ago."

"You knew about this, too?" Tae asked Leo looking hurt.

Mac didn't blame him. This was a huge engineering feat, and he was only now hearing about it. Tae and Leo had been together on the *Explorer II* for nearly six months and had trained together for nearly another year before that. Mac could see it on his face; they were the closest things he had to friends, and they hadn't let him in on the secret of the century.

Leo smiled impishly and said, "Sorry, Tae. I just found out about it myself."

Tae bit down on his bottom lip, too angry to reply and choosing to stay quiet instead. Mac decided she would have preferred if he yelled at them just to get it off his chest.

Mac started after the general and Brett, and Leo and Tae followed.

Leo stopped for a moment and removed his camera from his shoulder pocket to check it for a charge.

Mac called back to him, "No cameras, Leo."

Leo seemed to debate this order before he put the camera on a nearby crate and dashed after them. Seconds later, he reappeared, made sure no one was watching, and covertly pocketed the camera.

He caught up with Mac, Tae, the commando, and the general after they had already passed through the busy base command center and entered the elevator that would take them down seventy kilometers through the slushy ocean to Beta Base.

"Hold the door!" Leo said.

Mac rolled her eyes at her errant second as he slipped through the closing door.

"Is this it?" Mac asked the general as she nodded toward the big red-haired country-boy commando. "Aren't you bringing more men?"

"No," General Zimmerman said, "the pyramid's strictly need-to-know basis. I've already got one of my men down there securing the entrance." He checked the radio mic in his ear. "By the way, after this is all over I'll have NDA's for all of you to sign, no exceptions. Get used to not talking about it ladies and gentlemen, what you're about to see is classified."

There was a light hum as the elevator began its descent.

"Ah, is that normal?" Tae asked Brett, who stood next to him. He pointed to the sticky liquid that had begun seeping in near the floor.

"What, that? Oh, that's nothing," the commando replied somewhat unconvincingly.

Brett pressed a button and spoke into the microphone on the elevator's control panel. He crouched low so his lips were as close to the speaker as possible. "Hello, maintenance?" he said. "We've got some water leakage in the deep-sea elevator." Turning back to the group, he said, "Nothing to worry about — happens all the time."

For once, "Great" was all Leo could manage to say. Tae took a small step away from the puddle of dark water pooling at his boots.

Just then, everyone heard a resounding THUMP against the elevator shaft's outer wall.

"What was that?" Mac asked, struggling to hide the concern in her voice.

"Oh, that? That really is no cause for alarm." This time Brett's voice was more believable. "We call them 'Thumpers.'"

"You call them what?" Leo asked.

"We call them 'Thumpers' because they like to 'Thump' the sides of the station's walls." Seeing their apprehension, he quickly added, "Don't worry; they're perfectly harmless — about the size of an orca back on Earth. We don't have any clear pictures of them yet, only what the thermal imagers give us."

The commando rambled on about Europa's sea life, but Mac didn't hear him. She was thinking about the pyramid in the ocean's murky depths and her friend, in peril, within its walls.

The leaky elevator continued its 70-kilometer descent, and the doors finally opened on a cheerfully automated "You have now arrived at Beta Base level" to reveal the dimly lit underwater Beta Base, which consisted of little more than a basic command center and a modest laboratory. It was surrounded on all sides by cold, cloudy waters, visible through large rectangular viewing ports.

Surprised to find the base abandoned, Mac asked, "Where is everyone?"

"As a precaution, everyone was evacuated to the surface," the general said.

Brett added, "A few misplaced rounds from the sidearm your friend stole and then all the water out there would come rushing right on in here." He motioned to the view ports.

"Wait a minute," Leo said nervously. He stopped walking away from the safety of the elevator. "What did you just say?"

"Don't worry about it, flyboy," Brett said. "Just standard operating procedure."

"It's right through there," the general said as he stepped down into a smaller version of the aboveground OPS center.

Mac looked where the general was pointing and saw the entranceway to a tubular passage on the other side of the tiny OPS center.

Brett unslung his large black gear bag and dropped it to the floor, where it landed with a heavy THUNK. He unzipped the bag and pulled out a tactical vest. "Here you go, Commander. Put this on."

"I don't think that's necessary," Mac replied.

"Yes, ma'am, please put the vest on." Brett smiled. Clearly, she was going to put the vest on, without his help or with it.

Mac knew better than to argue with a commando, and it did make sense. Brett helped her put on the vest and tighten it.

"Wait a minute," Leo said. "Don't Tae and I get one?"

Brett looked at his bag and then back at them. "Sorry, I only brought the one spare."

General Zimmerman racked the slide to his pulse rifle and double-checked that there was a round in the chamber. "Just try and stay in the back, behind us," he said as he led the group toward the tunnel's entrance.

Once there, he checked in with a second commando, who had close-cropped blonde hair, bright-blue eyes, and a square jaw. The commando wasn't as tall or wide as Brett, but the fabric of his BDU strained from his ripped muscles underneath.

"Status?" the general asked him.

"No change," the blonde commando said with a curt German accent.

Quickly introducing them, the general said, "Commander MacKenzie O'Bryant, this here's the Coalition's finest elite-class commando, Sergeant Alan Stein."

"Just call me Mac," she replied before following the general and Brett into the tubular tunnel.

The big blonde commando watched her with an appreciative eye. As Leo went to step past him into the tunnel, the commando's large hand shot out with surprising speed and landed on Leo's chest, stopping him in his tracks. Leo looked down. The commando's hand was the size of a baseball glove.

"You're not going anywhere, I think," Commando Stein said in his thick accent, which brought to mind the dozen or so World War II videos Leo had watched during the six-month voyage to Europa. Mac glanced back and snorted at her lieutenant's wide-eyed gaze as he stared up at the commando blocking his way.

"Stand down," the general ordered. "He's with the commander."

Mac couldn't see the German commando's face but something must have flashed across it because Leo suddenly paled and took a half step back. The commando turned to let Leo and Tae pass. Leo gave the man a wide berth, casting furtive glances even as he followed the rest of them down the tunnel. Mac could see something working in his mind and she decided she really didn't want to know where his thoughts were taking him though she was sure she'd find out eventually.

They proceeded through the tunnel, which, according to Brett's recollection of the schematics, was 220 meters in length. Brett explained to Mac that the tube was made of a nanofiber matrix of the hardest acrylic glass known to man, but that they could've saved their money because visibility through the dark slush was nearly zero. If one waited for hours, he or she might glimpse a tail or fin passing near the glass, but that was about all.

On point, Commando Stein repositioned himself at the end of the tunnel, so he could use the temple's entrance as cover.

Mac found herself looking in the direction of Stein's boots. Pure white sand spilled amongst several roughly hewn temple blocks on the floor nearby, marking the spot where the original survey team had first broken through the outer wall. *This is it,* Mac thought. *This is the threshold where past meets present, where our conception of history changes forever.*

She instinctively ducked when a loud shot rang out and a bullet ricocheted off the frame surrounding the temple's entrance.

"Jesus," Leo stammered. He dodged to the rear, ducking back to where Tae was taking cover behind the party members actually wearing body armor.

"I missed on purpose!" Professor Bort yelled from inside the temple. "Anyone comes any closer and the next one goes right through the big blonde's exposed head."

Brett leaned over and whispered into Stein's ear, "She's right, you know. You did leave your head pretty exposed."

Stein ignored Brett's chide and announced in a harsh whisper, "General, I have a shot."

"Hold your fire, soldier," Zimmerman ordered.

Recovering her composure, Mac moved alongside the general. "General, she's my friend. Let me go in there and talk to her."

"I'd advise against that, General, she can negotiate from back here where it's safe," Brett said.

"Why are we debating this?" Stein interjected without looking away from his sniper scope. "I can take her out before she brings the whole place down on us."

Mac took an angry step toward the German commando, but Brett snatched her elbow and held her back behind cover. "Dr. Bort is a renowned extraterrestrial archeologist," she told the commando.

"Yeah, well right now she's a crazy lady with a gun," Brett said in Stein's defense. Mac tore her arm from his grasp.

"Noted," the general said. He turned to face Mac. "Okay, I've got the medics and additional security standing by. Why don't you try calling out to her first?"

Mac nodded, looked around at everyone for support, and took a step forward. "Joan, it's Mac. I'm coming inside," she yelled. Behind her, she could hear Brett's grumble of irritation as her actions overrode the plan to stay behind cover.

"Mac, is that you?" sobbed the professor. "Damn it, Mac, didn't you get my last message? I told you not to land on Europa."

"What message? I never got any message about staying away. Can I come in?"

There was a long pause. "Okay," Joan said weakly. She added more sternly, "But only Mac."

Mac took a few tentative steps into the open and stopped at the pyramid's threshold. She looked back at the group behind her. Brett was shaking his head, bidding her not to enter, while Leo and Tae were wide-eyed, wondering what she was going to do. Joan was her friend, mentor, and confidant. Mac knew that she didn't have any choice. She crossed the threshold between the buildings that spanned millennia and entered the outer room of the pyramid.

The moment she did, the lives of everyone in the pyramid were bound together and fated to alter the history of humanity forever.

Chapter 4

The Inner Chamber

STEPPING INTO THE narrow room of the outer chamber, Mac was overwhelmed by its cache of offerings, which included painstakingly sculpted stone statues that evidenced the skill and imagination of ancient and unknown artists. She was also stunned by the chamber's similarity to Earth's ancient pyramids, particularly when she considered that she stood not in Egypt but 70 kilometers beneath the icy ocean of Jupiter's moon Europa.

Mac had seen Dr. Joan Bort during her last trip to Europa. Joan was in her late sixties, tall and lithe for her age. She resolutely wore glasses, even though modern surgery could have easily corrected her vision.

The frail woman Mac saw inside the chamber now was a mere shell of the once proud mother figure and mentor in Mac's life. Joan wore her usual white, deep-pocketed lab coat, but the state of her hair and make-up suggested that she hadn't slept for days. She held a pistol in one shaky hand.

"Hi, Joan," Mac said.

"Oh hi, Mac," Joan replied a little crazily. "Why didn't you stay the hell away? Didn't you get my communiqués?"

Not wanting to get the professor in more trouble than she was already in, Mac made sure the general couldn't hear her. "I only got the one about the dead pilot you found in the pit and something about his journal."

This excited the professor, and her eyes perked up a bit. "And did you read what I had transcribed?"

"Yes, but it was only a partial transmission, and it didn't say anything about staying away."

Joan frowned and looked a bit like her former stubborn self. "Damn security must've intercepted my transmissions."

"Joan, what happened down here? What happened to you?"

"There isn't time. You have to leave," she said urgently.

"Why? What's down here? Why is it so important that we don't enter the inner chamber?" Mac risked a glance over Joan's shoulder.

Joan shook her head. Then, making up her mind, she said, "We had the corpse dated, and our results showed that the pilot arrived over 700 hundred years ago. I had the tests run three times. It just didn't make sense. So we focused our attention on the inscriptions on the walls."

Mac tried to see the pit and inscriptions Joan referred to, but they were farther inside the temple, in its inner chamber.

"They were similar to the ones found in the Mars pyramid and in the secret chamber beneath the Great Sphinx."

"Were you able to decipher any of them?" Mac asked. She tried not to focus on the shaking barrel of Joan's gun.

"Yes, yes," she said impatiently, "once we realized that the glyphs weren't solely Egyptian or Sumerian, but a combination of the two, it didn't take long to come up with a Rosetta matrix."

"And what did you find?"

Joan's eyes suddenly glistened with the awe of a small child. "Something wondrous.

The inscriptions discuss a device that forms a wormhole, or a portal, to another world, another galaxy, but the gateway's power source, a crystal that fits into a niche in the wall, is missing. The inscriptions also speak of an alternate power source, but my team and I have searched everywhere and found nothing. The only reference to an alternate power source is found with a hieroglyphic representation of the Europa moon over a cuneiform symbol meaning death. Before we could investigate any further, the base commander shut us down. But not before I grabbed this." She pulled out a dirty, torn journal from her coat pocket.

Mac recognized it from the photos Joan had sent. It was the World War II pilot's journal.

"I nearly read it too late. If the base commander hadn't shut us down, I probably wouldn't have gotten to it for months. I suppose, in a way, I should be thanking that fat pig."

Mac smiled. It was good to see a glimmer of her feisty friend. "What's in the journal? What did you find?"

For a moment, Joan had been her old self, excited about her most recent findings and eager to share them, but when Mac asked about the contents of the journal, the wild-eyed look of terror returned to Joan's face.

"I can't tell you, and you must never know," she said with finality. She slowly pocketed the journal in her lab coat. "The gods would be angry with me."

"What are you talking about?" Mac asked. She remembered that Joan had never cared much for religion. "Joan, listen to me. There are people outside with guns. They're professionals. Why don't you give me the pistol before anyone gets hurt?"

A look of fierce determination swept over Joan's face. "I'm sorry, but I can't do that." She leveled the gun at Mac. "I'm so sorry, but this is the only way to save mankind."

"What is? Save them from who?" Mac was acutely aware of the end of Joan's pistol and was suddenly terrified that she would never see her daughter again. Joan didn't look like herself anymore, not at all. She was no longer the woman who shared Mac's love for exploration and who had been like a second mother to Mac. This was a woman possessed, whether it was by fear or some Europa moon phantom, Mac didn't know. Whatever the case, Mac knew that Joan was prepared to fire to protect the pyramid's secrets.

"Everyone," Joan said. "I'm sorry. It's the only way."

All of Mac's tactical training from the academy went out the window, and she simply stood there, frozen with fear and confusion, and she hated herself for it. Her daughter would grow up, graduate from the academy, marry Leo, and have kids — and do it all without her. She closed her eyes and waited for the inevitable.

A single shot rang out.

Mac opened her eyes to find herself still standing and Joan's lab coat staining with an ever-increasing circle of blood. Stein had taken that preemptive shot after all.

"Heaven help us. It has begun," Joan said. The bullet had not blasted her backward, as bullets always did in Leo's old movies, but rather seemed to have just passed through her. She staggered for a moment and collapsed to the floor. Her fingers released their grip on the gun.

"Damn it, Stein! What are you doing?" Mac shouted back to the pyramid's entrance. She rushed to her friend's side.

"Bring in the medics!" General Zimmerman shouted into his radio as he, Brett, and Stein advanced on the scene.

"I need some help in here!" Mac yelled over one shoulder and turned back to her friend. The bullet had passed directly through Joan's lung, and Mac knew from her emergency trauma training that Joan's lungs were filling with fluid.

Stein, never taking his aim off the wounded professor, quickly moved in, confiscated her pistol, and checked her for more weapons. "She's clear," he announced.

"Get away from her!" Mac shouted as she shoved him out of the way, or at least attempted to.

Stein and the general moved farther into the temple to clear it of any additional adversaries and victims.

Mac lifted the professor's head and cradled it in her lap. Joan's hands trembled uncontrollably.

Brett stepped up to Mac. "Are you hit?" he asked.

"No, I'm fine," she stammered.

Brett ripped opened his trauma kit, yanked out a thick bandage, and applied it to Joan's open wound. "Don't worry. The medics are on their way."

"You hear that, Joan?" Mac said, choking up with tears. "The medics will be here any second, so you just hang on."

Joan tried to speak but only managed to produce a gurgling sound.

"What is it? What do you want?" Mac asked.

Joan put her hand in her pocket and removed the journal. She held it out to Mac in hands that shook more violently with each passing second.

"This? You want this?"

She tried to speak again, but only a mouthful of blood spluttered out of her lips.

"Don't worry," Mac said as she gently pushed the book and Joan's trembling hands back down. "I won't let anyone take it away from you."

"Hold this," Brett ordered. He placed Mac's hands over Joan's bandage while he used a syringe to pump Joan full of adrenaline.

The professor insistently pushed the journal toward Mac.

"You want *me* to take it?" Mac asked.

Joan nodded. She tried to speak again but couldn't. Mac used one hand to gently remove the journal from Joan's grasp, her other hand still occupied with holding the bandage over Joan's wound.

Just then, the paramedics arrived on the scene, and Mac felt two strong hands pull her backward and out of the way. As the paramedics worked on Joan, Mac dropped the journal and put a hand over her mouth to stifle a cry.

—— o ——

Nearby, Leo and Tae, who did not have emergency medical training, stood against the wall doing their best to stay out of the way. When the paramedics wheeled a gurney onto the scene, Leo had to step into the inner chamber to make room — at least, that would be his story, and he would stick to it.

Leo took one last look at the professor in the outer chamber and knew she was in the most capable hands available. Then Leo's feet, almost unbidden, began to carry him deeper into the pyramid. He knew that he should turn around but seemed unable to do so. He was surprised to see that Tae walked alongside him.

"What? Can't I see inside the discovery of the millennium?" Tae said. Clearly, he was still hurt that Leo and Mac hadn't told him about the extraordinary discovery.

They moved into the inner chamber together. It resembled the Egyptian-style outer room, except there was a deep pit in the center of the inner chamber that was encircled by the original survey team's floodlights. As they approached the pit, they saw the remains of rescue pilot Captain Harry Reed, still in his flight clothes.

"Whoa, look at this guy," Tae said.

"Yeah." Leo joined him at the pit's edge. "According to Professor Bort's report, the poor guy's plane and crew vanished in the Bermuda Triangle in the winter of 1945."

"How did he end up here?" Tae asked. His voice echoed off the tomb's walls. Fortunately, everyone in the outer chamber was too busy with the professor to notice their unauthorized entry into the inner chamber.

"Don't know," Leo said, but he was more interested in the inscriptions on the wall behind the pit.

He walked to the wall, which was lit by a light stanchion and covered in strange symbols. The symbols reminded him slightly of Egyptian hieroglyphics but looked more primitive. One drawing in particular held Leo's attention. It depicted the underwater temple and, next to it, several additional symbols, one of which resembled the Europa moon. Leo touched the moon symbol, and it lit up in bright yellow colors. He yanked his hand back. "Whoa, did you see that?"

Tae joined him, and Leo repeated the light show, only this time he was able to move the symbol around the wall, like a cursor on a computer.

Tae's eyebrows rose in surprise. "Uh, I don't think you should be messing around with that."

Ignoring him, Leo said, "I wonder why the scientists didn't discover this?"

"They probably photographed and airbrushed the site but never touched it with their bare hands," Tae said. "Only an idiot would touch an alien wall without some sort of protection."

Ignoring his friend's insult, Leo asked, "Why? What's the worst that could happen?" He continued to drag the moon symbol playfully around the wall.

"What's the worst that could happen?" Tae repeated. "Gee, I don't know. It's alien technology, and that's why we don't mess around with it."

"Huh, it kind of looks like there's a piece missing out of the temple symbol," Leo said. "I wonder what would happen if ..." He moved the symbol for the Europa moon into the drawing of the pyramid.

Leo couldn't read the ancient language, and he didn't know about the orbital gateway or its power sources. Nonetheless, he had just activated the portal's alternate power source: the moon itself.

The ground quaked under their feet.

"Uh, Tae?" Leo said nervously as he backed away from the wall.

"What did you do?"

"I don't know."

"Well, put the symbol back where you found it," Tae said.

"Good idea." Leo stepped back to the wall, but when he tapped the symbol, it neither lit up nor moved. The quakes increased in tempo and intensity. "Crap! Nothing's happening."

—— o ——

Back in the outer chamber, Mac stood out of the way while the paramedics loaded the professor onto a gurney. She looked at Joan and realized that the professor was staring intently at something on the floor.

A final breath escaped her mentor's lips.

"She's gone," one of the paramedics said.

Still in shock, Mac followed the professor's final gaze. She saw the journal lying open on the floor; it was now stained with the professor's blood. She quickly bent down, scooped it up, and stuffed it into her jacket pocket. In that moment, if she had looked closer, she would have seen a name written on one of the pages in Captain Harry Reed's handwriting: her own.

"I'm sorry, ma'am," the other paramedic said. They had strapped Joan onto the stretcher, and they offered Mac one last look at her friend's face.

Mac slid her hand gently over Joan's face and closed her eyes. "Good-bye, Joan," she said. The paramedics covered the professor's face with a sheet and wheeled her body to the elevator.

Mac's mind reeled. *What was so damn important that Joan was willing to kill or die for it?*

Suddenly, the ground beneath Mac's feet rumbled. And as usual, when something big went wrong, her future son-in-law soon burst on the scene saying, "It's not my fault!"

"Leo, what did you do?"

"Well, there were these symbols on the wall..." Another more powerful quake cut him off.

"A moon quake?" she asked.

"That's impossible," Tae shouted above the rumbling. "The tectonic plates of this planetoid have been inactive for nearly a century."

Mac nearly tumbled to the floor. "Yeah, I see what you mean," she replied sarcastically.

General Zimmerman popped his head back into the chamber. "Let's get the hell out of here!" he ordered.

The rumbling was steady now, so no one argued. They quickly retreated back through the tunnel and headed for the elevator. To their dismay, the elevator doors were already closing when they arrived.

"The elevator's leaving without us!" Leo yelled. He sprinted up the stairs to the elevator but couldn't catch the doors in time.

Another quake rocked the base, and it was followed by sounds of breaking glass and water rushing inside the tunnel.

Zimmerman cued his radio. "Base Commander, this is General Zimmerman."

"What the hell are you guys doing down there? That was a 12.7 on the Richter scale!"

"Shut up and listen to me. I'm ordering a full evacuation of all personnel. Evacuate! Repeat, all personnel are to evacuate Europa Moon Base Alpha immediately."

Alarms and red strobe lights were immediately activated. Although there were nearly a thousand colonists topside, they were all trained in evacuation procedures. The majority of them could be in orbit before the elevator reached the surface.

Leo looked back at the tunnel entrance where water was already starting to pool. "We're not going to make it!"

"The hell we aren't!" Tae said. He removed his trusty tool bag from his belt and knelt down next to the elevator's control panel. "Leo, help me get this panel off."

A survival knife's blade suddenly appeared behind the panel, courtesy of Stein. Great leverage was applied, and the panel clanged to the floor. "Done," Stein said. He re-sheathed his knife in one practiced move.

Everyone, including Mac, was in shock at the display. *Say what you wanted about Stein's attitude, but you sure as hell wanted him around in a crisis*, Mac thought. Maybe she should apologize for shouting at him; after all, he had likely saved her life. It couldn't have been an easy decision for the commando to make.

Still kneeling by the elevator, Tae generated a few sparks as he manipulated the wires that were spilling out of the panel. "There we go."

They all looked up at the elevator display. It indicated that the car had stopped its ascent and was coming back down.

"Good job, son," Zimmerman said.

"Yeah," Mac added, "I think you just earned your pay for the year."

Seconds later, they heard a loud crash followed by sounds of water roaring towards them from the far end of the tunnel. The subsequent ding of the elevator was the best sound Mac had ever heard.

Brett led the others into the elevator. "Move it people," Zimmerman ordered. As the commanding officer, he was the last one in to safety.

There was a tidal wave of dark water rushing toward the elevator, and Leo began pressing the elevator buttons repeatedly until he saw Brett calmly looking at him.

The big boy from Wisconsin was the proverbial rock in the storm. "You know, you've only got to press it once, right?" Brett said in his thick Midwestern accent.

The elevator closed just as the massive wave pounded into the doors.

—— o ——

After a seemingly endless ride filled with unsettling creaking sounds, the elevator arrived topside, and the doors parted. "You have now arrived at the surface level," the elevator's automated voice announced.

The Alpha Base OPS center initially appeared to be abandoned, but Mac spotted one of the paramedics pinned beneath debris from the partially collapsed ceiling. "Over here!" she shouted, as she knelt by the injured paramedic. Leo was the first to join her. "No, not you, Leo. You and Tae go prep the ship for take-off."

"Right," Leo said. He grabbed an inbound Tae, and they sprinted for the hangar bay.

Mac tried to pull the paramedic out from under the debris, but he screamed when she pulled on him. The general and Brett soon arrived, and each took a side of the largest piece of rubble that pinned the paramedic. Muscles straining, they slowly began to lift it off him.

"Almost there!" Mac said. She glimpsed a cantaloupe-sized rock bounce off Brett's shoulder. The commando didn't even flinch.

Mac was concentrating so hard on freeing the paramedic that she didn't see the remainder of the ceiling give way. "Look out!" she heard as Stein dove on her and expertly moved them both out of harm's way. It was the second time he had saved her life, the third if she counted his help with the elevator.

The paramedic wasn't so lucky. Only a bloody, pulpy mess remained beneath the new pile of rubble. Fortunately, both the general and Brett had dove out of the way just in time to escape injury.

"Thanks," Mac said while the big commando helped her to her feet. "I'm sorry about what I said before. I know you saved my life."

"Don't worry about it," he said. "C'mon, it's time to get out of here."

—— o ——

In the hangar bay, Leo ran alongside Tae and dodged another fissure that opened up before him. He pulled out his radio and contacted the *Explorer II*. "Jeannie, this is Leo. Begin take-off procedure."

Leo, a fan of *I Dream of Jeannie*, had programmed the computer to speak with Barbara Eden's voice, and her voice now responded, "Yes, master. Shuttle will be ready to launch in fifteen minutes."

Tae shook his head; yep, Leo agreed, fifteen minutes was way too long.

"Jeannie, ignore all safety checks and launch procedure protocol. Just open the rear payload bay doors and start the engines."

"That is highly irregular, master," the computer responded.
"I don't care. Just do it."
"Yes, master."

—— o ——

Seventy kilometers below, the Europa pyramid shot beams of
light energy into the heavens. Once in orbit, the energy beams
tore into the fabric of space and began to form a wormhole —
a wormhole that led, not to another part of the galaxy, but to
another dimension.

—— o ——

Still inside the crumbling Alpha Base, Mac risked a look over
her shoulder and saw the ground collapsing behind her, almost
as though the opening fissure were chasing her.

"Don't look! Just keep running!" Brett said. He and Stein
on either side of her, grabbing her arms to help her increase
her speed. They practically carried her the rest of the way to
the ship. The general, despite his age, was only a step behind.

The four of them dove through the hatch just as the
Explorer II began to move.

"All secure," Tae said into the intercom and slammed the
hatch closed behind them.

Mac tried to catch her breath. "What about the Europa
colonists?"

"The colonists evacuated the moment the earthquakes
started," the general replied, putting down his radio. "Their
shuttles are breaching orbit even as we speak."

A heavy bump launched Mac off the floor, and debris could
be heard impacting the ceiling. The ship was moving, but they
were still in the hangar bay. "You three strap yourselves in;
Tae, you're with me," Mac ordered before she bolted for the
cockpit.

When she arrived on the flight deck, Leo was maneuvering
the ship around another fissure, and the nosecone was just
starting to lift off the ground.

As she scanned the runway ahead of them, Mac dropped
into her seat and buckled her safety harness. She could see the
landmass dropping out beneath them. "Better punch it, Leo."

"You got it. Jeannie, you heard the lady. Full burn." Leo
and Mac were pressed back in their seats as the *Explorer II*'s

engines doubled in output and lifted the ship skyward. Leo whooped and hollered himself hoarse as the ship barely managed to slip away before the planet began to implode.

Once they were clear, Mac finally released the helm. "Let's see if we can hook up with the other shuttles and limp back to Jupiter station." She turned to the right of her console and pressed the communication button. "Tae, how's our fuel?"

He appeared on the flight deck behind her chair. "We're carrying a full load."

"Commander," Leo said cheerfully, "I've got the other shuttles on radar. They're quite a ways ahead of us, but I think we can catch 'em."

"Steady as she goes, Lieutenant."

"Aye-aye, Commander." Leo's jubilee abruptly cut short as his gaze snagged on something on his console. "Hey, Tae, you want to take a look at this?"

Tae leaned over and quickly scanned Leo's console. With a furrowed brow, he confirmed the readings on the engineering console behind him.

"What is it? What's wrong?" Mac asked.

Tae checked the readings once more. "We're firing all engines at full burn, but we're actually moving backwards."

A sick sensation settled in the pit of Mac's stomach. "Tae, if it's still attached, bring up the aft view camera."

Tae punched a few buttons and an image of the *Explorer II*'s tail appeared on her screen. Behind it, Mac saw the spiraling halo of atomic gas particles that had been incubated by the temple's cataclysmic reorganization of Europa's molecular photons. It was a damn wormhole...

Ten seconds later, the *Explorer II* vanished from the known universe into the crushing forces of the swirling vortex.

Chapter 5

The Specimen

HUMAN SPECIMEN 5924 awakened in a puddle of vibrant amber liquid. As he hacked and coughed like a man who had nearly drowned, he slowly realized that he had no recollection of who he was or how he had come to be there. His spew matched the amber fluid that he lay in as it flowed into what appeared to be little drain holes in the floor.

Trembling, he listened. Aside from a slight mechanical humming that matched the faint vibration in the floor, his breathing was the only sound that broke the silence. The taste of the acrid amber liquid lingered in his mouth, but there was another taste, too: the metallic taste of fear.

He glimpsed an empty cylindrical chamber beside him, which also contained remnants of the mysterious fluid. Realizing that his bare hands were wet with the stuff, he slowly sat up and wiped them on the sides of the brown leather bomber jacket he wore.

As he looked down at the jacket, he saw that he also wore some type of uniform resembling a flight suit. "CPT H. REED" was stenciled on the left breast pocket. The same name appeared on dog tags that hung around his neck. Alarmingly, the name meant nothing to the man. *But at least I know my name — my last name anyway*, he thought. An inventory of his pockets further revealed a standard issue .45 automatic pistol and two spare clips.

Wincing in pain, he pulled himself to all fours and looked around the room, which contained several rows of identical cylinders, all filled with the same amber liquid. He turned his throbbing head around and saw a man, wearing clothes similar to his, slumped over what appeared to be the controls to the empty cylinder. Exposed wiring stuck out of the mechanism, and the man's hands were scorched black, suggesting that he had been electrocuted.

The cylinder beside it contained another man. A hardened form of the amber liquid encased him and rendered his features nearly unidentifiable, but the captain could just make out the prisoner's mouth: it was frozen open in an eternal scream. The captain looked back at the empty cylinder and faced the terrifying realization that he had been its occupant.

Frantically, he tore around the room, searching for a way out. He exited through a hatch and stumbled into a hallway that had curved walls and smooth, but uneven, rubber floors. His legs pumped furiously as he sprinted away from his holding chamber. *I have to get out of here*, his mind screamed. He took off, unsure where his legs were taking him. Sometimes, his feet carried him off the ground, and he felt as though he could almost fly.

It has to be some kind of crazy dream. It has to be.

But then the dream became a nightmare. Captain Reed turned a corner and saw a green haze emanating from a room ahead. What he saw next stopped his frantic flight dead in its tracks. Shadows of small, thin bodies with oversized heads danced on the wall.

Gathering his courage and staying in the shadows, he slid against the wall and inched forward. Instinctively, he reached for his .45. He flicked the safety off and pumped a round into the chamber in quick, practiced movements. The feel of the steel in his sweating hand was comforting.

He moved closer to the threshold to take a peek inside the hazy green room. Just as he was about to peer inside, he felt long fingers, ice-cold to the touch, slither over the back of his neck like a squid's tentacles encircling its prey.

Without thought, he spun on his heel and raised his weapon. In the brief moment before he fired, he glimpsed a grey-skinned creature with enormous black eyes.

The gun roared. The sound echoed off the walls then died.

In the darkened corridor, the muzzle flash was so brilliant that for an instant he was blinded. When his vision finally returned, he saw that blue-blooded brains now stained the curved wall. At such close range, the .45 bullet had passed right between the creature's eyes and blown out the back of its head. Before he could investigate the motionless creature further, he once again became aware of movement in the shadows. *They heard the shot, and now they're coming for me.* There was only one thing he could do.

He ran.

He ran through the seemingly endless maze of dark, tubular corridors, desperately searching for an exit, until his lungs finally demanded rest. Gulping air, he found a small niche near a circular chamber and crawled inside. Here he could hide, catch his breath, and contemplate his next move.

Looking down, he noticed that the weapon, as well as his hands, face and arms, were splattered with flecks of bluish blood and bits of grayish brain matter. A feeling of revulsion washed over him as he furiously wiped the strange, sticky substance off his face and forehead with the sleeve of his jacket.

As he continued to gasp for breath, he expertly hit the pistol's magazine release with the thumb of his right hand and checked the spent clip. *Only one round short.* Fumbling for the spares in his pocket with his left hand, he inserted a fresh magazine and racked the slide. He was aware of the clacking noise it made more than ever before.

Weapon loaded, he peeked around the corner of his hiding place at the hallways that led from the chamber. *Which one? Which one?* He couldn't tell which — if any — of these hallways he had been down before. *One of these must lead out of this maze,* he thought. He heard a growing rustling sound and felt them drawing nearer. *It's now or never.* He boldly dashed into the chamber and turned down the first hallway on his right. He ran down the hallway until it dead-ended in a cavernous room that was about four times the size of any aircraft hangar back home.

Looking around, he realized that the cone-shaped room had to be some kind of storage facility, for it contained old vehicles, like a blue Ford truck and a 'kidney-crusher' motorcycle. In addition, five planes hung near the ceiling, like model planes on a mobile. The captain was surprised that he could identify the planes as TBM Avengers.

With these new sights, the captain's memory began coming back in tsunami-like waves. An image of himself in the cockpit of a different kind of plane flashed across his mind. He wasn't sure what kind of plane it was, but he knew it was flying over the Atlantic. Then he saw the faces of his crewmembers — all young, all smiles, all nameless to him. *They were doing something important ... searching for a patrol that had gotten lost. That's what it was: a training mission that had gone wrong. It was up to him and his crew to find fourteen souls lost in the Atlantic — fourteen souls that had been flying in TBM Avengers.*

The five Avengers had to be the lost torpedo bombers he and his crew had been looking for. Well, he had found them, by God. Only in doing so, he had become lost himself. Hell, he still didn't even know his own first name.

As he scanned the Avenger planes and the Ford truck for any signs of life, he saw the crown jewel of the whole damn collection and immediately recognized it: it was *his* plane, a Martin Mariner PBY flying boat, more affectionately known by her crew as the *Hail Mary*. All 124 feet of gorgeous wingspan. Normally, it was downed airmen floating in the Atlantic who swore that the big rescue plane was the most beautiful sight to behold, but to Captain Reed, she was now the Holy Grail. More importantly, she had every conceivable kind of rescue apparatus, from self-inflating rafts to a waterproof transmitter that could transmit a distress call for hours. *I have to get up there somehow.*

Just as he was contemplating climbing the room's honey-comb walls, the captain took one step into the open, and his legs were suddenly pulled out from underneath him. It was as though he were caught in a bamboo-tree snare trap, but instead of falling to the floor, he was immediately catapulted toward the ceiling at an alarming rate. Before the captain had control of his senses, he slammed face-first into the under-belly of the *Hail Mary*. He was stuck there, suspended at least forty feet in the air.

It took a moment to get used to being weightless, but the captain eventually used his hands to move from a gun turret to a steel strut and then to the side hatch. He clung to each handhold as if his life depended on it. While he figured he wasn't in any danger of falling, he wasn't sure he'd be able to get back up to his plane again on the first try.

He gained access to the cockpit through the side hatch and immediately made his way to the radio. He flicked a switch, and to his surprise, the radio still had a full charge. He picked up the mic lying on his seat and pressed it firmly to his throat. "Mayday, Mayday, Mayday. This is the *Hail Mary*."

Captain Reed repeated the transmission once more and then froze. Looking out the cockpit window, he saw that there was no ceiling to the cavernous storage chamber, only stars — stars that streaked by at impossible speeds. Until this point, despite all that he had seen, he hadn't really believed any of it was true. But it was true. He, his crew, and the crewmen of the missing torpedo bombers had been abducted by aliens that traveled amongst the stars.

The captain realized that he was still holding the microphone, and he dropped it in disgust. Still in a daze, he spotted what appeared to be a flight logbook floating in the lighter gravity just inches above the flight console. Its worn leather cover was also marked with the name "Captain Reed."

The captain's hand lunged at the suspended logbook and grabbed it. He took comfort in the book, part of a deeply ingrained practiced procedure, and suspected that it might help him cement his grip on reality. Gathering his thoughts, his right hand absentmindedly pulled a pencil from his left breast pocket. He began to write in the small logbook — slowly at first, and then rapidly — documenting the strange events of the last hour of his life — the only hour he could clearly remember.

—— o ——

Date*: Unknown*
Time: *Unknown*
Location: *Unknown.*

...

To anyone who finds this:
As incredible as it might sound, I suspect that I am

*being held prisoner on an alien spacecraft. My
abductors had encased me in some sort of amber
liquid that hardens, but I somehow escaped — I
believe with the assistance of one of my crew. Our
captors are hideous creatures with black, soulless
eyes; grayish skin; and misshapen heads, and
they appear to infest this ship. I killed one of them
with my service pistol. I'm going to attempt to
locate the rest of my crew. With their help, I hope
to take over the vessel.*

May God have mercy on our souls.

—— o ——

The captain was about to toss the journal onto the seat but
spontaneously stuffed it into his pocket instead.

Just as he was contemplating his next move, he glimpsed
something crawling across the windshield, and his mind went
numb with fear.

He suddenly felt what seemed like hundreds of cold hands
— hands with long thin fingers — slide across the nape of
his neck and over his face and shoulders, grabbing him from
behind. They yanked him roughly from his seat and threw
him to the flight deck.

As he lay on the flight deck and looked up between the
splayed blue fingers clamped over his face, he saw dozens of
penetrating eyes staring down at him. He felt his will rapidly
give way as more and more of the slender-fingered hands
enveloped him, and he began to slip out of consciousness.
As he struggled to stay awake, he heard a muffled scream. He
realized it was his own just before everything went black.

—— o ——

When Specimen 5924 came to, he was encased in a semi-
transparent cylinder in the same room from which he had
earlier escaped. The shock of cold fluid flowing over his body
had startled him to consciousness. He slammed his fist into
his cage and screamed for his captors to reveal themselves. He
thought he detected a flash of blue.

Amber liquid poured into the cylinder, swiftly rising to
the level of his knees, hips, chest. His legs and arms flailed,
trying to gain purchase on the slippery sides of the container.

He pressed his cheek against the ceiling in an effort to keep his head above the rising liquid.

Suddenly, his swishing legs began to feel more resistance. The luminous liquid started to thicken, rapidly turning from gel to solid. It encased his lower limbs and worked its way up his body, coagulating around his skin.

The liquid now covered his face. Blinking madly, his eyes tried to adjust to the gooey fluid. His lungs threatened to explode, and he pressed his face up to the glass to scream at his captors. The gelatinous fluid seeped into his mouth and hardened, forever preserving his final act of defiance. As his mind began to shut down for what he believed would be the very last time, he finally remembered his name.

It was Harry.

Chapter 6

Harry's Island

WHEN CAPTAIN HARRY REED regained consciousness, he found himself sitting in the cramped cockpit of a plane he knew well: the *Hail Mary*, or at least what was left of it.

His right temple throbbed. Touching his face, he felt dried blood that had trickled down from a two-inch cut over his eye. He winced in pain when he touched the wound. Harry's face and eyebrows were covered with frost, but he was grateful for the numbing cold because he realized that it was probably the only thing that had kept him from bleeding out while he had lain slumped unconscious in his chair, his hands still gripping the steering column.

Blinding white light, like that from a setting sun, shone through the shattered forward windshield. Harry neither felt motion nor heard engines roaring; his ship was grounded. The only sound he heard was that of a brisk wind whipping into the ruined plane and blowing snow inside.

Harry slowly turned his head to the side. Even though he was hurt badly, he realized that he had fared far better than the man sitting on his right in the co-pilot's seat. The windshield had collapsed, and the co-pilot and the right side of the cockpit had fused into one mesh of flesh and metal. Harry noticed that the co-pilot wore a flight suit, but the uniform was different than his own. The co-pilot wore a sky cap and a Mae West jacket, which led Harry to believe that the man was one of the TBM Avenger pilots for whom Harry and his crew had been searching. A blood-spattered nametag that read "BOOTS" appeared on the co-pilot's uniform, but the name didn't jog Harry's memory. Regardless, Harry thought that this was no way for an aviator to die.

Just then, visions of little grey men danced across Harry's fragmented memory. *These can't be memories*, he quickly told himself, *just bad dreams*. But the images kept coming. He envisioned himself running around a giant spaceship, just like Flash Gordon in the funny papers. Again, he told himself that these 'memories' couldn't be real. *This is real*, he thought. *The* Hail Mary *crashed somewhere, somewhere very cold, and everything else is the result of some fevered delusion, probably from my head injury.*

Summoning all his strength, Harry slowly got out of his seat. He was thankful that his body, though stiff, was in working order. He made his way to the rear of the plane and nearly toppled off the four-foot cockpit platform into the large payload area. He caught himself and, holding a bruised arm, carefully made his way to the ladder. As he climbed down into the cargo area, he noticed that the communications console, housed near the bottom of the ladder, was smashed and incapable of sending a signal.

He scanned the vast, dimly lit fuselage and was startled to see a small grey body on the floor. The creature resembled the alien monsters he had seen in his visions, although its forehead had a small hole in the center. It looked as though the creature's brains had been blown out the back of its head, for bluish-black blood and brain matter painted the wall behind it. The creature's soulless, black eyes stared vacantly at something across the fuselage.

Harry didn't want to look but did anyway. He saw the body of an older man, dressed in a crewman's uniform, propped against the opposite wall. The crewman held a .45-caliber automatic pistol loosely in his right hand, and there was a fresh bullet wound in his temple. Strangely, the man's left hand clasped his right wrist as though his left hand had tried to stop his right from carrying out his own execution.

White hair stuck out of the pulpy mess that remained of the crewman's ruined head. The man's bare hands were unscathed but seemed old. *He's too old to be a trainee pilot or a member of my crew*, Harry thought.

The man must have been part of Dougie's revolt. What? Dougie's revolt? What the hell am I thinking about?

Despite his jumbled memory, Harry made a promise to himself that he would carry out his mission and find any remaining pilots. He was a search and rescue pilot, and it was his job.

Although Harry didn't recognize the man, he nonetheless pitied him. Harry went to remove the pistol from the crewman's hand, thinking that an additional weapon might come in handy later on. As he gently touched the man's hand, he had another memory.

They stood on a freshly cut lawn at some sort of picnic for servicemen and their wives. A young man in his late twenties tended the grill and cooked burgers and dogs. Nearby, the man's young wife balanced a newborn baby boy on one hip, and a little girl in a Sunday dress chewed the end of an oversized hotdog. There wasn't a cloud in the sky, and the smell of the grill was enough to make Harry's mouth water and stomach ache.

"How do you like your burgers, Cap'n?" the young chef asked him. *"Oh, that's right. Chop off his horns, wipe his ass, and drag him across the flames."*

For a moment, the memory was so strong that Harry felt as if he were reliving the scene, but the smell of the grill soon faded and was replaced by the stench of rotting corpses.

Harry tried to sort out his memory. It seemed to be as full of holes as Swiss cheese. He remembered someone named Dougie Johnson talking about some sort of "jailbreak," but it wasn't Dougie as Harry knew him, rather an old-timer who claimed to be Dougie.

A freezing wind blew in from the ruptured cockpit and interrupted his thoughts. As he rubbed his shoulders and stamped his feet for warmth, he noticed that he could see his own breath. It just didn't make sense; when they had left the Florida coast, it was over ninety in the shade.

Regardless, he knew that the first order of business now was survival. *Better get moving Harry, or you're gonna freeze to death for sure*, he told himself. As his Officer Training School survival instructor used to say, "You can't rescue anybody if you're dead."

Harry rummaged through the remainder of his ruined search–and–rescue plane and soon found a pack filled with survival gear. He removed a first aid kit and set it to one side, making a mental note to bandage his injuries, starting with the cut over his right eye.

A small shaving/signal mirror spilled out of the rucksack. Harry stared at it for a moment. What if he had aged as the crewman who killed himself had? Harry's hands looked normal enough. He tentatively scooped the mirror up in one hand. A man in his mid-thirties with dark, wavy hair, with traces of grey at the temples, stared back at him. Harry wasn't sure, but he thought he was thirty-one, and he sure as hell didn't remember having any strands of grey in his hair. It seemed as if he might have lost about five years of his life, and he reasoned it had something to do with the little grey bastards.

Before venturing outside to look around, he switched out his flight boots for ground boots. Next, he pulled a lantern out of the rucksack, and to his surprise, it still worked. He danced the beam across the remainder of the fuselage and saw a second grey body, at least half of it anyway. It looked as though it had been sheared in half when the *Hail Mary* had closed its giant tail-bay doors.

"What the hell happened here?" the captain muttered to himself. *But where was 'here' anyway? Canada?*

He felt light-headed, and he knew he was beginning to lose control. He held onto the ship's cargo netting for support, and when the netting suddenly turned in his hands, he saw a third alien folded up inside it, presumably flung there during the crash. Harry quickly let go of the net and heard a maniacal cry escape his lips. He buried his mouth in the back of his hand, knowing that he couldn't take much more.

After unfastening the locks of a nearby hatch, Harry stumbled through the hatchway and fell into a fresh patch of snow. He dryheaved (it seemed as if he hadn't eaten in a while) and stared dumbfounded at the snow.

What the hell? How is this possible? We took off from the coast of Florida in the middle of summer. The Hail Mary *has*

*a flight range of 300 miles on its best day. We can't possibly be
anywhere near the arctic poles.*

Harry drew himself up to all fours and then sat on his
haunches. Looking at his immediate surroundings, he saw that
his plane had come to a stop at the end of a small box canyon,
which had snow-peaked mountains of rock and shale on either
side. The canyon's floor was little more than a barren, wind-
beaten stretch of land that sloped downward. The air was cool
and the climate arid. When he looked toward the twilight sky,
what he saw did not help him keep his grip on reality: he saw
three moons and a setting sun.

Harry knew that he could no longer deny the truth of his
memories. He realized that the small grey creatures had held
him prisoner; that was why he remembered trying to escape.
And now, now he had escaped, at least temporarily, but he had
ended up on another planet. The two men inside the downed
aircraft were probably all that remained of his crew and the
Avenger pilots.

Harry felt the temptation to give in to hopelessness, but
he remembered what his wise old Uncle Tony told him after
Harry had returned home from the war. After having witnessed
so many of his friends fall to the enemy, Harry had had trouble
leaving the house. He had lived as a recluse for several days
until his uncle had come into his room one afternoon and
said, "Son, you've got two choices: get busy living or get busy
dying."

Captain Reed knew that he faced that same decision now.
He could either accept the fact that he was marooned on
another world and try and figure out a way to get back home,
or he could put a .45 bullet through his skull as the crewman
inside the downed plane had done.

He decided to get busy living.

He stood up slowly, his body still stiff, and decided that
it was time to take a gander at his plane and surroundings.
The plane had settled in the ice, and the heavily damaged
nosecone was buried in a huge snow berm. He climbed on top
of it to get a better view of the crash. The plane's wings were
in surprisingly good shape, but its propeller blades were bent
and scorched as though they had been exposed to extreme

speeds. Even the drawing of the Virgin Mary on the side of the fuselage was scorched.

Jumping off the nosecone, Harry walked alongside the plane. When he reached the scorched emblem, he caressed it with a gloved hand. He remembered an old man telling him something about an escape plan — something about explosives going off the next time the aliens were in low orbit.

Hallucinating from fatigue, stress, and hunger, Harry envisioned the old man standing before him in the snow. The old man, Dougie Johnson — that was his name, tried to speak to him. His lips moved but made no sound. Frustrated, Dougie pointed to the cockpit of the *Hail Mary*.

—— o ——

Like a flash of a lightning bolt, Captain Reed had another memory. *He was back in the cockpit of his plane, which was parked in a cavernous hangar with honeycomb walls. Martians crawled all over the plane, trying to get in. He started the engines and was relieved beyond description when the last engine turned over and sputtered to life. He heard the rat-tat-tat of .50-caliber guns going off on both sides of the fuselage, and a quick look back confirmed that two of the TBM Avenger pilots he'd been sent to rescue manned the big guns. One of them stopped to reload and was yanked from his post by long grey arms. The shooter opposite him drew his pistol and unloaded it into whatever was trying to crawl through his buddy's gun port. The crewman turned toward the cockpit and shouted, "What are you waiting for? Get us out of here!" The man fought off two more aliens and hit the button to close the rear doors.*

Harry turned and suddenly heard a loud explosion that startled him so badly he nearly fell out of his seat. He then heard rushing wind and alarm klaxons that sounded like none he had ever heard before.

An alien crawling across the cockpit window was suddenly whisked off and carried upward, and the Hail Mary *followed. As Harry looked out the cockpit window at the alien ship's ceiling, which had cracked open like an eggshell after the explosion, the* Hail Mary *was ejected out of the Martian's spaceship into space.*

Captain Reed saw a planet below, impossibly far below, and the Hail Mary *was falling rapidly toward it. He gasped for air and quickly donned an oxygen mask. The plane began shaking like never before. He gripped the vibrating controls and …*

—— o ——

Harry found himself standing in the snow next to his plane, reeling from the distant recollection.

Looking back behind the tail of the plane, he saw the huge swath the *Hail Mary* had cut through the frozen tundra as it had skidded to a stop. *It must've been one hell of a landing*, he thought. Too bad he couldn't remember any of it.

The captain felt a huge gust of wind batter him from behind. Looking back, he saw the ridge at the canyon's edge, snow swirling off its edge in the wake of the wind's bombardment. He decided that, before the sun set completely, it might be a good idea if he got a look at the other side of that ridge.

Even though the ridgeline was only a hundred feet above him, it was slow going through the deep snow. For the last couple of feet, Harry had to crawl on the snow and spread his body weight out evenly, so he didn't sink. When he finally reached the top, what he saw on the other side nearly made him lose his tenuous grip on his sanity.

"Oh, my God!" Harry said, nearly toppling off the bluffs he lay upon. Looking down, he saw at least a 10,000-foot drop to the ocean's surface. Even worse, he realized that the landmass upon which he had crashed was moving. He was on some kind of giant floating island. And his wasn't the only floating hunk of rock, either, in the distance, Harry saw more floating islands at different heights and of different sizes. Some were stationary, and others were propelled by invisible forces.

Get busy living or get busy dying. Get busy living or get busy dying.

Chapter 7

Harry's First Contact

Date: *Day One (since arrival)*
Time: *Evening*
Location: *A floating island approximately 10,000 feet above an alien planet's surface*

...

TO ANYONE WHO MAY find this journal:

> *I'm not sure that anyone will ever read this, but I feel compelled to leave an account of what happened to my crew and me. I believe that writing in this journal will also help my fragmented memory and help me put these impossible circumstances into perspective.*

> *To begin, as unbelievable as it may sound, I seem to have crash-landed on another world. I recognize neither a single constellation in the sky nor any of the three moons orbiting this planet. Even the sun looks wrong.*

> *My memory is sketchy at best, but I do remember that my crew and I took off from Ft. Lauderdale Air Force Base on December 5, 1945 in search of five missing TBM Avenger bombers that had vanished in the Bermuda Triangle.*

> *I only have a slight recollection of being on the Martian spaceship, but the former journal entries that detail my captivity are written in my handwriting, so it must be so.*

I can only speculate that the members of my former crew and I did battle with our abductors. The three alien bodies I found in the plane's payload bay support my assumption. The bodies resemble those of the creatures that haunt my dreams, or what I now believe to be fragmented memories. The aliens appear to have died either by gunshot wounds or injuries from the crash.

We must've somehow departed the alien vessel while it was in low orbit of this planet. A high-altitude/high-speed descent would account for the heavy scorching on all frontal areas of the <u>Hail Mary</u>. It's a miracle she didn't just break up in the air.

Using their dog tags, I identified the bodies of the two human crewmembers I found as Lt. Gary 'Boots' Hughes and Lt. Albert Williams. I'll bury their remains in the morning. I have no way of knowing how long we were held captive on the alien ship, but one of my crewmembers seems to be in his late sixties, while I have hardly aged more than five years.

Having done a brief scouting expedition, I discovered that, despite the cold, this floating island is thawing. I can only guess that the island must have come from a polar region and is currently moving south.

Onboard rescue provisions are good, and I have more than enough food and water to last for about two weeks.

The ship's compass continues to spin without rhyme or reason, and I didn't think to time how long a day lasts here. I'll have to remember to do that tomorrow. Very tired now, must rest.

—— o ——

Date: *Day Two*
Time: *Morning*

While digging the graves, I spotted smoke on the horizon. I've decided that I'm going to make a break for it in the morning and see who made those fires.

As I learn more about my surroundings, I learn more about myself. I discovered that I wear a wedding ring, so I can only assume that I'm married. However, I can't remember my wife.

...

Afternoon:

I found a photo on the flight console in the cockpit today. It's a picture of me with a beautiful woman and an approximately nine-year-old girl standing on a white sandy beach. At first, I wasn't sure it was my family, but the young girl seems to have some of my facial features.

Having thought about them, I can feel them in my heart, even though I still can't remember them. At least now I know what they look like, and they motivate me even more to get home, however impossible it seems at the moment.

...

Dusk:

Despite the apparent hopelessness of my situation, I try to remain optimistic and look forward to exploring this new world. I've made a checklist of things I want to bring with me.

Checklist:

binoculars	*first aid kit*	*cigarettes*
rucksack	*rope*	*spare pistol*
flares	*matches*	*jacket*
knife	*sunglasses*	*canteen*
gloves	*cover*	*spare magazines*
flare gun	*canned rations*	*spare socks*
flashlight	*spare clothes*	*pocketknife*

—— o ——

The next morning, Captain Reed stepped out of the *Hail Mary*, closed the hatch behind him, and hefted a heavy rucksack over one shoulder.

He looked to the horizon, and the rising amber sun warmed his face. The temperature was cool but not so cold that he could see his breath on the wind.

He donned his aviator sunglasses to cut down on the glare from the ice and walked along the length of the plane. His boots crunched the melting snow.

As he passed the clamshell window near the tail end of the fuselage, he noticed the .50-caliber gun lying inside. Harry wished he could take the extra firepower but knew he had to travel light or he wouldn't get very far.

His hand lovingly caressed the aluminum fuselage one last time. Even with his Swiss-cheesed memory, Harry remembered that this plane meant a lot to him. They had been together for a long time. He wasn't sure of the details, but he knew they had seen their share of spilled blood.

Although he was packed up and ready to go, Harry dropped his rucksack in the snow and ducked inside the plane for a few minutes. When he reemerged, he held the emblem from the center of the plane's yoke controls — an emblem to which every captain had an unofficial right. He then walked away from the *Hail Mary* believing he would never see it again.

—— o ——

Date: *Day Four*
Time: *Morning*

> *Spotted smoke on the horizon again. Appears to be stationary. Hope to reach my fellow inhabitants of this floating island by midday.*

...

First Break

> *I've been stumbling up a mountainous trail over the frozen tundra for hours now. Thankfully, there's little wind.*
>
> *With the exception of evergreen-looking trees and prickly underbrush, most of the tundra is devoid of vegetation. I've also noticed rocks and boulders that float or levitate at different levels above the surface. I can only speculate that they are filled with varying amounts of the same ore that comprises my floating island.*
>
> *Before continuing my ascent, I took some time for a meal of canned rations, which I've not had the displeasure of eating since the war.*

...

Second Break

> *Crested my first mountain! I'm now in a valley that grows lusher by the hour as my island moves farther south. Is it south? Perhaps I merely find a concrete compass heading comforting to think of. Either way, it's getting warmer.*

> *During my descent, I saw that the valley teems with wildlife. I spotted about a hundred large wooly-mammoth-type creatures streaming through a mountain pass opposite me, and then I saw a small flock of tri-legged, goat-like creatures, some with an impressive array of horns, scampering over a large glacier.*

> *Upon reaching the valley floor, I passed a river and saw about a dozen bear-like creatures with fins on their backs. They fished in waters thick with eels that seemed to cry out when caught.*

> *This place is strange but nonetheless beautiful.*

> . . .

Third Break

> *I stumbled across an old campsite. I found it near a heavily used trail that slopes downward out of the valley. As I followed the trail, I came across enormous tracks and large smelly piles of dung.*

> *I can still see campfire smoke in the distance. I believe the camp is less than five miles ahead of me.*

> . . .

CAMPSITE!

> *Cresting a hill, I spotted the encampment. Lying low and keeping out of sight, I used my binoculars to take a closer look and saw a nomadic caravan that appears to be stopped. The camp includes about five drab pitched tents, with adjoining campfires, and one big, brightly colored tent that is adorned with flags.*

> *Four wide wagons that have no wheels are parked nearby. The wagons float in the air about three feet off the ground. I believe the wagons are made of the floating ore that is abundant on the island.*

Hideous oxen-sized creatures, which appear as powerful as they are ugly, are hitched to the wagons. They have flat, wide bodies, short thick legs with paws that face inward, and buck teeth. I didn't see anything in the camp that appears more modern than a covered wagon or pitched tent.

Staying low on the hill and zooming in with my binoculars, I saw small humanoid figures, about twenty in all, milling about the camp. With no known frame of reference, I guess they're about four to five feet in height. They are thin, but well-muscled, and have thick two-fingered hands and sickly purple skin that appears to have a rubbery texture, like whale blubber. They also have onion-shaped heads with big yellow, goldfish-like eyes; small mouths; and no noses.

All the purple onion-heads are dressed in little more than rags, despite the cold, and are seemingly unaffected by the temperature. They walk around with their heads lowered and seem to do chores, which leads me to believe that they are servants of some kind. They keep going in and out of the brightly colored tent at the camp's center, always bowing as they enter and exit. I thought the little purple servants comprised the caravan, but then I saw the giants, who look nothing like the others.

There are three of them. Although humanoid in form, the smallest of them is nearly twice the height of a normal man and easily three to four times as wide. If the little rubber servants are four feet tall, then these wooly giants are eight to twelve feet tall. With their thick girth, shaggy fur, and long — yet powerful-looking — arms, the beasts reminded me of an arctic mountain gorilla but are even taller and wider.

I zeroed in on one of the giants and saw that it has the muzzle and snout of a lion and wears armor akin to that of a samurai warrior. Its mouth hung open, and even from a distance, I saw rows of jagged, triangle-shaped teeth.

The giant wooly samurai not only look and dress differently than the smaller purple-skinned servants but also have an entirely different demeanor. Unlike the busy servants, the samurai quietly stand guard on the outskirts of camp.

Standing next to each of the wooly giants are what appear to be their mounts. The beasts look nothing like the buck-toothed oxen-type animals hooked up to the wagons and instead resemble enormous ostriches with two legs and thick feathers. However, the similarity stops there because the samurai's beasts also have tiny forearms, thick legs, and a long neck with a fin. These beasts definitely aren't ostriches.

As I adjusted my binoculars to focus again on the samurai, I noticed that one of them is bald on top and looks older, more scarred than the rest. It turned its head in my direction, as though it sensed me, and appeared to be looking right at me. This was impossible, of course, because I was still a good distance away, but I could have sworn it felt my presence somehow.

As dangerous as these three giant beasts look, I know I can't just sit here; I have to make contact.

—— o ——

Captain Reed threw the journal back into his rucksack, hiked the bag onto his shoulder, and moved across the thawing tundra toward the alien nomads' camp.

At about three hundred yards out, he began to hear the miscellaneous sounds of the camp and its purple, blubber-skinned servants: the clinking of pots and pans; the brushing of the buck-toothed, flat-backed oxen; and the beating of rugs on a clothesline. He also heard various conversations in a language that sounded like rubber bands being strummed.

Figuring it would be safest to wait outside the camp until he was invited in, Harry dropped his rucksack beside him and waved to the busy servants in the camp. "Hello," he said.

The purplish servants simultaneously ceased their labor and stared at him. The only sound Harry heard now was the wind.

Immediately, the bald samurai, the one who had seemed to sense Harry earlier, mounted his nearby 'ostrich' and headed toward Harry at a full gallop. A fatter, red-furred samurai quickly followed, and a more slender, black-furred samurai moved toward the brightly colored tent.

The tall bird-like creatures thundered toward Harry, raising ice-dust behind them, and suddenly Harry wasn't in as big a hurry to meet the local inhabitants.

He fought the urge to run or, at the very least, to draw his .45-caliber pistol. Instead, he remained still with his arms outstretched, palms open, in what he hoped was a universal signal for peace.

Looking back at the camp, Harry noticed that the small servants still had not resumed their chores; they stood watching him. He also saw a lone humanoid creature emerge from the brightly colored tent, followed closely by the black-furred samurai.

Although this latest creature had its head and face concealed beneath white coverings, it looked more human than the others. It was taller than the servants, although not by much, and it was thinner and frailer looking. Even from a distance, Harry saw that the thin humanoid's movements were graceful. It grabbed a tall walking staff that leaned against the tent and began moving toward him, trailing far behind the giant samurai riders on ostrich-back.

When the two samurai noticed the tent owner's presence, they protectively steered their mounts to block Harry's view of what seemed to be their master.

The red-furred rider was almost upon him when Harry realized that he'd lost sight of the old, scarred one. Hearing a sound behind him, he spun around and saw the missing samurai. *How in the blazes did he sneak up on me?* Harry wondered. *There's no cover on this open plain within a square mile.*

Harry soon found himself encircled by both furry samurai on their giant ostriches. The bald rider shouted something to him in a strange tongue; he had the gruff vocal chords of a lion. When Harry didn't answer right away, the rider urged his mount forward, and the ostrich beneath the saddle lowered its head and butted Harry in the chest.

Harry stumbled backward and crashed into the other rider's leg. He immediately received a powerful kick to the back that sent him stumbling toward the other rider.

"I'm sorry; I don't understand," he cried, but his pleas fell on deaf ears. The samurai continued to harass him with their mounts. The oversized birds' hooves pounded the ground, and Harry knew that if he wasn't careful, he'd be trampled.

Finally, Harry tried to make a run for it, but one of the ostrich creatures leaped into the air and landed in front of him. He doubted that the oversized birds could fly any better than a rooster, but they were certainly capable of making high leaps and jumps.

The birds' serpentine necks repeatedly battered at him. When one of the birds snapped at him with its sharp beak, it took off a piece of his ear. Harry's hand shot up to cover the painful, bloody wound, only to have the bird snap at his side. The other bird then slashed his arm with its tiny forelimb and cut through his jacket. Harry's sleeve puffed out from the blood.

"All right, that's it!" he shouted. He unsnapped his holster, drew his pistol, and flicked off the safety.

He intended to fire a warning shot, but before he could, the bald samurai deftly dismounted, far too quickly for its size. The ground shuddered when the beast landed.

Harry was right in his estimation of the creature's height. It was huge; its head easily would have touched the bottom of a basketball hoop. Harry aimed his pistol at the giant's chest and ordered it to stay back, but the creature seemed less afraid than intrigued by his weapon.

The creature's hide looked incredibly tough, but Harry was pretty sure a .45-caliber bullet would penetrate its chest armor and fur-covered skin, especially at such close range. He saw his own outstretched hand shaking in front of him, but he reasoned that he'd already killed a little grey alien this week, so why not a ten-foot yeti dressed like a samurai?

The samurai bared its rows of jagged, triangle-shaped teeth at him, as though sensing what he was about to do. Harry pulled back the pistol's hammer. He knew that the beast's buddy would probably get him from behind, but it wouldn't be before he emptied a clip into battle-scarred baldy.

As the hammer clicked back, the bald giant assumed a fighting stance that also reminded Harry of a samurai. Harry heard a blade unsheathing but never actually saw the giant draw his weapon. It seemed as if the bald samurai reached toward his scabbard one second and returned the blade to it the next.

Somewhere in between, a hand-shaped balloon flew through the air and landed in the snow about six feet away. It held Harry's gun.

Captain Reed had lost his hand.

Harry blinked in disbelief as blood spurted about three feet in front of his severed limb. The furry giant had cut off his hand at the wrist. He clutched the bloody stump in his left hand and fell to his knees, muttering "Oh, Jesus" over and over again.

A lesser man might have passed out, but Captain Reed had seen men's limbs blown off in the war and knew he had to act fast. His survival training kicked in, and he removed his scarf and tied a tourniquet around his right wrist using his left hand and mouth. He knew that he would still bleed out in a matter of minutes unless he cauterized the wound, but without a flame, he didn't know how he was going to managed that. He suddenly remembered the pack of flares in his rucksack. It was going to hurt, but he knew he had little choice: the flares would have to do. He rapidly crawled across the melting tundra to his pack and struggled to remove the clasp.

A shadow appeared over him, blocking out the sun. Harry looked up to see the bald samurai. The giant picked him up as effortlessly as a little girl picks up a rag doll and held him at eye level. Harry felt his legs swaying off the ground beneath him.

The bald giant barked something unintelligible at him. When Harry didn't reply, the alien samurai dropped him roughly to the ground. Somehow, Harry landed on his feet, and the bald giant shoved him backward with one hand. Still standing and now delirious, Harry pushed back.

"You cut off my hand, you son-of-a-bitch!"

The battle-scarred samurai raised an eyebrow, seemingly impressed with Harry's bravado, and then backhanded Harry so hard he thought his jaw was going to fall off.

Harry flew through the air and landed in a heap. In his weakened condition, he could no longer offer much of a fight; he simply clutched his bloody stump. The second samurai, the red-furred one, dismounted, and Harry felt the beast's fur-skinned claws wrench his arms painfully behind him, nearly pulling them out of their sockets, and then the creature forced his head down.

Before his face was forced into the dirt, Harry saw the bald samurai remove his weapon from the scabbard on his back. This time, he got a good look at the weapon. It was about the length of a sword but had numerous jagged teeth that curved toward the handle in scimitar fashion. Judging from the noise it made when unsheathed, the weapon was very, very sharp.

Harry knew that the samurai was going to finish him off in one quick, smooth stroke, and he didn't doubt the warrior's proficiency.

He let out a cry as his arms were pulled even farther behind his back. He got a glimpse of the swordsman raising the blade high, executioner style, against the backdrop of the bright arctic sun.

This is how it ends, he thought. *I survived so much, only to die now.*

"Ey'och!" said an ethereal voice. The words were as alien and gruff as the giant's had been, but the voice was softer and definitely female.

Before losing consciousness completely, the captain looked up to see his benefactor — and saw an angel instead. He realized that the humanoid walking with the staff was not a thin man, as he had first thought, but a young woman, perhaps a teenager. When she pushed back her head coverings onto her thin shoulders, Harry saw that her extremely narrow face was hardly human but still exquisitely beautiful. She had short purple hair, pointed ears, fair skin, luminous green eyes, and a painted face. She reminded Harry of drawings he had seen of fairies and wood nymphs.

So angels exist, too. Why not? Harry had seen little grey men inside a giant spaceship, crash-landed on an alien planet, and had his hand cut off by a giant samurai-like mountain gorilla. Why couldn't this vision before him be an angel?

While the second giant samurai held Harry firmly from behind, she grabbed him by the chin. Instinctively, Harry yanked his face from her grasp, and another samurai quickly removed his sword as well.

"Ey'och!" the wispy angel cried again. She glanced angrily at the samurai with a sidelong glance, and he resheathed his blade.

Her curious eyes focused on Harry once more. With her hand under his chin, she turned his head back and forth, examining him as a rancher might inspect a horse at market. Her own head turned side-to-side as she did so, like that of an inquisitive bird.

Harry felt a wave of nausea sweep over him. He'd lost too much blood. The furry giant released him, and he fell onto the soft tundra.

Captain Reed knew he was going to die whether the giant samurai finished him or not. Giving in to pain and shock, he closed his eyes and waited for heaven. After seeing the angel, he figured he was halfway there.

Chapter 8

Crash-land

WHEN COMMANDER MACKENZIE O'BRYANT awakened, she lay on her back with a bandage wound tightly around her head. Still groggy, she found herself looking up at three moons in a green-tinted sky. The air was so clear and pure that it seemed possible to see every contour of the moons' surfaces, that is, until the underbelly of an enormous island glided in the way — — and obstructed her view — just like a cloud might drift lazily across the sky back home.

She heard water lapping against something solid and felt ocean spray on her sun-baked face. *Where did we land?* she wondered, feeling alarmed. Sitting up, she discovered that she was lying on the underbelly of the *Explorer II*, which floated upside down on a multi-tinted ocean.

After sitting up too quickly, she realized that her head throbbed. She felt that her head was bandaged, but when she raised her fingers to examine her wounds, Leo stopped her.

"Don't touch it!" he said. His smiling face appeared before her, blocking out the sunlight. "You've got a concussion, but I'm glad to see that you're awake." The young lieutenant turned and yelled over his shoulder, "Hey, Brett! Mac's awake."

Mac turned and saw Brett and Stein standing on one of the *Explorer*'s partially submerged wings. Each held a piece of tubing and stared intently at the water. Brett handed Stein his tubing and tapped him on the back before making his way over to Mac and Leo.

Leo followed her gaze. "If it weren't for the commandos, we probably wouldn't have gotten out before the cockpit flooded." He added somberly, "I know I wouldn't have."

"What happened?"

"Well, that depends. How much do you remember?" Leo tried to regain his cheerful tone.

"You mean after we broke orbit?" she asked. When Leo nodded, she replied, "Not much. Bright light. My daughter." She shrugged her shoulders. "That's about it."

"Well, that's not what happened!" Leo said. "In case you haven't guessed, we were sucked back through the wormhole and spit out above this alien planet. Without main power, we couldn't sustain orbit for long and dropped right through the atmosphere. When we first cleared the lower atmosphere, we couldn't get a proper altitude reading; the computer couldn't figure out where ground zero was. That's when we first discovered these floating islands, and we navigated right through 'em." Leo pointed skyward. "We set her down on one of those islands up there but ran out of land and teetered off. The ocean was about ten thousand feet below us. If Tae hadn't gotten the anti-gravity generators back online, we would've pancaked on the ocean for sure."

Mac looked up once more at the floating continents and then back at her co-pilot.

"I tried to set it down for a nice easy belly landing on the water, but we hit a freak wave that flipped the *Explorer* right over on its back."

Mac ran the events through her mind as Leo told her about them. It couldn't have been easy for the junior pilot. "Sounds like you did one heck of a piece of flying up there, Lieutenant. Good job." She saw the young man's chest swell with pride.

"Thanks, Commander. Feel free to tell Emma about it when we get back home." Leo grinned. With genuine concern in his voice, he added, "Hey, I'm just glad you're okay."

Brett came over with his medical kit and knelt down next to Mac. He pointed a pen light in each of her eyes and asked, "How ya feeling, Mac?"

"Right as rain, considering." She left out the part about her head feeling like it was about to combust spontaneously.

"Well, your eyes look good, and the bleeding's stopped. I can give you some aspirin for the pain."

"Who said I was in pain … uh … ouch." A wave of lightning zipped through her brain, cutting her off and causing her to grimace. Frowning, Brett tapped out two shiny pills from a small plastic bottle and offered them to her. Leo passed her a bottle of water to wash them down.

As she downed the pills, Mac attempted to gather her thoughts. *Think, Mac, think. Ship and crew.* Although it seemed callous, Mac knew that the ship came first; without the ship, the crew wouldn't last long. The *Explorer II* shifted slightly beneath them — not much, but enough to send the water bottle skidding across its surface.

Mac took in her surroundings. The *Explorer II* floated upside down. Fortunately, NASA had designed the shuttle with built-in floatation devices that deployed in the event of a water landing. As long as the bulkheads were sealed and the main cargo bay doors were closed, the shuttle could probably float indefinitely. Mac doubted that NASA's engineers had ever imagined the crew would actually use the floatation system on an ocean on another planet, or, for that matter, in another universe.

"How's the," she began, but her throat was dry and sore, and her voice cracked. Leo offered her more water, and she carefully sipped it. "How's the crew?" she finally managed.

"Tae broke his forearm. Brett set it, and it hasn't kept Tae from working. Stein, Brett and I got off with minor cuts and bruises."

"Where's Don — uh, General Zimmerman?" she asked.

Leo's hesitation fueled her annoyance. She knew Leo was only trying to give her the bad news in doses, but his plan was backfiring. "Leo, focus. Where's the general?"

Brett answered for him in a somber voice. "General Zimmerman got pretty banged up in the crash. I think his back might be broken. I'm keeping him sedated and stationary; we've got him secured to a door panel. As for the rest of us, only minor cuts, bumps, and bruises."

Mac could tell by his answer that he might have been closer to the general than one would first assume, perhaps some sort of father figure? Mac felt a sudden pang of sympathy for the man.

She tried to stand up, but the pain in her head told her to lie back down.

"Maybe you should take it easy for a while," Leo said.

Mac wouldn't have it. "Help me up, flyboy, or get the hell out of my way."

Leo and Brett helped her to her feet, and she looked around. She saw the general strapped to the door panel, just as Brett had described.

"What's the status of the ship?"

"Well, it's sinking," Leo said. "It got damaged pretty badly when we skirted around the mountains on one of the floating upper continents. The good news is that Tae has used an EVA suit to swim down into the shuttle's cargo bay and open the payload doors. He plans to release the cargo containers from the bay and float them to the surface. They're airtight, so they should float right up."

"That's great, but for what purpose?"

"He's going to use the soilmover that's stored in one of the cargo containers for a propulsion system. He thinks he can reconfigure the tires with paddles. If we string all the cargo containers together using wires from the avionics bay, we'll have ourselves a floating wagon train."

Mac harrumphed in surprise. "That's actually a pretty good idea." Looking around, she saw that someone was missing — someone dear to her.

"Where's Joan?" she asked. She shielded her eyes from the sun and tried to locate her friend.

Brett and Leo exchanged worried glances.

"Joan!" she shouted.

"Mac," Leo said, "Joan didn't make it. She died back in the pyramid on Europa. Don't you remember?"

Mac stifled a cry and bit down on her lower lip. As she pushed a hand through her sea-sprayed hair, it all started coming back to her: the underwater base, the pyramid, the bullet wound, Joan's shaking hands and gasping breath. Tears welled up in Mac's eyes.

"Maybe you should lie back down," Brett said. He held her gently by the forearm and attempted to steady her.

"Don't." Mac yanked her arm away from the big commando. "Just don't."

There was a loud splash as the first cargo container breeched the foamy surface of the water. "I'm gonna go see if Stein and Tae need a hand," Leo said, excusing himself. He ran over to help Stein reel in the bobbing container. Tae floated near the container in his helmeted space suit.

"So, is there anything else I should know?" Mac asked Brett. She wiped away tears on the back of her hand and sucked in a breath through her congested nose.

Clearly anxious to change the subject, Brett said, "Well, we used up the remaining oxygen in the suits to bring supplies up from the ship, so we'll have to start going in the water without oxygen and without the added protection of the suits."

Mac nodded and placed her hands on her hips. She was eager to concentrate on something other than her friend's death. "This means we're going to have to run some tests, tests on the water."

"Right. Plus, we don't know what kind of creatures are swimming around down there."

"Yeah, we've got to take slow, calculated steps."

"Cannonball!" They heard Leo's distant voice and then a large splash. Mac and Brett turned to see Leo land in the water next to Tae.

"Or, we could just dive right in and hope for the best," Brett said dryly as he watched Leo climbed up the side of the floating container.

Leo straddled the top of the bobbing container like a cowboy riding a rodeo bull. He whooped and hollered to complete the illusion. Stein threw him a rope, and he caught it on the first try. Brett and Mac joined Stein to help reel Leo, Tae, and the cargo container back to the ship.

They spent the rest of the day working on Tae's plan. First, they unloaded the remaining cargo containers from the payload area and lashed them together using scavenged wire from the avionics bay. Tae then worked to make the enormous soilmover seaworthy. He attached paddles to the tires to jury-rig four paddlewheels, which resembled those on old steamboats.

The following day, after a few trial runs, the cargo-container wagon train was ready to go. The group transferred the supplies to the new sea-train, and the general, still sedated and hooked up to an IV, was loaded into the last car, which Brett had fitted with a removable sunroof. By dusk, the group got underway.

The *Explorer II* had begun sinking more rapidly after the payload doors had been opened to unload supplies, and as the sun set on the horizon, the group watched the ship slip beneath the turquoise waves. No one said a word.

——— o ———

The next morning, Tae's sea-train motored happily along a random course that coincided with the current. The train moved slowly — no more than about six knots — but it was something, and the solar cells would keep the motor running indefinitely. Although they still had plenty of bottled water, they rigged up canvas sheets to catch rainwater. Other than catching rainwater and fish, and keeping the soilmover's engine running, there was little else for the group to do.

On the afternoon of the third day, Mac rediscovered Captain Reed's journal in her inside jacket pocket. She took it out and fought back a sense of overwhelming grief when she saw that some of the pages were stained with Joan's blood.

Mac leafed through the dead pilot's journal. She saw a few strange sketches here and there and was startled to read Harry's description of an alien planet that had floating islands — just like the ones she saw in the sky above her. But there was no way to know for certain whether the pilot had gone crazy or whether he had indeed been transported to another world, let alone the world that Mac and her crew were now on. Above all, Mac wondered what the journal contained that was worth dying — or killing — for?

Sitting in her command chair, which Leo had removed from the *Explorer II*'s cockpit, Mac settled in for the watery journey ahead of them and started to read.

Chapter 9

The Caravan

HARRY DRIFTED IN and out of consciousness.

He finally awakened to the sounds of rain slapping a leather tarp draped over his head and distant thunder. The aroma of cooking meat greeted his nostrils, and the heat from a nearby fire warmed his skin.

The pain in his wrist was excruciating. Still in shock, he wasn't coherent enough to wonder why he was still alive.

Mixed with the sounds of the rain, Harry began to hear groups of aliens talking amongst themselves as they milled about the camp. He decided his analogy of snapping rubber bands was definitely accurate and he couldn't think of anything else to describe the sound of the small, light-footed creatures. The other group on the other hand, the giant gorilla lions, had a serious and threatening tone that reminded him of waves crashing against a rocky shoreline.

The light-footed creatures scurried off, and for a time, the camp was silent. But then Harry heard a third type of voice from within a nearby tent. Harry wasn't sure if this creature was speaking or singing; her voice was that lovely. He believed the voice belonged to the little fairy nymph he had seen earlier. Desperate to see her again, he forced his eyes open, but the angel was nowhere to be seen, and the lovely voice ceased as quickly as it had begun.

Weak and moving as little as possible, Harry risked a look around. He lay in a hammock made of leather hide. It was tied to two small boulders that levitated in the air. Tents that surrounded his immediate area blocked most of his view, but he was able to see the campfire about ten feet to his left. He saw one of the fur-skinned giants sitting near it, and his blood ran cold.

The wooly beast in samurai armor sat on a log underneath a similar leather tarp and toasted something on the end of a poker. The fierce-looking giant wasn't the same samurai who had cut off his hand. This one was much larger and was covered in mounds of sun-fire red fur that not only sprouted wildly from all parts of his armor and tunic but also framed his muzzled face.

The beast didn't seem to notice that Harry was awake, for he continued to sit near the fire with his eyes closed and hands open in what seemed to be some type of meditation pose. Abruptly, the samurai opened his black eyes and stared at Harry through the campfire's smoke.

Harry stared back and suddenly realized what the samurai cooked over the fire: a human hand. He would have cried out if he had been stronger. Instead, he looked at his right wrist, hoping against hope that what he saw wouldn't validate his most recent nightmare, but bloody bandages at the end of a stump confirmed the worst: his hand had been severed.

Harry looked back at the furry giant across the campfire. The red-haired samurai slipped the freshly cooked hand off the end of the poker, hesitated to glance up at Harry, and took a bite. Even over the sounds of the heavy rain, crackling fire, and talking servants, Harry heard a loud crunching sound as the samurai bit into his blackened hand.

"Oh God!" Harry cried. His arm started to bleed through the bandages.

Another fur-skinned samurai suddenly appeared next to him and quickly took his wounded arm in its clawed hands and began unwrapping the bandages. The captain thought that this black-furred samurai was probably female because she was far more slender than the other two (although still twice the size of a man), and her movements were nurturing, like those of a nurse.

Once the bandages were off, she grabbed a thick cloth and thrust it into his left hand. She put the cloth over his bleeding stump and applied pressure, indicating that she wanted him to hold the cloth firmly in place. Harry did so, and the samurai rewarded him with a quick, gentle stroke on his forehead. Her fur felt luxuriously soft on his skin.

The black-furred giant then removed something from a worn leather pouch that was slung over her shoulder. It looked like a root of some kind. She inserted it into her mouth and chewed it heavily, the way a dog might chew a thick bone. Her lips smacked loudly.

Just as Harry was feeling slightly relaxed, she quickly grabbed his severed forearm in both her hands and startled him. The bloodstained cloth fluttered to the ground.

She opened mouth wide and reared back her head. Harry saw her gaping maw of triangle-shaped teeth and struggled, but she effortlessly pinned him with her elbow. Her head shot forward with surprising speed but stopped short of his severed wrist. There was a loud THWOOOTTT sound as she spat a black, tar-like substance onto his bloody stump. He heard a hissing sound and felt his flesh burning beneath the tar.

Harry continued to struggle, but she held fast. He realized that she wasn't trying to help him, as he had thought, but rather was tenderizing him. His hand was nothing more than an appetizer. She was getting him ready to be the main course.

Harry screamed.

—— o ——

To Harry's surprise, he woke up the next morning. The rain was gone, and it was no longer chilly but a comfortably warm day. A gentle breeze swayed his hammock.

Harry was even more surprised to realize that his arm didn't hurt anymore. He quickly looked down and saw that a hard black shell covered his wrist. He gave it a few practice hits with the knuckles of his left hand, and it produced resounding thunks. The covering was rock hard. In fact, Harry felt better all over, although he was ravenous. The black-furred giant had been trying to cure him, after all.

Harry heard the purple servants moving about the camp, but clinking sounds coming from the opposite side of the smoldering campfire grabbed his attention.

Still sitting on the log where he had parked himself the previous night, the red-haired samurai dug through the rucksack Harry had taken from his plane. The large beast sniffed a pack of Lucky brand cigarettes. He took a tentative bite out of the pack and chewed for a second before shaking his head wildly in disgust and spitting out the tobacco. He continued to spit for the next minute or two.

Realizing that Harry was watching, the beast looked at him suspiciously and growled. The message was clear: "Don't even think about messing with me."

Next, Big Red, as Harry had come to think of the giant wooly beast, took out a can of rations. More carefully this time, he tasted the can with the tip of his tongue and seemed to smell the food within. Big Red bit right through the can with a loud crunch and proceeded to lick the can's interior with his long blue tongue. Harry realized the beast could easily do the same to his bones at any time.

Big Red continued to dig through Harry's pack. He systematically removed the binoculars, flares, and spare clothes and threw anything inedible onto the tundra. Suddenly, Harry's hopes rose. He remembered that the rucksack contained a spare pistol and clips and reasoned that the beast would chuck these items to the ground with the rest of his supplies.

As if on cue, Big Red removed Harry's spare pistol, barrel first. He was about to toss the pistol to the ground, just as Harry had predicted, but then seemed to sense Harry's keen interest in the metal object.

Harry's hopes were dashed, but then Big Red pointed the weapon directly at its own face, and its thumb dangerously close to the trigger.

"That's right, you son-of-a-bitch," Harry heard himself say. "Go ahead and pull the trigger."

Big Red heard this and stopped fiddling with the weapon to glare menacingly at Harry.

Harry held his breath and remained quiet. He quietly hoped that the stupid creature, which had taken part in severing his hand, would pull the trigger and blow its damn head off.

Just when Harry thought nothing was going to happen, there was a loud BANG as a single shot rang out.

The purple servants let out cries of surprise and scampered off, but the old, battle-scarred samurai arrived on the scene with a leap and a roar. The black-furred nurse soon followed.

When the gun smoke cleared, Big Red still sat upright, but his eyes were open wide in surprise. The bullet had partially penetrated his skin, right above his muzzle and directly between his eyes.

The battle-scarred samurai seemed to ask him what had happened in a crude language. Big Red responded with an animated speech that included gestures to the pistol on the ground, to Harry, and then to bullet that was still lodged in his face.

Black Fur stepped forward with a dagger and easily pried the piece of metal from Big Red's face. Battlescar let out a hearty laugh at his friend's expense.

The ridiculousness of the situation suddenly hit Harry, and he started laughing and quickly lost control. He laughed so hard that he fell out of his hammock and kept laughing as he rolled back and forth on the ground while holding his sides, which felt as if they might split.

When he finally settled down, he looked up and saw all three fur-skinned giants staring down at him, along with half the little purple servants in the camp, who had come over to witness the spectacle.

Harry didn't care; it was just so darn funny — like watching one of those new Bugs Bunny cartoons with the dopey hunter. He took another look at Big Red, who rubbed the tiny bullet wound, and started laughing again.

When Big Red realized that this laughter was at his expense, he let out a lion-like roar, jumped to his feet, and headed toward Harry. Black Fur tried to stop him but didn't even succeed in slowing down the much bigger samurai. Harry wasn't laughing anymore. Big Red's jaws were inches from Harry's throat when he suddenly stopped.

The wood nymph was back.

The purple servants dropped at her feet, pressing their faces firmly into the ground, and even the fur-skinned giants (with the exception of the older one) took a respectful step back.

The lithe nymph moved over to Harry and planted one sandaled foot on his chest, but she was so light that he barely felt any pressure. With the flexibility of a contortionist, she crouched low, so her face was close to his, and gently caressed his face, exploring it with her hands. Her long, thin fingers danced across his skin. She felt its texture and frowned in disapproval when she pricked her delicate fingers on the stubble of his beard.

The fragrance of her hair reminded Harry of autumn rain in the forests back home. He couldn't tell if the scent was natural or the result of incense, but it was intoxicating nonetheless.

"How did I get here?" Harry asked, resigned to his fate but wondering at it none-the-less.

She seemed surprised at either his ability to speak or at his language. She touched his lips, waiting for him to speak again.

"My name is Harry," he said. It was something to say; he wasn't really expecting a reaction.

She turned her head from side to side like an inquisitive bird, just as she had done at their first meeting. She looked back at Black Fur as if to see if the wooly guard understood his words any better than she did, but when Black Fur didn't respond, she turned back toward him.

"Harry," she repeated questioningly.

He stared at her, "Yes, that's right." He smiled. "My name's Harry."

"Harry," she repeated more confidently.

When Harry pointed to her, she placed her hand on her own chest with the same questioning look. When Harry nodded, she said, "Asha."

There was a quick bark from Black Fur, a respectful but gentle reminder of some kind? Asha rolled her eyes at this and added, "Dan-Sai. Dan-Sai Asha."

"Well, it's nice to meet you, Dan-Sai, Asha." Harry presumed that Dan-Sai was some sort of a title, like princess.

There was a loud grumbling sound, but this time it came from Harry's stomach and not from one of the large guards.

Princess Asha's eyes went wide at the sound.

"Sorry. Just a little hungry," Harry explained.

The princess seemed to grasp the situation immediately. She stepped off Harry and quickly uttered commands to the groveling servants.

The captain watched as the servants rose to their feet, without lifting their eyes from the tundra floor, and quickly scampered off to do her bidding. When Harry looked back at the princess, she was gone, as were the giant samurai.

Finding himself alone, Harry gathered up his gear one-handed and placed it back into his rucksack. When he thought no one was looking, he picked up and holstered his gun.

Harry didn't notice the battle-scarred samurai watching him from the shadows.

Chapter 10

The River

TAE'S CONVERTED SOILMOVER SEA-TRAIN hadn't been motoring over the vast open ocean for more than five days when its passengers spotted land of the non-floating variety.

A few hours later, with Tae still at the helm, the wagon train approached a mainland abounding with a dark, foreboding jungle and bordered by tan sandy beaches. For a time, the group was concerned about washing up against a menacing-looking barrier reef, but the tide washed them through a wide opening in the jagged rocks and guided them right into a fifty to sixty-foot wide, Mississippi-style river.

On either side of the river, an array of multicolored leafy canopies and thick trunks shrouded a lower layer of palms and ferns, creating a dense and nearly impenetrable blockade.

Leo was eager to wash the saltwater from his pores and cool his sun-baked skin, and he dove into the inviting river. When he surfaced, his future mother-in-law (he hoped) called to him in a mothering tone, "Leo, stay near the boat."

"Okay, Mom," he chided, but he still stayed alongside Tae's water train as the current carried it lazily along.

Leo dove beneath the waves. The water was brisk but refreshing, and it was so clear that he could see all the way to the bottom, which was about 100 feet below. He saw beautiful reefs under the surface, along with an abundance of fish of all shapes and colors. Leo suspected this was how Earth's waters must have looked long before pollution and overfishing.

At first, Leo was a little frightened, especially when one of the strange fish brushed up against his skin, but the majority of the fish were small and extraordinarily beautiful. He wished he had scuba gear with him.

After gazing at a school of oddly shaped, multi-colored fish, he turned around and saw a very large grey face next to his. The creature had gentle, lazy eyes, extremely long whiskers, and a large protruding nose, and it was the largest creature he had seen all day. Leo shot out of the water like a bullet.

—— o ——

Out of the corner of her eye, Mac caught sight of a huge splash of water as Leo broke the surface on a gasp and flailed backwards as a large grey creature closed in on him. "Leo?" Mac shouted. She jumped one container at a time from her train car to the nearest one, her heart in her throat, expecting at any moment to see her nearly-son-in-law get eaten by a giant alien whale.

Mac shielded her eyes with her hands and saw that Leo had abandoned his frantic splashing and was now swimming calmly alongside the water-train, twenty feet off its port side. Looking more closely, she saw the large grey creature about the size of a car floating next to him, just under the surface. The water creature had several blowholes, and when it breathed through them, it produced flute-like sounds. Her lieutenant trod water next to it and was playfully splashed water into the creature's open mouth. "Leo," she shouted to him, "you okay?"

Leo stopped splashing his new aquatic friend, which resembled a manatee with frilly wings. "Yeah, just making some new friends." He smiled broadly. "The big guy gave me quite a scare at first, but he seems really friendly."

The mammal turned over and allowed the pilot to rub its belly. Leo added, "Real friendly. Maybe we could keep him as pet."

"Yeah," Mac said, "I'm sure Emma would love to have a flute-playing manatee for a goldfish."

Leo continued to tread water and give his newfound friend the belly rub of its life. The creature rolled over and began nudging Leo's chest. Leo laughed, "Hey, stop that..."

A loud RAT-TAT-TAT sound cut Leo off, and his face was suddenly splattered with the creature's blue blood.

"No!" the lieutenant screamed. Huge bullet wounds punctured the creature's side, and its flute-like noises were replaced by heavy groaning.

Mac turned to see Commando Stein staring through his sniper scope. Crazily, she realized that it was the same scope he must have stared through when he shot Joan. "Stein, what the hell are you doing?"

"What does it look like I'm doing?" he asked. "I'm saving Leo's life." He yelled to Leo, "Leo, get out of the way. You're in the line!"

Leo didn't hear the commando; he was too busy watching the creature bleed into the water. Sobbing in alien squeaks and whistles, the dying water beast began to sink beneath the waves. "No, no, no!" He put his hands beneath the creature and kicked madly to keep it above the surface, but he couldn't hold the beast up, and it descended to the riverbed floor.

Mac turned to face Stein and grabbed the barrel of his gun, attempting to yank it away. "Stand down, soldier," she said in a gruff voice.

Stein held fast. "Back off, lady."

His tone alarmed Mac, but not as much as the bloodthirsty look in his eyes. "No. Give me your gun, Stein," she ordered, standing her ground.

Leo climbed out of the water and walked over to them. "What the hell is wrong with you?" he asked. Leo was angrier than Mac had ever seen him.

Stein easily yanked his weapon free from Mac's grasp and turned to face Leo with that same murderous stare. "I saved your life," he countered. "I thought it was going to eat you."

"But it wasn't attacking me," Leo shot back.

"I didn't know that," Stein said vehemently. He looked at Leo as though he were about to beat the young astronaut within an inch of his life and enjoy it.

Leo refused to back down. Mac knew he didn't have the training or experience to fight Stein. Sure, Leo could land a crippled space shuttle and navigate Orion's belt without a navigational computer, but up against a trained Security Force Response commando like Stein, Leo would lose. And Mac knew Leo hated to lose. Yet here he was, squaring off against the giant commando like Emma's honor was on the line. Right then and there, Mac decided she'd happily let him marry her daughter if they ever got off this planet.

"You two had better step back unless you want your heads blown off," Stein warned Leo and Mac.

This time, a much more capable hand clamped down on the barrel of Stein's automatic weapon: Brett's.

"Now, Stein, what in this gosh-forsaken world did you go and do that for?" Brett asked, his Midwestern accent thickening.

Moving closer to Brett, Stein explained, "I thought Leo was in trouble, and we also have to know if our weapons will have any effect on these creatures."

"Why? They're not trying to hurt us," Leo, who stood behind Brett, countered.

Stein tried to yank his weapon out of Brett's hand, but Brett held fast. The two men squared off.

Mac admired Brett's response. His good-natured smile was replaced by a glare that nearly equaled the German commando's. Stein was taller than Brett, but Brett outweighed him by a good forty pounds.

Brett jutted his square jaw out. "Stein, I crap bigger than you." More quietly, he asked, "Do you really want to throw down over a fish?"

"I didn't feel like fish anyway," Stein muttered. He relinquished his rifle to Brett.

Once he was out of earshot and Leo had gone off to find a towel, Brett turned to Mac and handed her the rifle. He said quietly, "You know, in Alan's defense, at first I thought the creature was attacking Leo, too."

"Well, it wasn't, Brett," Mac said angrily. She took the rifle from Brett and checked to see that the safety was on. "You watch him, Brett. You watch him close."

In the distance behind the wagon train, there was a loud wailing sound that resembled the call of the manatee-like creature Leo had befriended, but this water beast's song was somber and marked with great mourning.

—— o ——

For the rest of the afternoon, the group saw numerous indigenous life forms, such as an iguanodon-like creature that frolicked near the riverbank. They also saw more creatures like the one Leo had befriended, but none of them would approach the wagon train, despite the lieutenant's best efforts. It seemed that word had gotten out that they were murderous killers on the river. *There goes the neighborhood*, Mac thought.

Hours passed, and they traveled farther down the river. After checking on the general's condition, Mac found herself sitting alone, trying to think happier thoughts. Sailing the river reminded her of when she had helped Emma with a class project on Huck Finn and Tom Sawyer. Instead of just typing up a report, they had built a raft similar to the one in the novel and sailed it down the Tennessee River, which ran just behind their house. They had filmed the adventure and edited it, and Emma had received an A for the project. These thoughts turned sour at the thought of never seeing Emma again, which pained Mac greatly. She suspected that Leo was going through the same thing.

As night approached, the expedition spotted a great wall in the distance that ran parallel to the river. It was several miles off, but they could judge its immense size because it towered over the plentiful forests. It was the first sign they had seen of any kind of civilization.

The river narrowed as they got closer to the wall, and Mac ordered Tae to land on the next beach. Less than ninety minutes later, Tae's soilmover train landed. Leo commemorated the occasion by planting a little flag.

Their celebration was cut short, however. When they went to unload General Zimmerman from the train, they discovered that he had died sometime between approaching the shore and actually landing on it. This had been one of the few times Brett had left the general's side and Mac could see that he intended to blame himself for the general's death. Not that there was anything they could have done. Mac debated bringing it up and decided to leave the commando to his grief, feeling an echo of it herself.

They dug a grave near the tree line, and Mac presided over a service. Leo said she did a good job, but Mac felt that no amount of words would do it justice. As the group departed from the gravesite, Mac lingered next to Brett, the commando holding his silence like it was a tattered battle standard. Mac decided she could speak for him and so she opened her mouth to tell the general that she would miss him and that she wished he were there now because they all could use his strength.

Brett heard her words and placed his large hand on her shoulder. Mac fought back tears, realizing she hadn't had the chance to bury Joan. Instead of breaking down, she turned to the commando and said, "You know, he never said anything, but I could tell that he loved you like a son."

Brett's lips tightened and a single tear rolled down his cheek before he looked away. He started to say something, clearly wanted to say something, perhaps that he'd known it and that he'd loved the general like a father, but he didn't speak. Instead, he walked off to be alone.

Mac caught up to the four remaining members of her crew. "We'll make camp on the beach tonight and then head toward the wall in the morning," she said.

By nightfall, they had made a respectable camp; the cargo containers made excellent tents. Mac assigned Stein to take the first watch.

Everyone was tired, everyone but Mac who was convinced the chaos of her thoughts would never let her sleep. Instead of crawling into her container, she curled up next to the fire with Harry's journal. She told herself that the journal would distract her mind from the circling thoughts of death and that it might offer a clue as to how to get off the planet safely — if, indeed, the captain had been on the same planet they were on now. She did her best to ignore the bloodstains and picked up where she had left off.

Chapter 11

The Stray Dog

WRITTEN IN MESSY SCRIPT:
Day 7

> *In my last entry (four days ago), I wrote that I was about to meet the natives of this planet for the first time. As I am now writing with my left hand (my captors cut off my right one), it goes without saying that my first encounter with the aliens didn't go well.*

> *Despite this, one of my wooly samurai captors has not only tended my wounds but has now also become my unofficial teacher (perhaps at the request of the princess?); she attempts to teach me the aliens' language. Although there are three distinct species in the caravan — the Mooks, the Awump-ai, and the princess — they share a common guttural language, and this is the language I've been trying to learn. I've also learned a great deal about the caravan and its members over the last week, and I'll jot down some of my observations.*

> *First there are the Mooks ...*

> *...*

Mooks

> *The Mooks are the little purplish servants that I spotted first in the camp. They have onion-shaped heads and goldfish-like eyes. They are gentle by nature and, despite their resilient-looking bodies,*

are not physically threatening in any way. In fact, the Mooks are particularly adept at prostrating themselves before the princess. In less than the blink of an eye, they can go from fully functional to prostrate, almost as if they were designed to assume the latter position. When the princess walks through camp, I hear light thumps as the Mooks fall before her.

The Mooks do all the work — from striking the camp to pitching the tents, and everything in between. They also feed me morning and night. I suspect that the princess instructed them to do so.

...

<u>Awumpai</u>

Next are what the Princess refers to as the Awumpai (pronounced a-womp-hay), which resemble over-sized mountain gorillas but have the head, mane, and muzzle of a lion. The smallest of this species is over ten feet tall and three times the width of a normal man. Their bodies are covered in thick, shaggy fur, and they wear leather body armor akin to that of a samurai.

They have large black eyes and a mouth full of triangular-shaped teeth.

The Awumpai are extremely protective of the princess. In fact, protecting her seems to be their main purpose. I rarely see the Awumpai do anything in the way of manual labor.

—— o ——

Day 10

After spending the last several days with the caravan, I learned that the three Awumpai are not as similar as I first thought. Each Awumpai has a unique name and a unique role within the caravan.

...

<u>Fu-Mar</u>

Fu-Mar, the battle-scarred Awumpai, is the one who severed my hand from my arm. Physically, he's the shortest and stockiest of the three, but he also appears to be the toughest and most skilled. I don't know whether Fu-Mar is naturally bald or whether he plucks his hair, but I get the sense that he is older than the other two Awumpai.

Fu-Mar seems to be the natural leader of the group. He's very serious and always scans the horizon, scouts the trail ahead, and checks the rear for unseen enemies. Fu-Mar is always awake when I go to sleep and awake when everyone rises in the morning, and I've never seen him eat! I know that the other two Awumpai do eat and sleep because I've seen them do both. In particular, the fat, red-haired Awumpai named Hu-Nan seems to eat enough for all three, and his snoring would put a grizzly bear to shame.

...

Hu-Nan

Hu-Nan, whom I previously dubbed "Big Red," is the largest and strongest of the group. I once saw him uproot a small tree and use it to scratch his back. He is as tireless as he is powerful, but he has no leadership qualities whatsoever. He doesn't carry a weapon and doesn't need to; he could simply pull his enemies apart.

I think that, in addition to being the princess's protector, Hu-Nan also serves as her playmate. He has the mind of a child and makes her laugh at every opportunity. Yesterday, he threw her high into the air, and she landed in a tree, much to her delight. She jumped back down, and he caught her. This went on several times until Fu-Mar arrived and cuffed the oafish Hu-Nan heavily, presumably for endangering the princess.

...

Ba-Tu

Ba-Tu, who has black fur, is the tallest and slenderest of the three and, I suspect, female. She serves as a mother, mentor, and doctor to the princess, on

*whom Ba-Tu dotes. Ba-Tu doesn't seem to carry
a weapon but rather a large leather pouch con-
taining medicinal herbs. Nonetheless, as Ba-Tu is
always close to the princess, I suspect she serves
as the last line of defense. Ba-Tu is the one who
first tended my wounds and who teaches me their
language.*

That brings us to Dan-Sai Asha.

...

Asha

*Dan-Sai Asha reminds me of a fairy wood nymph.
(I believe "Dan-Sai" means "Princess" because
of the reverence with which the servants say the
word.) Asha is roughly five feet tall and weighs
about 80 pounds. She has short purple hair, elfin
ears, and luminous green eyes.*

*For a time, I believed that Asha painted her face or
perhaps tattooed it the way desert women back on
Earth do, but now I believe otherwise. I've never
actually seen her paint her face, yet the patterns
and colors on it change daily, sometimes more often. At first I thought I was imagining these changes, but I sketched the patterns over the last few
days and documented how they differed. I suppose that Asha could still be applying some sort
of paint to her face each day or having the Mooks
do it for her, but it's my belief that she's capable of
controlling her skin's pigmentation. I'll continue to
observe this further.*

*The princess and I haven't spoken since our initial
encounter. She spends most of her time in her
tent, schooling with Ba-Tu, learning to fight with
Fu-Mar, or playing with Hu-Nan.*

*Ba-Tu seems reluctant to understand my questions
pertaining to Asha and continues to mutter the
word "Joppa-Cal" over and over, which may be
another name though it bears a unique weight.
The one thing I could piece together seems to be
that the caravan is tasked with protecting the prin-*

cess and getting her somewhere. Perhaps deliver-
ing her to this Joppa-Cal.

—— o ——

Captain Reed stopped writing and set the journal down on the log beside him, the simple action taking extra steps without a second hand to do half the work.

It was a morning like any other on the floating island: the sun was rising; the three moons were vanishing with the night sky, and the Mooks were striking camp. Harry had long ago stopped trying to help or talk to the little servants; they had little interest in anything that wasn't an assigned duty.

Harry still had no idea where the caravan was headed, but he had grown accustomed to the daily routine. After the Mooks packed up camp in the morning, the caravan traveled all afternoon until the Mooks made camp for the night.

As he reached for the last can of coffee in his rucksack, Harry heard light thumps from the Mook servants hitting the ground, which indicated that the princess was heading his way. Harry also heard Fu-Mar's heavy feet.

As soon as the princess passed within earshot (and Fu-Mar passed out of striking distance), Harry mustered his courage and said, "Comp-pai." He believed that this was the morning greeting he had heard her use with several of the Mooks and two of the Awumpai.

Harry had incorrectly estimated Fu-Mar's range. Before he even saw Fu-Mar's hand, it landed a blow that knocked Harry across the campsite. His ears rang and his vision blurred. He staggered to his feet, stumbled around like a drunk, and fell to the ground behind a nearby ore cart.

The princess appeared over him. She knelt down and gently touched his forehead. "Are you okay?" she asked.

Harry noticed the delicateness of her slender neck and wrists. And her eyes were not one color but many swirling shades of light blue. He felt as if he could get lost in them; they were almost hypnotic.

Harry blinked stupidly in surprise when he realized that she was actually speaking to him in perfect English. He nodded. "How is it that you are speaking my language?"

"I'm not," she responded. Harry realized that her mouth wasn't moving with her words.

He rose to his feet and dusted himself off. "Thank you," he said.

"You are welcome, Harry," she responded tentatively, aloud this time and definitely in English. She turned to leave.

"Wait," he said, grabbing her tiny arm.

He heard Fu-Mar's blade unsheathe, and he quickly put his head down in submission, raising his one remaining hand to show that it didn't contain any concealed weapons. He heard the princess say "ray-nock" to her big bald protector.

"You should be more careful," she told Harry.

"What do you mean?"

"They do not like it when anyone touches me." She gestured behind him.

When Harry turned around, he saw that all three Awumpai had gathered behind him. Fu-Mar stood closest, well within striking distance, and had his blade unsheathed. Harry had no doubt that the Awumpai could have easily lopped off his head with a flick of its thick wrist. Hu-Nan stood behind Fu-Mar and appeared ready to pounce, while Ba-Tu crouched by a nearby tree and aimed some type of projectile weapon at him.

The Dan-Sai said something loud to them in Awumpai, and Hu-Nan and Ba-Tu backed down and moved off. She had to yell at Fu-Mar a second time before the bald Awumpai finally sheathed his sword and thudded away, complaining loudly to himself as he did so.

The princess watched her Awumpai go and then turned back to Harry. "Yes, Harry," she said. He could tell she liked saying his name.

"I have so many questions."

She turned her head to the side, as though listening to a distant voice, and then turned her attention back to him. "Joppa-Cal," she said.

"What?"

"You want to know where it is we are going," she said. "Joppa-Cal."

Harry shook his head in surprise. "You can read my thoughts?"

"Yes," she said impishly, easily transitioning between a noble princess and a little girl. "But I am not good at it."

"Can I ask you more questions?"

Asha thought this over before answering. "I am already late for practice with Fu-Mar, so maybe we could talk for a little while."

A little while turned into the better part of the day. Asha had the ability to speak telepathically, but to make him feel more comfortable she used her mouth and spoke in English. She explained that the Awumpai and Mooks were lower life forms, whose crude languages needed to be spoken aloud. By contrast, her language was sung.

She told him that her father, who was king of their land, had sent her to the city of Joppa-Cal to pay homage to the coming gods and that the Awumpai, who had been with her since birth, served as her protectors on this journey.

When Harry asked where the Awumpai came from, she placed her hand on his temple. In his mind's eye, he saw their city, Valhalla, which lay in a dormant volcano. Only Awumpai had permission to enter this forbidden city. In exchange for peace with neighboring lands, the Awumpai served as bodyguards for kings and royalty.

As the caravan's oxcarts moseyed down a rugged trail for the remainder of the day, Harry and Asha continued to converse in English and occasionally in Awumpai. Asha was curious about Earth. Harry told her about Earth's skyscrapers and different cultures, and she inquired about its animals, again revealing her youthfulness.

The Dan-Sai learned English quickly, and she was not only a patient learner but also a patient teacher. Whenever Harry got frustrated with the Awumpai language, she laid her delicate hand on his in encouragement. Her hand felt as light as a feather. Harry remembered that his Uncle Tony once had said, "A good martini should feel like a cloud in your mouth," and this was exactly how her hand felt on his — like a cloud.

That evening, as the Mooks finished setting up camp, Harry and the princess sat by the fire together. After a loud commotion among the servants, whose language still sounded like rubber bands being strummed to the captain's ears, one of them approached the princess. The servant, who was dressed slightly better than the other servants, dropped a pile of Mook clothing at the princess's feet and then prostrated himself before her.

"Rise, Ode," she said harmonically, despite her use of the crude Awumpai language.

The creature rose but kept his gaze on the forest floor.

"What troubles you, Servant Master?" she asked.

The creature, whose name Harry realized was Ode, spoke his rubber-band-like language at a fever pitch. Harry saw several anxious Mooks peek out from behind a nearby tent flap to watch the event unfold.

When Ode was done, the princess thanked him and said words in an assuring tone as if to promise that the matter would be addressed. Once he was gone, she nodded to Ba-Tu.

Ba-Tu must have anticipated the princess's request, for she walked over to a nearby ore-cart, reached behind it, and pulled out a sheepish-looking Hu-Nan. Ba-Tu brought the enormous Awumpai to the princess, and the princess gave him a sound verbal thrashing. She pointed her finger angrily at the Mook clothes on the ground and then at Hu-Nan. Harry saw a side of the princess he didn't expect, and he found it slightly humorous to see the formidable beast, which could have easily bitten the princess's thin body in half in one bite, stand before her with slumped shoulders and downturned eyes, looking like a scolded child.

Harry's Awumpai was still hazy at best, but he believed that Hu-Nan was getting his butt chewed out for dining on a Mook servant.

When Asha asked Hu-Nan what he had to say for himself, he belched and shamefully handed her a soggy leather wrist bracelet that he had just burped up. This further infuriated the princess and led to another verbal thrashing.

Following Ba-Tu's lead, Harry slipped away to his hammock. Sore from the day's journey, he climbed into it slowly where it hung between its customary floating rocks. He took out his journal, propping it open with the stump of his right hand, and began writing down everything he had learned that day about the princess, the Mooks, the Awumpai, and their trip to

Joppa-Cal. He even started an Awumpai-English dictionary at the back of his book.

—— o ——

Awumpai Dictionary

Ah-stew-bleef – Please

Asha – I'm not sure of the literal translation, but I believe the word means something to the effect that her voice is a gift to the gods.

Comp-pai – Good morning

Dan-Sai – Princess (I think)

Dewy – Bye

Muck-locks – Four-legged, buck-toothed beasts of burden with flat, table-like backs and feet that turn in. They chew cud constantly.

Ray-nock – Stop

...

In closing, I'm eager to meet these "gods" of whom Princess Asha speaks, she seems to think they are real enough. Perhaps they can offer me some assistance in locating the rest of my crew and returning home.

Furthermore, I no longer feel like a captive in the nomad caravan I stumbled across. Now I feel more like a stray dog that they have accepted into their fold.

Chapter 12

The Wall

THE WALL WAS MASSIVE.

Putting her hands on her hips, Mac arched her head back as far as it would go and stared at the structure. The colossal wall they had seen from the river was higher than most skyscrapers back home and extended as far as the eye could see in either direction. A rampart ran the length of the wall, and there were sentry towers placed on top at quarter-mile intervals. It reminded Mac of the Great Wall of China but was much higher.

Three quarters of the way up the wall, Mac saw what she guessed to be birds. They looked like a cross between vultures and giant bats. The birds flew in and out of the clouds that were burning off in the morning sun, and some of them nested on the wall's jutting sandstone blocks.

It hadn't been an easy trek through the dense forest to the wall, but looking at the towering wall above her, which had no obvious point of entry, Mac knew that getting inside was going to be even tougher.

Earlier that morning at base camp, Tae had wanted to reconfigure the soilmover with wheels, but the big mover couldn't penetrate the dense forest, and they had left it behind. They had talked about leaving someone behind to guard the camp, but no one had wanted to stay. Mac also preferred to keep everyone together. They had left everything they weren't taking in the cargo containers and locked them. They also had left a note at the campsite in case a rescue party had received the signal from their emergency locator transponder and came looking for them. That done, they had set out for the wall. It had taken them less than three hours to reach the enormous wall's base.

Standing on a quarter-mile wide slab of stone that served as the wall's base, Mac and the others took their first break of the day.

"Looks like there's some sort of sentry tower over there, near the top," Brett said. He stood next to Mac and peered at the wall through his binoculars. "Looks like some sort of an elevator up there, too." He passed the binoculars to Mac.

Mac pointed the binoculars where Brett indicated and saw the small bastion atop the wall. Just below it hung a rickety, jury-rigged wooden platform that looked as though it had been added to the wall as an afterthought. The 'elevator' was little more than a platform that dangled from a worn rope-and-pulley system.

"I see it," she said, "but it doesn't look very solid."

"Well, I don't see an opening down here for miles. It might be our only option."

She returned the binoculars to him. "Yeah, but how the hell are we going to get up there?"

Brett swallowed hard before answering. "I guess one of us will just have to climb up there and lower the elevator down for the rest of us."

Mac noticed that Brett blanched at the thought of climbing the wall. Clearly, he was not thrilled at the prospect. "Brett, are you afraid of heights?"

"Lady, I'm not afraid of anything," he said. But his attempt to conceal his discomfort failed miserably.

"Yes, you are." She grinned. She found it hard to believe that the big bad commando was afraid of anything. "You're afraid of heights."

"I'll climb it," said a voice behind them. It was Stein's.

Both of them turned to face Stein, who was already dropping his gear and disrobing down to his tank top. Stein, with his lithe, muscular body, seemed to offer the only viable option. "I used to climb in the Alps with my father when I was a boy," he said. "I'll be up there in a few hours."

Brett was Mac's first choice for the mission. If anyone was going to make first contact with the aliens, she wanted it to be Brett, especially after the incident with the river creature. However, having watched Brett pale at the sight of the climb, Mac knew that Stein was the best possible candidate. Stein was certainly the most physically powerful, and with his background in rock climbing, he was the most qualified. *Besides*, Mac thought, *a small part of me wouldn't mind if the murderous bastard fell to his death. No*, she cursed herself silently, *Stein's still a member of my crew, and I can't have thoughts like that.*

"Okay, Stein. You've got the OP," she said.

Stein nodded and began emptying one of the packs and selecting items necessary for his ascent: a rope, bottled water, food, and so forth. Tae helped him with his gear, but Leo chose not to.

To his credit, Stein had been going out of his way to be helpful and avoid confrontation with Leo and the others since his little performance on the river. She tried to keep in mind that the commando had shot the water beast to protect Leo, just as he had shot the professor to protect her. Mac's inner voice kept repeating that there was definitely a pattern there, but she tried to ignore it.

Sensing her thoughts, Brett said, "You know, if you really want me to, I'll make the climb."

"No," Mac said. She watched Stein stretch and was surprised at how limber the heavily muscled man was. "You were right. If we're to go forward, Stein's the best man for the job."

She didn't mention her concerns about what might happen if Stein was to make first contact, and Brett didn't bring it up. It was a risk and they both knew it.

After she wished him luck, Stein moved to the wall and began his ascent. The bricks had been laid in a jigsaw pattern, and they jutted out randomly, affording him plenty of handholds. Still, the climb, which would be at least sixty stories high, was a massive undertaking.

Stein climbed only two feet and slid back down. Had he been over thirty feet, the same fall would have been fatal. And Stein had to climb over six hundred feet. The fall hardly inspired Mac's confidence.

"Don't worry," he told her, spying her concerned look. "I'm just testing the handholds. I'd rather do it down here then up there."

"Be careful," she said with genuine concern.

Hesitating for a moment, he replied in a gentle tone, "Since when do you care about my well-being, Commander?"

"Since the day you boarded my ship," she said.

"Don't worry. I'll be back in — how do you say? — a jiffy." With that, he climbed ten feet in less than a minute. Stein stopped climbing long enough to turn back toward Mac. "Just one more thing, Commander."

"Yeah, what's that?" she shouted up at him.

"We're no longer on board your ship."

Before she could reply, the commando resumed his speedy ascent.

Tae stepped next to her. "If he maintains his present rate of climb," he said, doing some mental figuring, "he should reach the top in about an hour and six minutes."

"Not much else we can do until he reaches the top. We might as well break out some food and have lunch."

As the others began unpacking their gear and settling in, Mac continued to watch Stein. After twenty minutes, she was finally satisfied that he wasn't going to fall to his death, and she took some freeze-dried apples from Leo and sat down in the shade of a tree. She removed the Europa journal from her pocket and held it in her hands.

As she contemplated the book, she wondered if her shuttle had landed on the same planet that Harry had described in his journal. Both planets had the same amount of moons, and they also had similar features, notably the floating landmasses. *But if Captain Reed were here*, Mac wondered, *how long ago was it? Seventy years ago? A thousand?* Professor Bort had told her that Captain Reed's corpse was over seven hundred years old. *Is time even relative when traversing through a wormhole?* She made a note to ask Leo or Tae about that one in the near future. Just not right now. She wasn't in the mood to hear a sixty-minute dissertation on wormholes. Instead, she opened the Europa journal and began reading.

Chapter 13

The SongBird Goddess

DAY 11

I have been poisoned.

——— o ———

As the bile from his stomach rose in his throat, Captain Reed tore away from the evening campfire and ran into the surrounding thick underbrush. He should have known better than to accept a morsel of food from Hu-Nan, the big fat Awumpai. Hu-Nan never gave up food. Harry could still hear the Awumpai laughing.

Obviously, they weren't trying to kill him, for they could easily do that with a flick of their wrists. No, stupid, stupid, stupid Hu-Nan was having some fun with him. The big red Awumpai was probably trying to get even after the gun incident.

Harry tripped over a root but caught himself before he hit the forest floor. Normally, a combination of one or more of the three moons lit one's way at night, but only the smallest of the moons was visible this night. It didn't help that Harry was beneath a canopy of leafy trees and had forgotten his flashlight.

In the past week, the caravan had journeyed out of the mountains, and the terrain had changed from valleys of tundra to thick forests. Although it still snowed on some of the cooler nights, it usually melted by midday.

At present, Harry searched for a creek that he had seen near camp during the daytime. He knew he just had to get through the thick undergrowth. Feeling the bile rise up again in his mouth and hearing the babbling brook, he quickened his pace. He was only one tree line away from the creek when he started hearing what sounded like singing.

Harry had read Homer's *Odyssey* as a kid and had always wondered what the Sirens might have sounded like. He knew now, though, that the Sirens' song couldn't have sounded more beautiful than what he heard just then in the alien forest. He was drawn to the song, the nausea fading from his mind.

As he made his way through the woods, moving parallel with the river, he glimpsed a vaporous cloud of sparkling lights above the river. In his haste, he was far from stealthy. His footsteps cracked fallen tree limbs, and his shoulders snapped off dead branches. Suddenly, another voice joined the first, and both sang in harmony. It was beautiful. The light was just ahead near an opening, like a small beach, next to the water's edge. He was almost there.

Harry burst through the trees and didn't see the short embankment that encircled the small beach landing. He fell over the embankment and landed face first in the sand. In the brief moment between bursting through the trees and planting his face so far in the dirt that he would have made an ostrich proud, Harry glimpsed the most wondrous thing he had ever seen in his life.

In those brief seconds, he saw Princess Asha floating about twenty feet above the center of the river. A shimmering aura surrounded her tiny form, and she spoke — no, sang — to an angelic head that appeared on a luminescent cloud. The angel had swirling multi-colored eyes, like Asha's, and her face was surrounded by long golden curls that floated upward, almost as though her head were submerged in water.

Stunned, and slightly hurt from the fall, Harry lifted his face out of the dirt. As he hastily brushed sand out of his eyes with his one good hand, the singing abruptly stopped. Before he could raise his head, the light he saw reflected on the beach faded away.

When Harry's vision finally cleared, he thought he saw the princess's dainty bare feet step off an invisible stairway that bridged the river and the beach. He looked for the angelic face in the cloud but didn't see it, and Asha's aura was gone as well.

"What's wrong, Harry?" Asha asked. She had her hands clasped easily behind her back and an impish smile upon her face.

"What the hell was that?" he stammered.

"I don't know. What did you see?" she asked coyly.

What had he seen? He had only caught a glimpse of the big cloud, and most of it was through the trees. Had he seen fireflies or some sort of gas cloud that had ignited?

"I ... I don't know what I saw," Harry said. "A beautiful woman, almost angelic. She looked kind of like you, only older."

The Dan-Sai gave him a pitying look and helped him to his feet. To Harry's surprise, she explained what he had seen. "That was the SongBird Goddess, Harry; that's who you saw. She asked me to say 'hello'."

Asha turned to go, but Harry roughly grabbed her by the arm. Realizing what he had done, he quickly released her in case there were any Awumpai nearby. "The SongBird Goddess," he stammered, "who is that?"

Asha thought about the question for a moment before answering. "She is many things: mother of all creation, brother to Khaos, and the balance to the universe — or, at least, she was."

Asha's beautiful face focused on him for a moment and suddenly contorted, as though she were inflicted with great pain. Once it passed, she asked, "Would you like to see her?"

Before he could answer, Asha took a step toward to him and lightly tapped his temple with her middle finger. Harry suddenly found himself standing on pure white sand in a cavernous room, the walls built of massive sandstone blocks. Looking around, he saw a pool of water in a circular pit that was not more than twelve feet across. On the wall behind the pool, he noticed strange writing. The symbols reminded him of Egyptian hieroglyphics and Japanese characters.

Harry was about to examine the writing further when he glimpsed ripples on the water. Moving to the pit's edge, he looked into the water and saw the SongBird Goddess of whom Asha had spoken. The beautiful woman floated just beneath the surface of the crystal-clear turquoise water. Her long hair flowed gently over her head, and a glowing white aura surrounded her. She peered up at Harry, and he saw a look of sadness upon her angelic face.

She reached out to him, her fingers making ripples on the water's surface, and suddenly, as if he were in some kind of crazy dream, he found himself underwater staring up at her as if he had been transported to the bottom of the well to stand at her feet. The water was ice cold against his face and he instinctively held his breath. The Goddess towered over him, over ten feet tall, and he was surprised by the look of agony on her face. It appeared that she was nearly drowned, her arms limp to either side, her head tipped back as if in hopeless desire for the air above, and, as Harry watched further, he determined that this was the perpetual state of her existence: forever drowning in an aqueous tomb.

Harry felt an overwhelming urge to free the enigmatic, wondrous being. Looking down at her feet, he saw that one slender ankle was shackled to an enormous chain, which, in turn, was fastened to a semi-circular hook on the pit's floor. The chain was only long enough to allow the ends of her hair to break the surface.

Worse yet, she wasn't alone. Two dragon-headed eels slithered doggedly around her floating form. Each of them was six feet long and had a mouth lined with four-inch-long, needle-like spikes. Harry saw one of the serpents lunge toward the goddess and take a bite out of her side. She grimaced.

The bite wound began to heal immediately, but even though the goddess's skin regenerated, it was clear she had felt the pain of the injury. It was a torture endured beyond mortal comprehension. Harry had to do something.

He was running out of air. Nonetheless, he swam to the chain and reached for it. His single hand passed through the links as though it belonged to a ghost, but his movement drew the attention of one of the serpents. It reared its head back like a cobra, opened its jaws, and darted for his face. When Harry opened his mouth to scream with the last of his breath, the horrific scene vanished, and he found himself back on the beach.

He felt Asha's tiny hands try and steady him, but his wobbling legs gave out, and his body dropped to the beach. He tried to process what he had seen and couldn't be sure if he'd left the beach or whether the scene had played out only in his mind. Regardless, he knew that the goddess existed and that her suffering — such agony! — was real.

Feeling overwhelming sadness for the beautiful being, Harry asked, "Hasn't anyone ever tried rescuing her?"

"Many have tried, and all have failed." A sad look washed across Asha's face. "Only the scepter of power can break the bindings that hold her."

Harry recalled the thick chain that bound the SongBird Goddess's ankle. He doubted that a welding torch could even dent the heavy links. "Who would do such a thing?" he asked.

"Her brother, Atum-Khaos," Asha said without trying to hide the contempt in her voice. "It was he who imprisoned her for all eternity."

"Why would he do that to his own sister?"

Asha took a deep breath before answering, but once she began, her response poured from her delicate lips like a heavy downpour of Florida rain. "Long ago, when the universe was still a gaping shapeless void — even before time was set in motion — there was a great battle among the gods. Atum-Khaos, first born to Anu, the Father of all Gods in heaven and all creation, was Anu's greatest general. After defeating Anu's enemies, Atum-Khaos was declared second only to Anu himself."

"Let me guess," Harry said, interrupting her. "That wasn't good enough."

Surprised, Asha tilted her head to the side. "You have heard this story?"

Harry rubbed his calloused hand over his stubbly chin before answering. "Let's just say we have similar stories back where I come from. But I'm sorry. Please continue."

Asha considered this information for a moment and then continued. "Yes, well... Atum-Khaos gathered all those loyal to him and rose up against the Father of the Gods, but Anu was much too powerful and cast Khaos from the heavens."

"But what does any of this have to do with the SongBird Goddess?" Harry asked.

"I am getting to that, Harry. Be patient." Asha gently stroked his arm. "The SongBird Goddess's only crime was that she did not wish to see her brother perish in the fall, so she stood with him. But, she herself never lashed out at the Order of the Universe."

"So it was Anu who did this to her?" Harry asked.

"No, it was her brother, Khaos. After she suffered the same fate as her brother and was cast down from the heavens, she and the other fallen ones did many wonders with the few powers they still possessed. They bore many offspring by joining themselves with the local inhabitants of worlds that they helped nurture and create."

"But again, Khaos was not satisfied with sharing all of the power," Harry guessed.

"Yes, that's correct. It did not please Atum-Khaos that some of his own followers began to worship his gentle and more benevolent sister. So, in a fit of rage, he wiped her offspring from many worlds throughout existence."

"Didn't she and her followers try and stop him?"

"Yes, and it was a battle that lasted nine millennia. Just as Khaos was about to be defeated, his followers held three races of her offspring hostage: my people, the Awumpai, and the Adamah.

"Declaring a truce, the SongBird Goddess agreed to banishment as long as her brother swore not to harm her people. Unfortunately, she didn't know the terms of the banishment when she agreed. Since the SongBird Goddess is still an immortal and cannot be killed, Khaos banished her to a secret temple. He knew that she would still be able to reach out to her followers in dreams and whispers upon the winds, so he devised a punishment that would keep her in agony and distract her from communicating with her followers. As you saw, she drowns in a pit of sorrow, torment, and damnation while twin serpent guardians feast continually on her regenerating flesh."

Harry asked, "Is there anything we can do?"

"No," Asha answered. "At least, I do not think so. Her suffering is eternal."

Then, as if that explained everything, Asha picked her way through the nearby brush and dashed off into the forest, presumably heading back toward camp. Harry sensed that Fu-Mar was close behind.

Even more confused than before, Harry was about to follow, but he was suddenly — and violently — reminded why he had ventured into the dark forest in the first place. He started heaving from whatever it was that Hu-Nan had slipped him as if only Asha's presence had been keeping it at bay and now, with her absence, his body was free to revolt as it willed.

His sickness continued well into the next morning; and by morning, he had resolved two things: first, to get revenge on Hu-Nan (he recalled that he had a ration of laxative in his first aid kit), and second, to rescue the SongBird Goddess. He was a rescue pilot, after all.

Chapter 14

The City

RELAXING IN THE afternoon sun, Mac sat on a pack and rested her back against a crumbling stone block that had probably tumbled off the massive wall at some point in its past. She took a break from Captain Reed's journal and put it back in her coat pocket.

Thinking about the Awumpai, Mac felt that, in a way, Brett, and Stein were like her own Awumpai protectors. It was funny, she thought, that she already seemed to know the aliens in Captain Reed's book so well. She was sorry she wouldn't ever get the chance to meet them; they were probably dead and gone centuries ago.

Mac decided to check on Stein's progress. Despite his earlier comment, he was still a member of her crew. It had been nearly an hour since he had begun his climb.

Borrowing Brett's binoculars, she saw that Stein was a mere fifty feet from the top of the wall. Moving her gaze upward, she focused on the sentry tower and noticed that a sentry had taken up a position at the post. He appeared at the window and, to Mac's surprise, resembled one of the Mooks Captain Reed had described in his journal. The sentry seemed to be looking out at the distant ocean and had not seen Stein climbing below.

"What the hell is that?" Tae asked, looking through his own set of binoculars.

"I think it's a Mook," Mac said. She suddenly liked the idea of playing the role of tour guide and pointing out indigenous life forms. Reading the journal had paid off, after all.

"A what?" Leo asked.

"A Mook," Mac repeated.

"How would you even know that?" Tae asked.

Mac removed the Europa journal from her pocket. "I read it in Captain Reed's journal. He even drew pictures of them. See?" She flipped to several small sketches in the book.

"That's it all right." Tae passed his binoculars to Leo. "Can I read that when you're done?"

"Where did you even get that?" Leo asked.

"Joan gave it to me just before she died," Mac said. She swallowed the memory of her departed friend.

Brett stood nearby and heard their conversation. "Does it say if they are dangerous?" he asked.

"Captain Reed says they're harmless enough and are usually servants. It's the Awumpai you have to worry about."

"A-wump-ah-what?" Leo asked as Brett got on the radio and warned Stein about the Mook sentry.

"Awumpai — sort of like a cross between a yeti and a samurai," Mac explained.

"Sounds delightful," Tae said.

Mac didn't reply. She saw through her binoculars that Stein was just below the sentry house, and she watched intently. He had stopped his ascent to listen to the radio that he had mounted on his shoulder. Unable to free his hands and aware that they would be watching him, he nodded in response to Brett's message.

"Did the sentry spot him?" Tae asked Leo, who was still holding his binoculars.

"Nope," Brett replied for him. "Looks like the little guy is still looking out at the ocean."

"I hope he doesn't hurt him," Mac said.

"Are you kidding? Stein is an elite-class commando; those guys put Navy Seals to shame."

"I was talking about the Mook," Mac said dryly. "Captain Reed wrote in the journal that they're fairly docile creatures."

"Well, the little guy is armed with a spear," Brett countered.

Mac watched as Stein pulled himself up and slipped stealthily over the side wall of the sentry post. Stein towered over the little sentry, but the Mook didn't even notice the big commando behind him. A second later, Stein cupped his hand over the Mook's mouth, and both vanished from the sentry window, apparently falling to the floor of the watchtower.

The few seconds that passed felt like an eternity.

"Does anybody see him?" Mac asked.

"No. Do you think maybe one of us should go after him?" Leo asked.

Her shoulders tired, Mac dropped the binoculars and turned to look at him. "No, let's give him a few more minutes." She heard Brett already gearing up for the climb.

"Oh, crap!" Leo said.

Mac looked up in time to see the little Mook's body fall the last hundred feet. It hit the ground in front of them with a loud THUMP, which sounded like a big bag of water hitting the ground.

"Oh, my gosh!" Leo said, running over to the body.

"Brett, grab the first aid kit," Mac ordered. She looked at Stein, who now appeared in the tower window. His hands rested on the balcony, and he looked oddly pleased with himself. He had apparently hit some kind of release switch for the elevator; the flimsy-looking platform began to descend slowly on a thick rope.

Mac joined the others around the Mook, or the pulpy mess that was left of him. Even in his present state, the dead alien resembled the Mooks about which Captain Reed had written. He was small and thin, and his sickly purple skin appeared rubbery, like that of a seal. He also had big yellow eyes, one of which hung out of its socket, and two-fingered hands.

Leo touched the rubbery skin. "It's like touching a dolphin."

Tae frowned. "When did you ever touch a dolphin?"

"Didn't you ever go to Water World? They let you swim with dolphins and everything now."

Mac didn't hear the two men squabbling. She was certain of only one thing: she should have sent Brett.

—— o ——

The rickety elevator reached the ground. Mac decided they would ascend two at a time. She and Brett would go first. She was furious with the German commando and couldn't wait to get up there so she could give him a verbal thrashing. *Two first contacts in as many days and Stein kills them both. Nice.*

As they stepped into the elevator Tae asked, "What do you want us to do with the body? Hide it?"

"Might not be a bad idea," Brett said. "The locals might not be too happy when they find out we killed one of their sentries."

Against Mac's better judgment, she told Tae and Leo to hide the body in the woods for the time being. Maybe after they made some headway with the locals, they could explain the death as a misunderstanding. *Damn Stein for putting me on the spot like this!*

Above them Stein began operating the crank and the elevator ascended in jerky movements. The wooden platform creaked and groaned. The rope didn't sound much better.

When they were about thirty feet off the ground, Mac looked over at Brett and knew that he hadn't been kidding when he said he wasn't exactly comfortable with heights. He gripped the thin wooden railing so tightly that he caused the wood to creak even more.

"You okay over there, soldier boy?" she asked.

"Me? Uh, sure." He tried desperately to sound calm.

"Try not to look down." She smiled. "Look, you can see our camp from here." She pointed in the direction of the beachhead where they had left the soilmover and cargo containers.

As they ascended higher than the treetops, they had a great view of not only the base camp but also the distant ocean and the river on which they had traveled.

Mac heard Stein cranking madly away as the elevator approached the tower. It had taken him nearly an hour to crank them up. He had rested in ten-minute intervals, but she knew he had to be exhausted.

After they reached the tower and Stein locked the lift in place, Mac headed right for him. He rested against the wall, his muscles swollen and his body drenched in sweat. Despite his weakened condition, she delivered a strong right cross to his jaw. He didn't flinch, but his lower lip bled a little.

"Stein, what seems to be your major malfunction?" she said. Before she could lash into him further, she glimpsed a magnificent city out the window behind him.

Mac moved past him and out the sentry tower onto the open rampart, which was as wide as any two-lane highway back home. The city was so vast that her eyes couldn't take it all in at once. It was medieval in design and its stone walls, cobblestone streets, and thatched roofs reminded her of the thirteenth-century towns she had visited when traveling in Europe. This definitely wasn't Europe; the majestic city's size exceeded anything she had ever seen in Europe, or on Earth for that matter. Even more strange and wondrous, she also saw numerous floating castles, which were anchored to the wall with heavy chains, and a variety of floating ships.

"She's beautiful, yes?" Stein asked, sidling up next to her.

Mac ignored him. Despite the view, she was still too furious to grace him with words.

After a time, Brett asked, "What do you want to do next?"

"We need to get Tae and Leo up here first, and then I want to take a look around."

They took turns cranking Leo and Tae up. Then, after gathering their gear, they made their way down to the cobblestone streets below via one hundred and twelve flights of stairs.

—— o ——

When they reached the city, Mac and her crew moved about unchallenged and largely ignored by the local residents. It didn't take the new arrivals long to discover the city's basic social structure.

The little Mook servants, who wore rags, seemed to be lowest on the social scale. They served as the labor force and were seen doing a variety of menial tasks, including carting wagons, sweeping streets, and picking up dung. They didn't seem threatened or alarmed by the humans at all.

The city's middle class, which included shop owners and business people, was comprised of more human-looking creatures. In fact, upon first spotting these creatures, they looked human. However, a closer look revealed that they had several decidedly alien characteristics: bulbous heads; hairless, grey skin; long fingers; and black eyes.

Mac speculated that these creatures were some sort of a cross between humans and the grey aliens mentioned in

Captain Reed's book. "Captain Reed writes about little grey aliens, who abducting humans during his century," she said. She whipped out the journal and flipped to one of the pages. "See? He even drew pictures of them. Maybe the grey aliens abducted humans in order to breed them and populate this world and who knows how many others."

"What are you saying?" Leo asked. "These creatures are some sort of hybrid species, like the guys from Roswell?"

"She's right," Tae answered for her. "I mean, just look at them. They look like they're half-human and half-alien."

"They don't look human to me," Leo said disgustedly.

"I said 'half-human'."

Leo ignored Tae and soon spied a new type of creature. "What's that thing?" he asked.

Mac turned. A tall, well-dressed, beautiful woman, who resembled a blue-skinned elf, appeared amongst the Mooks and human/alien hybrids. She had striking black eyes that seemed to encompass nearly a quarter of her small head, and she towered above the other creatures. She had a large entourage about her and was obviously someone of great wealth and importance. Some of the human hybrids removed their head coverings and bowed as she passed, while the Mooks prostrated themselves before her.

"She kind of looks like an elf," Brett said.

"An elf?" Tae exclaimed. "I didn't see any pointy ears. And did you see those enormous black eyes?"

A sly grin spread across Leo's face. "I'm gonna go talk to her." He crossed the street and walked toward her.

Mac was about to stop the young co-pilot, but up to this point, despite the crowded streets, the townspeople had paid little attention to Mac and her crew. They had to make contact with someone at some point. Why not the elf?

Mac watched her future son-in-law approach the tall blue creature who was in deep conversation with members of her entourage. He attempted to get the female's attention, but she just looked down her nose at him. If anything, she looked annoyed. She glanced through a window and resumed shopping, and three hybrid creatures in her entourage blocked Leo from following.

Obviously shocked by the alien's behavior, Leo wore a frown as he started across the street toward Mac and the rest of the crew. Mac winced as he was nearly run over by a floating oxcart that was drawn by a flat-backed oxen with six legs and oversized buckteeth.

"No luck, huh?" Tae asked once Leo had managed to rejoin them safely.

Leo shook his head. "Nope. And she doesn't look like an elf up close. For one thing, she's got totally black eyes like the hybrids. Maybe she's a higher species of them, or something."

"Maybe will have better luck at one of the castles," Brett said.

"I'll tell you one thing," Leo said. "It looks like the author of *Chariots of the Gods* had it right after all. Now we just have to find Bigfoot, and we've solved just about every last unexplained mystery."

As if on cue, a tall, scary-looking creature clip-clopped around the corner and startled them. It wasn't Bigfoot but something far stranger.

The creature reminded Mac of a centaur because its body seemed to be a combination of two separate creatures. The lean upper half had a trapezoid-shaped head and two long, sinewy arms that ended in pincher-like fingers. One 'hand' carried a twelve-foot pike. A large diamond-like gem protruded from the center of the creature's face, and Mac guessed it served as some sort of eye. Two oval-shaped holes on the side of its head seemed to serve as ears.

The creature's lower half moved on thick, powerful legs the size of a Clydesdale's; however, unlike a horse, this creature moved on three legs that ended in heavy three-toed hooves. As the 'Tripod', as Mac came to think of it, moved toward them, she noticed that it moved both awkwardly, like two people in a three-legged race, and efficiently: it could immediately move in any direction, like a spider, and its top portion seemed to float about the lower legs as they moved.

"Kind of looks like a centaur," Leo whispered beside her.

Mac was about to concur, but the Tripod beat the base of its long pike against the stony street and spoke to them for the first time. *Where the hell is its mouth?* Mac wondered. She soon realized that it wasn't the Tripod speaking to them but rather a hologram. The hologram appeared to be projected from a disc that had been spot-welded onto the Tripod's left shoulder. The disc glowed brightly as it projected a hologram of a human/alien hybrid.

"Yo-ten-Nay, Hock!" the hologram bellowed at them. Simultaneously, the Tripod creature gestured for them to halt and pointed its long pike at them.

Brett and Stein racked the slides on their weapons and took aim.

"No," Mac said, stepping in the line of fire, "no more killing."

"You're in the line," Stein said through clenched teeth without averting his gaze from his rifle sight.

"You might want to tell him that, Commander," Brett said. He, too, refused to lower his weapon. The beam of his laser scope and Stein's centered on the Tripod's forehead, just above its gemstone eye.

"Hock!" the Tripod's hologram said again. Not receiving the appropriate response, the projected face then turned toward the Tripod's head and began speaking to it in the form of clicks and whistles, as though issuing a new set of orders in the beast's native tongue. As it did so, three additional Tripods clip-clopped out of the alleyways behind them, cutting off any hope of escape.

They were trapped.

Chapter 15

Millwood Junction

DAY 20

As the floating island continued to drift lazily toward the South Pole on magnetic, core-induced winds, the crisp arctic air grew warmer with each passing day. This day was the warmest one yet.

As the Awumpai rode their ostrich mounts alongside the caravan, Harry saw that the wooly giants' tongues hung low out of their gaping maws and their fur glistened with sweat. Hu-Nan, in particular, was shedding enough hair from his winter coat to make an entirely new Awumpai.

Asha and Harry rode in the lead ore cart, which had poked along a bumpy dirt road that spanned a barren sea of tundra wasteland for the last three days.

Lifting his tired gaze, Harry finally saw the end of the road. Up ahead, just visible on the horizon, he saw a little frontier town.

"What's that?" he asked, pointing on instinct with his right hand and feeling silly for waving a stump around.

"That? That is the town of Millwood," Princess Asha said. "It means 'city between many crossroads.' According to my studies with Ba-Tu, it was once home to an immense forest, thick with many trees, which extended as far as the eye could see."

Harry looked at the barren wasteland around them. "What happened?"

"About one hundred years ago, the gods came and took all the trees with them. Now it is just a crossroads in the middle of nowhere."

"Well, then why are we going there?" Harry asked grumpily.

"We need to obtain passage to Joppa-Cal," Asha explained. Her eyes were wide with wonder, and she was clearly delighted by the imminent change of scenery.

"Passage?" Harry asked. "Isn't this Joppa-Cal?"

The princess giggled. "No, Harry. This is only Millwood Junction."

—— o ——

The caravan stopped just outside the tundra town near the intersection of five roads that pointed in as many directions. Captain Reed examined the signs that accompanied each road. While he guessed that the inscription on the sign pointing toward town read 'Millwood', he was unable to read the wedge-shaped writing on the other signs.

Harry was surprised that only Ode, the Mook master, exited the ore wagon. Generally, all the Mooks scrambled out at once when the caravan stopped. Harry saw Fu-Mar give Ode a brown sack of currency.

"The Mooks, aren't they coming with us?" Harry asked.

"No. This is as far as they go. Besides Mooks can't go on the ship," Asha said.

"Ship? What ship?" Harry asked. He hadn't seen anything larger than ponds filled with glacier run off, let alone anything to sail a boat onto.

The princess smiled at him and leaped nimbly off the ore cart.

Asha ran toward a wooden promenade deck about thirty yards off the main road. When Harry didn't immediately follow, she turned back and yelled, "C'mon, Harry!"

Harry stepped off the cart as fast as his sore, trail-worn muscles would allow and walked off the dirt road after her. When he caught up with her, she was standing on the deck, which overlooked open air.

She pointed downward.

Harry knew that their caravan had been running parallel to the island bluffs for the past day or so; once during their journey they had passed over a swaying bridge where he had seen a ten-thousand-foot drop on either side. Partial prepared for what he would see, he carefully peered over the windy side.

Far below a lush green mainland was just floating into view.

"That's Joppa-Cal?" Harry asked. He pointed, left handed this time, at the vast jungles below that contrasted sharply with the arctic tundra through which they had been traveling for weeks.

"No, but we must go down there to get to Joppa-Cal."

"Well, how the heck are we gonna do that?"

As if in answer, an enormous vessel suddenly hovered into view. It came up from below the balcony on which they stood and silently rose above them. Then it turned sharply to its port side and proceeded toward the town. The ship passed so near to them that it startled the young princess and sent her into Harry's arms. Harry instinctively hugged her and shielded her from the wind with his back.

"That's how," she said. Her voice was muffled by his chest.

"What is it?" Harry shouted to be heard above the torrents of wind. He gazed at the ship's carved stone underbelly and deduced that it was made of the planet's floating ore.

"It's an ore ship," she said happily. She braved the winds to look up at him but still didn't let go.

Harry hoped that the Awumpai knew that he wasn't hurting the Dan-Sai. He wanted to live so he could ride in one of those magnificent hovering ore ships.

—— o ——

Shortly thereafter, the Mooks turned their oxen around and headed back the way they had come. Aside from a few supplies, the Mooks took everything in the caravan with them, even the Awumpai's ostrich mounts. Asha, Harry, and the three Awumpai were to continue on alone.

Harry hiked his rucksack onto his shoulder, and they headed toward the town. He checked his sidearm, which was set up cross-draw fashion in a holster on his right hip. Much to the Awumpai's displeasure, he had done a little target practice on the trail one day and found that he was as rusty as hell with his offhand but his early years on the range training with both hands hadn't faded entirely through disuse. At least he wouldn't be completely useless in a fight. The revelation made him happier than he'd felt in days. With one magazine loaded, two clips in the magazine pouch on his belt, and another three clips in his rucksack, Harry had a total of sixty rounds of ammunition. He would've liked to continue with his practice but he knew better than to waste those bullets. All in all, until he had something worth shooting, it was as good as it was going to get.

As they approached the town, Harry saw that Millwood Junction was little more than two rows of buildings with a paved dirt road between them. Covered plank walkways ran along both sides of the street and reminded Harry of photos he had seen of frontier gold-rush towns in Alaska.

What made this town unique, however, was the enormous building at the far end of the main street. The large, heavily lumbered building dominated all the other buildings in town. It was crowned with numerous wooden stairways and platforms that seemed to branch out from the huge building in no particular order. The individual platforms varied in size but most were large enough to receive the enormous ore ships. Seeing all the marvelous wood construction it was little wonder that the forests were all but gone.

As Harry looked at the structure, he saw the ore-ship that had flown over them earlier pull up to one of the station's platforms. Lines were tossed to waiting Mook longshoremen, and after the ship was tendered, gangways were lowered, and passengers and crew began to disembark.

This wasn't the only ship docked at the busy hub. Harry saw a variety of ships, in many different styles, embarking and disembarking. One large ore ship circled the docks, waiting for an open tender.

The ore ships were basic in their design and resembled old sailing ships. As a pilot, Harry was curious about how the ore ships' pilots controlled the vessels' yaw and pitch. Once they were on board, he vowed to speak with the pilot (or the equivalent) and see for himself.

—— o ——

Entering the town, Harry was surprised to see other humans. Elated, he ran up behind a short fellow dressed in a tunic, leather pants, and knee-high boots. Harry tapped on the man's shoulder and said, "Hi, I can't believe it! I thought I was the only human on this miserable ..." Harry stopped short when a half-human/half-alien hybrid turned to face him. He pulled back in revulsion at the sight of the alien's bulbous head and black, soulless eyes and fought the urge to draw his pistol.

The creature blinked at him a few times and shrugged its shoulders before spinning on its heel and walking away.

Looking at the other citizens on the streets around him, Harry saw that the town was comprised primarily of Mook slaves and human/alien hybrids. Some of the hybrids looked more human than others, but the black eyes were a dominant trait. Harry remembered the touch of long blue fingers, and the memory nauseated him.

"Friend of yours, Harry?" Asha caught up to him and hung on his elbow.

Harry's face had turned grim. "No, Asha. That thing will never be a friend of mine."

Asha frowned. She searched out his eyes, staring him squarely in the face. Suddenly Harry had a quick review of all his memories regarding his abduction.

She's reliving my memories.

The flash of memories was over in seconds and Asha patted him on the arm in understanding.

"Harry, you should never judge the many by the actions of the few."

Harry glanced away, feeling suddenly foolish.

They watched the hybrid townsperson duck into what Harry guessed was the equivalent of a general store. Harry saw what looked like farm tools, feed, and coarse woven bags amongst other miscellaneous goods for sale inside.

He identified other buildings, too, and was amazed at how similar this frontier town was to ones back home. He saw a hybrid sheriff standing out in front of a building that had bars on it, which he assumed was the local jail. The sheriff was a bit larger than most of the other hybrids, and he cradled a large rifle that resembled a musket. A thick but short deputy, who wore a bandolier loaded with enormous shells, stood nearby.

Directly across the street, music and laughter emanated from a large open-air building, which he figured to be some sort of saloon. Harry gave the saloon a wide berth; he had seen too many western Bs. The last thing he wanted to do was get into a bar fight — not that it would be much of a fight with the three Awumpai in tow.

Before they reached the ore-ship station, they stopped at what served as a post office, so Asha could send word to her father.

The post office in no way resembled the mail-carrier hubs with which Harry was familiar. First, the structure had no back wall. Second, instead of counters, the building had individual booths, like those in a shooting range. A colorful three-foot tall bird sat on perch in each booth.

A hybrid clerk sat near one of the sidewalls, and Asha carried a sack of coins to him. Harry noticed that the patrons stood before the birds and talked. Once done, the patrons fed the birds morsels of food they got from slots in the booths' walls — slots that the birds couldn't get into with their talons. The birds then recited the patrons' messages back to them while mimicking their voices perfectly.

After having paid the 'postage', Asha took Harry by the arm and led him to a cherry-red bird that had flames of orange on the backs of its wings.

"Now you have to be quiet while I do this, or it may confuse the poor thing," she said.

"Okay, but what is it?" Harry asked.

The princess made a face at Harry's ignorance. "It's a messenger bird. Don't they have them on your planet?"

"No." Harry shook his head. "Well, not really."

"Then how do you communicate with one another?"

"Huh? Oh, the telephone and sometimes the telegraph." Realizing that she didn't know the meaning of such words, he added, "We send our voices over wires strung over vast distances."

Asha shook her head. "And you find my world strange?" She lifted the soft velvet blind that covered the messenger bird's eyes and began singing a message to her father.

Her voice was too lovely for words.

The other patrons in the busy mail office must have thought so, too, for they stopped reciting their own messages just to listen.

Chapter 16

Ore-Ship Station

WHEN HARRY, DAN-SAI ASHA, and the Awumpai entered the crowded ore-ship depot, he was reminded of a train station he had visited in Amsterdam during the war. Both hubs had many seats lining the walls and vendors selling food and wares. However, in Millwood Junction, Harry saw hybrids with humanesque faces moving about the hub with many different types and sizes of luggage. Passengers stood in long lines before several ticket booths to buy heavy, eight-sided tokens about the size of a pancake. Each token had a strange symbol on it that Harry was unable to decipher.

Just as he and Asha got behind one of the shorter lines, the depot's double doors far behind them were violently thrown open. Harry and everyone else turned to look and saw a tall, slender, black-furred creature, wearing a white tunic, step from the brightly lit street into the building's darker interior. The creature carried a dangerous-looking scythe and reminded Harry of images he had seen on an Egyptian temple walls in National Geographic magazines.

The beast, which walked upright on two thick, dog-like legs, probed the immediate area with all its senses: its curved snout sniffed the air; its erect, square-tipped ears turned as if on a swivel, and its golden eyes scanned the crowd.

The jackal-like guard then raised one arm and said in a deep, thunderous voice (in Awumpai), "Make way for Queen Apsu!" He roughly shoved aside a passing hybrid to allow room for an elaborately festooned litter that was carried by a dozen Mook slaves.

As the litter entered the depot and moved to the line one over from Asha and Harry, more jackal guards, about half a dozen, appeared and encouraged other hybrid patrons to vacate to another line, which they did.

The litter's bejeweled gossamer curtains parted just enough for Harry to see the royal traveler riding Cleopatra-style within. The lone occupant was a humanoid female, who wore the brightly colored robes and gaudy jewelry of a rich queen. When the queen turned toward him, Harry got a good look at her hairless head, floppy ears, and long face, which was marked by oversized lips and a heavy brow.

She and her entourage of servants and guards stopped in front of the ticket counter. A short hybrid, who Harry guessed was the equivalent of her valet, seemed to have a difficult time with the ticket master in the booth. After arguing with the clerk in hushed tones, the well-dressed hybrid darted back to the queen's litter and whispered in her ear.

Upon hearing the valet's report, the queen swung her long legs over the side of the litter and walked down an improvised Mook stairway to speak with the ticket taker personally.

Before the ticket master could utter so much as a word, the aristocrat held up a long six-fingered hand and silenced him. "Ticketmaster, are you aware of who I am?" she asked in a crisp, concise tones that, to Harry, sounded vaguely British.

"Yes, your eminence," the unhealthy-looking hybrid behind the counter replied in a tiny voice. "You are Queen Apsu of the Southern providence of Skandaha."

"That is correct. So why did you tell my valet that the deckhouse has been booked?"

The hybrid swallowed and replied, "I'm sorry Queen Apsu, but, as I told your royal valet, the last rooms have already been taken. But, we still have plenty of room on the outside deck."

"On the deck? On the deck? This is an outrage. My valet booked this passage over seven hunter's moons ago."

The ticketmaster leafed through his reservations and tried to answer, but Queen Apsu cut him off. "And do you think it will do for Queen Apsu to sleep out in the open and ON THE DECK?"

The ticketmaster seemed to shrivel before her like a slug

showered in salt. "No ma'am." He rapidly flipped through more pages. "If you like, I can put you in the deckhouse on a flight two moons from today."

"Two hunter's moons from today?" she roared. "The gods will have come and gone from Joppa-Cal in two hunter's moons!"

When Harry realized that she was heading for the same destination they were, he rolled his eyes. The aristocratic giraffe would probably behave like this the entire voyage.

Just then, another hybrid clerk climbed up on a platform, picked up a cone-shaped, metallic bell, and clanged it with a rod several times. Hearing this, the majority of the waiting passengers below departed the depot and headed for their waiting ships. The depot was nearly empty, except for the tall queen, her slaves, and her bodyguards. The ticket booths began closing one by one, and Harry saw that it was growing dark outside the hub windows.

"I'm sorry, your highness, but the only room that still isn't occupied was booked eight hunter's moons ago."

The queen raised her painted eyebrows when she realized that there might be a stateroom available after all.

"And who, may I ask, is this patron?" she said.

The ticket master adjusted the writing utensil behind his ear, coughed, and pointed toward Dan-Sai Asha. "Well, your highness, it is she."

The queen turned and looked at Asha, who stood quietly in line at a different ticket booth. When Asha realized that the towering queen glared at her, she simply waved and said, "Hello."

Harry noticed that Queen Apsu immediately took note of the formidable Awumpai flanking Asha and appeared to size them up against her jackals. She seemed to decide that the barbaric beasts would be little match for her honor guard.

Ignoring Asha's greeting, the queen turned back toward the ticket taker. "I will not have this common rabble shedding their mounds of disgusting hair all over my new robes the entire voyage. Why, what would the gods think?" She shook her robes haughtily.

This comment received a heavy growl from Hu-Nan, but Asha held up a small hand to silence him.

Hearing the growl, Queen Apsu spun toward Dan-Sai. "You! Call off your dogs, little one, before my honor guards take them out into the street and teach them how to conduct themselves before royalty."

"Oh, I wouldn't do that if I were you," Asha said innocently. She shook her head, a worried frown on her lips. Harry was amused to realize that her concern was for the queen's safety.

Queen Apsu was turning away from Asha but whipped her head again toward the princess after hearing this comment. "You wouldn't do that if you were me?" the queen sputtered. "You wouldn't ..." she sputtered again.

Harry had dealt with enough high-society types to know that Queen Apsu was up to something. The queen probably figured that if her guards beat Asha's protectors into submission, it might open up her room in the deckhouse. Before Harry could warn Fu-Mar, the queen turned to the jackal guard nearest her.

"Ghanta," the queen said.

"I'm Chephren, your highness," the guard replied with a slight nod of respect.

Queen Apsu dismissed him with a wave. "Take these curs outside and teach them how to behave in a manner that is befitting my station."

Hearing this order, Fu-Mar stepped forward and took point. He carefully ushered the princess back to Hu-Nan, who, in turn, guided her behind his back.

Chephren gave the queen a nervous look. He leaned in close and whispered, "My Queen, those are Awumpai ..."

"And you are a royal bodyguard!" she snapped, cutting off any further discussion. "Remove these peasant vermin from my sight!"

Hu-Nan and Ba-Tu quickly moved the princess near one of the sidewalls, out of the way. Only Fu-Mar remained in the center of the room.

Harry could see the royal bodyguards were easily twice his size. And he knew he would be instantly broken in half the moment the fighting started. Despite this, he took his place next to Fu-Mar.

The battle-scarred warrior took note of this and Harry thought he detected a small turn of the corner of the Awumpai's lips.

Did Fu-Mar just grin at me?

Fu-Mar grunted something under his breath and suddenly Harry felt Ba-Tu's large paw on his shoulder. She pulled him backwards until they were standing against the wall next to Hu-Nan and the Princess.

Hu-Nan took up a position protectively in front of the princess and Harry could see the big red Awumpai grinning with delight. Asha grabbed her protector from behind, putting her frail arms around his waist, and peered through the crack between the crook of his elbow and his side.

Harry watched the eight royal jackal guards encircle Fu-Mar. Their confidence seemed to build as they realized that Hu-Nan and Ba-Tu would not join the fight.

"I'm worried about Fu-Mar," Harry said to Asha as he watched the older Awumpai pant heavily in the heat. "He looks overheated."

"Oh, he's fine," the princess said. She seemed surprisingly unconcerned for the well-being of one of her Awumpai.

Fu-Mar panted more heavily now, and his tongue hung out his open mouth. Clearly, the afternoon heat had taken its toll on the older Awumpai, and he was not up for a fight. Harry had never seen Fu-Mar look so bad before. Heck, the big guy could barely stand.

"Aren't you going to help?" he asked Hu-Nan.

Hu-Nan seemed perturbed by Harry's interruption. He glanced at Harry in annoyance and resumed watching the fight.

"Well, if you're not going to do anything." Harry whipped open his jacket and removed his .45 pistol from its holster in a cross-draw with his left hand.

He had taken one step toward Fu-Mar before Hu-Nan's baseball-glove-sized hand fastened again on his shoulder like a vice and roughly pulled him back. Hu-Nan hadn't given him so much as a glance.

"What the hell are you doing?" Harry asked. He looked to Ba-Tu for assistance, but the female Awumpai was leaning against the wall at her back. She sighed heavily, and, to pass time, removed knitting needles from her bag and began working on a blanket that she had started on the trail. The material was the same color as Hu-Nan's red fur.

What the hell was wrong with them? Couldn't they see that their friend was in trouble and in no condition to fight?

Fu-Mar already looked beaten. He stood there with his arms hanging loosely by his sides, as if he were too weak to raise them or his weapon. He panted heavily as the royal bodyguards slowly advanced on him from all sides. Stricken, Harry believed he was about to watch the old Awumpai get killed by the advancing jackal bodyguards.

Suddenly, Harry noted that Ba-Tu and Hu-Nan didn't seem to have any problem adjusting to the warmer climate.

When the jackals had Fu-Mar surrounded, Chephren brought his weapon to bear and lunged forward. He thrust his scythe toward the Awumpai's throat.

For a moment, time seemed to slow. Fu-Mar immediately straightened and darted to the side. He grabbed the shaft of the guard's weapon, pulled it toward him, and backhanded the guard in the chest. The force of the blow sent the jackal flying backward into the ticket booth.

Everybody but Asha and the Awumpai were stunned. Hu-Nan chuckled to himself and rubbed his palms together. While he was clearly excited to watch the show, Ba-Tu looked slightly bored and continued with her knitting.

The jackal guards looked at their fallen comrade, who lay unconscious among the debris of the former ticket booth, and then at Fu-Mar. Enraged, they all charged the Awumpai at once.

It was the first time Harry had ever seen Fu-Mar truly smile.

—— o ——

Harry watched the queen duck behind the counter and join the ticket master. As the queen watched Fu-Mar toss her honor guard all over the depot, the ticket clerk removed a messenger bird from its cage and spoke to it. The bird quickly flew out the depot ceiling.

As the battle raged on, a formidable-looking dagger slid

across the floor and stopped at Ba-Tu's paws. A jackal guard went to retrieve it but froze when he realized its close proximity to Ba-Tu.

Everyone waited silently to see what the female Awumpai would do with the discarded blade. When she realized that she was the center of attention, she sighed once more, put down her knitting, and picked up the weapon.

The fear in the royal bodyguard's face turned to confusion when Ba-Tu flipped the knife expertly into the air, caught it blade first, and offered the weapon back to him. Thinking it a trick, the guard refused to reclaim his weapon.

Ba-Tu offered it a second time, only this time she outstretched her hand farther.

Harry saw that Fu-Mar didn't seem bothered by Ba-Tu's action in the least and that Hu-Nan smiled with delight.

"Don't worry," the small princess said from behind the protection of Hu-Nan's thick hide. "She won't hurt you. You should probably take it."

After a few tentative reaches, the guard snatched the weapon out of Ba-Tu's clawed hand and darted backward to rejoin the fight. The knife didn't help him much, for Fu-Mar easily disarmed him a second time and threw him into one of his advancing comrades.

Just then, the result of the Queen's messenger bird arrived. The sheriff and his deputy burst through the main entrance. Unfortunately, the hybrid sheriff made the mistake of approaching the princess with his rifle. "You there, halt!" he told her in guttural Awumpai.

Hu-Nan's lion-like roar nearly knocked the sheriff off his feet, so Harry could hardly blame the sheriff for aiming and firing at the oversized Awumpai.

In the blink of an eye, Hu-Nan turned and hugged the princess to shield her with his back. The buckshot struck the thick armor on his back, denting it, and, in a few places, even punching through.

Once Hu-Nan was satisfied that the princess was unharmed, he stomped toward the sheriff. A retreating royal jackal guard got in Hu-Nan's way and was swatted away effortlessly.

The sheriff took another round from his quivering deputy and attempted to reload but, seeing that the enormous Awumpai was almost upon him, turned on his heel and attempted to flee. Before he could do so, Hu-Nan grabbed him by his collar and the waistband of his pants. The sheriff's body flew through the air and smashed all the way through the wall by the window. His body left an outline in the wall behind him.

When Hu-Nan turned toward the timid deputy and roared, the deputy retreated out the door through which he had come.

Meanwhile, still hidden behind the ticket booth, the queen ushered up two of her guards and pointed at Asha who was now standing alone, "Go grab her. Grab the little one," she ordered the two guards before ducking again behind the clerk's desk.

Harry tensed, reaching for his gun again, but the princess was not alone; Hu-Nan was only the second line of defense. When the two honor guards were nearly upon the princess, they discovered the third: Ba-Tu.

Ba-Tu's slender body moved between the two jackals in graceful, fluid motions. She struck them multiple times with her knitting needles before they even knew she was there. Their dead bodies, punctured with dozens of holes, hit the floor within moments of their fatal attempt to grab the princess. When a third jackal tried to attack Ba-Tu from behind, Hu-Nan appeared and tore the jackal's body in two.

Harry realized that anyone who approached the princess with the intention of harming her received the death penalty. The sentence was swift and sure. The royal bodyguards fighting Fu-Mar were still alive only because they posed no threat to the princess. In fact, during Fu-Mar's fight with the guards, he never drew his blade. As Harry watched, the last royal bodyguard dropped at Fu-Mar's feet, dazed but alive.

Fu-Mar stepped over the stunned guard and ripped the ticket counter from the floor. He threw it aside to reveal the queen responsible for it all. Queen Apsu backed against the wall and shrank into the floor.

Fu-Mar slowly withdrew his sword and held his blade to the queen's throat.

Asha picked her way through the debris and moved alongside Fu-Mar. She whispered something up to Fu-Mar's ear and gently moved his sword away.

Asha then knelt down beside the queen and said, "There, there old mother. Do not fear. Let me help you to your feet." She helped the older woman to stand, and two badly beaten royal bodyguards assisted.

Asha turned to the ticket clerk and handed him a sack of coin. "Here. This should compensate you for any damages my protectors may have caused. My apologies, noble ticketmaster. With your permission, please allow Queen Apsu to reside in my accommodations."

The clerk, happy that Princess Asha was speaking to him, replied, "Thank you, Dan-Sai Asha." Looking inside the bag, he added, "You are most generous, but I hardly think someone such as you should give up your stateroom for the likes of her."

"Please, grant me this, Ticket Master, and I will be forever in your debt."

The clerk blushed. "As you wish, Dan-Sai."

Hearing this, Queen Apsu dusted off her clothes and resumed her arrogant stature. She threw her scarf over one shoulder and, limping on one broken sandal, boarded the ore ship ahead of Asha's group.

Harry watched the way the clerk interacted with Asha and realized that the hybrid not only recognized her but also loved her, as Harry suspected most of the people of this world did. It was easy to see why; she was generous and noble beyond anything Harry had ever known.

Her kindness made him think of his own wife. Although his memory still had more holes in it than a block of Swiss cheese, one thing he remembered was that she was kind. He felt his heart physically ache for her. He had to get home to his family. Whatever the cost, however impossible, he would never stop trying.

Their tokens cashed, Asha, Harry, and the Awumpai boarded the ore ship that would take them to Joppa-Cal, the city of the gods. And quite possibly, the way home.

Chapter 17

The Ore Ship

AS TWILIGHT IN the darkening hemisphere turned to night, the light from three incandescent moons lit the magnificent ore ship's way while it sailed on a sea of clouds.

Standing in the bow of the ship, Harry watched Asha and her Awumpai prepare for slumber. He noticed that the other passengers kept their distance from the wooly samurai.

Harry was impressed that Asha had given up her stateroom to the snobby queen, but it bothered him that Asha would have to sleep on the frigid deck with the commoners, while the arrogant queen slept in the warm stateroom. However, watching Asha gaze at the starry sky, he realized that she probably preferred it this way.

The captain of the ship had given Asha several thick animal-skin blankets. She had gratefully accepted these and then quickly given them away to other passengers who shivered in the chilly winds.

Fu-Mar stood guard while Ba-Tu and Hu-Nan bedded down for sleep. Hu-Nan patted down his chest fur, as he did each night, so the princess could curl up there and go to sleep.

Harry took his own bedroll from his rucksack and lay down upon it. He was surprised when Asha chose to lay her head on his chest instead of Hu-Nan's. The big Awumpai was dumbstruck at her decision. When he realized that the Dan-Sai was not going to come over to him, he grumbled loudly enough for everyone on the boat to hear and roughly turned his back to Asha and Harry. Harry knew that he'd have to stay out of the big Awumpai's way in the morning.

The princess snuggled up to Harry. Her body was as light as a feather.

Just when he thought her asleep, she said, "Harry?"

"Yes, Dan-Sai."

"I'm afraid."

"Afraid of what, Asha?" Harry asked, using the same tone that he would speak to his own child, but Asha was already fast asleep.

Ba-Tu soon came over and tucked them in with the blanket she had made. It was as soft as it was warm.

"What's it she is afraid of?" Harry asked in hushed tones.

Ba-Tu briefly thought this over. "Harry," she said, "what do you think 'Dan-Sai' really means?"

He shrugged. "I thought it meant 'princess'. Why?"

"It does not mean 'princess'."

"What does it mean, then?"

Again Ba-Tu hesitated, unsure of her place. Of all the Awumpai, she was the most concerned about propriety.

"It means 'offering'," she said finally and walked away.

Harry grimaced and looked down at the little girl who slept on his chest. Did Ba-Tu mean Asha was being sent off to marry one of the gods? Maybe arranged marriages were the norm for this world. Of one thing he was certain, no harm would come to her, not as long as he was alive.

Looking up at the night sky, he drifted off to sleep and dreamed of home.

—— o ——

The next morning Captain Reed awakened to daylight on the deck of the ore ship and found himself wondering which reality was the dream world.

He shielded his eyes from the glaring sunlight overhead; it had to be at least noon.

"Bad dreams?" Ba-Tu asked. She sat on the wooden deck nearby.

"How do you know that I was dreaming?"

"You talk in your sleep."

"I dreamt about my family," Harry said. "I've got to get back to them somehow."

"Perhaps you could ask the gods when you get to Joppa-Cal," Ba-Tu suggested.

"Harry!" said the princess cheerfully. She no longer slept on his chest but leaned over the starboard railing. "Come see! Quick, or you'll miss it!"

He joined her at the railing and looked over the side just in time to see the ship clear the highest and longest wall he had ever seen in his life. The extraordinariness of the wall was matched only by the magnificence of the city that lay inside it. Numerous castles floated over the city, but nothing compared to the Olympian palace that hovered above it all.

They had arrived at Joppa-Cal, unquestionably the city of the gods.

Chapter 18

The Prophet

MAC SHUFFLED AWKWARDLY down the carpeted hallway in leg-irons and manacles. Per the Tripod's instructions, she kept her gaze on the floor and led her crewmembers, who were all shackled behind her — just like an old chain-gang in the South — into the throne room.

The throne room had once been lavish, but its faded carpets, slightly tattered curtains, and torn upholstery suggested that it had long since seen its prime. It was clean, however. Mook servants milled about performing various household chores, from dusting to scrubbing floors.

Much to Brett's and Stein's objections, Mac had thought it best to surrender their weapons without a fight. Given their present condition, it might not have been the wisest of choices, as both commandos made a point of reminding her at every opportunity. They had discovered that any deviation from the Tripod's orders resulted in a swift kick. The Tripods had paraded the humans through the city's cobblestone streets to the castle in the city center, but for the most part, Mac and her crew were unharmed.

"Aye-yock," the lead Tripod's hologram said. The creature halted in front of a tattered red carpet that lay over wide semi-circular stairs that led up to an even wider dais.

Risking a blow to the head from the guard's hooves, Mac looked up to see that they had stopped in front of a throne. A hunched-over, humanoid-looking figure in black robes stood next to it and had his or her back to the group. The humanoid read from a scroll to a hybrid servant, who nodded at his every word.

The lead Tripod's hologram uttered something to effect of "ya-touche," and the robed humanoid turned to face them. To Mac's surprise, the humanoid was actually a fully human man, who appeared to be in his late sixties or early seventies. He had a large nose, thick eyebrows, and a bushy, graying beard. For a moment, the man stood there and blinked at them in surprise.

"Ba-toi, dial kay?" he asked. He spoke a language that was similar to the Tripod's. Letting out a short laugh, he said something in a different language. It sounded like a question and he was directing it at them.

Leo's head popped up. "Hey, that sounded Greek."

A Tripod clip-clopped toward Leo and raised his spear. Leo quickly lowered his head.

The robed human held up a hand to stop the guard.

"You speak Greek, Leo?" Tae asked under his breath. He kept his eyes fixed firmly on the floor.

"No, but I know enough of it to know that he just asked who we are."

The robed man walked over to Leo.

"Say something, Leo," Mac said. She leaned out of the line-up to make herself heard and then quickly stepped back in line when the nearest of the Tripods struck its front hoof on the palace floor.

"I told you. I don't speak Greek."

"You speak Ang-lish," the robed stranger said, to everyone's surprise. "You spake Eng-Lash," he said again.

Mac answered for her stupefied lieutenant. "Yes, we're with United Coalition of Planets. Our ship crash-landed on your planet after traveling through a wormhole."

"Too fast, too fast," the robed man said, shaking his hands in the air. "First, I am Enoch, Prophet of the Gods. Welcome to Joppa-Cal!" He widened his arms in a gesture of welcome.

They looked at one another in surprise, except Leo, who asked, "I don't mean to sound rude, but do you think we could dispense with the irons?"

When Enoch gave him a questioning look, Leo shook his manacles for emphasis.

"Yes, yes, of course." He shouted commands at the Mook servants, who quickly scrambled to unlock the heavy bonds. "First, you must be hungry. You will be fed. And later, later I would hear of your tale."

Mac dropped the heavy chains to the floor, and they landed with a loud CLUNK. She rubbed her wrists and watched the Mooks release Brett and Stein from their bonds.

Tae and Leo stepped next to Mac. "You don't think he could be the same Enoch from the Bible do you?" Tae asked.

"No," Mac said in disbelief.

"Wait a minute. What are you talking about?" Leo asked.

"Didn't you ever go to Sunday school?" Tae asked him.

Leo shook his head and then shot back, "Oh, and I suppose you did?"

"As a matter of fact I did," then in a softer tone he turned to Mac and explained, "Before I was accepted to M.I.T. my mom wanted me to be a priest."

"Your point, Tae," Mac said exasperated.

"Genesis 5.24: 'Enoch walked with God; then he was no more, because God took him away.' The book of Enoch in the Jewish Bible is even more specific: 'And so it came to pass that Enoch rose up to heaven in a storm, on fiery steeds, in a fiery chariot.'"

"Why would it be the same guy? How could he still be alive?" Leo asked.

Before Mac could answer, Tae pressed his argument. "Why not? According to the Bible, Enoch was three hundred and ninety-five years old when he rose up in a fiery chariot, and his son, Methuselah, carried on for another nine hundred years after he left."

"I don't know," Leo said, "that's a pretty big stretch. What do you think, Mac?"

But Mac didn't answer and instead stared at the bearded man in robes. She knew that Tae and Leo didn't want to know what their commanding officer really thought, for they would think that she had gone mad. And that just wouldn't do.

——— o ———

A short time later, Mac and her crew sat at a dining room table that was long enough to serve over seventy people. Like the throne room, the enormous dining hall had once been lavish but had long since fallen into decay. Mook servants ran in and out of the kitchen with the marvelous feast they had prepared.

By the time Enoch finally joined them, the group had finished a seven-course meal. Mac couldn't make heads or tails of the first six items but the main entrée smelled, looked, and tasted like an oily roast pheasant — it wasn't half bad.

Enoch inquired about the group's adventures, and Leo recounted most of the story, although, to Mac's relief, he left out the murders of the river creature and the Mook sentry. Instead, Leo told Enoch about the Europa Moon Base, the wormhole, their crash-landing, and their trip to the city. The old prophet listened intently and occasionally nodded or asked Leo to repeat something he didn't understand.

After what seemed like hours, Mac became exasperated that the conversation wasn't a mutual exchange of information; they had learned nothing about Enoch. More abruptly than she had intended, she demanded, "Enoch, what is this place and who are you?"

Everybody in the room, including the Mook servants, stopped what they were doing and turned to look at her.

To her surprise, the old prophet answered her directly. He seemed to understand her frustrated curiosity. "This place is Joppa-Cal. And, as I have said, my name is Enoch. What else it is you wish to know, Ko-man-dier Macleansy?"

Mac frowned, suspecting that this was going to be tougher than she had thought. "How long have you been here?"

"I arrived here about two hundred years ago, and I was told by those who carried me to the stars that several millennia will pass in my absence from my house."

"How is that possible?" Leo asked. "In our timeline, you lived over seven hundred years ago."

Enoch spread his arms to the heavens. "Only by the grace of the gods."

"Are you the ruler of this place?" Brett asked from the far end of the table.

"Oh, no." Enoch smiled. "I am merely its caretaker for the gods."

"Do you have interplanetary transport?" Mac asked.

When he didn't answer, Leo added, "Uh, chariots that go from one planet to the next, like the one that I told you about, the one that brought us here."

"Ah. No, but the gods do."

"Are the gods here now?" Stein spoke up for the first time since dinner. He sat opposite Brett at the far end of the group.

"Yes and no," Enoch said. Seeing their confusion, he explained, "Khaos, greatest of all the gods, first born of Anu — he who gave birth to the universe — sees everything through the eyes of his followers, but he and his brethren will soon be amongst us once more. It will be a great day of celebration."

Mac noted that although Enoch tried to portray this event as a happy one, the look on his face did not match his words. Whether this Khaos could indeed see through the eyes of his followers or not, it was clear that Enoch believed the gods would hear any negative words said about them and issue severe punishment.

"What's that down there?" Leo asked, breaking the silence. When Mac turned to the co-pilot's seat, she found it abandoned. The young pilot stood in an alcove that ran parallel to the dining hall and pointed to a paved, mile-long ramp that sloped upward and ended abruptly.

"That," Enoch said proudly, "is the Royal Mile. When the gods arrive, the trumpets shall sound in all their glory, and the gods, the gods themselves shall descend from the heavens and be among us."

"Who are these gods you speak of?" Stein asked. Mac was surprised at the commando's curiosity.

"Surely my descendants told you about God, the one who made us? I went to a great deal of trouble to construct a place where my scrolls of knowledge would survive." Enoch looked at them worriedly.

"Well, the safe you put them in survived, anyway," Tae answered. Seeing looks of confusion, he elaborated. "Enoch is credited with building the Great Pyramids of Egypt."

"Wait a minute," Leo said. He rejoined them at the table and grabbed a piece of cheese. "I thought Cheops was the architect of the Great Pyramids."

"That's what modern day Egyptologists will have you

believe, but the ancient Egyptians regarded Enoch as the pyramids' builder."

Enoch seemed unfazed by this discussion, and he resumed his tale. "Shortly after, the gods brought me here in a fiery chariot and made me caretaker of this place."

Tae began speaking again in the voice he'd used for quoting the Bible, "And they sought them at the place whence Enoch rose up to heaven. And when they came to the place, they found the earth covered with snow, and upon the snow lay great stones like unto hailstones. They each spoke to the other: 'Let us dig away the snow and see if we may not find those who accompanied Enoch.'"

"And did they find them?" Enoch asked, looking troubled.

"Yes," Tae said soberly. He looked directly at Enoch. "They found the bodies of hundreds of your followers. They hadn't heeded your warnings to stay away and were burned to death. But your remains were never found."

"I did not know that," Enoch said sadly. "I warned them to stay away."

Mac gave Tae a hard stare.

Lifting his gaze, Enoch asked hastily, "And my son — my son Methuselah — was he killed as well?"

"Uh, no," Tae said. "He lived to be 969 years old. I think he was the oldest man in recorded history."

Enoch nodded at this good news, but Mac saw that the old prophet was still overwhelmed with grief over his followers' deaths.

"I am sorry, but I am an old man, and I am suddenly very tired," he said. "Please excuse me. My servants will show you to your bedchambers."

"Wait, Enoch. We still have so many unanswered questions," Mac said.

"Tomorrow, after you have rested and eaten, I will answer all of your questions." Turning to Tae, he said, "And if you like, young man, I will give you a guided tour of the city of Joppa-Cal."

Tae beamed. "I'd like that very much."

"Good then. My servants will show you to your rooms." Enoch rose from his chair.

"Please, Enoch, just one more question," Mac begged.

Enoch sighed heavily. "Only because you are such a lovely woman. What is your question?"

"How did you learn English?"

Enoch sighed again. "Out in the desert, several hunter's moons ago, a great fiery chariot fell from the sky. Not long after, Khaos descended from the cosmos, and a stranger then came to the palace. The stranger was dressed as you are, but Khaos was very angry with him. He and his friends were punished severely for their blasphemy and placed in my care. Then, after the Gods left, the man escaped. But before he did, I often visited him in his cell. He taught me how to speak Anglash and play a game he called chess."

"Where did he go?" Leo asked.

"My young friend, you're just as impatient as Harry was." Enoch smiled.

Everyone around the table immediately froze.

Brett was the first one to break the silence. "Hey, Mac, isn't that the name of the guy in your book?"

"You knew Captain Harry Reed?" Mac asked. "What happened to him?"

"Oh, now you want to know about Harry?" Enoch said. "Another time perhaps."

"No, now Enoch," Mac ordered.

A Tripod guard burst into the room. The prophet assured the Tripod that he was fine, and the sentry returned to its post outside the dining hall.

Despite the guard's appearance, Mac pressed the issue. "I'm sorry, Enoch. I know you're tired, but this is very important. What happened to Captain Reed? How did he die?"

"Die? He didn't die. At least, I do not think he died."

"Wait a minute. Are you telling me he's still alive?"

"Yes, yes. Well, he was alive when he left for the ruins, the ruins that fell from the sky. However, I'm afraid I haven't seen him in some time."

"Enoch," Tae said, "how long ago did you see him?"

"Let's see, the DaMookie celebration was last moon ... about six Awumpai moons ago."

"Tell me more about these ruins, these ruins from the sky," Mac said.

"Please, I am a very old man. I have answered your questions, and I must now go to bed."

"All right, Enoch. I'm sorry, but can you take me to these ruins in the morning?"

"No," Enoch said, "we can't go into the desert this time of the year. It's very dangerous; it's lyquest season."

"Lyquest? What's that?" Leo asked.

"Lyquest? Lyquest are carnivorous insects about the size of your head."

Leo turned to his commanding officer. "Mac, what do you want to go there for? These gods obviously have interstellar travel. Let's wait around for them and see if they can hook us up with a ride back home."

"That seems like the best bet to me," Brett added.

Mac stared at the two men in disbelief. "We have to find out if Captain Reed or anyone else from the Lost Patrol survived. And if these lyquest things are as dangerous as Enoch says, that's all the more reason to go out there and look for the patrol sooner rather than later."

"Mac," Leo pleaded.

"I'm going with or without you," she said. "It's settled. We'll go out to these ruins tomorrow and search for any survivors."

"I really wish you wouldn't go, but if you insist, I will arrange for my personal chariot to take you there," Enoch said.

"That's very kind of you. Thank you. I'm truly sorry for keeping you up so late."

The old prophet shuffled over to Mac. He reached up and tapped her cheek lightly with his weathered hand. "It's okay, my dear. I enjoyed your company. As for the rest of you, I bid you good night."

As the group got up to leave the table, Leo's face contorted as he clearly struggled to make sense of the information they had received. "Wait a minute; I'm confused," he said. "Enoch left Earth about seven centuries ago, but he wound up here less than two hundred years ago. Then the World War II pilots disappeared in the Bermuda triangle in 1945 and showed up here six months ago. We left Earth in 2168 and showed up here less than a week ago. It doesn't make sense."

"Unless this place is some sort of nexus," Tae said.

Everyone looked at him. "Care to elaborate on that?" Mac asked.

"We all know that a wormhole is a non-recurring, randomly generated pathway between two distinct space-time dimensions." He picked up a napkin from the table and folded it into the shape of a tunnel. "But what if, instead of a tunnel shape, our wormhole was shaped more like a funnel? Like this." He folded the napkin accordingly. "And for the sake of argument, let's say Enoch is here." He pointed to the wider, outer ring of the cone. "And we're closer to here." He pointed to the smaller end of the cone. "If this cone represents the shape of the timeline in a wormhole, then, regardless of when you traveled through it, ultimately everyone arrives at this point in the galaxy at roughly the same time."

"You lost me, partner," Brett said while pocketing some fruit from a bowl.

"In other words, Enoch left seven centuries ago, but he still travels to the same point in time and space as we do, except that he arrives a couple hundred years earlier. The missing pilots left Earth back in 1945, so they arrive say six months ago. We leave Earth in 2168 and arrive a week ago. We're all moving toward the same zenith in the wormhole."

"Yeah, but why is the wormhole cone and not tunnel shaped?" Mac asked.

"Well, my theory is that the wormhole must be closing on this end first; otherwise, it would be shaped like a tunnel."

Pondering Tae's theory, the group followed the Mook servants out of the dining hall and up several spiral staircases to their rooms.

As they gathered in the hallway before their respective doors, Mac turned to the group and bid everyone good night. Stein and Tae immediately disappeared into their rooms, but Brett called out to her in a low voice.

"Hey, Mac, is it okay if Leo and I talk to you for a minute?"

Here it comes, Mac thought. As they had walked up the long staircases, she had heard Brett and Leo going on about something in the rear. They joined her at her door, and she asked, "What's on your minds, gentlemen?" She hoped that having the conference at the door, rather than in her room, would keep it short. "Go on; spit it out."

"'Flesh eating locusts the size of your head,'" Brett said, reciting Enoch's words.

"Yeah, that doesn't exactly sound like Club Med," Leo added. "Maybe we should skip the ruins and wait for these gods."

Brett moved closer to her. "You know I'll back whatever decision you make, but these ruins sound pretty dangerous. Maybe Leo's right on this one. Maybe we should wait to talk with these gods. After we're better equipped and have more information, we can go out after Captain Reed."

"He's right," Leo said. "Besides, if these ruins are as dangerous as Enoch says, Captain Reed might not even be alive."

Mac looked at them as though they had sprouted multiple heads. She couldn't believe what she was hearing. "Look, Leo, if there's even the slightest chance that Captain Reed is still alive, I'm going out after him." She turned and unlatched the door to her bedroom.

"Why? Why do you have to go?" Leo asked.

"Because he's a rescue pilot, and he was lost trying to find pilots like you and me. The least we can do is look for him."

Brett removed his hat and looked as if he were about to say something else to Mac, but he seemed to change his mind.

"Well, if there's nothing else, gentlemen, I'll see you in the morning." She went into her room and closed the door.

Defeated, Brett turned from the closed door and saw Leo smiling at him. "What are you grinning at?"

"You like her," Leo said. "You like the commander."

Brett shook his head. "Go to bed, Leo."

As Brett walked down the hallway to his assigned room, he heard Leo taunting him. "Big bad Brett's got a crush on Mac."

—— o ——

Mac's bedroom resembled the rest of the magnificent, yet slightly rundown, castle. Flopping onto the bed, she smiled to herself. Captain Harry Reed was still alive, and she was going to meet him.

She rolled over onto her back and removed the journal from her pocket. After fluffing up a few dusty, old pillows, she settled in to find out what had happened when Harry had met with the gods. But before her eyes even focused on the open book, she fell fast asleep.

If she had stayed awake to read the next entry, Commando Brett Harper might have lived.

Chapter 19

The Palace

AS ASHA, HARRY, and the Awumpai marched up the long stone walkway, the so-called 'Royal Mile', to the magnificent floating palace of the gods, Harry noted that the palace contrasted sharply with the drab, medieval-looking city of Joppa-Cal.

The palace was breathtaking. To Harry, it reminded him of all those pictures he had seen in National Geographic. It was as though the designers of the Taj Mahal, the Parthenon, the Mayan temples, and the Egyptian pyramids collectively had built the palace. Or perhaps it was the other way around, Harry mused. Maybe the designers of Earth's greatest architectural wonders had been inspired by the floating palace. Either way, Earth's monuments paled in comparison with the enormous palace.

The entrance alone was two-stories high. The great doors were propped open to receive the myriad worshipers, who arrived with tributes of jewels, livestock, and slaves.

Captain Reed had seen many strange beings since he left Earth, including light-bulb-headed Martians, purple-skinned Mooks, wooly samurai, and fairy wood nymphs. However, the two guards that flanked the palace's entrance blew them all away in the category of weirdness. The humanoid creatures stood on three powerful legs and had giant gemstone eyes. Their lower bodies clip-clopped around like horses, but these orange-skinned creatures were far from horses.

As they passed between the two guards, Asha moved a little closer to Harry's side and squeezed his hand. Harry wasn't afraid to admit it; he squeezed back.

The Awumpai snorted with distrust when they moved near the creatures, and Harry knew that Fu-Mar, at least, kept his hand near the hilt of his sword. If the tripod-legged creatures were afraid of the Awumpai, they didn't show it.

The group passed through the doors and came to a stop. A line of worshipers had formed in the inner hallway, and it took Harry, Asha, and the Awumpai another hour to progress to a second set of giant doors. As Harry neared the doors, he saw the reason for the holdup: a royal announcer, a tiny hybrid who bore an uncanny resemblance to a Siamese cat, stopped the line to announce each newcomer as he or she entered the palace.

Finally, it was Asha's group's turn. "Announcing Dan-Sai Asha of the Province Mukara."

Within the palace, the air was cool and smelled sweet.

"Ah, can you hear the music?" Asha asked Harry.

But Harry heard nothing besides the announcer's annoying voice, the echoes of shuffling feet, and the joyful chattering of the worshipers. Looking at Asha, he saw that she was clearly entertained. Her eyes were ablaze as though they looked at something wondrous. However, when he followed her gaze, he saw nothing.

Sensing his frustration, Asha finally looked back at him. "Oh, I'm sorry, Harry. I forgot." She reached up and lightly touched behind his ear with her middle finger, just as she had done by the river to show him the vision.

Harry felt a slight shock and suddenly heard beautiful harp-like sounds. When he looked up, he saw glowing female forms in translucent gowns playing strange, yet wonderful, instruments. The smell of an intense, pleasant fragrance flooded his nostrils, and his body instantly felt lighter.

"Do you hear them now?" Asha asked.

His senses were so overwhelmed that he had nearly forgotten her presence. "Yes," he said, "but what did you do?"

Asha thought about his question before answering. "I helped you," she finally said. She grabbed the inside of his elbow, and they continued to move deeper into the palace with the masses.

As they neared a hallway leading to one of the outer chambers, an effeminate male voice addressed Asha and said, "Ah, Dan-Sai Asha, we've been expecting you."

Harry saw a tall, thin, elf-like man standing amongst the numerous marble columns that flanked the hallway. The elf's velvet clothes were adorned with glittering jewels, and he had multiple rings on each of his fingers.

"Do you know him?" Harry whispered.

"No, do you?"

"Please, Dan-Sai, right this way." The elf, who was nearly as thin as Asha, gestured for the group to follow him up a large marble staircase that was hidden from the masses by the thick columns. Every inch of the walls around the staircase was adorned with decorations composed of precious metals.

"Thank you," Asha said in her language. Harry understood her perfectly and assumed this was another benefit of her 'help'. He found himself wondering why she hadn't 'helped' him before now. Perhaps it was something that had taken her time to figure out or maybe it wasn't until after the bar fight she had deemed him worthy.

After ascending the staircase, they were ushered into a white tiled room where numerous visitors received spa treatments from dozens of Mook slaves. Some visitors received manicures, while others received haircuts or deep-tissue massages. The room reminded Harry of a very fancy version of his mom's beauty salon back home in his youth.

When the Mook beauticians weren't scrambling about in a frenzied state, hurriedly obeying their master's commands, they were dancing on the balls of their two-toed feet, anxiously awaiting their master's next command.

"Don't worry, Dan-Sai. We'll have you looking fabulous in no time," the head beautician informed Asha.

"Thank you, Master Beautician. You are most kind."

Seeing Captain Reed's haggard appearance, the master beautician raised a nostril and said to his assistant, "Put the strange one into a susha bath right away."

"Get your damn hands off me!" Harry yelled when two Mooks grabbed him without warning. He heard a PHOOT sound, and when he turned toward it, he saw one of the Mooks concealing a small tube in his white tunic.

Suddenly, a susha bath didn't sound so bad anymore. It actually sounded pretty good.

"It's okay, Harry," the princess said. "They're just going to give you a susha bath."

"A su-sha bath?" Harry's eyebrows raised as the room seemed to tilt at an odd angle.

"Don't worry. You'll be fine." She allowed the Mooks to lead him away, and she herself was led to another beauty chamber.

"What about his clothes?" an assistant asked the master beautician.

"Destroy them," he replied.

Assistants immediately began tearing Harry's clothes from his body. His prized bomber jacket had survived World War II, an alien abduction, and a crash-landing, only to be destroyed now.

"No, wait," the beautician said just before the Mooks threw Harry's soiled and torn clothes into a nearby furnace. "Give his clothes the full number six cleaning treatment and repair them."

The Mooks gave Harry's clothes to the tailor's assistant, who was so short he could barely see over Harry's garments and boots when they were piled into his arms.

"What about his hair?" another assistant asked.

The master beautician thoughtfully rubbed his narrow chin. "Shave him bald."

Harry's eyes glanced questioningly at the assistant, who signaled another Mook to bring the clippers to the barber. The clippers were activated and began vibrating loudly. It seemed as if the buzzing sound of clippers was universal. Harry's drugged body tensed up slightly, but the Mooks holding him tightened their grip on his arms.

The tailor's assistant dropped one of Harry's boots, and as he bent down to pick it up, a photo fell out of Harry's bomber jacket.

The photo fluttered slightly and landed near the master beautician's velvet slippers. He picked it up and examined it.

It was the photo of Harry, Julie, and their daughter in front of their Florida home.

"Wait!" the master beautician said to the barber with the clippers. "Cut his hair like this." He held out the photo.

The barber turned the photo this way and that and examined it up close and at arm's length as if there would be serious consequences for any deviation from haircut in the photo.

Meanwhile, another set of Mooks retrieved a ladder, set it next to Harry, and climbed it at various heights.

Without warning, the floor parted behind Harry. He glanced over his shoulder, and his eyes went wide when he saw a tub filled with thousands of small, diamond-shaped fish — susha, he presumed.

The susha resembled suckerfish, but the sushas' bodies were lined with thousands of little frilly fronds. These fronds scrubbed off the outer layer of dead skin and scooped it up into the sushas' tiny mouths, which were located near their bellies. As they fed, the fish secreted a pleasant cologne.

The Mook on the ladder's top step placed a cap on Harry's head, and the other two Mooks pushed his drugged body over. He fell backward like a towering oak tree and landed right in the tub.

Despite the drugs he had been given, Harry was terrified when he felt the susha scrambling all over his body and imagined that the small creatures were eating him alive. He gripped both sides of the tub and attempted to climb out, but several Mooks shoved him back under the waves of susha. Harry screamed as they did so, but his scream was muffled by the squishy sounds of the squirming parasites.

After every pore of Harry's body had been cleansed, but violated, he was removed from the susha bath and given a robe. The Mooks drugged him for a second time and moved him to a cushioned chair for his haircut, manicure, pedicure, and facial.

As Harry was getting his treatments, an assistant asked the master beautician, "Sire, what do you want to do about the Awumpai?"

"Send them in one at a time."

"Are you sure that's a good idea?" the assistant asked nervously.

"Of course I'm sure. Why wouldn't I be sure?"

"Well," the assistant gulped, "the big one's already eaten one of the Mooks."

Needless to say, the Awumpai never got susha baths. Harry figured that Hu-Nan would probably just eat the fish anyway.

—— o ——

After his treatments, Harry waited for Asha in a room near the palace's main audience chamber. He wore his uniform, which now looked brand new, and he had never been cleaner or sweeter smelling in his life.

"Hi Harry," Asha said as she walked through the room's double doors with her Awumpai behind her. "You look very pretty."

"I've never felt so violated before in my life," Harry said.

But Asha didn't hear him. Her face suddenly turned serious, and she grabbed his hand and led him to a nearby couch.

"What are you doing?" he asked, concerned by the serious look on her face.

"Before we go inside, I want to give you something."

"Okay."

"Do you remember the SongBird Goddess?"

"Yes," Harry replied immediately. He still felt compelled to rescue her. "Is she here?"

"No, at least not really," Asha whispered, as though to admit such a thing were a crime. "What I give you now is not from me but from the SongBird Goddess. I am merely a vessel. And she, she got it from the Father."

Asha took Harry's severed wrist in her small hands. "I would have given it to you sooner, but I wasn't ready." She blew on his wrist, her breath sweeter than jasmine. "And I may not get a chance to give it to you later." She blew again, and this time lights resembling tiny butterflies escaped from her bluish lips.

Instinctively, Harry tried to pull away, but Asha held fast. Her delicate frame was surprisingly strong. "It kind of burns,"

Harry said. The butterflies encircled his entire body, and he found himself in a tornado of the butterfly lights.

"Hello in there! The gods will see you now," an assistant said from behind the audience chamber's double doors. He knocked and called to them again, but a vicious roar from Fu-Mar ceased any further inquiries.

A few seconds later, the butterfly lights dimmed and disappeared. Asha, Harry, and the Awumpai walked to the doors that would lead them into the god's audience chamber.

Harry opened the door for Asha — and used his right hand.

Chapter 20

The Offering

THE AUDIENCE CHAMBER was roughly the size of a small football arena and had ceilings at least four stories tall. Despite its enormous size, nothing in the room was unadorned; every surface, from the walls to the furniture, was artfully and intricately decorated. If the décor itself didn't overpower the senses, the contents of the room were sure to stagger the mind.

Harry took one step inside and noticed alien orchestras floating in the air. The musicians played unique instruments and danced near the ceiling. He also saw a large body of clear cerulean water suspended in the air like a giant teardrop or drop of rain. When he walked beneath it, Harry saw blue-skinned, mermaid-like creatures frolicking in the water. One of them stopped to peer down at him. She had sea-green eyes, gills, and waist-length, braided hair that was clasped with tiny seashell clips. Although the mermaid initially took his breath away, she subsequently reminded him of the SongBird Goddess, who suffered in her aqueous tomb.

Harry figured there had to be at least a thousand worshipers in the audience chamber. While some worshipers prostrated themselves in prayer, others enjoyed the festivities. The jubilant music was nearly drowned out by the worshipers' laughter, talking, and singing as they honored the gods of their choice.

Asha explained that royalty from every province of the known world was in attendance to pay tribute to the gods in the forms of gold, livestock, and slaves. Harry even saw Queen

Apsu and her entourage. Her Mook slaves and the remainder of her jackal bodyguards pushed through the crowds while carrying her in her litter. Despite their recent unpleasant encounter at the ore-ship depot, Harry was glad to see a familiar face, even one as disagreeable as Queen Apsu's.

The queen's jackals did a fair job of clearing a path until they encountered about thirty male humanoids who resembled Asha. Whoever they were, it was clear to Harry that the jackal honor guard wanted to mess with them about as much as they wanted to go another round with Fu-Mar.

Asha saw Harry looking at the humanoids and explained, "Those are Mukarian Bowmen. Their bows are the most feared weapons in the land."

Harry looked closely at the Mukarians, who wore similar mauve- and wine-colored tunics. He realized that what he had mistakenly assumed were animal bones on their backs were really curved bows.

"They come from my father's kingdom," she added. One of the largest and most fierce-looking bowmen caught Asha's eye and nodded respectfully.

Asha curtsied and bowed her head in reply. Harry thought that he saw Asha blush slightly, which once again reminded him of her youth.

Harry also saw that more of the powerful-looking Tripod sentries lined the walls and were sprinkled strategically amongst the crowd. The curious creatures stood watch and did not participate in the festivities. Harry saw Fu-Mar observing the Tripods, too.

When they moved deeper into the room, Harry finally saw the 'gods'. To him, every last one of them looked like they belonged in Frankenstein's zoo. A demigod sitting in an alcove was the first to catch Harry's attention. The god sat on a lavish throne that was engulfed in icy blue flames, and he was surrounded by worshippers. Everything the demigod touched blazed with icy flames until he released it. When Harry saw him put down a glass of wine, the goblet was frozen with ice.

Looking at the gods, Mooks, hybrids, jackals, Mukarians, Tripods, and Awumpai, Harry recalled the fantastic creatures from Greek mythology and decided that this palace and the wondrous beings within its walls would surely give any Grecian or Roman Olympus a run for its money. *Or perhaps they are all the same?* he wondered.

As Asha led them toward the front of the room, Harry saw a large circular dais. A towering, beautiful man with wolf-like facial features and sun-colored hair floated on a throne above it. He wore a form-fitting tunic that accented his powerfully built, twelve-foot-tall body. The man's size was staggering; his skull alone was the size of a barrel, and he was at least a head taller than the Awumpai.

"Who's that?" Harry asked Asha in a hushed tone.

"That is Atum-Khaos, ruler of all the gods, ruler of us all."

Harry could tell from her tone that she wasn't happy about this situation. Despite Asha's obvious mistrust of the god, to Harry, Khaos appeared to exemplify benevolence: his arms were outstretched, his palms face up, and he smiled down on his admiring worshipers. His energy seemed to extend throughout the room, and he also seemed to absorb and revel in his worshipers' attention.

The god's followers crowded around him. Their hands were interlocked, and their bodies swayed rhythmically while they sung him praises. Harry was mesmerized by the scene, which was more fantastic than anything he had ever seen or imagined. Khaos seemed nothing like the cruel villain Asha had described. Harry felt as if he could stare at Khaos and admire his statuesque beauty for hours. Khaos was a living, breathing work of art — that is, until he looked back.

Harry saw the god's face and was startled to notice his dark, liquid eyes, which enveloped a quarter of his head; his mouth filled with rows of shark-like teeth; and his six-fingered hands. Harry had seen those black, soulless eyes before on the aliens that had abducted him and on the hybrids at Millwood Junction. It suddenly dawned on Harry that the aliens and hybrids were Khaos's offspring. Somehow, Khaos must have crossbred himself with early versions of the Mooks to create hybrids, the same way his mother used to crossbreed her flowers in her garden back home.

But that didn't explain Asha and the Mukarian bowmen. They looked nothing like Khaos. *Whose offspring are they?*

Harry wondered. He suddenly remembered the SongBird Goddess's swirling multi-colored eyes — eyes that resembled Asha's and the Mukarian bowmen's — and realized that they must be the goddess's offspring.

Spying a large gleaming baton near the armrest of Khaos's throne, Harry asked, "What's that on his throne?"

"That's the scepter of power," Asha said. "It was forged by the one true Father, Anu."

So that's the only thing in the universe capable of freeing the SongBird Goddess, Harry thought. To him, it looked like a glowing storm lantern on a stick, except the lantern portion appeared to be at least three feet tall and two feet in diameter, while the stick portion added about another twelve inches in length. The scepter was engulfed in a white-hot light. Harry suspected that to look at it was to risk blindness.

Before Harry could inquire about the scepter further, there was a loud, THOCK-THOCK- THOCK near one of the sidewalls. Everyone turned and saw a black-robed old man with a bushy beard. He beat his wooden staff, which was a foot taller than he was, onto the floor of a balcony that overlooked the entire room. The music stopped, and the talking ceased. Not a sound could be heard within the chamber.

Seeing that he had everyone's attention, the old man raised his weathered staff and shouted at the top of his lungs, "All hail Atum-Khaos!" His face beamed with love.

"All hail Atum-Khaos!" the crowd boomed back in response.

"All hail he who brought the universe from the Great Darkness!" the old man shouted.

"All hail Atum-Khaos!" the crowd cried more loudly and jubilantly than before.

"All hail he who did battle with the evil gods for his children and was victorious!"

"All hail Atum-Khaos!"

"Do you love your god of your own free will and with all of your heart?" the robed man asked.

Around Harry, Asha, and the Awumpai, the crowd thundered, "With all our hearts, we do!"

"Then let the tributes begin!" the old man bellowed, his lungs nearly bursting from his chest.

There was a loud cheer from the followers. The orchestra once again played joyous music, and a long procession of tributes from numerous kingdoms began. Each kingdom, along with its tribute of precious gems, ore, livestock, or slaves, was announced in turn.

Watching Khaos bless his followers as they showered him with offerings, Harry found himself wondering what he was really looking at. Had everything he had been taught in Sunday school been a complete and utter lie? Was this really the god who spoke to Moses on Mount Sinai?

A Mook servant carrying a platter of hors d'oeuvres bumped into Harry and interrupted his thoughts. Harry looked down at the small creature, which offered him what looked like a susha wrapped up in a little doughy roll. When the hors d'oeuvre blinked back at him, Harry declined.

"You are wondering if he is God," the Mook waiter said.

"Are you talking to me?" Harry asked. He was surprised that he and the Mook were able to communicate but surmised that it was another result of Asha's 'help' when they had first entered the castle.

"Yes," the Mook said. "Are you here to pay homage to the greatness that is Atum-Khaos?"

"No. Well, yes. Well, not really."

"You seem confused."

"You have no idea." Harry looked around for Asha, but she was playing the role of ambassador with a portly king from another province.

"Well, maybe you could ask the great Atum for guidance," the waiter said.

Harry frowned. "I doubt Khaos will make time to speak to an insignificant speck like me."

The Mook smiled broadly, something Harry did not think Mooks were capable of. "Atum-Khaos loves all of his children. Just love him back with all of your heart and soul, and he will grant you what you desire the most."

Harry shoved his hands in his pockets and pretended to ignore the annoying waiter. He hoped the waiter would just go away.

But he didn't. Instead, the Mook asked, "Do you know what it is you want the most?"

"What? Yeah, uh, sure. For starters, how about helping me find my missing crew and the pilots I was sent out to find? And, oh yeah, help us all get back home to Earth and our families."

"I sense your pain," the Mook said.

"Yeah, well, there's really not much you can do about it," Harry said irritably.

"Certainly there is." The Mook's voice grew more calm and loving by the second.

"Really, and what's that?" Harry asked.

"Just know that you are not an insignificant speck," the waiter said, seemingly reading his thoughts. "I love all my children. I am that which you seek. I am the creator of your forefathers and all of things. And yes, I will send you home to your children. All that I ask is that you worship me above all others."

Harry couldn't believe his ears. When he looked back down at the waiter, he noticed that the waiter's eyes did not resemble the normal goldfish-like eyes of a Mook but rather the eyes of the twelve-foot being floating on the dais. Harry decided that this was definitely not some run-of-the-mill Mook slave. *Can it really be? Can I really be standing before God himself, who has taken the form of a Mook waiter just to talk to an inconsequential dot in the universe like me?*

Harry was nodding and about to say 'yes' when he heard an announcement that drowned out even his innermost thoughts. "Dan-Sai Asha from the Kingdom of Mukara!"

Harry looked up and saw that it was Asha's turn to present Khaos with a fitting tribute. When he turned back to the waiter, the Mook's eyes had returned to their normal dull yellow color.

"Who are you?" Harry asked.

But the waiter responded in the rubber-band-like Mook language, and Harry couldn't understand a word. When Harry didn't take an hors d'oeuvre from the waiter's serving plate, he shrugged his shoulders and sauntered off. Whoever or whatever the Mook waiter had become, it was that no more.

A feeling of elation washed over Harry. Was there really a chance that this Atum-Khaos would take him and his men back home to their families? Heck, why not? He had helped the Awumpai safely deliver the Dan-Sai to the gods, after all. Harry decided he would take a glass of wine from a passing waiter's platter. He even felt like dancing. He didn't. But he felt like it.

Instead, he decided to join Asha. He was working his way to the tribute pen, where he had last seen her, when the music died down and the lights in the chamber dimmed. The only lights now visible came from Khaos's scepter and from Asha.

Pushing his way through the crowd, Harry saw Asha's tiny form crumpled on the floor before Khaos. She had a glowing aura about her that resembled the one Harry had seen when she conversed with the SongBird Goddess above the river.

A hush enveloped the audience as Asha slowly and delicately lifted her head and began to sing. Her song resembled the one Harry had heard that night by the river, but it was sadder and more poignant. Then, just as she did at the river crossing, Asha slipped her terrestrial bonds and rose above the adoring crowd, singing with even more fervor. She was truly an angel among mortals, and the crowd sighed as she sang.

This must be what Ba-Tu meant by 'offering', Harry thought. He had been worried that Asha herself was going to be the tribute, but maybe it only meant that she was going to offer Khaos a song.

The crowd's adoration for Khaos began to transfer to tiny Asha. Even Harry, a mere mortal, felt the energy in the room shift from one god-like being to another.

Harry was just as captivated by Asha's singing as the rest of the crowd, but because he had heard her sing twice before, once by the river and once in the post office, he alone noticed that something strange was happening to Atum-Khaos. The god's white-hot aura deepened into a reddish-purple. The god fidgeted, and the more the people adored Asha's angelic singing, the more the god's aura deepened. It became a dark, venomous red.

"ENOUGH!!!!" Khaos bellowed, jumping to his feet. "I AM NOT PLEASED!" His booming voice shattered windows, goblets, and chandeliers. Many worshipers screamed and fled the room and his wrath.

Asha abruptly ceased her singing but continued to hover before Khaos.

"THIS IS THE SEED OF THE SONGBIRD GODDESS AND WOULD DO HARM TO YOUR GOD!"

The remaining followers cried out at this statement, and the Tripods slammed their pikes into the floor.

Harry was dumbfounded. The throngs of loving worshipers, who only moments ago were sighing with admiration for Asha and her singing, turned into an angry mob filled with murderous rage. Even Asha's bowmen screamed obscenities at her. When Harry looked into their eyes, however, he saw that their once multi-colored orbs had become all black, like Atum's.

As the crowd continued to yell at little Asha, Khaos ignited his scepter of power, causing it to glow even more powerfully, and silenced them all. He lifted his scepter and held it outstretched toward Asha.

The vibrant colors swirling about the tiny princess first dimmed and then began moving toward Atum's outstretched hand. As the energy transference took place, Asha weakened, and her small body slowly descended toward the floor. Her aura turned from the color of autumn leaves to black, and her beautiful icy-blue skin faded to grey.

Harry stepped forward, "Stop it! You're killing her!" But Harry's warning fell on deaf ears. The god was in rapture as Asha's life force drained from her body to his. Harry turned to Fu-Mar. He was certain that the Awumpai would protect Asha, no matter what the odds.

To Harry's surprise, Fu-Mar instead signaled that it was time to leave. The Awumpai spun on his heel and started toward the exit. Ba-Tu followed him through the mesmerized followers.

Harry pushed his way through the crowd and quickly caught up with him. "Fu-Mar, stop!" He blocked the Awumpai's path. "Where are you going?"

Fu-Mar easily shoved him aside.

"Ba-Tu," Harry pleaded.

"I'm sorry," she said, "but this was our purpose. We were charged to deliver Asha to the Atum, and we have done so."

"So he can kill her?" Harry asked.

Ba-Tu hesitated.

"Look at her, Ba-Tu. She's dying. Look at her!"

Ba-Tu began to turn her head, but Fu-Mar pushed her toward the exit.

"I'm sorry." She walked away without a backward glance.

"Well, to hell with this," Harry said. He attempted to draw his pistol, but Fu-Mar quickly restrained him. Harry saw tears well up in the Awumpai's eyes, but Fu-Mar held fast.

"You bastards!" Harry said. "You bastards! I'll kill you all for this!"

Fu-Mar again attempted to lead Harry to the door but suddenly seemed to notice that Hu-Nan was missing. He turned. The big red Awumpai had remained near Asha. Fu-Mar growled at Hu-Nan, but the shaggy Awumpai ignored him. When Fu-Mar repeated his command, Hu-Nan shook his head in defiance and refused to look the older Awumpai in the eye.

Harry had never seen Hu-Nan (or anything else for that matter) disobey the old warrior. Fu-Mar immediately shoved Harry aside and moved toward Hu-Nan. But before Fu-Mar could stop him, Hu-Nan stepped forward and growled thunderously at Atum-Khaos.

Hearing Hu-Nan's roar, Khaos lowered his scepter, and Asha's nearly lifeless body collapsed to the floor. Atum glared at the big red Awumpai and shouted at his Tripod guards, "REMOVE THOSE FILTHY AWUMPAI FROM MY SIGHT!"

Hu-Nan rushed to Asha's side with surprising speed. Two mighty swipes from his oversized arms sent the approaching Tripods flying. He then reached down and scooped up Asha's body. He held her in the crook of his arm, as a parent holds a newborn.

The crowd gasped in bewilderment. Some fearful worshipers darted for the doors, while others were rooted to the spot, paralyzed by their surprise.

Hu-Nan held Asha protectively to his chest. Two Tripods with long pikes moving toward him, and he released a deep, throaty growl that stopped the duo in their tracks. The Tripods shuffled their hoofed feet nervously before moving away from the large Awumpai to wait for reinforcements.

Seconds later, the Tripods reinforcements appeared, and a dozen of the creatures encircled Hu-Nan. The Tripods jabbed their long pikes at him, and one blow slashed his arm and grazed Asha's head.

The small cry that escaped Asha's lips sounded like a crack of thunder to Harry where he stood frozen between Hu-Nan in the center of the room and Fu-Mar near the door. The small sound seemed to reach Fu-Mar's ears as well because the old Awumpai stopped dead in his tracks.

The Tripods continued to jab and strike at Hu-Nan with pikes and axes. The big Awumpai was losing blood from several wounds. Nonetheless, Hu-Nan remained defiant and clutched the princess to his chest.

A Tripod with a double-bladed ax stepped behind him and prepared to deliver the killing blow. Free of his paralysis, Harry drew his gun, but before the blow fell or he could fire a shot, the Tripod's head was severed from its shoulders. The severed head flew through the air and landed in the overhead aquarium while the body took a few halting steps and collapsed to the ground.

The crowd parted to reveal Fu-Mar, who stood in a samurai stance with his hand on the hilt of his sword. Most of the remaining audience members fled for the exits while two Tripods charged the old Awumpai

Neither of the Tripods saw the black Awumpai leap through the air behind them while firing bolts from her projectile weapon at the backs of their heads. The thick-shafted bolts protruded from their faces; alien centaurs turned into grotesque three-legged unicorns. Ba-Tu landed between their bodies, paused for a moment, and moved off before their lifeless forms even toppled to the floor.

Simultaneously, a third Tripod leaped before Fu-Mar and hoisted his mighty battle-ax. He confronted Fu-Mar with an impressive ax demonstration and took a mighty swing at the older Awumpai. Fu-Mar dodged under the swing and bolted past the Tripod with a burst of speed. The Tripod's body split in half at the waist and crumpled to the floor in two pieces behind Fu-Mar.

A fourth Tripod drew back its arm to throw its pike into Fu-Mar's unprotected back, but Harry's .45 rang out five times. All five shots made a pulpy mess of the Tripod's face. The creature fell to two of its knees, but the third limb remained extended and kept the inert body at an odd angle.

Harry moved over to Hu-Nan's side to relieve the Awumpai of the princess. He scooped the princess up in his arms, and Hu-Nan rose painfully to his feet. The Awumpai nodded in thanks.

The red Awumpai roared as he joined the fight. The battle turned in the Awumpais' favor, and they more than held their own against the seemingly inexhaustible supply of Tripods that surrounded them. Harry did his best to stay between the three giant protectors and, because he held the princess, could only watch as Fu-Mar and Hu-Nan kept the Tripods at bay.

As he jumped back from a pike thrown at him, Harry turned to find a Tripod rearing up its front two legs in order to trample him. Before Harry could so much as cry out, Ba-Tu appeared on the Tripod's back, reached around to the front of its throat with a captured knife, and slit its throat. As before, she was gone before the Tripod's body ever found the floor.

Harry didn't see Khaos signal the Mukarian archers to attack, but the god must have done so because scores of arrows suddenly hit each of the Awumpai protectors.

The Awumpai cried out in pain. Fu-Mar, roaring at this newest threat, grabbed a nearby set of chairs in each hand and flung them at the archers, who were reloading their bows.

The missiles struck three of the bowmen to devastating effect, but several more archers took their places.

Fu-Mar and Hu-Nan overturned a heavy banquet table and motioned for Harry to duck behind it. As he did so, the long tabletop was struck by a score of arrows.

Harry gently laid the tiny princess on the floor behind the table and reloaded his pistol. Seconds later, Ba-Tu joined him and they stood up together to gun down several more members of the bowmen infantry: he with his pistol, she with her crossbow.

More enemies took their places.

Harry removed his second pistol from his waistband with his left hand, needing to double his effort to keep the archers busy. Aiming at the nearest archer, Harry saw that it was the same bowman who had nodded to Asha earlier. Like the other worshipers, the archer's eyes now resembled Khaos's, and he aimed his bow directly at them. Harry fired left-handed. His first two shots went wide, but the third hit the young Mukarian between the eyes.

Just when it seemed as though the Awumpai, Harry, and the princess could make a break for it, a ball of kinetic energy appeared out of nowhere and struck the table barricade with a horrific BOOM. It left a small crater in the floor and knocked all of them off their feet.

"ENOUGH!" Khaos yelled while holding the scepter of power.

His ears ringing, Harry said, "Wow, that thing really packs a punch."

He'd lost count but knew there had to be nearly fifty more Tripods clip-clopping into the room and just as many archers aiming their bows from the walls. Before any of them could recover from Khaos's blow, the Awumpai, Harry, and the princess were surrounded once more.

Fu-Mar pulled Harry to his feet, and the group quickly formed a circle around Asha. They kept their backs to one another and faced the enemy, who, for the moment, held their fire.

Harry and Fu-Mar exchanged a grin. "Hell of a way for an Awumpai to go out, don't ya think?" Harry asked. The old Awumpai grunted in reply.

"KILL THEM! KILL THEM ALL!!!" Atum ordered.

The Tripod's moved in but halted at the sound of a quiet voice that was so lovely, so pure, it demanded attention.

"No," Asha pleaded.

The Awumpai unwillingly parted to reveal the princess. Harry noticed that her normal ice-blue color had turned completely grey. She held her side with one arm and leaned heavily on Ba-Tu with the other.

She started to say something else but coughed up crimson blood. Ba-Tu steadied her, and she tried again. "Please, Atum, let them go," she begged.

Harry realized that the jealous god had already delivered the fatal blow. Asha would die whether they managed to escape the palace or not.

"Mercy, Atum!" a worshiper in the crowd cried out. When Harry tried to identify their benefactor, he was surprised to see that some of the eyes of Khaos's followers had returned to their normal colors.

"Mercy!" shouted another.

"Mercy!" shouted Queen Apsu, who was flanked by her honor guard.

Although ready to strike, Khaos considered the audience's cry for mercy. His sinister, murderous grin was replaced by a brief look of confusion over this latest development, and then his smile took its place once more.

"My Atum," Asha said, "I will give my life willingly if you will but spare my friends."

Atum thought this proposition over and responded, "I WILL BE MERCIFUL AND SPARE YOU AND YOUR FRIENDS, BUT YOU MUST CHOOSE WHICH OF YOUR BELOVED AWUMPAI SHALL DIE IN YOUR PLACE."

"I'm sorry, my liege, but I can no more choose one of my Awumpai than I can choose a favorite star in the night sky." The small princess trembled.

"IF YOU DO NOT CHOOSE ONE, I WILL KILL THEM ALL," Khaos warned.

Asha turned and looked at her battle-weary protectors, who now helped each other to stand and to remove the well-placed arrows from their bodies.

Asha turned back toward the jealous god and shook her head. "I'm sorry, but I cannot choose."

"BUT YOU HAVE ALREADY CHOSEN. IT IS THE AWUMPAI WHOM YOU LOVE MOST, AND THAT LOVE HAS NOW BETRAYED IT."

Without another word, Khaos formed another kinetic fireball with his scepter. This one was larger and more menacing than before. It burned brighter and brighter and was accompanied by a shrill sound that crescendoed in volume and pitch.

Before releasing it upon the chosen Awumpai, the angry god turned again toward his audience of followers. "ALL KNOW THIS: HER BETRAYAL KILLED THE ONE WHOM SHE LOVED MOST."

Hu-Nan stepped forward and braced for the blow. It was Hu-Nan with whom the young princess played, laughed, and cried the most. She tied ribbons in his hair, slept on his mighty chest at night, and ran to him when she had bad dreams. He dropped his weapons to the ground, outstretched his arms, and waited for the inevitable.

Atum held the kinetic ball of power on his scepter for a few more seconds and then flung it toward the Awumpai.

But the mighty fireball streaked past the red-haired Awumpai ... and struck Ba-Tu instead. The blast tore open Ba-Tu's chest and created a cavernous wound that exposed her ribs.

Tears streamed down Asha's face, and she rushed to the fallen Awumpai's side. Ba-Tu could not move her head, but her eyes focused on the princess.

It took Hu-Nan a moment to realize that he had not been hit, and then he instinctively bared his teeth at Khaos and moved toward the angry god, flinging the nearest Tripods out of his way.

A small army of Tripod's stepped in Hu-Nan's path, and Fu-Mar struggled to hold Hu-Nan back.

"No, Hu-Nan, no!" Harry yelled. He stepped in front of the big Awumpai, his arms raised, "Please Hu-Nan. Another time."

Still fighting and still furious, Hu-Nan thrust Harry aside and reached forward to crush a Tripod's head in his claws before several more Tripods piled on top of him.

"DO YOU WISH TO DIE, FILTHY ANIMAL?" Khaos asked. He conjured up another fireball above his scepter.

"No!" Asha cried out from near Ba-Tu's fallen form. "You made a promise. Let them live."

At Asha's cry, Hu-Nan stopped his struggles and fell limp in his captors' arms.

Khaos looked at the followers still in the room. "SO BE IT."

Except for Ba-Tu's labored breathing, there was silence. Harry, Fu-Mar, and Hu-Nan moved near Asha and surrounded their fallen friend.

A small army of Tripods encircled the group. The Tripods took no chances and pointed their weapons at the Awumpai.

The Mukarian bowmen, who were no longer under Khaos's spell, slung their bows upon their backs and bowed their heads in shame. Asha collapsed over Ba-Tu with grief. She looked into Ba-Tu's eyes, and so much love passed between them with that look that Harry's throat ached. The princess embraced Ba-Tu, and the Awumpai closed her eyes. When the Tripods pulled Asha away, Ba-Tu was dead.

Hu-Nan knelt beside his fallen friend. He took Ba-Tu's hand in his, and a long sorrowful howl escaped his lips.

Harry clenched his fists and stepped toward the murderous deity. "I don't know who or what you are, but you are not my God!"

Several Tripods had formed a barrier between Harry and Atum, and they lurched forward, causing Harry instinctively to take a step back.

Despite their presence, Harry shouted, "What kind of a god would kill a creature as noble as this!" He gestured toward Ba-Tu.

"YOU WORDS ARE BLASPHEMOUS, AND YOU SHALL DIE FOR THEM!" the deity said. He formed another fireball and flung it. The energy force streamed toward Harry but struck the princess in the back instead. She had freed herself from the guards' grasp and leaped into Harry's arms in one last selfless act, taking Atum's vengeance in his stead.

Harry fell to his knees while still holding Asha. His face close to hers, Harry watched the life force drain from her eyes.

"Don't lose faith, Harry," she said. "Don't lose..." She died before she could finish her sentence.

Harry hugged her to his chest. He attempted to hold back his sobs but failed. He didn't even feel the guards' hands remove her lifeless body from his arms. The kinetic deathblow might as well have torn through his chest as well, for his heart felt as though it were no longer beating. He heard the Awumpai struggling against the tidal wave of Tripods that now swarmed over their bodies, but Harry just didn't care anymore.

Asha had been sacrificed to the gods after all.

Chapter 21

The Ruins

MAC PILOTED THE open-air hover chariot over and around numerous hilly peaks while the wind whipped through her hair. With the exception of a few sharp projections, the terrain had been similar since they had left Enoch's castle. The chariot flew east, toward the approaching ginger-colored dawn, and Mac was enjoying both the scenery and the flight.

Looking behind her, she saw Stein and Brett on either side of the chariot, rifles slung but at the ready. Enoch had returned their gear that morning before sending them out into the wastelands. Tae sat between the two commandos clutching his backpack to his chest as if he'd thought he'd never see it again. His fingers, meanwhile, were twitching as he stared around with wide eyes at the strange aircraft. She knew he would have loved to tear the chariot apart and put it back together again, just to see what made it tick.

Leo, wearing sunglasses, sat beside her in the front seat. He looked as though he were enjoying a Sunday afternoon drive. In fact, he had asked to drive several times, but Mac wasn't ready to give up the wheel just yet.

"How will we know which ruins are the ones," Leo made quotation signs with his fingers, "that fell from the sky?"

On the horizon, Mac had just spotted a crashed spaceship that resembled the Roman Coliseum. It had crashed on its side as though it had taken a nosedive into the planet, more specifically into the side of a mountain. "Oh, I think we'll know," she said.

Tae leaned forward and stuck his head between them. "Looks like a crashed UFO."

Leo finally saw the spaceship. "Look at the size of it!" he said. "It's gotta be the size of a football stadium!"

The chariot made a low pass over the enormous vessel and the vast amount of wreckage surrounding it. Mac spotted what appeared to be the remains of a single TBM Avenger plane mixed in with the crashed spaceship. Yep, definitely the right one.

Mac saw a nice open landing spot near the wreckage. "Okay, everybody hang onto something. I'm gonna try and put this bucket down in one piece."

"Uh, could you say that again but with a little more confidence next time?" Brett asked from behind her. She glanced back to see him white faced and clutching his seat. She tried not to laugh.

Much to Brett's surprise and relief, the hover chariot landed safely and within walking distance of the Avenger wreckage they had spotted from the air.

"This way," Stein said. He got his bearings and led them up a trail that wound through the wreckage, which reminded Brett of junkyards he had frequented as a kid back home.

Looking back, Brett saw that the commander brought up the rear. She had been through so much, but he had never seen her waver. She reminded Brett of the early pioneer women in the West who had hacked their stake right out of the untamed wilderness alongside their men. She was definitely the kind of woman he'd want to settle down with one day.

Despite his feelings for her, Brett was a realist. *Even if we weren't stranded on an alien planet in another galaxy and even if she weren't a superior officer, there's no way someone as strong and beautiful as Mac would ever fall for a big dumb country boy like me*, he thought. These and thoughts of alien locusts devouring them before they could escape occupied Brett's mind for about fifteen minutes, and then he spotted the first Mook.

The group had been walking steadily up the mountainous trail when the first of many native Mooks revealed itself. It stayed partially hidden amongst the wreckage on the side of the trail, but it certainly took note of their presence. And it had friends. Lots of them.

"These don't look like your garden-variety Mooks," Brett heard Leo say. Brett spied a Mook that hid atop a pile of wreckage. The Mook peered down at him with a menacing look on its face, and unlike the Mooks with which they were familiar, had bones and jewelry piercing its face and skin.

"I don't think these Mooks are exactly tame," Tae said nervously after spotting yet another Mook. This one wore some kind of war paint and had animal bones sticking through its limbs.

"Maybe they're an indigenous species," Brett said. His head swiveled as he scanned their surroundings. Moving closer to Stein, he whispered, "I count at least twenty." He casually flicked off the safety on his rifle.

"More like thirty-five," Stein replied. His rifle's safety had been off since landing.

"It's okay. They're harmless, remember?" Mac reminded them. Brett could tell that she was eager not to repeat the wall-sentry incident but he was starting to get the vibe that it wasn't going to be peaceful encounter either way.

PHOOTTT! A six-inch dart from a Mook blowgun hit Mac's shoulder.

"Harmless, my ass," Brett said. He fired a quick burst at the Mook holding the blowgun. The direct hit blew the Mook clear off the junk pile on which he stood.

"Mac, you okay?" Leo ran beside her and pulled the dart out of her shoulder.

A mob of angry, rubber-band-like shouts came from the bottom of the trail. Brett turned to see about a hundred Mooks running up the hillside toward them. A few more jumped out of the wreckage on either side of the trail.

"Oh, cripes!" Mac said.

Brett and Stein each emptied a magazine into the nearest of the Mooks. "Reloading," they shouted in succession as they dropped spent clips and inserted new ones. For the moment, they kept the closest of the advancing Mooks at bay, but the hundred or so coming up the hillside was another problem entirely.

Both men dropped to their knees, pulled out some charges, and stuck them in the ground on the trail. Brett looked at Mac and the others. "What are you waiting for? Run!" he said.

Looking at the swarm of angry Mooks, Leo and Tae didn't need any further urging, and they darted up the trail.

"What about you?" Mac asked.

"Don't worry. We'll catch up," Brett said.

Stein had already finished setting his charge. He jumped to his feet and sprayed a quick burst at the advancing Mooks. Half a dozen went down on the trail and slowed the pace of those behind, but the tidal wave of Mooks continued to advance at an alarming rate.

"Time to go," Leo said as he came back down the trail to retrieve Mac, who had frozen in place. Leading her by the arm, he dragged her up the hill.

Brett finished with his charges, and both commandos soon followed Leo and Mac. The light-footed Mooks were almost upon them.

"Hit the deck!" Brett yelled while diving behind nearby wreckage for cover. Once Brett was sure Stein was safe, he clicked the detonators three times. "Fire in the hole!"

The explosion engulfed the first twenty Mooks and blew them apart. Brett and Stein sprayed the few Mooks that had gotten through ahead of the crowd and were stumbling around, stunned by the explosion.

"That should buy us a little more time," Brett said. He took one last look over his shoulder, and they were off once more.

The two commandos easily caught up with the astronauts. The group rounded a bend in the trail together, and then the trail bottlenecked through a tight entranceway that led into a wide, circular dead-end.

A solid wall of the crashed UFO blocked their path, and the walls of wreckage on either side were just as impassable.

"Dead-end," Leo said.

"No kidding, really?" Brett reminded himself to thank Leo for stating the obvious if they ever got out of this predicament. "How many charges you got left?" he asked Stein.

"That was my last." Stein set up behind a small wall of junk that would serve as cover. He began removing his magazines and placing them within easy reach on a slab of scorched metal.

Brett unslung his rifle and removed his sidearm. He checked that the pistol had a full magazine and a round in the chamber and then threw it to Mac. "Mac, here. Try and keep them at the entrance. We have limited ammo, so pick your targets." Brett then removed a second pistol from his vest and gave it to Leo. "Here, take these mags and divide them up with the commander," he ordered.

Although Leo outranked the commando, it was pretty clear that Brett was the man currently in charge. Leo took the weapon and the magazines from him.

"You know how to use one of those?" Brett asked.

"Yeah, this end goes toward the bad guys," Leo said.

Brett had to admit it; the young pilot was keeping his cool. Just then, the first three Mooks ran into the bottleneck entrance.

Stein was first on the trigger and mowed them down. "Reloading," he yelled while replacing his spent magazine with a fresh one.

"Covering fire," Brett yelled back to him, but for now, no more Mooks appeared.

"How many more of those do you have?" he could hear Tae ask Stein.

"Six," Stein answered. He seemed to think for a second and then removed his pistol and handed it to the engineer. "Spare clips are in my magazine pouch on my belt."

Tae was reaching for the spare clips when the Mooks swarmed into the funnel. As the commandos knocked the first ones down, other Mooks climbed over their fallen brethren. And when those Mooks fell, the Mooks behind used the pile of bodies for cover as they flung spears, blew darts, and shot arrows at them. When a second arrow flew past his head, Brett decided he was getting tired of playing cowboys and Indians. Fortunately, they had excellent cover and a little bit of range, which made it difficult for the Mooks to hit them.

"Persistent little guys," Leo said to Brett.

The commando noticed that Leo hadn't wasted a single shot. "Good shootin', Lieutenant. You would've made one hell of a commando."

The Mooks abruptly stopped advancing. Everybody held their breath.

"I think they finally gave up," Leo said.

"No," Brett said, "I hear them climbing the wreckage around us. Alan, how much ammo you got left?"

"Two magazines, you?"

Brett sighed; he had hoped for better. "I'm down to my last one, six rounds at that."

"I'm out, too," Mac said.

Stein looked at Tae, who also had a respectable kill ratio. "How much ammo do you have left?"

Tae ejected the magazine from his pistol and saw no ammo. "I've got one round left in the chamber."

"You might want to save that for yourself," Stein said.

Tae threw Stein a dirty look.

Brett hoped Stein wasn't right, but these Mooks were savages. Who knew what kind of torture they were capable of?

A Mook suddenly jumped up on the wall behind Brett and Leo. Neither of the two men saw it aiming its spear down on them. BANG! The dead Mook fell off the wall and landed between the two men. *Well, that decides that*, Brett thought as Tae stared at the dead Mook through the smoke of last shot.

"Thanks, Tae," Leo shouted. He asked Brett, "So what do we do now?"

"Ain't nothing but a thing, chicken wing. We just beat them the good old fashion way." Brett grinned and unsheathed his long, jagged survival knife. He buried it in the soft metal nearby for when the time came.

He reached for the knife only seconds later when the Mooks again swarmed the entrance. Brett and Leo were closest to the entrance and went first to hand-to-hand combat. Brett used every trick in the book: he tossed Mooks right and left, bashed their heads against the walls, stabbed them, and sliced their throats. Leo had trouble with just the two Mooks in front of him and the third on his back.

Mac came to Leo's aid and whacked one Mook upside the head with a pipe she had found amongst the wreckage, but she, too, was soon overwhelmed by Mooks.

Stein fought like a man possessed and killed Mook natives as fast with his knife as he had earlier with his gun. But even the big giant was wearing down. One Mook sliced his knee, while another blew a dart into his back.

Their little Alamo had been overrun, and there was no escape. In a matter of seconds, it would be over, and they would all end up in Mook stew.

Brett knew it. They were finished.

TAT-TAT-TAT-TAT-TAT-TAT-TAT-TAT-TAT-TAT-TAT-TAT-TAT-TAT!

Heavy machine gun fire from overhead dropped scores of Mooks around the humans. Mooks were shredded by the dozens, and those that tried to flee were cut down from behind.

When the shooting finally stopped, Stein and Brett made short work of the remaining Mooks and then stood guard near the entrance. Tae joined Mac and Leo, who looked up at the wall behind them and tried to spot their benefactor.

Just then, a man appeared. He had dark, wavy hair and wore khaki pants and a bomber jacket. He put his boot up on the edge of the wall and peered down at the group. The distinct nose of a .50-caliber machine gun was visible on the ground next to him.

"It's freaking Indiana Jones!" Leo exclaimed. Brett stared at the pilot, worried he'd taken a hit to the head and then realizing at the last moment that it was a classic movie reference.

"Who?" Tae asked.

Before Leo could answer, the man in the bomber jacket called down to them, "You all right down there?"

"Yeah," Mac said, "thanks to you." Brett found himself frowning at her tone. Captain Harry Reed was alive, and he had just come to their rescue, and Brett wasn't at all sure that he liked the effect it was having on Mac.

Chapter 22

Final Resting Place

MAC COULDN'T HELP but stare at the rescue pilot sitting across the smoldering campfire, resting his elbows on his knees and holding a tin cup of sweet-smelling coffee in both hands. He was taller than she would have imagined and had dark-brown hair, with graying temples. His wavy bangs had grown out and hung over his eyes. Unlike her former husband, who was always clean shaven and wore a suit to work every day, Captain Reed had a rugged look, with his five-o'clock shadow and his worn flight jacket.

Mac did some quick mental calculating and determined that he had to be at least 254 years old: it was 223 years since he had vanished in the Bermuda Triangle, and records showed that he was thirty-one at the time of his disappearance. The ruggedly handsome pilot didn't look much older than thirty-five. Mac decided that he was precisely the sort of man who could build the frickin' Swiss Family Robinson tree house — complete with a two-car garage and a swimming pool fed by a bamboo aqueduct — after being dropped in the jungle with only a pocketknife.

—— o ——

After Harry had saved them from the Mooks, he had lowered a rope into the ruins. Brett and Stein had climbed up first and then pulled the rest up.

Introductions had been made, and then Harry had led them to his camp, which was about a quarter of a mile farther up the grassy mountainside. To Mac's surprise, it was a fairly respectable camp that included a pitched tent, a small fire pit, a clothesline, and an aqueduct system that caught and stored rainwater. Harry had rigged the aqueduct system to serve as a shower, too, which only confirmed Mac's Swiss Family Robinson tree-house theory. He had also mounted a .60-caliber gun on a makeshift tripod behind a homemade metal bunker.

Despite Harry's assurances that the Mooks rarely bothered him, Brett and Stein had set up a perimeter using his .60 and another one scavenged from the wrecked TBM Avenger plane they had seen from the air. Brett and Leo had taken the first watch, while Stein and Tae had turned in for some shut-eye.

Harry and Mac sat around the campfire and swapped stories of their journeys to and adventures on the alien planet. The captain confirmed everything Mac had read in his journal. However, she never did find out what happened after his group had arrived at the palace. All she knew was that he and the Awumpai had headed to the floating palace to deliver the princess to the gods, and she had learned from Enoch that Harry subsequently had been imprisoned by the gods and had escaped.

After story hour was over, Mac decided to take a closer look at the TBM Avenger sitting in the midst of the alien wreckage. It was hard to believe that the search plane skipper who had been sent to find the missing torpedo bombers in 1945 had finally found the Lost Patrol. The TBM Avenger torpedo bomber looked just as it had the day it disappeared in the Bermuda Triangle two centuries before.

At the moment, the unscathed bomber had its engine cover off, and the nose cone was surrounded by makeshift scaffolding and a jury-rigged pulley system made from scavenged parts. It appeared as though Harry had just lowered a new engine into the canopy's housing when he'd been interrupted. *That's probably when he saved our lives*, Mac thought. Various tools lay around and a makeshift ladder that leaned against the nosecone, but for the most part, the infamous plane had escaped the ravages of time.

Mac was wondering where he had found all the spare parts when she noticed a second Avenger lying in a heap in a big pile of alien wreckage. This was the damaged plane they had seen from the air. The plane looked as though it had been dropped from a great height; it was totally smashed to bits, and its broken wings lay off to one side.

She spotted a third Avenger in another nearby heap of wreckage. It, too, was heavily damaged and looked as though it had been dropped from a great height. However, she also noticed that parts were missing from the plane, seemingly removed rather than sheared off in the crash. She realized that the captain was scavenging parts from the two most damaged Avengers to rebuild the least damaged one.

Looking over the remains of the TBM Avengers, Mac knew she was looking at one of history's greatest unexplained mysteries. Historians and scientists had speculated about what had happened to the Lost Patrol and the search plane that had gone out after it, and here they were. The pilots hadn't simply lost their way and ditched in the ocean, or been sucked into an ocean sinkhole. One theory had even proposed that they had returned to Florida in cloud cover and crash-landed in the everglades, only to be eaten by alligators. *No*, Mac thought, *the paranoid sci-fi dorks had been right all along. The Lost Patrol had really been abducted by aliens.*

Harry entered the makeshift hangar and walked slowly toward her.

"Wait a minute," Mac said after a few moments. "I see three of the Avengers. Where are the other two?"

Harry had been standing quietly next to her, giving her time to absorb everything. He looked at her, and then his eyes gestured for her to look up.

Mac followed his gaze and saw two perfectly preserved planes suspended in a green-hued stasis field. Despite the massive devastation, it seemed that there was still some power left in the alien spaceship.

Now she understood: the stasis field must have protected the Avengers from the crash, but when the field was partially switched off during the crash, three planes had fallen free. The other two remained in the still operational areas of the storage field.

"Even after the crash," Harry said, "this thing still has power. I've tried everything to get them down but no luck. I don't suppose you know a good alien mechanic?"

"Wow," Tae said, joining them, "this place is so cool." He sounded more like a little kid in a toy store then one of the space program's best engineers.

Mac looked at Tae then turned back toward Harry and smiled. "You know, I just might."

"Hey," Tae said, interrupting them, "do you guys realize there's still power running through this ship?"

Spotting them in the wreckage, Leo abandoned his post to join them. He circled the planes and caressed them, touching history. "Did you ever find the crews?" he asked in an uncharacteristically solemn voice.

Harry regarded the young man for a second before answering. "Some of them. Come this way." He led them deeper into the maze of alien wreckage and into one of the few rooms that had survived the impact. Several canisters lined the room's walls.

Mac walked over to a canister that had become dislodged from the wall and saw a man lying half-in and half-out of it. Some sort of thick amber gel remained inside the broken canister, and it had preserved the portion of the man that it touched. Mac saw a scream frozen on the man's face. She took a closer look at the others canisters and saw that they contained human abductees as well. All were dressed in World War II pilot uniforms.

"What are we looking at?" Tae asked Leo quietly, so as not to be heard by Harry.

"The missing bomber pilots," Leo said.

"The what?"

"You know, the five bomber planes that disappeared in the Bermuda Triangle in the late 1940's."

"Oh."

The group continued to examine the pilots in the smashed hibernation chambers until Mac broke the silence. "How many have you accounted for so far?"

"Well, twelve of the fourteen Avenger bombardier bodies are here, and I know of at least another one that crashed in the *Hail Mary* with me."

"That makes thirteen of the fourteen," Leo calculated aloud.

"And what about your crew? Did you find them, too?" Mac asked.

"I've accounted for half of them here; one died on the alien ship." Harry shuddered at what must have been a chilling memory. Mac remembered the scattered fear from the first entries of his journal. "And another one died when my plane crash-landed."

Mac watched Harry stare at a partially preserved corpse. The half that was exposed to the air had long since rotted and been picked off by the local scavengers, but the part that wasn't exposed remained intact and was visible through the amber gel.

As horrible as the circumstances were, Mac had to admit that the storage container was fantastic. NASA had been attempting cryo-sleep for years but had never come close. The bright liquid seemed to have preserved the occupants perfectly. She found herself wondering if it was still possible to revive any of the poor souls trapped inside the chambers.

"You knew this man personally?" Mac asked, stepping beside the captain to offer her support.

"He was my co-pilot," he replied, seemingly surprised at the recollection. When he continued, he struggled with his words as if his memory was slow to resurface.

"He was also my best friend. We flew thirty-seven missions together over the Pacific in a plane called the *Hail Mary*."

"The *Hail Mary* — wasn't that the same plane you were flying when you disappeared?" Leo asked as he walked up behind them.

"Yep. Originally, she was only built as a spotter plane, but it didn't take the War Department long to figure out that the PBY's could sneak up on Japanese destroyers at night and drop torpedo bombs."

"That's right," Leo recalled. "They strapped the bombs to the bottom of the wings. You guys followed the luminescent trails the destroyers left when they stirred up the ocean's algae and then dropped them on in."

Mac realized that Leo had come to idolize the captain. She herself had come to enjoy reading about his adventures, but

Mac believed it was more than that for her junior officer. She recalled that Leo, for the most part, had been raised by his mother and suspected that, even in his mid-twenties, Leo still craved a father figure.

Harry regarded Leo for a second, genuinely impressed by the young man, and then flashed him a lopsided grin. "Yep, that's right. They never saw us coming."

"What happened to your PBY?" Leo asked.

"I crash-landed it in a mountain range on one of those floating continents."

"What do you want to do about your friend?" Tae asked, gesturing towards Harry's former co-pilot.

Harry's grin faded. "You know, you're right. I hadn't really thought about it until now." He walked to the young Korean, unceremoniously spun him around without warning, and removed the shovel strapped to Tae's backpack. After looking around for a few seconds, he picked out just the right spot and began digging.

It didn't take Leo long to find a second shovel and join in.

—— o ——

Mac watched Captain Reed and the boys dig the grave. She saw the way the captain looked at his friend's corpse. It wasn't more than a week ago that she had looked down on his.

The only thing they had told Harry was that two centuries had passed since he and his crew had vanished in the Bermuda Triangle. The captain had told them that he had figured as much and explained that he had run into one of his crewmembers who seemed to have aged over a hundred years. Everyone had agreed not to tell Harry about the journal until the time was right, but Mac wondered when the time would be right to tell Harry that his journal had been found near his corpse inside a strange pyramid. The poor man had been through so much. They all had.

—— o ——

After the men finished burying the pilot, Mac and Harry walked back to camp and settled in around the campfire once more. Leo returned to his post, and Tae remained in the wreckage to work on the stasis field.

"Tae's gonna be working on that thing all night," Mac said, smiling to herself.

"He should get some sleep," Harry replied while gazing at the burning embers.

"Hah, good luck with that one. Back on Earth then call him 'Tireless Tae'. He won't rest until he figures it out."

Mac saw that the captain had taken out his journal, the original one, and had laid it on his knee. It was far less tattered then the one she carried in her coat pocket. She wondered if he was going to write about them.

Suddenly, a realization hit her like a bolt of lightning. It finally dawned on her; she finally understood what Professor Bort had been trying to warn her about. Joan must have seen their names in Captain Reed's journal. That was why she was so adamant about not letting them into the pyramid: she was trying to prevent them from opening the wormhole. That was what Joan was trying to tell her before she died.

Mac felt like an idiot. She'd been carrying around a crystal ball in her pocket and hadn't realized it. Not only did the journal document the past, but it also documented the future — everything that would transpire until the time poor Captain Reed ended up in the Europa pyramid. She fought the urge to whip out the journal right there in front of him. If she knew events in advance, she might even find a way to prevent his death.

She had seen enough science-fiction movies to understand that knowing one's future often alters the original timeline. But this train of thought lasted only about a second before Mac reached for the journal she kept in her inside coat pocket.

It wasn't there.

Mac frantically tore at her other pockets and checked her backpack, but the journal was nowhere to be found. Had one of the others taken it out? She looked up to see Harry watching her.

"Lose something?" he asked.

"Yeah," she replied. *But what should I tell him?* The last time she remembered seeing the journal was in her bedchamber at Enoch's castle. That had to be it. She must have left it in her bedroom.

The captain still waited for an answer. So this was it. She would tell him everything. She would tell him that two hundred and twenty-three years after he had disappeared with his crew in the Bermuda Triangle, his body had been found in an underwater pyramid on one of Jupiter's moons.

"Harry, what would you say if I told you that..."

"Hey, I got it!" Tae yelled from the nearby stasis field. The captain took one last swig of his coffee and quickly joined the engineer.

"Saved by the proverbial bell," Mac said dryly and then followed.

It took some experimenting, but it wasn't long before Tae figured out how to disengage the stasis field. He was able to do so at a gradual rate, enabling the Avengers' tires to touch down on solid ground for the first time in over two centuries without a scratch. The group now had three workable planes.

Secretly, Mac had hoped to find equally preserved pilots in the planes, but the cockpits were empty. Judging by Harry's face, she could tell that he had been hoping for the same thing.

Mac and Harry spent the remainder of the night going over the planes, making small talk as they did so.

"This one's got about a half a tank of gas, too," Mac called from the top of a makeshift ladder that leaned on one of the plane's wings.

As they worked through the night, they talked about each other's families. Harry told her about his wife, daughter, and the little one on the way, while Mac told him about her daughter and her dream of commanding a space station. The discussion of the space station piqued Harry's interest, and he wanted to know all about the space program.

"Maybe we should siphon gas out of the plane you rebuilt and put it in these two?" Mac suggested. Harry agreed, but she saw that he wasn't happy about it. He had obviously worked hard to rebuild the plane using spare parts from the wrecked ones. Spying an old Ford truck overhead, Mac asked, "You think there's any gas in that old beater?" After saying that, Mac realized that the antique truck was probably state of the art when he had left Earth. Harry didn't catch her slip, however. He seemed happy just to be talking with someone for a change.

It was therapeutic for both of them.

—— o ——

The next morning, Brett and Stein returned from a brief scouting expedition and reported their findings to Mac. Just as she suspected, the Mooks had torn the hover chariot to pieces. Mac knew that Enoch wasn't going to be happy.

Seeing the commandos' return, Tae and Leo joined them.

"What's going on?" Leo asked.

"Well, it seems we just lost our ride," Mac answered. "The Mooks tore it apart."

"I could take a shot at fixing it," Tae offered.

"Not before those little bastards ripped you apart," Brett said.

"How many did you see?" Mac asked.

"More than the ammo we got twice over," Brett replied glumly.

Looking around, Mac asked, "Where's Harry?" When she had finally turned in last night, Harry was still up, draining fuel from the wing of his rebuilt plane into a homemade barrel.

"Oh, its Harry now, is it?" Brett asked.

Mac glared at him until she realized he had tried to make his comment sound like a joke, but it had come out wrong.

Mac hit him playfully with her hat to lighten the moment. She was not unaware of Brett's feelings, and a part of her welcomed them. But somehow, things were different now.

"He's clearing a runway," Leo said.

Just then, the Ford truck rumbled past on a nearby plateau. It dragged a large piece of alien wreckage behind it.

"He's been at it since I got up this morning," Tae added.

Mac looked at the planes and then over at the cleared area on the plateau. There was a significant amount of debris and rough terrain between the makeshift hangar and runway, but it was certainly manageable with a lot of hard work.

"Well, boys, let's go give him a hand." She donned her hat and pulled the brim down over her eyes to block out the rising sun. Despite their desperate situation, she found herself smiling. She didn't notice Brett watching her as she walked off to help Harry.

—— o ——

By mid-afternoon, they had nearly cleared a path to the plateau that would serve as their runway. Only Tae was excused from runway duty; Mac ordered him to poke around the alien ship to see what else he could find. She gave him a pistol and some extra ammo, and told him to be wary of the Mooks.

They took shifts covering the camp with the .60 caliber, but so far, Harry was right: the Mooks rarely ventured anywhere near his campsite. She suspected they had found the pilots' corpses and feared the place.

After a quick lunch of rations, they were back at it. Mac and Harry leveled a hill with shovels, while the others continued to clear the bigger debris with the old truck.

"Harry, what happened to you? I mean, after the gods killed the princess?"

Harry stopped digging for a second and wiped his brow with a handkerchief (something men had stopped carrying in the late-twentieth century). "I told you already. They killed two of my friends; the rest of us were imprisoned; the gods left, and I escaped. My friends were left behind." He dug with more fervor.

Mac suspected he wasn't telling her everything, particularly about his escape. She suspected that Enoch probably had helped him escape and that Harry was covering for Enoch. In fact, Harry hadn't even mentioned the prophet, let alone their conversations and chess games.

"Hu-Nan was the one who died, right?" she asked.

"No, it was Ba-Tu." Harry stopped digging for a moment. "Wait a minute. I never told you any of their names, did I?"

Tell him, her inner voice screamed, *tell him about the journal*. "You must have," she said instead. "So once we get these planes on the runway, what's your plan? To fly back and rescue your friends?"

"Pretty much."

"You should know, Enoch told us that the gods are due back anytime now."

"I know," he said.

"You know?"

"Yep. They return once a year to pick up tribute. That's why I have to hurry up and rescue Hu-Nan and Fu-Mar before they arrive."

Mac knew she had to choose her words carefully. "You do know that they are not really gods? I mean, you do know that they are just some sort of advanced race of aliens, right?"

"Just because I was born two centuries before you, doesn't mean I'm stupid," Harry said defensively. "I knew in my heart that Khaos wasn't my god the moment he killed my friends."

"Good. Because I'm going to meet the gods and ask them to help us get back home."

Harry stopped digging and stared at her. "Are you crazy? Weren't you listening? They killed my friends." He practically shouted at her.

"I know, but if they're nothing more than astronauts, I figure they can be reasoned with. It's the only way for my crew and me to get back home. If you could get back home to your family, wouldn't you at least try?"

Harry removed his flight gloves and pushed his right hand through his thick hair, as he often did when he was frustrated. "Yeah, that's what I thought, too. Right up until they murdered my friends." He stabbed his shovel into the dirt. Before Mac could reply, he added, "You know, they'll kill you and your men if you go to them — maybe worse."

"I know, but I've got to try — for the sake of my daughter, I've got to try."

For the rest of the day they worked in silence and only spoke to one another when it was necessary for the task at hand.

Chapter 23

Mook Attack

BEFORE THE SUN set on a vibrantly painted sky the following day, they had cleared a path to the plateau and taxied the two planes onto the runway. Mac and Harry checked the engines one last time before they turned in for the night. Everyone else was back at camp.

"Purrs like a kitten," Mac said loudly enough to be heard over the engine's roar. She crouched on the wing of the lead plane while Harry ran up the engine. He ran it up one more time and switched it off. Mac noticed that he had fastened the emblem from his old plane onto the Avenger's console.

As the props came to a halt, he smiled with satisfaction. "Okay, that's it for today. We'll get a good night's rest and then strike camp and head for Joppa-Cal first thing in the morning."

"Sounds good to me, Captain." Mac beamed. It had taken some doing, but the planes were ready for takeoff.

They had decided that Harry would fly one of the planes with her and Tae, while Leo flew the other with Brett and Stein. They were heading back to Enoch's castle, so Harry could rescue his friends. He had made it very clear that if they still wanted to wait around for the gods, they were on their own.

—— o ——

While Harry and Mac readied the planes, Leo strolled happily through camp. He thought about the hero's welcome he would receive when they got back home. He could see the headlines now: "Lieutenant Leo Dalton Solves Mysteries of

the Universe." He completed a mental checklist. Builder of the
Pyramids? Found. Lost Patrol that disappeared in the Bermuda
Triangle? Found. Theory of wormholes? Ah, best leave that
one to Tae. Extraterrestrial contact? Check. And he could also
chronicle everything they had seen and done. There had to
be a multi-billion-dollar video deal in there somewhere. Best
of all, he and Emma could finally get married and not worry
about what anyone would think because they'd be rich beyond
their wildest dreams.

He walked past Brett, who had just finished giving the .60
a thorough cleaning. "Hey, Brett. How's it going?"

"Good," Brett said as he reloaded the weapon. "So when
we leaving?"

"First light."

"Sounds good to me." Brett racked a round into the heavy
machine gun to keep it ready for action.

Leo found his backpack where he had left it, up against
the old truck. He opened it up and took out the last piece of
fruit he had pilfered from Joppa-Cal. As he took his first bite,
he saw Tae about fifty yards away, walking out of the bowels
of the UFO. No, Tae was running. Leo took another bite and
wondered what the engineer was so excited about. *He must've
found something good*, Leo thought.

Just then, Leo noticed a Mook warrior, with a painted face
and a bone through its forehead, standing in the middle of
the camp. Oblivious of Leo, it poked at Stein's backpack with
a small spear and took a few tentative sniffs. When it finally
noticed Leo, it immediately raised its spear at him and growled
menacingly, like a small dog.

When Leo looked back at Tae, he saw a small army of
Mooks flooding after the engineer.

—— o ——

Harry and Mac were walking back to camp, sharing a laugh,
when they heard the heavy thumping of the .60 caliber.

"That sounds like the .60," Mac said.

Harry's eyes went wide with worry. "The Mooks!"

They started running toward the camp, but Harry grabbed
her by the arm and stopped her. "Mac, listen to me. Go warm
up the planes."

She opened her mouth to object but closed it again as he watched the reality of the situation settled in on her face. She nodded and turned back for the planes.

Harry sprinted the rest of the way back to camp. When he got there, the camp was overrun with Mooks. Leo grappled with a Mook on the ground over a spear; Stein sliced and diced Mooks left and right with his knife, and Brett fired away on the big gun.

Harry arrived at Leo's side first. He removed his .45 and shot the Mook in the head. After he helped the young astronaut to his feet, he said, "Leo, go help Mac prep the planes for take-off." Leo started to object, but Harry cut him off. "Don't argue. Just do it."

Leo nodded in compliance. He quickly grabbed his pack and ran to the airstrip.

Tae arrived in camp with scores of Mooks a hundred yards behind him. Harry leaped into action. He uncovered the second .60 caliber and let her rip. He cut down several Mooks running into the camp, and then, spying the old Ford truck near the advancing Mooks, he fired several rounds into it. The truck burst in shower of flaming parts, scattering the nearest hoard of Mooks.

The Mooks retreated for the moment, but Harry knew it wouldn't be long before they regrouped and returned. It was now or never. It was time to go.

Brett, who had so many blow darts sticking in him that he looked like a human pincushion, fired the first .60 until it went dry. "I'm outta ammo!" he shouted.

A Mook scout leaped over the bunker wall behind him and buried a hatchet in the commando's back. Brett's vest slowed the blow down but didn't stop it. "You son-of-a-bitch!" he yelled. He grabbed the Mook and broke its back over one knee. He pulled the ax out of his back just as another Mook came over his makeshift bunker wall. Harry watched Brett bury the newly acquired ax in the Mook's face.

Harry was about to go grab Brett, but Tae shoved him out of the way. A Mook with a club had leaped off of the wall behind them. The creature's club coming down even before

Tae had pushed Harry out of the way. The engineer took the blow to the head instead. His body went down like a rock.

Harry swung the heavy gun around on the tripod. He squeezed both triggers and shot the Mook point blank, blowing it in half.

"Stein!" Harry shouted at the big commando, who was covered in Mook blood. "Go grab Brett. I'll cover you."

Stein looked at the wounded commando, who was bleeding in several places and riddled with blow darts. "He's already gone," the German said, but Brett rolled over and moaned.

"No, dammit he's still alive," Harry yelled as he finished reloading the .60 with the last box of ammunition.

He heard the familiar sound of the Avengers' engines. He covered the German commando and waited for the next wave of Mook attackers, the Mooks were busy regrouping again.

Stein moved past him with Brett's arm over his shoulder, and the two commandos hobbled toward the airstrip. Brett was seriously injured, but it looked as though he were going to make it.

Harry squeezed off more rounds and scattered a few more Mook scouts, which he hoped would buy them at least a running start for the airfield. At his feet, the engineer was still unconscious and bleeding from the back of his head. Harry scooped Tae up and onto his back in a fireman's carry and made a run for it.

He caught up with Stein near the end of the runway. Stein was making slow progress while carrying the heavy commando, so Harry sent them to the closest plane. "Stein, you two take the rear plane; Tae and I will take the lead." Harry then broke off to head for cover alongside the runway.

—— o ——

Just after Harry left them alone, Brett's legs gave out. Stein couldn't hold the man who outweighed him by at least forty pounds and dropped him heavily to the ground.

Stein looked down at Brett. One of Brett's eyes was swollen shut, but his one good eye focused on him. "I can make it," Brett said, coughing up blood. But Stein knew neither of them would make it — not with him carrying Brett, anyway.

Three more Mooks jumped out from the surrounding alien wreckage not thirty feet behind them.

"Stein, I can make it," Brett said. He rolled onto his belly and then to all fours.

But Stein's legs backed away from his fellow commando and led him to the waiting planes. The German aimed and shot his pistol at two of the advancing Mooks but missed the third, who was now almost upon Brett.

"Stein. Stein, I can make it," Brett said. He stumbled to his feet, his wounded arm hanging loosely by his side.

The Mook that Stein had missed tackled Brett to the ground just after the farm boy had stumbled to his feet. Stein finally stopped, not twenty feet away. He took aim and pulled the trigger, but the hammer landed on a dry chamber. The Mook raised its ax for the kill.

"Stein, wait," Brett pleaded. Those were his last words. The Mook's ax hit the back of his skull with a sickening crunch. A half a dozen more Mooks ran up from behind and swarmed over his body. Stein watched for a second as they began ripping it apart with their bare hands. Then he turned and ran.

—— o ——

When Stein arrived at the airfield, he saw Harry loading Tae's unconscious body into the lead plane with Mac's help. He told himself there was nothing he could have done for Brett and jumped onto the wing of the rear plane.

"Where's Brett?" Leo asked him while focusing on the Avenger's controls.

"He didn't make it." Stein slipped into the tail gunner's seat.

A wave of grief swept across Leo's face. The young pilot swallowed. "C'mon, strap yourself in, and pray I can fly this antique."

Leo's plane began to taxi down the runway as several Mooks ran up alongside its tail section.

"Go, go, go!" Stein shouted. Then, for the first time in his life, he froze in combat. Looking at the edge of the airfield, he watched one of the Mooks raise Brett's severed head on a pike. One of Brett's eyes was open and seemed to stare right at him.

Stein didn't even realize they were safely airborne until Mac's voice crackled over the radio. "You guys okay back there?"

Leo, his hands strangling the controls, carefully picked up the throat mic. "Mac," his voice choked up, "Mac, Brett didn't make it."

For a moment, there was only static over the airwaves, but then Harry's voice came over the tiny speaker. "Leo, you listen to me. You concentrate on flying that plane. You hear me? We already lost Brett today, and I don't want to lose you, too. Drop in on my wing, and let's get the hell out of here."

"Aye, sir," Leo said. He dropped the microphone into his lap and wiped away his tears. Stein didn't say a word for the remainder of the flight.

Leo maneuvered the torpedo bomber plane in on Harry's wing and followed Harry as he circled over the downed UFO in a fly-by salute to the final resting place of the Lost Patrol and Commando Brett Harper.

In the canopy of the lead plane, Mac finished bandaging Tae's head and laid him back in his seat. The young engineer was breathing, and she was thankful he was still alive. She turned in her seat and looked down at the ruins of the crashed spaceship, which slowly grew smaller behind them.

Brett gone. She wasn't even sure how she was going to process that one. She didn't know him for very long but their adventures together had seemed like a lifetime. He was a good man, the best of men. And now he was gone. The fact that he was sweet on her only made his death harder to bare.

"Good-bye, Brett," Mac said silently and after wiping the tears from her face she put one hand on the canopy. "Thank you for saving our lives."

Both planes headed due west, into the sunset and toward Joppa-Cal.

Chapter 24

The Oasis

IN LESS THAN an hour, they saw Joppa-Cal on the distant horizon.

In the lead plane, Harry was within two miles of the city when he saw a glittering palace the size of a small mountain perched above the old, tattered city like a vulture above a carcass on the African savannah. The gods' palace, which combined every great feat of architecture on Earth and more, had returned.

This changed everything.

Captain Reed knew that he was too late, too late to save his friends. He gripped his throat mic with one hand and veered off his plane with the other. "Break off! Break off!"

"What's wrong?" Mac asked. She leaned forward and saw the massive palace floating over the medieval city. "Oh, the gods are early."

Leo followed Harry's plane back to a long-abandoned quarter of the city. After making a few passes, Harry put the plane down right in the middle of one of the quarter's main streets. He knew that even though the planes had backtracked a few miles, the slave quarter was still well within visual range of Joppa-Cal and the monstrosity that hovered above it, so he and Leo taxied and parked their planes next to a hovel at the edge of town.

Everyone climbed out of the cramped planes, including Tae, who had regained consciousness. "Anybody got any aspirin?" he asked. He grinned, clearly happy to be alive, but then the grin faded as he noticed the rest of their long faces.

"Tae, Brett didn't make it," Leo said before the engineer could ask.

"Yeah, so what did happen, Stein?" Harry asked. He hopped down from the wing of his plane. "The last time I saw you, you were both making a beeline for the runway. You should have been right behind me."

"What is it you're trying to say?" Stein shot back.

"I'm not trying to say anything. Just answer the question."

Stein glanced between Harry and the others as the rest of them focused on him. "We got jumped by the Mooks, okay? Besides, he was already dead when they started climbing all over us. I was lucky to make it out alive."

Mac, Leo, and Tae held Stein's gaze for a moment and then moved off to unload the planes. Harry didn't look away.

"This isn't World War II anymore Captain Reed," When no one responded, he shouted, "Oh, would you prefer that he had made it instead of me? Is that it? You can all just go to hell!" and he stormed off.

"Stein!" Mac called after him.

"Let him walk it off," Harry said.

Later that night, the Palace of the Gods was lit up like a beacon, and it could be seen for miles. Looking at its glittering splendor, Mac guessed it could probably even be seen from space.

Stein had cooled off and rejoined them. Mac made a few attempts to reconcile with the commando, but he blew her off every time.

The five of them gathered around a campfire; Stein standing apart and glaring at the empty buildings that surrounded them. They had agreed that they would stow the planes in the abandoned slave quarter and walk to Joppa-Cal in the morning, and now they sat in silence. After what had happened to Brett, nobody felt much like sleeping.

Mac saw that Harry couldn't stop staring at the glowing palace on the horizon.

"Harry, why don't you wait here?" Mac asked. "If all goes well, we'll come back for you."

"No, I've got to rescue my friends," he replied without hesitation.

Behind them, Leo poked the fire with a stick. "Harry, if we don't make it, and these 'gods' are as bad as you say, shouldn't you wait a few days and then go after your friends? I mean, it's going to be hard enough getting inside, but with the gods here, won't it be next to impossible?"

Harry turned toward Mac. "Does that mean you've reconsidered?"

"No, I'm still going to make contact with the E.T.'s, but if I'm wrong, getting yourself killed isn't going to free your friends either."

Harry frowned. "That's a chance I'm gonna have to take."

"Captain Reed," Tae said, "have you considered that your presence might agitate the E.T.'s and ruin our own chances of a peaceful first contact?"

Mac noticed that this line of thought affected Harry the most. It was clear from the look on his face that he hadn't thought about endangering their lives. Mac wanted to tell him that she didn't give a rip what the 'gods' thought and that he could come with them if he wanted to, but she sensed that they were beginning to sway him to stay, which she knew would be safest for him.

"Tell him," Stein said as he stepped out of the shadows and into the campfire's light.

"Shut up, Stein," Mac said quickly.

"Tell me what?"

"Tell him or I will," Stein threatened.

Mac gave the commando a hard stare.

"Maybe you should," Leo added, much to Mac's surprise.

"What is it?" Harry asked again.

Mac sighed. So this was it. As it turned out, it proved easier than she had thought. Once she started, the information that she had kept bottled up for so long just flowed right out of her. "Harry, I knew about your Awumpai because I read about it in your journal." She saw Harry reach for the logbook that he kept in the pocket of his pants. "No, not that one — one we found on your body in a pyramid that lies beneath the ice of a moon that circles Jupiter."

"That's why it's too dangerous for you to go with us," Leo added.

"You want to run that by me again?" Harry said.

Mac did, and early the next morning, just before dawn, they left on foot for Joppa-Cal, without Harry.

In the light of the rising sun, Captain Reed watched Mac, Tae, Leo, and Stein through his binoculars. He saw them hike toward Joppa-Cal on a worn-out road and then eventually disappear from view. He was alone once more.

He was moving back toward the campfire when a bright light suddenly rose up behind him. It was so bright that it illuminated the outline of his form on a nearby wall that the early morning light still had not reached.

"Hello, Harry," a disembodied voice said in greeting. Its tone was music to his ears.

When he spun toward the light, he was surprised to see the same vibrantly colored cloud that he had seen Asha singing to by the river. "Who are you?"

"You know me, Harry. I am the SongBird Goddess of whom Asha spoke."

"I thought you were..."

"I know," the cloud giggled, "fireflies or igniting gas. It is common for your kind to try and explain that which you do not understand."

Harry looked down at the ground.

"Why do you despair?"

"Oh, haven't you heard? God seems to be nothing more than an alien astronaut. If that's true, then my wife and daughter aren't really waiting for me in the afterlife, are they? They're nothing more than rotting corpses in the ground. Everything I've ever believed in is a lie."

"Why do you doubt your faith, now?" asked a less god-like voice behind him. The voice belonged to his radio operator, Dougie Johnson. He now appeared before Harry as a young man, not as the decrepit old man he had become on the spaceship. But it wasn't really Dougie. Looking into his swirling multi-colored eyes, Harry realized that it was still the SongBird Goddess talking; she had just assumed Dougie's form.

"Shouldn't I? The facts are pretty overwhelming."

"The one who killed Asha and her mighty Awumpai guardian — who do you think he was?"

Harry shrugged his shoulders. "He told me he was God."

"And do you believe that?"

"No, not God." As he thought about this question more, his eyes widened.

Dougie disappeared, and Ba-Tu now addressed him. "That's right, Harry. He is the Fallen One."

"Khaos is—" Harry asked, but in his heart, he already knew the answer.

When Harry looked up, Ba-Tu was gone. He now saw Brett standing by a low wall. The good ole country boy had his arms crossed and one foot propped up on the wall. Harry noticed that he had various Mook weapons sticking out of his bloody corpse and a swollen eye.

"That's right, Harry," Brett said while walking toward him. "You must remember who Khaos is: he is the Father of Lies. If you knew the secret of all life, you would know this."

Harry backed away from Brett's corpse and tripped over his own feet. When he looked up, he saw the crewmember from the downed *Hail Mary*, the one who had committed suicide, standing over him. The crewmember, who was no longer wounded, extended a hand to help Harry up.

"What's the secret?" Harry asked him. The pilot didn't respond but rather put his hands on Harry's shoulders and spun him around to face little Asha.

"Hi, Harry," she said.

"Asha?"

"Yes, Harry. I'm here with the SongBird Goddess, but I can't stay very long." She crossed over to a nearby fountain and hopped onto the ledge of its basin.

"Why are you here?"

Asha playfully dipped her toes in the water. "I came here to warn you."

"To warn me of what? What's the point of this? What's it all for?"

She hopped down and looked up at him. "Harry, knowing the answer to that question risks the time you have left in your terrestrial body. In the history of existence, no mortal has ever been told the secret of human life. To know it while you are still in this terrestrial form is to risk almost certain death."

"Oh, haven't you heard? I already know how I'm going to die, at least where my body is going to end up."

"That's true," Asha said. She turned her head to the side like a bird, the way she often did when she was alive. "You are a unique soul, Harry Reed, but again I must warn you: to know the secret in your present form is to risk your physical body and your immortal soul. Do you still wish to know?"

Harry considered this for only a second. "Yes," he answered. He was prepared to pay the price, whatever that price might be.

"Okay," Asha said. She stood on her toes and gave him a kiss on the cheek before backing away from him and fading away into hundreds of glowing fireflies.

Harry looked around. No one was there.

Looking skyward, he clenched his hands into fists. "I said I wanted to know!" he shouted, but his words only echoed on the walls of the slave quarter and died on the wind. Then he saw her. She sat by the fire with her back to him.

"Julie?" he asked. *No, SongBird Goddess, this is too much*, Harry thought. *Not Julie.*

"Then I shall tell you and try to speak in terms you can understand." It was Julie's voice, but Harry knew in his heart that the SongBird Goddess was speaking through Julie's form. She stood up and faced him. He recognized her summer dress and sandals from his dreams.

"What defines humanity is your faith," she said as she walked toward him. "Angels cannot have faith, for they have been in God's presence since their inception. They did not ask for this privilege. What Khaos says about your origin has some truth, but what he neglected to tell you is that what is inside those bodies was put there by *his* creator."

"You mean our souls?"

"Precisely. You terrestrial beings have only your faith to guide you, and that is why the one true Father loves you most."

"Thank you, thank you for telling me this. But what must I do?"

Julie disappeared, and a shimmering cloud took her place. "You will know when the time comes."

"Can you help me fight him?"

"You already have what you need."

"I don't understand."

"You will. As you are well aware, you near your hour of death, Harry Reed. I've told you the secret to prepare for what you must do, but beware of telling others because to tell them is to risk their mortal lives as well."

"I will," Harry said solemnly.

"Oh, and Julie and your daughters wanted me to give you a message."

"They're — they're with you?" Harry choked back his tears.

"Yes, in a way."

"What .... what's the message?"

"She misses you, and you will see each other soon. There's just one more thing you have to do first. Most of all, she says ... have faith."

The light of the SongBird Goddess faded away.

Harry knew what he had to do. That thing that had killed Asha was not God, but the Father of Lies, and Mac and the others were headed straight for it, thinking they were just going to meet another alien.

The captain grabbed his gear out of his plane, checked his pistols, and set out after them. Despite the overwhelming odds against him, he walked with determination.

Harry had his faith back, and he was damned if he was going to lose it again.

Chapter 25

Prisoner of the Gods

MAC AWAKENED IN complete darkness and felt as if she couldn't open her eyes. *Am I blind?* she wondered. The only sound she heard was the clink, clink, clink of metal, and she felt something cold and hard encircling her wrists. It didn't take her long to figure out what it was.

There was a loud buzzing in her ears, and when it began to subside, she heard voices — familiar ones. Leo and Tae talked to one another, but Leo's voice sounded funny; he slurred his words like someone who was intoxicated.

"All I'm saying," Leo said with the volume of a drunk, "is that this proves that God was an alien astronaut who made humans by combining his own DNA with that of prehistoric monkeys. Everyone wonders what the missing link is. Bingo!" He paused to collect his thoughts. "It's 'dis guy."

"For what purpose?" Tae asked in a straight and steady voice.

At least one of them is sober, Mac thought.

"What do you think? For slaves to mine Earth's natural resources." Leo snorted. "The 'gods' sure as heck weren't going to get *their* hands dirty. Plus, let's not forget good old-fashioned butt-kissing worship."

"If that's the case, then where's your proof that these guys even visited Earth?" Tae asked, not giving up without a fight.

"Proof? You want proof?" Leo stalled, but then the answer hit his inebriated brain. "Sumerian pictographs reveal that mining metals was part of daily life, and there's a great deal of evidence of prehistoric mines in South Africa, which even today is a major source of gold."

"You're delusional," Tae retorted, but Mac had to admit there was some merit to what Leo said, especially after everything they had seen since entering the palace of the gods.

"Am I? Am I, Tae?" Leo said loudly, and then he subsided, seemingly having lost his train of thought.

Open your eyes, damn you. No. It hurts too much. Don't want to see anymore. Open your eyes. No. Too painful. Mac decided to listen for a little while longer instead.

"Where was I? Oh yeah, what about the 'Summerian spike'? Huh? What about that?" Leo asked.

"The what?" Tae clearly didn't care, but there was little else to do.

"The ancient Sumerians are going on, just like all the other unsophisticated cultures around them, like the nearby Semites, and then, bam! Within one generation, they've got the first written language, astrology, two-story buildings, mathematics, the wheel, and more. What about that, huh?"

Mac hated to side with Leo, but her future son-in-law made a good point. Scientists agreed that the first civilization seemingly appeared overnight in Sumer near the barren wastelands of the Eastern desert around 3800 B.C. The Sumerians' crude language was the original script from which all other writing derived, and scholars considered the Sumerian wheel to be the greatest invention of all time. Tae still wasn't willing to give up, though.

"Maybe they had a savant — you know, like Da Vinci or Michelangelo? Did you ever think about that?"

Leo fell silent for a moment. "Yes, yes, I did. But then we met the angels, and that changed everything."

"You mean the aliens," Tae corrected.

"Angels, aliens — what's the difference? They're both the same thing."

"How do you figure that?"

"The word extraterrestrial means 'not of this earth,' right? Well, all I'm saying, either way, is that whether they were little green men or fallen angels, the term extraterrestrial still applies."

Now it was Tae's turn to be silent while he thought this over. Finally, he said, "Look, I'll give you that the guys we saw today might be the same thing as the Greek mythological gods and might even be the same gods who visited ancient Greece and Egypt. But you're trying to tell me that God and the angels are just greedy miners who spliced us together with prehistoric monkeys, so we could mine Earth's precious metals?"

"Well, according to Sumerian tablets, more specifically, it was a brother and sister named Enki and Ninharsag who combined their DNA with a Homo erectus to produce a suitable hybrid laborer to mine gold for the ancient astronauts, who needed to replenish their home planet's dwindling resources."

Tae frowned. "Leo, where do you even get this stuff?"

Leo didn't answer. Instead, he said, "Hey, look! Mac's finally decided to wake up."

Mac opened her eyes and saw that they were imprisoned in some sort of jail cell, just as she had suspected. Her wrists were manacled in irons, and she was shackled to the wall behind her. Leo and Tae were shackled in a similar fashion. They were being held in a circular room that was shaped like a tower in a castle. Judging by the room's dilapidated walls, they were no longer in the lavish, glittering palace suspended above Joppa-Cal.

"Morning, Commander," Tae said.

"Hi, Mom! Wakey, wakey!" Leo said. "Hey, hey, hey, see that small window over there? That's for the rats. After we die, the rats will come in through that window and pick our bones clean. It's sort of like a medieval garbage disposal. Isn't that cool?"

"Lieutenant, have you been drinking?" Mac asked, although she already knew the answer.

"No," Leo lied. He tried to keep a steady face, but the attempt only lasted about a second, and then he burst into a fit of laughter. "Okay, okay, I admit it. I'm drunk, but don't tell Emma. She'll be really, really mad."

"Nectar of the Gods," Tae explained. "Leo had a little too much to drink at the party with some guy named Bacchus."

"Nectar of the Gods," Leo explained. "Leo had a little too mush to drank at the par-tay." Leo thought about this for a second. "Par-Tay. Hey, that sounds just like your name, Tae. Par-Tae, get it? Maybe that's where your name comes from?"

Ignoring him, Mac focused on Tae, who seemed to be a little more coherent. "Aside from Prince Sumeria over there being drunk off his ass, are you two okay?"

"Yeah, we're okay. That fall nearly killed us." Tae gestured to a trapdoor in the ceiling about twenty feet overhead. "But luckily we didn't break anything. How about you? How's your head? You smacked it pretty hard on Leo's knee when we all came crashing down."

Mac gingerly touched the back of her head. Her scalp and hair were moist and sticky, but it felt as though the wound was clotting okay. "I'm okay. Where's Stein?"

Tae's face answered before he could. "Didn't you see it happen? Stein's dead, Mac. They cut him in half."

Suddenly, it all came flooding back in a mass of jumbled memories: the splendor of the amazing palace, the throngs of worshipers, the endless parade of mythological beings, and the god known as Khaos.

—— o ——

AUDIENCE WITH A GOD

Mac was never much for parties. For her, making small talk ranked among the top ten things she hated most, which was probably why she wasn't good at it.

Perhaps that was why she found herself standing alone on an expansive balcony with a goblet of nectar in her hand while everyone else enjoyed the festivities inside. The wind whipped by her ears and turned them red and numb with cold.

She peered over the railing and saw the rooftops of Joppa-Cal hundreds of feet below. It was a long drop, at least five hundred feet, to Joppa-Cal's highest rooftops.

Moving between two immense red tapestries, Mac reentered the stately palace, which reminded her of the castles in Austria that she and Emma had once visited. The palace's interior rooms, just like those in Austrian castles, were massive; the smallest of the rooms had ceilings at least two stories tall. In addition, nothing in the palace was unadorned. Elaborate woodwork and alabaster carvings appeared on every surface, and cream-colored tapestries with intricate blue designs covered the walls.

Unlike the Austrian castles, however, the palace she now entered had a swimming pool and an orchestra that floated near the ceiling. Mac found the experience of the alien palace overpowering, and the display of species in the palace's audience chamber certainly contributed to this feeling.

She entered the chamber and found herself amongst a sea of otherworldly beings that surpassed anything she had ever heard or read about. The crowd around her was composed predominantly of the hybrids and the tall royal citizens they had seen upon their arrival in town. Mook slaves weaved in and out of the crowd, serving food, waiting tables, and performing other menial tasks, while three-legged Tripods stood guard at every doorway. Mac also saw several new beings, such as a humanoid engulfed in ice-blue flames and canine-like creatures that looked as though they belonged in ancient Egyptian drawings.

Nearby, Mac did see something familiar, however: Stein loading his plate from a banquet table. The commando still wore a weapon on his tactical sling, but he had finally begun to relax over the last couple of hours. She had lost Tae and Leo about an hour ago when they had wandered off with Enoch.

After downing her own food, she continued to split her time between the chamber and the balcony while she waited for Enoch to return and let them know when they could have an audience with the being called Khaos.

Sometime later, Tae stepped up beside her. "Are you enjoying the feast, Commander?" he asked.

"I'm fuller than a stuck pig," she said, but she couldn't pass up another delicious hors d'oeuvre from a passing platter. "Where have you been for the past three hours?"

"Enoch set me up on a tour of the palace with one of the hybrid technicians. This place is amazing."

"So did you figure out what keeps it afloat?"

"Yeah, and it's definitely not magic." Tae's response led Mac to suspect that he and Leo had had a great debate over that exact subject.

Knowing Leo, Mac thought, he was probably just pushing Tae's buttons. Tae interrupted her train of thought by launching into an enthusiastic description of his palace tour. He sounded like a little kid describing his most recent visit to Disney World.

"You should see the size of the anti-gravity generators holding this place up! They've got to be the size of small buildings. Oh, and their engineering complex is massive. They've got stuff that you wouldn't believe. When we get back to Earth, I'm going to be the first to volunteer for the exchange program. It's going to take years just to come up with a working interface. I've already started building a schematic of the main complex on my PC, but that's only the beginning..."

"Tae," she said, interrupting the over-stimulated engineer, "Tae, where's Leo?"

"What? Oh, I saw him hanging around with some guy surrounded by blue flames and a bunch of water nymphs."

"Great," Mac said sarcastically. Just then, she spotted Enoch standing near a pillared entrance, the entrance to Khaos's inner sanctum. Enoch gestured for her to join him.

Quoting one of Leo's favorite old movies, Mac said, "Looks like the great and all powerful wizard is ready to see us now." She signaled Stein, who was still stuffing his face with food.

With her flight engineer and the German commando in tow, Mac strode toward the inner sanctum. She was confident that she would be able to negotiate with aliens who tried to pass themselves off as phony gods.

—— o ——

They followed Enoch through an elaborate entranceway and down a long pathway that was flanked by rows of enormous pillars. If there were walls behind the seemingly endless number of pillars, Mac certainly didn't see any.

It was a shame Leo wasn't with them. She made a mental note to wring his neck once she found him later. *Damn that future son-in-law of mine. Never around when you need him.*

When she looked up at what appeared to be a throne room at the end of the hallway, she saw Khaos for the first time. The beautiful humanoid male, who had wolf-like facial features and sun-colored hair, was so tall that she had mistaken him for one of the giant statues that littered the palace. That is, until he moved.

Looking at him, Mac realized that the hybrids had to be his offspring. The Mooks must have been the original inhabitants of this planet, but after Khaos introduced his DNA into the mix, he produced worlds of followers.

Khaos stood before his large throne, which was the size of a school bus turned on one end, while his aide spoke to a convoy of pilgrims. The aide was small in stature and resembled nothing Mac had ever seen. He was alien even in this palace of the gods.

"His eminence is most pleased with your offering, Queen Apsu," the aide said in a compassionate voice. "Go in peace with his blessing."

The lanky queen bowed and said to Khaos, "Thank you, your eminence. It is my and my people's privilege to serve such a loving god."

"TELL YOUR PEOPLE THAT I LOVE ALL OF MY CHILDREN," Khaos boomed.

"Thank you, thank you, your grace." The queen bowed again and her head nearly touched the floor.

"Well, I'll be darned," Tae said. "God has a Korean accent. He talks just like my uncle back home in South Korea."

"No," Stein countered, "he's speaking in German — Southern German, to be precise."

But to Mac, Khaos sounded like her Baptist preacher back home in South Carolina. His voice reminded her of Sunday afternoons at church with her parents.

"I think it's all three of them," she said. "I think it's some sort of telepathy."

This is going to be easier than I thought, she said to herself. *If he's capable of this, then we're as good as home.*

They waited with Enoch until Khaos's aide signaled to them. Enoch then ushered them ahead, and they approached the being that Mac guessed was easily twice the size of an ordinary man. The hybrid aide, who stood next to Khaos's throne, only came up to his kneecap.

From afar, Khaos had seemed disarming and benevolent, but up close, he was downright scary. The god's dark, liquid eyes frightened Mac the most. They reminded her of a sociopath's eyes. And when those eyes looked at her as though she were the only thing that existed in the universe, ice ran up and down her spine.

Mac waited for a full minute for someone to say something before she finally took a deep breath of courage and stepped forward. "Your eminence, my name is Commander MacKenzie O'Bryant, and this is my crew..."

The aide stepped forward and held up a slender six-fingered hand to silence her. "His eminence knows who you are." That said, the aide took a step backward to stand again by his master's side. He reminded Mac of her grandpa's dog back home, who used to sleep by her grandpa's rocker on the porch.

Mac waited once again for someone to speak. She risked a quick look back at Enoch, but the old prophet had mysteriously vanished.

After waiting another sixty seconds, she said, "It is my hope that..."

Again, the small aide stepped forward and held up his hand. "Do not speak to me. I am Lahmu, aide to the Atum. Speak only to his eminence, Atum-Khaos — he who is higher than the most high."

Mac nodded and said to herself, *Okay, this could be going better.* To Khaos, she said, quickening her tone, "Your eminence, Khaos, it is my hope that we could obtain passage..."

Lahmu stepped forward and cut her off for the third time. "Your eminence knows why you are here and how it is you came to be here."

Mac's mouth was still hanging open from the last time the aide had interrupted her. It only made sense that Enoch had briefed his boss on who they were and what they wanted, but she was still speechless and unsure how to proceed. She looked to the others for help.

Tae shrugged his shoulders, and Stein, whose eyes took in the Tripod guards around them, remained as impassive as ever. Before she could utter another word, the towering deity spoke to her in a thunderous voice.

"HOW MANY?" he asked. When he spoke, he revealed a mouth filled with triangle-shaped teeth.

Mac nearly jumped out of her skin when the deity spoke to her, and she hoped her body didn't show it. She briefly glanced at the others to see if they understood the question any more than she did. *Was he asking how many needed a ride back to Earth?*

"HOW MANY LIVE ON YOUR WORLD?" the colossal deity asked with a hint of impatience in his voice.

The pilgrims before certainly had gotten better treatment, Mac thought. She considered his question for a moment. Why would this deity, alien, whatever, want to know how many people lived on Earth? Having received military training, she was reluctant to hand over information. She wondered just how much information she should share with an extraterrestrial, especially one that Captain Reed had so adamantly warned them about.

Tae, still jubilant from his tour, didn't seem to have any such quandaries. He stepped forward and said, "Per the last census, conducted in August of 2167, there are nearly eleven billion citizens residing in our solar system on and around six major planets." Smiling broadly, and happy he could be of help, Tae nodded to Mac as if to say 'you're welcome' and stepped backward.

Mac glared at the young engineer, but he didn't seem to notice her irritation.

Khaos sniffed the air as though smelling the humans' very essence. It was apparent from the look on his face that he caught the scent of something he didn't like. Mac had a bad feeling in the pit of her stomach.

Khaos's look must have bothered Stein, too, for Mac heard a familiar CLICK as the commando took off the safety on his rifle. Other than his thumb, the soldier hadn't moved so much as a muscle beside her. She wanted to tell him to stand down, but in truth, she was getting nervous; her stomach acted up with more fervor. She was comforted by the fact that she had her own .45 strapped in a shoulder holster that she had taken from one of the Avenger pilots, but at the same time, she doubted that bullets would bring down such a formidable being as Khaos.

The god sniffed the room a second time. "YOU'RE ESSENCE IS OF MY SISTER, THE SONGBIRD GODDESS."

From the way he said it, Mac could tell that it wasn't a compliment. Just as she was going to say "maybe this isn't such a good idea," Khaos pointed at her.

The aide quickly commanded the Tripods, "Take them away until they can be properly interrogated."

Mac and Stein tried to back toward the door, but four Tripods quickly encircled them.

"Get your hands off of me!" Stein jerked free of a Tripod that had grabbed him from behind. He spun on his heel and sprayed bullets into the Tripod's face.

The three-legged being grabbed its ruined face and took off as fast as its three legs could carry it. It ran into a nearby stone pillar and knocked itself out while also breaking part of the pillar.

Mac drew her own pistol and pointed it at the nearest advancing Tripod. She shot one time in the air, and the creature skidded to a stop. It then began moving laterally.

Stein was reloading when a Tripod conked Tae on the head from behind. Before either Mac or Stein could fire a second time, she saw the towering deity rise to his feet, remove a staff from his throne, and cast a beam of light at the German commando.

"Stein, look out!" she shouted, but it was too late. The beam of light cut Stein in half.

When Mac was distracted, the Tripod that had initially advanced on her attacked again. It reared up a foreleg and one thundering hoof connected with her face. Lying on the cold floor, as the darkness enveloped the last of her senses, she could just make out Stein, who lay beside her with his body in two pieces.

—— o ——

While the unconscious Adamah bodies were dragged away, Atum-Khaos turned his attention to his aide, Lahmu, who had leaped down from the dais to pick through the dead infidel's remains.

The aide dipped two slender fingers into the blood on the floor, and after a brief sniff, he flicked his long, forked tongue over the blood, as a snake does when it scans for food.

Seemingly reading his master's thoughts, the aide said, "The Adamah's DNA is consistent with that of the miners in the colony near the Sol system."

Khaos pondered this information for a moment. "DID WE NOT DESTROY THAT COLONY FILLED WITH MY SISTER'S DISGUSTING OFFSPRING?"

"We did, sire, in the form of a great flood about thirty-six thousand Sars ago, but it seems that some of her progeny somehow survived." Lahmu thought for a moment. "Perhaps your sister warned the Adamah of the impending flood before you so wisely banished her."

Lahmu knew that the thought of an entire planet filled with his sister's descendants would not sit well with Khaos. The SongBird Goddess's offspring were too difficult to control; they were artistic and sometimes even clever. This would not do.

"How shall I dispose of him, your eminence?" Lahmu pointed to the severed Adamah, Stein.

Khaos took a deep breath through his nose. "HE IS NOT OF HER BUT OF ME. EVEN AFTER CENTURIES, I CAN STILL SENSE MY OFFSPRING." Khaos looked at the fallen Tripod that his progeny had killed.

"As you wish, your eminence." The aide clapped his hands at nearby Mook servants and gestured for them to remove the Adamah's body parts and take those, as well as the dead Tripod, to the medical facility.

"I WILL SPEAK WITH MY SISTER NOW," Khaos announced abruptly. He rose from his throne and walked to the wall behind it, which contained a plain-looking wooden doorway that resembled the pi symbol. He paused before stepping through the seemingly solid matter. "AFTER TRIBUTE, PREPARE FOR ACENSION. WE WILL TAKE CARE OF THE REST OF HER VILE OFFSPRING ONCE AND FOR ALL."

"As you wish, my grace."

After the aide had followed the Mook slaves out of the room, Enoch stepped out from behind the one of the nearest pillars, where he had been hiding. He had a worried look on his face as he removed a weathered book from the pocket of his robes.

He recalled the story young Tae had told him about how his followers had been burned ruthlessly when the chariot of the gods had taken him away. He said solemnly to himself, "And when they came to the place Enoch had departed from, they found the earth covered with snow, and upon the snow lay great stones like unto hailstones."

Chapter 26

Back in the Cell

MAC REMEMBERED. STEIN was gunning down a Tripod when a white bolt of lightning seared him in half. She had been standing right next to him when he'd been struck down. That was the last thing Mac remembered: lying with her face on the floor and seeing Stein's severed body.

Looking at the whitewashed cell wall around them, Mac assumed that they were being held in the prisons of Joppa-Cal. She wondered whether this was where Harry had been held captive and whether Fu-Mar and Hu-Nan were still being held nearby.

The sound of the door unlocking interrupted her thoughts. She fought down her hopes that it was Enoch, coming to the rescue. A door that was invisible inside the cell swung open.

"He wants that one," a Tripod's hologram commanded from the hallway, pointing at Mac. Two Mooks moved in, unhooked her manacles from the wall, and led her away in chains.

Still groggy from her head trauma, Mac was too weak to put up a fight.

"Where are you taking her?" Tae asked but was ignored.

"Bye, Mac. Say 'hi' to Khaos for me!" Leo said as she was dragged from the prison cell.

The door slammed shut behind them, and Mac was gone.

There was a moment of blessed silence before Leo started up again. "You know, in ancient Greek mythology, the gods would often descend down from Olympus to make love to beautiful women."

"Shut up, Leo."

———— o ————

As they dragged Mac down the torch-lit hallway, she reviewed the latest turn of events. She had underestimated Captain Reed's grasp of the situation. She had thought that his twentieth-century mind was too easily fooled by these alien posers, when, in fact, these beings were so advanced, powerful, and seemingly omnipotent that they could be easily classified in the category of 'gods' by anyone's reckoning. And because she had underestimated the situation, another member of her crew was dead. Worse still, if Khaos had discovered the wormhole, all of Earth might be in danger.

Mac had no doubt Khaos would torture her, Tae, and Leo for every scrap of information he could glean about the inhabitants of their solar system. She'd fight them, of course, but if it came right down to it, she'd kill herself at the earliest opportunity before she let them pick her brain. Her deepest regret was not getting the chance to see her daughter one last time. No one could possibly save her now.

"Hi there," said a familiar voice in the hallway just ahead of them — a human voice. "There's been a slight change of plans."

Utterly defeated, Mac had been looking at her feet the whole time. With Herculean effort, she lifted her head and saw Captain Harry Reed.

The Mooks holding her were just as surprised to see him as she was. Before either of them could react, Captain Reed knocked out one with one punch. The second one uttered a short growl that reminded Mac of a small, scrappy dog and jumped at him. Harry backhanded the Mook, slamming it into a wall. He moved in, pinned the dazed Mook to the wall, and unsheathed the survival knife he kept on his belt.

There was fear in the little Mook's eyes. These weren't the same wild Mooks that had killed Brett at the ruins. These were domesticated servants that were merely obeying their master's commands.

Mac saw the frightened look in the Mook's eyes. "Don't kill him," she said.

Harry rolled his eyes but did as she asked. He flipped the knife around in the air and bonked the little guy on the head with the handle. The Mook fell to the floor unconscious.

"Miss me?" Harry asked. He still hadn't noticed Mac's appearance. When he did, the look in his eye finally broke her down.

She wanted so badly to be tough and reply with some quip like "it's about time you got here," but instead, she simply fell into his arms and cried. After everything in the universe had been thrown at her, she was finally broken. She had seen it in his eyes.

Mac buried her face in Harry's jacket, and he held her until her sobbing finally slowed.

"It's okay, Mac. Hey, it's okay," he said soothingly. He sat down with her on the stairs and rocked her gently. "You cry as long as you need to."

Mac did. When she was able to stand, Harry helped her to her feet. "C'mon, I'm getting you out of here," he said.

"Wait a minute. We've still got to save Leo and Tae," she said. The spark in her had rekindled slightly.

"Which way?" Harry asked without hesitation.

"Um, back this way."

—— o ——

Soon they were back in the lowest regions of Joppa-Cal's prison. Mac leaned out and peeked around a corner. She could see Leo and Tae's cell, but it was guarded by one of the gigantic Tripods. She turned around to face Harry, who had been following just behind her. "It's just one guard, but it's a Tripod, and he's a big 'en."

Harry checked his .45 pistol.

"You can't use that," Mac stammered. "You'll bring every guard in the castle down here."

"Hmm, you're right." Harry holstered his weapon and walked out from their hiding spot — out into the open.

"Wait a minute. What are you doing?" she whispered harshly after him.

He stopped. "I'm going to get Leo and Tae."

"Are you crazy? What about the guard?"

Harry turned and looked at her. She noticed now that there was a light about him. She couldn't put her finger on it, but he seemed more alive than before. It gave her hope. Her own spark was beginning to turn into a flame — a small one — but a flame nonetheless.

"Mac, trust me," he said. He headed down the dungeon's hallway as if he owned the place.

Mac decided Harry had gone crazy but followed timidly after him, on the balls of her feet, just the same. She trusted him. As they got closer, she noticed that this particular Tripod wasn't wearing a hologram projector and was thankful for small favors.

Harry walked up to the Tripod sentry and said, "Excuse me, but my friends are in there. Would you mind opening up and letting them out?"

The Tripod looked at Harry in disbelief. Seeing that he and Mac were alone, it shrugged its shoulders haughtily and struck one hoof on the dungeon floor for emphasis.

Mac stepped up behind Harry. "Shoot him," she whispered into his ear. "Shoot him now!"

Instead, Harry held up his hands, palms up. "Whoa, whoa, hold on there, big guy."

The Tripod paused, looking confused.

"You might want to check with them first." Harry pointed behind the Tripod.

The Tripod's confident demeanor turned to one of pure fright when he heard twin lion-like roars behind him.

Mac peeked out from behind Harry's shoulder and saw yeti-looking behemoths standing directly behind the Tripod guard. Their muzzled heads scraped the ceiling, and their shoulders brushed both sides of the corridor.

"Awumpai!" she breathed. She recognized the enormous beasts from passages in Harry's journal.

As the Awumpai crouched like tigers, ready to strike, Harry turned back toward her. "You might wanna look away for this," he said.

Mac took Harry's advice, and although she looked away, she still heard ripping sounds and what sounded like buckets of liquid splattering the walls.

When she looked up again, Harry was lifting the key ring from the pulpy mess and severed limbs that remained of the Tripod. After several attempts, he opened the cell door.

He freed her of her shackles and motioned for her to enter the cell. He held the door for her while he watched the entryway for guards.

Taking the keys, Mac stepped inside the cell. Tae lifted his head, and his eyes went wide when they saw her.

"Mac!" Tae beamed. "I'm sure glad to see you two," he added as Mac unlocked his manacles, and Harry entered the cell behind her.

"It's good to see you, too," she said. She moved over to Leo. "Leo, wake up. You okay?"

Leo groaned in response. "What's wrong with him?" she asked Tae.

"I think he's finally hung over from sampling all that god nectar."

"C'mon, Lieutenant." She slapped him. "It's time to go."

"Aw, Mom, but I don't want to go to school," Leo said groggily.

"Nice to see you haven't lost your sense of humor, Lieutenant," Mac shot back while freeing him.

As Mac led them to the door, one of the Awumpai, the bald one, stepped inside the tiny cell. He had to duck his head to get in through the eight-foot doorway.

"Whoa, what the hell is that?" Leo asked. He and Tae, with eyes as big as saucers, backed away as quickly as possible.

"That, my friends," Mac said, gesturing to Fu-Mar, "is an Awumpai."

"Looks more like a yeti to me," Leo replied. He eyed the creature with trepidation.

"C'mon, we might not have much time," Harry said while ushering them toward the door. He had to push Leo and Tae past the Awumpai.

Mac led them into the corridor and nearly slipped on the Tripod remains that littered the floor. Nearby, Hu-Nan smiled happily while he chewed a large Tripod drumstick.

Harry introduced the two of them. "Mac, Hu-Nan. Hu-Nan, Mac."

"Hi," she managed. She stared at the enormous Awumpai, whose head towered over her even though he sat on his haunches. The Awumpai merely grunted and continued to eat.

"What? He's hungry," Harry said in Hu-Nan's defense.

"What are you doing?" said an old man's voice behind the big red Awumpai. It was Enoch. Mac smiled as he tried to maneuver around Hu-Nan and slipped on the Tripod's insides. Regaining his feet, he said nervously, "This is not the time for introductions. We've got to get all of you out of here before Lahmu's Tripods realize you've escaped."

"Enoch," Mac said, "what are you doing here?"

"I thought you could use some help." Enoch squeezed past Hu-Nan and made his way to Harry. "Harry, my old friend," he said, hugging him.

"I'm old but not as ancient as you, old man," Harry quipped. The greeting confirmed Mac's theory that the two had become friends during Harry's imprisonment.

The prophet turned to Mac, and a look of concern washed over his face. "Are you hurt?" he asked.

"I'll be fine, Enoch, but why are you helping us? Won't you get in trouble?"

"I was wrong about everything. These foul creatures are not the God of my ancestors. I know that now."

"What changed your mind?"

Enoch struggled to remove something from his robe. When he finally did, Mac saw that it was a small, tattered book that was stained with blood.

"I found your journal. You left it in your bedroom. We have much to discuss. Now come. My personal chariot awaits."

They made their way to the landing bay unchallenged, thanks to Enoch's assistance.

—— o ——

Enoch was about to enter the chariot when his Mook servant appeared. Enoch motioned for the others to board the chariot, and he turned to converse with his servant.

"Listen to me, my friend," Enoch said in ancient Hebrew. "Now is the time we discussed. Do you understand?"

The Mook nodded his head vigorously in reply. He took Enoch's hand and laid it upon his head.

"Bless you, child. The one true God blesses you," Enoch said. He patted the Mook gently before boarding the vessel.

Before Enoch took his seat, he grabbed Harry by the shoulders. "Listen to me, Harry. Before I die, I must tell you something very important."

—— o ——

On her way to the front seats, Mac paused as she heard Enoch's words behind her. She turned to glance at Harry.

Harry shook his head. "What are you talking about, old man? You've lived for over a century. You're not about to kick the bucket now."

But even Mac saw the knowing look that Enoch was giving him. It was the same one Mac used to give Emma when she was a child. Enoch knew something about the future. Mac guessed it was something he had read about in the journal.

"You are probably right," Enoch said, patronizing him, "but I must warn you — warn you all…"

"What is it?" Mac asked, concerned. Tae joined them while Leo began preflight.

"Atum-Khaos plans to return to the place of our birth and destroy everyone."

"He must be planning on using the wormhole," Mac said.

"And we opened it right up for him," Tae added. "Or rather, Leo did."

"Hey, how was I supposed to know?" Leo shot back from the helm.

"Anyone that survives the initial attack will be turned into mindless slaves, just like on this world."

"How is that possible?" Tae asked. "Sure this place is impressive, but he's only one guy."

"The palace is only his personal yacht. Khaos has an entire fleet of warships at his disposal."

"Not only that, but he's also capable of manipulating people's minds so they become his willing followers," Harry said. "You saw them in the audience chamber; they'd do anything for him."

"So let me get this straight," Mac said. "Khaos will attack Earth and then pass himself off as some kind of messiah? I don't know. Even with his fleet of warships and the ability to brainwash his followers, I still have a hard time believing he's capable of enslaving everyone on Earth."

The prophet stepped close to her and looked directly into her eyes. "Why not, little songbird? He has already done so on hundreds of worlds. Why not one more?"

Mac held the old prophet's gaze a moment longer and then heard the engines winding up.

"Hey," Leo shouted from the helm, "can we discuss this later and get out of here now, please?"

Mac took her seat beside him and ordered, "Punch it, Leo."

—— o ——

Left behind on the docks, Enoch's Mook servant watched his master depart in the flying chariot. When the chariot had cleared the palace, the small slave abruptly tore the clothes from his body. He then knelt down and dipped his fingers in a nearby greasy puddle and smeared the substance on his face, like war paint, before he ran off to do his master's bidding one last time.

—— o ——

Nearly a mile overhead in the palace, Lahmu, Khaos's aide, entered the inner sanctum and waited for his master's acknowledgment. At the moment, Khaos stood in a small alcove that served as his sacrificial chamber. It contained a beautifully carved granite altar that was lit by four torches, one at each corner.

Four robed hybrid priests, all of royal bloodlines, held down a Mukarian female on the altar. At first, she had been a willing sacrificial victim, but when she saw Atum's chest crack down the center and open, she screamed. She struggled against her captors when the turbulent, churning ball of energy within Atum's chest began sucking the life force from her body like a vampiric succubus. The female's eyes turned black, like those of Atum and the other royals, and then her skin rapidly aged, and her hair turned white.

When Khaos finally took notice of the aide, Lahmu said, "My Atum, the Adamah have escaped. A disemboweled Tripod was found outside their cell door."

"ENOCH?" Khaos asked knowingly in his thunderous voice.

"He's nowhere to be found. It is my belief that he assisted with their escape."

Just then, a hover chariot flew by the open balcony window. Recognizing the sound of Enoch's personal chariot, Khaos glanced at his aide, but the aide was already in communication with palace defenses.

"Atum, somehow all palace defenses have been disabled," the aide reported in disbelief.

With tension on his face, Khaos walked to his throne and removed his scepter from the armrest. He carried it out of the inner sanctum, through the main audience chamber, and onto the balcony. His eyes reflected the white-hot light from the lantern portion of his staff as he formed a kinetic ball of energy. "I DAMN YOU, ENOCH! I DAMN YOU TO DWELL IN DARKNESS FOR ETERNITY!"

Khaos hurled the ball of energy at the fleeing ship. The blast pursued the small craft like a guided missile and finally struck it solidly.

A devilish smirk graced the deity's broad face when the smoking vehicle hobbled for a moment and threatened to fall. But when the tiny craft recovered and resumed its course, the smile faded from his lips.

—— o ——

The lightning bolt struck the right rear of the chariot's passenger compartment and blew a huge hole in the hull. Only twisted and melted crossbeams remained in that section of the chariot. The jagged edge of the hole glowed with white-hot energy.

Enoch had been sitting on a bench near the aft section of the ship and was severely injured by the blow. Mac helped Harry lay the prophet's burned and trembling body on the deck. She was bitterly reminded of how Joan had died in her arms back in the temple, which had set everything in motion. *If only I had listened*, Mac thought. *If only I had read the journal, no one in my crew would have died, and no one on Earth, especially sweet, sweet Emma, would be in danger.*

"Harry," Enoch said nearly inaudibly. "Harry!"

"How you doin' there old timer?" Despite his attempt at a cheerful tone, Harry's eyes betrayed his realization that his friend was about to die. "You just hold on there."

"No, my friend. I am sorry to say it, but I cannot go with you. I go to be with my fathers and my sons."

"No, Enoch. You can't die," Harry said. He held Enoch's ruined hand in both of his own.

"Release the SongBird Goddess from her prison," Enoch said while tapping Harry's hand gently with his one good hand. "Release her, and Khaos will fall. Balance will be restored to the universe."

"But I don't even know where she is."

"Throne." The prophet coughed, then shivered more heavily than before. "Find the doorway behind the throne." With these words, Enoch went the way of his fathers and departed this world for the next.

"Oh my gosh, the book!" Mac shouted. The Europa journal was stuck on one of the damaged girders, and its pages had started to burn. The wind threatened to whisk the journal out the gaping hole at any moment. Mac lunged for the book, but the wind was too strong for her to approach the breached hull. Looking around, she grabbed some cable sticking out of the ruined compartment and, after a few practice tugs, tied the loose part expertly around her waist.

"What are you doing?" Harry asked.

"What do you mean, what am I doing? I'm going to grab your journal before it blows out the damn hole." Mac made sure the knot was tight and began making her way toward the hull breach.

"Why don't you just let it go?" Harry called after her, but she could barely hear him above the flapping wind.

"I can almost reach it," she said. Her fingers were within inches of the book when the cord began to rip out of the wall. Mac fell to her knees and would have been swept out the hole had Harry and Tae not dived on the broken end as it ran the length of the fuselage.

"Let it go! It's not worth your life!" Harry shouted. He and Tae strained to hold her inside the ship.

"I've almost got it!" Mac stood and fought against the torrents of wind, but the wind whisked the burning book out the hole just ahead of her grasp. Mac thought she saw the book flash into a small fireball as it departed the chariot.

"Pull her in" she heard Harry say and felt the line tug on her waist. They didn't stop until she was back in Harry's arms.

"You okay?" Harry asked her. Tae began untying her makeshift harness.

"I lost the book," she said matter-of-factly. She looked up at him through her bangs, which now covered her eyes.

Harry pushed her bangs off her forehead. "Maybe it's for the best."

"What do you mean?"

"Well, everyone who has ever read that damn book has died." Looking deep into her eyes, he added, "And I couldn't bear the thought of losing you, too."

But she could still see that he was wondering what he had written in the book that should never have been read.

Chapter 27

Angle of Attack

MAC WAS THANKFUL that only one of the three moons was visible in the partly cloudy sky that evening. The sun had just set on the horizon in the direction she called west, but with the spinning compasses aboard the Avengers, there was no way to be sure.

The hover chariot had landed back in the slave quarter, and they were now safely hidden amongst the ruins. Joppa-Cal seemed to be northeast of them; the river, southwest. They were somewhere smack in the middle.

Mac shoved her hands in her jacket pockets. Now that the sun had set, a brisk wind from the ocean swept across the abandoned city streets. It chilled her to the core.

Once again, she and her crew had managed to evade any pursuers. How many escapes had she been through in the past two weeks? She mentally ticked them off in her head: the underwater Beta Base, where they had nearly drowned; the Alpha Base, which had collapsed into a wormhole; the crash-landing that had brought them here; the Mook attack (not once, but twice); and the angry deity's fireball. Mac shivered at that last one. The memory of Khaos's demonic smile was still fresh in her mind.

Other hover chariots, troop transports, and small fighter-like crafts had zoomed overhead, but so far, they had not been detected. Tae theorized that the magnetic ore around them that made their compasses spin was also probably interfering with the 'gods'' more efficient sensors. Mac decided it was either their first lucky break or just plain dumb luck. Either way, she figured they were overdue for some luck.

Once they were sure that they were free of any pursuers, their first order of business had been to bury Enoch. The old prophet's death hit Harry particularly hard. Next, they had prepped the planes for immediate takeoff, should the need arise.

They had been so busy doing what needed to be done that they hadn't come up with any sort of a plan. Mac suspected that Harry would suggest leaving in the morning and putting as much distance between them and the 'gods' as possible. Harry had been right when he'd advised her not to meet with the phony 'gods'; her decision to do so had cost another crewmember his life.

Knowing what they were up against, she wouldn't blame Harry for wanting to leave, but she had a duty to protect the billions of humans in the solar system on the other side of the wormhole. And it wasn't a question really, with her daughter being one of those billion, whatever the opposition, they had to stop Khaos from entering that wormhole.

Mac shivered again and pulled her jacket tighter around her small frame. This time, it wasn't from the cold.

Tae, Leo, and the red-haired Awumpai were putting together something she hoped would pass for dinner. They had made a campfire in one of the surrounding hovels. Mac saw the smoke rise up through the broken roof, but it was barely visible in the moonlight, and she doubted any passing patrols would spot it.

Wondering where Harry was, she heard a flapping noise on the wind. Movement overhead caught her eye, and she saw a beautiful red bird land on Fu-Mar's outstretched arm. Harry stood next to the Awumpai on the roof of a nearby hovel. The large bird seemed to be talking to the big Awumpai.

Curious, she climbed the stairs on the side of the small house and joined them on the roof.

The bird had just finished reciting something to Fu-Mar when she arrived. The big Awumpai then launched the bird into the air, assisting its takeoff. Mac only got a glimpse of the beautiful bird and was sorry she didn't have time to take a closer look at the strange, yet wonderful, creature.

"Hi Harry," she said when Harry and Fu-Mar turned to look at her. Mac got the feeling that her presence wasn't exactly wanted. "Am I interrupting?"

"No, not at all," Harry replied and smiled at her.

Ever since he had rescued her from the palace, he had seemed different somehow. Mac couldn't put her finger on it, but he seemed more at peace.

Fu-Mar grunted in greeting and went down the stairs.

"I saw the bird, and I was wondering what you two were doing up here," she said.

"Oh, just checking the mail."

"Checking the mail," Mac repeated dryly.

Pushing a hand through his hair, Harry said, "Fu-Mar's people aren't coming. Fu-Mar says the Awumpai are sympathetic to our cause, but even with ore-ships, there is no way they can possibly reach us before Khaos's palace lifts off."

Mac knew the situation had just become much more dire. "What about Asha's people, the Mukarians, or Queen Apsu? Have you tried them?" she asked.

"What's the point? They still think of Khaos as their one true god." Harry wasn't being pessimistic, just realistic.

"So, you mean to tell me that we — you, me, Tae, Leo, and two nine-hundred-pound gorillas — not only have to defeat Khaos but also his army of Tripods and throngs of brainwashed followers?"

"Well, I'd say they're more like fifteen hundred pounds, and I wouldn't exactly call them gorillas, but yeah, that's the general idea."

Mac bobbed her head a couple times before answering. "Okay, I'm in."

They stood there looking at each other for a moment. In another life, they could have been lovers who gazed at one another in the moonlight: Mac, with the wind blowing through her hair, and Harry, leaning on the smooth railing with a lopsided smile on his face and an adoring look in his eyes. They could have been just as easily standing on the deck of a cruise ship, sailing across the Pacific. *What was that saying? Two ships passing in the night?*

Mac yearned for Harry's arms to be around her once more, and she moved closer to him. They were within inches of each other when …

"Hey, Mac!" Leo yelled from below.

Mac looked down from the roof and saw Leo standing outside the hovel that contained the campfire. He hadn't seen them yet, and he was cupping his hand, getting ready to call out in the darkness once more.

"Up here, Leo!" she shouted.

Surprised to see her up on the roof with Harry, Leo did a double take before shouting, "You and Harry might want to come down and take a look at this."

"Be right down," Mac replied. She raised her eyebrows in resignation at Harry, and both of them moved toward the stairwell.

Their ships had passed.

———— o ————

Mac and Harry walked inside the hovel and over to the campfire where Tae and Leo sat. Their shadows danced on the walls in the firelight.

They heard loud slurping and chewing from the broken corner of the building. Hu-Nan was eating, as usual. His bloody meal looked similar to a gazelle-like creature she had seen earlier. The big Awumpai's back was to them, and he constantly checked over his shoulder to guard his kill. *At least he didn't finish off the last of the rations*, Mac thought as she took a seat beside Tae.

Much to her disappointment, the two men had not prepared anything in the way of a meal. "Okay, you two want to tell me what it is you were doing that's so important your commanding officer has to go without dinner?" she asked, trying to keep it light.

Leo, not missing a beat, pulled out a can of rations from the Avenger plane packs and tossed it to her. "Show her," he said to Tae.

Tae opened his laptop, which he had been carrying in his backpack since they had arrived on the planet, and laid it on a large, flat rock near the fire. "Okay, we know the aliens are aware of the wormhole," he said.

"Atum-Khaos," Leo said, correcting him.

Tae sighed. "We've been through this already. They're just aliens."

"What difference does it make?" Mac interjected. "Either way, he and his armies are going to travel through the wormhole in a fleet of warships and enslave the entire solar system on the other side."

Tae paused for a moment to allow this to sink in. "Well, the way I see it, we have two choices. We either a) destroy the wormhole, or b) destroy Khaos. Since we can't reach the wormhole..." The engineer tapped a few keys on his computer pad, and a holographic image of the palace appeared over his laptop.

"Hey, that's pretty neat!" Harry said and gingerly touched the hologram. It surprised Mac that after all he'd seen, he could still be impressed by a simple hologram schematic.

Tae continued, "Okay, three anti-gravity generators are the only things holding up the floating palace. The generators are these three basins here." He pointed to each of them with a laser pen. As he did so, each one lit up and flashed red.

"When did you do all this?" Leo asked.

"Well, while you were busy flirting with that water nymph and getting drunk on nectar, I got a tour of the palace that included the engineering sections. I scanned it with my computer as we walked."

"Good work, Tae," Mac said, patting him on the back. She was reminded just how good an engineer Tae really was. Although she had been surrounded by the best of the best for the last several years, she had resigned herself to being little more than a 'glorified truck driver' during her shuttle runs to Europa and back. She had forgotten that she and the other astronauts were some of the best that humanity had to offer. This realization not only rekindled her hope but also gave her courage.

"Hey, I was not flirting with any water nymph," Leo said defensively. He looked at Mac, worried she might tell Emma.

Tae was about to continue with his presentation, but he stopped and looked squarely at Leo. "You were flirting."

Mac stifled a laugh as Leo shrugged his shoulders then rolled his eyes skyward. Even in their dire situation, it was nice to see Tae come out from behind the books and stretch his wings.

"Now, as I was saying, if we can disable the generators while the palace is in flight, it should fall."

"How are we going to do that?" Mac asked.

"Well, naturally, the generators are shielded, but if we can disrupt the main power systems here," Tae pointed to a spot at the center of the palace's platform basin, "that should turn off the shielding long enough to give us time to blow up the generators. But it's going to have to be some pretty heavy-duty explosives. Those generators aren't small."

"The Avengers' torpedo bombs are still attached," Harry said. "They should be big enough."

"My thoughts exactly," Tae said eagerly.

"Now, will that shut power down all over the palace?" Harry asked.

"No, that's what the main power generator deep inside the palace basin is for. I never got a good look at it, but I do know that it's heavily guarded. But the main power supply for the shield generators, which protect the anti-gravity generators, is hardly guarded at all."

"Yeah, but we only got two planes," Leo said to Tae, "and you said there were three generators."

"We only need two."

"What?" Mac asked.

Tae explained, "If we take out two generators, it will keep them from achieving orbit. If we take out the third generator, the palace will fall like a stone."

Leo shook his head. "Wait a minute. Are you guys even listening to yourselves? We barely got out of there alive. I mean, I'm all for saving Earth and everything, but c'mon! Get real! We're just four guys with a couple of antique planes. Who are we kidding?"

"C'mon, Leo. This is a good plan. It just needs some fine tuning," Mac said soothingly.

"I'll say it does," Leo said. "Look, I'm no coward. I just don't see how getting ourselves killed is going to help anyone back home."

Mac looked at him. This was it. Leo was going to have to decide whether to cowboy up or turn tail and run. "Look, I'm not going to order you to do this, but if we don't stop Khaos, a lot of people on Earth, including Emma, are going to die."

Tae was the first to commit. "Hey, I'm in. We've got too much to lose if we don't try." He turned toward Harry. "Besides, Harry saved my life. The least I can do is trust him now."

Leo shook his head again and said, "This is crazy." But, after sighing heavily, he agreed. "All right, I'm in."

Harry clapped Leo's shoulder with one hand and Tae's with the other. "Okay, let's do it."

Pointing at Tae's schematic again, he asked, "Tae, if Fu-Mar can sneak you back into the palace, do you think you can disrupt the anti-gravity generators' power supply?"

Tae bit down on his lower lip. He wasn't the type to answer before he was one-hundred percent sure. "I can, but it sure would help to have Leo along in case I have trouble figuring it out."

"Hey, you're the engineer," Leo said. Mac could see he was still not totally on board with the risky plan.

"Need I remind you that you're the one who opened the wormhole in the first place?" Tae shot back.

Leo shrank at this and quickly responded, "Okay, okay, fine. I'll go with you."

"Once Tae and Leo disengage the power supply feeding the shield generators," Harry said, "Mac and I will be able to torpedo two of the anti-gravity generators."

"And bingo!" Mac said. "The palace falls out of the sky, or at the very least, we keep it from entering the wormhole."

"How soon do you want Leo and me to infiltrate the palace?" Tae asked, there was an edge of excitement in his voice.

"Couple hours, tops. According to what Enoch told me, tomorrow is the last day of tribute," Harry said. "After that, you can bet that Khaos is going to pack his bags and head for Earth."

"Okay. I think I can be ready to leave within the hour."

"Better take Hu-Nan for back-up," Harry added.

Leo looked back at the oversized Awumpai. "Uh, he doesn't exactly blend in."

"Don't worry. He's a lot stealthier than he looks," Harry replied, but just then, Hu-Nan erupted with one of his infamously loud farts. Hu-Nan looked at them apologetically with a dopey grin on his face.

Tae was in the middle of packing up his things when he stopped suddenly and took a few tentative sniffs; Hu-Nan's gas had wafted in his direction. "Oh gosh, gross. Do you guys smell that?"

Mac was trying to open a can of rations. "What?" she asked irritably, wondering what Tae was going on about.

Tae held his nose. "Are you telling me you don't smell that?"

Mac sniffed and gagged. She covered her mouth with the back of her wrist. "Oh my," she said. Tears welled in her eyes, and bile rose into her mouth.

Harry scolded the big Awumpai, but Mac couldn't help it; she just had to laugh. Harry chased the big Awumpai out of the hovel, which made her laugh even harder. Seeing her lose it, Leo and Harry soon started laughing, too.

"That's not funny," Tae said. "I'm serious. He shouldn't be doing that near an open flame."

—— o ——

Later that evening, Harry walked up to one of the TBM Avengers hidden amongst the city's ruined walls.

He saw Leo sitting in the open cockpit, trying to turn the engine over with little success. Judging by the heavy sputtering and black soot chugging out of the exhaust, the boy had probably flooded the engine.

It would be dawn in a few hours, but the group was leaving within the hour. Harry told himself that he was just checking on the lad, but part of him wanted to make sure that the young lieutenant wasn't having second thoughts and wouldn't decide to crank up the Avenger and fly away. Harry didn't want to believe it, but it was obvious that the young man still wasn't entirely on board with the seemingly hopeless plan of attack. He considered calling Leo down for a moment, but when the engine cranked heavily again without success, he climbed onto the wing.

"Sounds like its flooded. Best let her settle for a while." Harry knelt down next to the cockpit.

Despite Harry's advice, Leo defiantly tried the engine one more time. It bucked, chugged for a few seconds, and then both men got a heavy dose of a black cloud laden with gasoline before it died once more.

"Geez, I can't even start the engine, and we're supposed to take on Khaos," Leo said. He removed the flight gloves he had been wearing and threw them on the dash.

"Don't worry. We'll be fine." Harry said while wiping soot from his face with a grease-stained rag he kept in his back pocket.

"Yeah?" Leo said, his voice cracking, "What makes you so sure, Harry? What makes you so sure that we won't just get ourselves killed?"

Harry handed him the rag. "Hey, haven't you read the Bible? As long as God is with us, how can anyone stand against us?"

Leo snorted. "God is with us? Ha, that's a laugh." He wiped his face with the rag. "I hate to be the one to tell you this, Harry, but I think we've pretty much confirmed that these so-called 'gods' are nothing more than an advanced race of extraterrestrials. They're probably the same ones who mixed their DNA with prehistoric monkeys to create mankind for their own selfish purposes." There, he said it. He didn't like doing it, but he had to make Harry see reason. There was no God.

"Son," Harry said and then paused.

Oh, boy, here it comes, Leo thought. *The old timer's gonna impart some wisdom, and he probably doesn't even know about Darwin's theory.* But Harry surprised him.

"Son, let me tell you something. When your doubts are the greatest, that's when you have to have faith in God the most."

"Faith?" Leo asked incredulously, "How can you still believe in God after everything we've seen? We've got proof that these aliens, fallen angels, whatever, have been visiting Earth since the days before the flood. Given everything we've seen, how can you still believe in God?"

Deep in thought, Harry rubbed his scalp for a second. "Well, let me ask you this: if these advanced extraterrestrial beings created mankind, who created them?"

Leo started to answer but realized that he didn't have an answer. Scientific journals and excavations of the ruins on Earth, Mars, and Europa never had provided evidence of who created the creators. The only thing that Leo recalled was the first sentence of the Bible: "In the beginning God created the heavens and the Earth."

Harry remembered the SongBird Goddess's warning about sharing the secret of life and knew he had to choose his words carefully. "Look," he said, "there's nothing wrong with being afraid. During the war, when I was flying missions over the Pacific, I was scared silly lots of times."

Leo snorted. "C'mon, Harry, you were afraid?"

"You'd better believe it. But in every man's life there comes a time when he realizes that there are things out there that are more important than himself. So, back then, we acknowledged our fear and then did what had to be done the best way we knew how. It wasn't always easy and sometimes it was downright terrifying, but we got the job done. And you know what? You will, too."

Harry was fully aware that no amount of scientific data would ever convince Leo of the existence of the one true God — it was a personal journey for everyone — but he saw that he was getting through to the boy. "Now try it. Turn it over."

"What? Oh." Leo flicked the ignition switch. The plane's engine began to turn over. It sputtered a few times, so Harry reached into the cockpit and adjusted the choke to give it a little less fuel. The engine kicked over and roared to life, much the way Leo's courage was starting to.

"Better let it idle for a bit," Harry said. "Do you think you and Tae can be ready to go within the hour?"

"Huh? Oh sure," Leo replied. He was slightly dazed and dumbstruck from their conversation, but Harry saw a spark in the boy's eyes. Leo had just begun his journey.

"Good." Harry jumped down from the wing and left Leo alone with his thoughts.

Chapter 28

Leo and Tae's Impossible Mission

"**I THOUGHT YOU SAID** you knew where this place was?"

Leo and Tae skidded across the palace's heavily polished floors and hid in the shadows of an expansive, but abandoned, hallway.

"I do, I do, but this place is huge. Just give me a second," Tae said. He consulted his hologram schematic once more.

Leo was not happy about this plan, not happy at all. But even he had to admit that so far things had gone pretty well. With the hover chariot, Fu-Mar's and Hu-Nan's uncanny stealth techniques, and Tae's familiarity with the layout, they had easily penetrated the palace. The oversized Awumpai had effortlessly dispatched what little resistance they had encountered. Naturally, the red-haired Awumpai had taken a little piece of each foe as a 'snack'. Leo noted that the Awumpai seemed particularly partial to the Mook servants.

Leo theorized that they had encountered so little opposition because the majority of the guards were either dealing with the thousands of worshipers paying tribute to Khaos or out searching for the humans in the forests. Khaos must have thought that only idiots would launch a counterattack on the palace — idiots like him, Tae, and the Awumpai.

"Okay, got it. The main generator is this way." Tae checked to see that the coast was clear and darted quietly down the hallway.

He's actually enjoying himself, Leo thought as he followed.

—— o ——

The main power supply for the anti-gravity generators consisted of an hourglass-shaped power core surrounded by machinery that was as alien as it was complex.

Fu-Mar and Hu-Nan had made short work of the two Tripod sentries guarding the room and the Mook and hybrid technicians manning it. At present, Hu-Nan ate one of the Mooks outside in the hallway, and Fu-Mar guarded the room's only entrance.

Leo was wondering if the big Awumpai ever stopped eating when he spied Tae, who stood in front of the massive power generator and peered inside an open panel.

Leo moved next to him. "Okay, we're here. Now what?" he said.

Tae was biting his lower lip again, which was never a good sign. "Well, it is pretty intricate."

"Well, do you know, or don't you?" Leo asked.

Tae turned toward him. "Look, this isn't one of your movies. I can't just magically understand alien technology that's far more advanced than anything I've ever seen or even heard about."

As Tae began fiddling with the alien circuitry, Leo noticed a Mook wearing war paint standing outside in the hallway. Leo recalled the indigenous Mooks at the ruins and swallowed nervously, but then he saw that Fu-Mar was talking to the Mook.

"Hey, isn't that Enoch's Mook?" Leo asked Tae.

Frowning at the interruption, Tae took a quick look and then did a double take before returning to the task at hand. "Yeah, I think so, but what's with the war paint?"

"I don't know," Leo said thoughtfully.

Tae sighed with exasperation. "That's it. I give up. Maybe if I had about a year to build some sort of interface I could understand all this, but there's no way I'm going to figure it all out in the next five minutes."

Leo unslung his pack and removed its contents. "Well, can you understand this?"

Tae leaned over to peer into Leo's backpack. It was filled with homemade explosives. "Where the hell did you get those?"

"Harry gave them to me," Leo said. "He's been working on them for months."

"Well, why didn't you say so before?" Tae asked.

"All part of the plan — need-to-know-only basis." Leo saw that Tae was angry and added, "Harry made me promise not to tell anyone in case one of us was captured."

Leo handed Tae one of the charges and then noticed that the Awumpai were no longer in the hallway. "Wait a minute — where are Fu-Mar and Hu-Nan?"

"I don't know. They probably went off to find someone else to eat."

Leo didn't think that was likely — Hu-Nan, perhaps, but not the older one.

Tae looked at his watch. "C'mon, Leo," he urged. "Harry and Mac are going to start their attack run in about twelve minutes."

Leo nodded and helped Tae wire the charges in and around the generators, but he still wondered where the Awumpai had disappeared to.

—— o ——

Less than ten minutes later, Tae was just finishing up with the last of his charges when Leo heard a noise near the entrance. He spotted Commando Alan Stein walking on the other side of a long row of machinery. Strangely, Stein looked about four feet taller than Leo remembered, but Leo assumed that he was walking on a platform behind the machinery.

"Stein, you're alive!" Leo exclaimed, but then he realized that Stein wasn't exactly himself anymore. "Oh crap!"

Stein now sported a Tripod's body where his legs should have been. He carried a large trident in one hand and wore thick body armor made of leather.

"Uh, Tae?" Leo said.

"Yeah?" Tae plugged the last detonator cord into the master detonator just as Stein stepped out from behind the machinery.

"You might want to hurry things up a bit!" Leo called over to him. Tae must have seen Stein, too, for he seemed to pick up the pace.

"Hello, fellows!" Stein boomed.

"Stein, is that you?" Leo asked.

"Don't be ridiculous, Leo, of course it is me. Khaos returned me to life, so I could serve him. It is my calling."

Leo and Tae exchanged nervous glances. Leo remembered that Hu-Nan was still in the hall. "Uh, Hu-Nan?" he cried meekly.

"If you're waiting for that filthy animal friend of yours to save you, I wouldn't hold my breath," Tripod-Stein said. He planted the pole of his trident loudly on the floor and licked one of its bloodstained points.

"You killed him?" Leo asked.

"It was no small task, mind you. He killed three of my Tripods in the process and fell out a window, but fortunately for us, we got the drop on him while he was eating."

Leo noted that Stein hadn't said anything about Fu-Mar.

"Damn you, Stein!" Leo said. "You didn't have to kill him." Leo spied Tae sneaking behind Tripod-Stein toward the generator to set the last of the charges. If he could buy his friend a few more seconds, they could still complete their part of the plan. Harry and Mac were due any moment now, and if they didn't blow the shields, the entire plan would come to nothing. *In every man's life there comes a time when he realizes that there are things out there that are more important than himself.*

"Khaos doesn't judge me," Tripod-Stein said. "He accepts me for who I am."

"Stein, are you off your rocker? Khaos may be an omnipotent alien, but even you have to see that he's nothing more than a psychopath." Leo saw that Tae had set the last of the charges and was tiptoeing toward the detonators.

"You shouldn't say that about such a benevolent being."

"How can you say that? Hello, Stein? He cut you in half."

"Yes, but he also put me back together. He is merciful, but I am not." Stein abruptly spun at the waist and flung his mighty trident at Tae with no more thought than someone swatting a fly. It seemed as though Stein had seen Tae sneaking behind him, too.

"Tae, look out!" Leo shouted, but it was too late.

Tae's face registered a look of surprise as the massive trident slammed into his midsection like a nuclear missile. It carried him backward through the air and pinned him to the generator housing behind him. His legs dangled off the floor.

The two outer points of the trident had passed clean through Tae's body. The engineer gripped the trident's shaft with both hands and tried unsuccessfully to remove the weapon.

Tripod-Stein clopped over to Tae, took the trident in his hands, and wrenched it back and forth. Tae cried out and coughed up blood. "Hurts, Tae?" the Tripod asked him with a nearly demonic voice.

"Leave him alone!" Leo screamed. He ran toward them, and Tripod-Stein quickly removed the trident from Tae's body and turned to face Leo.

No longer pinned to the generator, Tae dropped to the floor.

Leo skidded to a halt in front of Tae. He saw Tae slumped over on his side, attempting to hold his intestines inside his torso.

Tripod-Stein stepped into Leo's field of vision. "I don't want to have to kill you, too, Leo."

Leo reached for his pistol, but before he could fire, Tripod-Stein expertly spun the trident over his head like a Bo staff and, in one swift blow with its pole end, smacked Leo's hand and sent his gun flying.

Leo remembered that he still held one of the detonators. He brought it up to his chest and tried to depress the button, but before he could do so, Stein swung the staff again and delivered an uppercut that sent him soaring backward through the air.

Leo dropped the detonator and landed on his back with his lungs deprived of all breath. Before he could even think about getting up, Tripod-Stein clip-clopped over to him and rested a hoofed foot on his chest. The pressure was unbearable. Leo gripped Stein's hoof and tried to remove it but couldn't. Stein peered down at Leo the way a bird might look down on a worm.

"You know, Leo, I think I'm just going to have to kill you after all." He raised his bloodstained trident and aimed it at Leo's head.

Leo's last thought was that there were three points to the trident, and they would soon be stained with the blood of three deaths: Hu-Nan's, Tae's, and his.

But before the trident made its fatal descent into Leo's skull, a hologram appeared beside Tripod-Stein's head. "Bring him to the inner sanctum," the disembodied voice commanded.

"Yes, my master," Tripod-Stein replied. He removed his hoof from Leo's chest and picked him up off the floor with one hand

Dazed and breathless, Leo watched as Stein removed a short piece of rope from his saddlebag and, in one deft move, dropped a noose around Leo's neck.

"Come with me," Stein said. He moved past the pilot and pulled the noose tight. As Leo was dragged out the generator room, he saw Tae lying on his side with both arms clutching his stomach. Tae's eyes stared at him but were devoid of life.

—— o ——

Khaos's aide, Lahmu, stood in the palace's main control tower behind a hybrid being, whose brain and veins were hardwired into the glowing fiber-optic cables that surrounded and suspended him.

The hybrid had the singular distinction of being the augur, the eyes and ears of Khaos. He looked as if he were caught in the nexus of a thousand giant spider webs, and he was, in fact, a living, breathing oracle who was wired into everything: every last warship and every single Tripod. He was the nexus of every communication system in the empire.

"Augur, how long until the fleet arrives?" Lahmu asked.

"Working." The augur's synthesized voice resounded over the room's speakers. He no longer utilized his mouth, as his nervous system was hardwired into the system around him.

Lahmu clasped his hands behind his back and paced back and forth. He let his mind wander while he waited for the augur's answer and contemplated the fact that there had been fewer, and less jubilant, worshipers this year than last. He blamed the small wood nymph from the Kingdom of Mukara for this and realized that he had previously underestimated the people's love for the tiny princess.

He wasn't worried, however. He knew that although his master preferred to rule under the guise of love, he was unafraid to rule by fear. Perhaps when the fleet of warships arrived, Atum would raze the princess's kingdom, so it would serve as an example to others who dared to oppose him.

The aide turned from the augur to see his new Tripod Prime, the earthling who once called himself Stein, standing before him. The other pesky human, the one called Leo, lay at his hoofed feet and struggled to remove a leather noose from his neck.

"Ah, Lieutenant Leo Dalton, back again, I see. Where's your friend?" a sly glance at Tripod-Stein confirmed what the aide had seen already on the boy's face. "Oh, I see," he said, feigning sympathy.

"You murdered my friend!" Leo yelled, his voice hoarse.

"Why, I did no such thing. My Tripod Prime merely defended himself and everyone in this palace."

"Stein, don't you get it? These guys are going to wipe out Earth!" The young Adamah ripped the noose the rest of the way from his neck and threw it to the floor.

"Oh, come now. There's no reason to be so melodramatic. You're much too smart to believe in God — much smarter than the others. Why, I'm sure you were the first one of them to figure out that mankind was created by Atum-Khaos, not by some non-existent deity to whom billions and billions of your kind have needlessly prayed over thousands of years."

"Harry said you would say that," the Adamah replied while looking for an exit.

"Did he now? Well, then, since you won't worship His Benevolence, I guess the only alternative is for you to die." He took a threatening step toward Leo, who attempted to back away but was held in place by Tripod-Stein.

The augur's voice suddenly filled the room. "Lahmu, let his eminence know that his fleet will achieve orbit within three hours."

"There, you see? You'll be back home before you know it. But, by the time Atum-Khaos is finished with it, it may not be the home you remember."

The aide was about to dismiss the Tripod to carry out his bidding, but the Augur's voice addressed him once more. "That's not all, Lahmu." He gestured toward a three-dimensional holographic projection that appeared in the center of the room. The projection displayed two planes heading directly for the palace. "Two crude unidentified chariots approach the palace from the east," he said. "Shall I inform Atum-Khaos?"

The aide scoffed. "And interrupt him while he is attending tribute? I think not. Do they present any danger to the palace?"

"Our scanners show that the crude craft do seem to be carrying large explosives." The augur zoomed in on the torpedo bombs that were strapped to the planes' wings.

"Will the bombs do any damage?" Lahmu asked, trying to sound unconcerned in front of the Adamah.

"No, all critical areas are heavily shielded."

Lahmu looked at Leo and said, "That's what you and your engineer friend were doing in the main generator's power-supply room. You thought that if you could disrupt the power system, it would shut down the shields protecting the anti-gravity generators and the gun batteries. A good plan. That is, until my Tripod stopped you."

Turning toward the augur, he commanded, "As soon as they're in range, lock all batteries on them and disintegrate them. Also, prepare for immediate ascension. We'll rendezvous with the Atum's fleet in orbit."

"And any followers still within the palace?" the Augur asked.

"Enlist the Mukarian bowmen for additional security but remove the rest. Have the Tripods throw them over the side if you have to." Lahmu turned back to Leo. "I don't think your primitive friends will be able to reach us at higher altitudes," he said. "Once the Atum's fleet arrives, I'll blast this planet back into the Stone Age. They'll be talking about this day in song for centuries."

Tripod-Stein struck the control room floor with one hoofed foot. "And what do you want me to do with this one?" He gave the boy a good hard shake.

Lahmu smiled. "Bring him to the sacrificial chamber."

Leo was dragged from the room, fully aware that Harry and Mac weren't coming to the rescue but rather flying to their deaths.

Chapter 29

Bomb Run

"WE'RE TOO LATE!"

"What?" Harry asked. He banked the nose of his Avenger for a better view, and he saw it, too. Mac was right. They were still several miles out, but even from this range, he saw that the mountain-sized citadel suspended over Joppa-Cal was slowly beginning its ascent toward the heavens.

"Harry, look at the palace. It's starting to climb."

Worse still, the shimmering shields over the anti-gravity generators were still visible. Both pilots knew that dropping their bombs prematurely would waste their one and only shot.

"Yeah, I see it. And it looks like Tae and Leo haven't managed to shut down the shields yet, either."

When they were within two miles of their target, the palace's main guns opened fire. Within seconds, a barrage of deadly flak engulfed both planes. The onslaught was far worse than anything Harry had experienced during the war.

"Break off, break off!" Harry yelled into his microphone as he yanked his stick over to complete a high-speed turn.

Mac followed suit, and both planes arced away. They ducked behind a nearby range of mountain peaks and hid out of the line of fire.

The gun battery assault stopped as abruptly as it had begun. Passing between a gap in the mountain tops, Harry saw a half dozen small attack craft explode from the palace's launch bay like a disturbed nest of angry bees and rocket after them at uncanny speed.

"Bogeys closing in on our nine o'clock," Mac said into the microphone.

"I see 'em. We may be in a bit of trouble here." Harry realized that was probably a vast understatement.

"What do we do?" Mac asked. She dove the nose of her plane down to generate every last ounce of speed out of the Avenger.

But Harry knew that there was nothing they could do against the superior craft. Their one chance had been the element of surprise, and now, even that was gone.

With the shields still covering the generators, they were finished, and they both knew it. It was only a matter of time before the alien fighters closed in on them and blasted them from the sky, dashing any hope of saving humanity from annihilation.

—— o ——

Tae awoke in the fetal position with his back against the generator he had come to destroy. He had been either dead or asleep. He wasn't sure which. Either way, he'd had the most wonderful vision of a young girl who floated above a river and sang the most beautiful song. And now, somehow, he was still alive.

There was a dull ache in his stomach, and he felt wet, sticky blood on his fingertips and chin. But more than anything else, he was cold. He couldn't stop shivering. The young engineer saw bloody, bluish guts piled on the belly of his shirt, and he knew that he was dead. His brain simply hadn't realized it yet.

Tae had heard that soldiers in battle feared stomach wounds the most because these wounds took so long to kill. But he thought it wasn't so bad, considering. *Now, what to do with the time left?* he wondered. He suddenly spied Leo's backpack, which contained the detonators.

If only he could sit up. Tae knew that if Stein's trident had severed his spinal cord, it wouldn't be possible. He would just lie there, with his face pressed to the palace floor, and bleed out until his brain finally caught up with the rest of his body.

Before he decided to try and move, he remembered something Leo had said — something Leo, in turn, had heard from Harry. What was it? *Something about believing in a cause greater than oneself.*

—— o ——

"Get your damn hands off of me!" Leo shouted at four hybrid priests who held his jerking limbs. The priests carried him high over their heads and roughly placed him atop an altar that looked to Leo as though it belonged in an Aztec pyramid.

Leo turned to see Stein, who stood nearby to watch him squirm. The former commando seemed to be enjoying himself. Leo cast him an angry look. Everything had come down to Stein's betrayal. If it weren't for Stein, he and Tae would have disabled the shields and Harry and Mac could have blown up the anti-gravity generators and kept the psychopathic deity from reaching Earth. But there was no hope of success for their plan now.

But then Leo remembered the words Harry had spoken back at the slave ruins, and he smiled.

"Why are you smiling, little Adamah?" Atum-Khaos asked. He startled Leo by speaking in an almost normal voice before stepping into view. The towering deity, with his wolf-like features and oversized eyes, was even more frightening up close than afar.

"Something Harry told me," Leo said through trembling lips. "Harry said that when things are at their worst, that's when you have to have faith the most."

"Faith?" Khaos's chest cracked down the middle and revealed his glowing essence. Leo squeezed his eyes shut and looked away from the brilliant, throbbing light. "I AM YOUR GOD!" Khaos's voice softened as he said, "Do you think that your God cares about an inconsequential fleck of molecules such as you?"

But Leo didn't have to answer him. The massive explosion that shook the palace walls answered for him. Tae had reached the detonators after all.

—— o ——

As they scudded their Avengers precariously through a narrow, twisting canyon, Harry realized that the more advanced fighters were designed for space warfare and had a difficult time flying on this side of the atmosphere. The smaller spacecraft constantly overshot their targets and took miles to circle back.

"I'm getting low on fuel!" Mac voice shouted at him over the cockpit speakers. "I'm not sure how much longer I can keep this bird in the air."

She was right. If Leo and Tae didn't act soon, their planes would simply drop out of the sky and save the alien fighters the trouble. Harry decided to make one last pass over the generators.

"All right, I'm gonna try for one more pass," he radioed back to her. "If the shields are still in place, we'll drop our bombs anyway and hope for the best."

Harry expertly looped his plane around and flew head-on between two closing fighters, causing one of them to dodge out of the way and crash into a canyon wall. "Starting attack run," he said as he center-lined his nosecone on the palace.

The palace's main guns opened fire, but Harry dived his plane below the flight deck and flew on beneath the onslaught of plasma fire. The guns couldn't hit him there without damaging the palace's own buildings.

Moving within range, he topped the great wall and wound his way through the narrow streets of Joppa-Cal. Then, flying underneath the palace (while praying the hovering citadel didn't have belly turrets), he looped his plane around the palace's outer wall and closed in on the generators.

He saw his target dead ahead but also saw that the glittering shields were still in place, confirming his worst fears. Grabbing his throat mic, he relayed back to Mac, "No good! No good! Shields are still in place."

But just as he was about to veer off, he took one last look at the shimmering shield, saw it wink out several times, and then vanish completely. Harry wiped his eyes on his sleeve and blinked several times to be sure before he radioed Mac. "You're not gonna believe this. The shields are gone. I'm starting my bomb run."

Harry knew that this was the most important bomb run of his life, and for humanity's sake, he prayed he wouldn't miss. "Torpedo away!" Harry held his breath as the falling missile sailed toward the anti-gravity generator. He flew over the generator, and for a moment, nothing happened behind him.

And then, as he was gaining altitude, BOOM! The explosion was massive. He banked his plane in a 180-degree turn, so he could survey the damage. There was a huge smoking hole where the generator housing had been. The floating city now dipped on the damaged side. Its ascent continued, but at a much slower rate. Harry whooped and hollered. "One down, and one to go!"

Suddenly, two fighters closed in behind him. "Uh-oh," he said. "I may be in a little trouble over here. Better start your run." He began evasive maneuvers and weaved in and out of the palace's towers.

"I could use some help over here myself" Mac replied, but Captain Reed couldn't hear her. He aimed his plane for a gap between a pair of Arabian-looking towers, unsure if the Avenger would even fit through them. He banked sideways at the last moment and hoped for the best.

—— o ——

Mac heard an explosion behind her and feared the worst. Harry wasn't answering her radio summons, which meant only one thing. After delivering his bomb, the second explosion she had heard must have been his plane. Help wasn't coming.

The bogey on her six fired a volley that streaked down the side of her plane. The enemy plasma fire dotted the wing and just missed her bomb. The antiquated plane was just no match for the superior fighter craft. She had used every trick in the book to evade them, but she knew that in a few more seconds she'd be little more than cloud vapor. She imagined the alien pilots behind her gazing at their advanced consoles as their targeting sensors locked onto her ancient plane.

She suddenly heard a burst of heavy machine gun fire behind her, which was followed by a succession of explosions. Risking a quick look, she saw Harry's Avenger shooting down her pursuers. The last one trailed smoke as it took a swan dive into the floating palace.

Captain Reed had come to her rescue once again.

This time, Mac found enough courage for a quippy comeback. "It's about time," she said.

Even over the radio waves, Mac heard the jubilance in Harry's voice when he replied, "Hey, you gonna drop that pig or just carry it around all day?"

Harry dropped down on her wing, and they passed over the two towers Harry had banked through earlier, or rather, they flew past the remains of the towers. It was evident that Harry's two pursuers had crashed through the buildings rather than flown between them.

Spying her own target, Mac radioed, "Lining up for final attack run." With Harry's plane covering her, it was going to be a milk run. A minute later she was over the target. "Bombs away," she said into her microphone and pulled the release mechanism.

But nothing happened.

Mac watched as Harry's Avenger moved onto her wing, but Mac didn't need him to tell her that her torpedo hadn't disengaged.

Just then, two more alien fighters arrived and fired upon the Avengers. A salvo of lasers hit the side of Mac's plane, shredding the fuselage, but the plane stayed aloft. Mac smiled. *These old birds are built to last.*

Harry quickly engaged the fighters. He maneuvered between them, and the alien pilots became so focused on shooting him down that they crashed into one another.

Meanwhile, Mac aimed the nose of her plane downward, which fanned the flames that had sprung up on her nosecone. She hoped that an unlikely blowout would extinguish the flames on her engine's housing, but it didn't happen.

As if that weren't bad enough, her plane suddenly sputtered. It was lower on fuel than she had realized. She tapped the fuel gauge, but the little white indicator arrow failed to move off empty. She knew she only had seconds to act before the flames licking her fuselage ignited the vapors in her empty gas tanks.

Quickly doubling back and lining up for a second attack run, she picked up her mic and held it to her throat. "Do me a favor, will ya?" she asked as she aimed the nose of her plane at the second generator.

"No, Mac, there's got to be another way."

But they both knew that she didn't have time to land; the palace was entering the upper atmosphere, where they would no longer be able to reach it. Mac doubted they would get a second shot at this. The Avenger's engines screamed in protest, and her plane began vibrating heavily. Fire and smoke streamed past her cockpit. There just wasn't time.

In the cockpit of his Avenger, Harry saw Mac's burning plane fly toward the second generator in a textbook kamikaze attack. About twenty seconds before the impact, Harry received Mac's final words. "When you get back to Earth, kiss my daughter for me."

—— o ——

When Lahmu regained his feet after the first explosion, he knew that one of the anti-gravity generators had been hit, for the palace slanted ten degrees to the right for several moments until the other generators compensated and slowly returned the palace to level. Lahmu had just finished navigating the tilted palace halls and was about to enter the main audience chamber when the second explosion nearly knocked him flat.

This is not possible! he thought as he picked himself off the floor. With the second generator destroyed, the palace began descending slowly toward the planet. *Who knows what kind of damage will be inflicted on the palace in an uncontrolled descent!*

Entering through the main doors and rapidly moving into the inner sanctum, Lahmu saw Atum in the sacrificial chamber presiding over the sacrifice of the young Adamah, despite the fact that the floor was now at a forty-five-degree angle.

"I SENSE DOUBT IN YOU" Lahmu heard his master say to the boy. When the young man jerked his head from Atum's hands, he saw the young Adamah's eyes had already turned all black. *And yet he continues to resist,* Lahmu said to himself, *most impressive.*

"AIDE, REPORT!" Khaos said in an annoyed voice without looking up.

Lahmu quickly bowed, his nose nearly touching the carpet, and trembled as he did so. "Two anti-gravity generators have been disabled, my Atum," he announced.

"WHY HAVE THE MAIN BATTERIES CEASED?"

"It's the Mooks, my Atum—" He paused and wondered if it was a good idea to be the one to give him this information.

Khaos raised an eyebrow. "Yes, go on. What about them?"

"They've gone crazy. They're killing everyone they come into contact with. They ripped my assistant apart with their bare hands."

As if on cue, they heard a loud THUMP in the main audience chamber. Khaos signaled for the robed priests to keep the Adamah pinned to the altar and walked into the main chamber with Lahmu following. They reached the chamber just in time to see one of the Adamah's winged craft soar by.

Seconds later, the main doors burst open and three of Atum-Khaos's royal offspring burst into the room with Mooks crawling all over them, stabbing them, and tearing at their bodies. Even from fifty yards away, Lahmu heard cries in the outer chamber — the cries of more royal hybrids.

Hordes of Mooks, dressed like the indigenous species of the planet, had stormed the palace. The Mooks that couldn't negotiate the crowded floors climbed the walls and ceilings. Two Awumpai, those that used to serve the Dan-Sai, led the rebellious horde.

Although concerned, Lahmu wasn't worried. There were at least six full regiments of Tripods between them and the Mooks, and Mukarian bowmen loyal to Khaos lined the walls. In addition, the third anti-gravity generator was already returning the palace to level, albeit slowly. Lahmu also knew that it wouldn't be long before Atum's fleet arrived in orbit and sent down reinforcements. Still, the aide would have felt better if his master had brought the scepter of power with him from the inner sanctum.

Instead, Atum grabbed a heavy sword from a nearby Tripod warrior and, with a smile on his face, led a charge toward the advancing Mooks.

The final battle had begun.

—— o ——

Meanwhile, in the sacrificial chamber, Leo struggled against his captors but to no avail. Although the robed hybrids' limbs seemed frail, the four of them were strong enough to keep him pinned to the granite altar.

In the midst of his struggles, Leo glanced upward and saw a young girl — a child, really — who looked like a wood nymph from fantasy stories. She walked toward the altar on dainty bare feet. If the priests saw her, they didn't show it.

"Hello, Leo," the nymph said in perfect English. When she saw Leo look at the priests and then at her, she said, "No, they cannot see me."

"Are you the SongBird Goddess?" Leo asked.

He was rewarded with an adorable giggle. "No, silly. I'm Asha." She grew serious. "Leo, you must free the SongBird Goddess. The scepter of power will show you the way."

Leo saw Khaos's scepter near the throne and figured that it had to be what the wispy little girl was talking about.

"I'm a little tied up at the moment," Leo said. "I don't suppose you could help with that?"

Asha swiped her transparent hand through the nearest priest to demonstrate her present condition. "I am sorry, but in my current state, I cannot."

"Great, well, thanks for nothing," Leo said tiredly.

One of the priests turned his head to see whom Leo spoke to. Although the priest didn't see Asha, he seemed slightly uncomfortable, as though he sensed Asha's presence.

Asha thought for a moment. Then, looking down at him, she bit down hard enough to make a resounding chomping noise with her teeth. "Have you tried using your teeth?"

Leo raised his eyebrows in response but decided it was worth a shot. He relaxed to make the priests believe that he had given up, waited a moment, and lunged forward, latching his teeth onto one of the priest's forearms.

"Ahhh!" The priest cried out in pain and released him.

Before the bitten priest could grab him again, Leo shoved him backward and sent him to the floor. When another priest tried to pin his chest, Leo reared up a booted leg and kicked him to the ground.

Before the other priests could recover from the surprise attack, Leo jerked his right leg and arm free and rolled clear of the altar.

Asha jumped up and down on her toes and clapped her hands. "Grab the torch! Grab the torch!" she shouted.

The four priests had nearly backed Leo into the wall but paused when Leo removed a nearby flaming torch from its holder.

When the first priest finally attacked, Leo lit the priest's robes ablaze. He swung the torch at the other three, and they fled from the chamber, presumably to seek help.

"Wonderful!" Asha yelled with glee. "Now grab the scepter! Grab the scepter!"

"What?" Leo asked, but then he saw the glowing scepter on Khaos's throne. He tossed the torch away and ran to the throne.

When he touched the scepter, he felt as though he'd grabbed an electric fence. He yelped as a powerful surge of current passed through his limbs and sent him to the floor.

Leo looked at his burned hands and then at Asha with a betrayed, hurt look on his face. "What the hell?"

Asha shook her head sympathetically. "You have to believe you can carry the scepter. Try again."

"You might have told me that the first time," Leo said. He was growing weary of playing hero.

Jumping to his feet, he shook out his hands and took a deep breath. But before he could step toward the scepter once more, a large three-legged form appeared between him and the magical staff.

"Going somewhere?" said the Tripod once known as Stein.

"Get out of the way, Stein!" Leo shouted, but Stein continued to block his path.

"I don't think so, boy." Stein twirled his heavy trident over his head before pointing it at Leo.

"Over here! Over here!" Asha shouted. Leo saw that she stood next to a statue that held a squat, but formidable-looking, short sword.

Leo ran over to it, grabbed the sword, and faced the Tripod warrior once more.

Stein threw his head back and let out a hearty laugh — just before he charged.

Chapter 30

Final Battle

STANDING ON THE BALCONY that overlooked the main audience chamber, Lahmu had the best seat in the house to watch the battle below.

He saw Atum Khaos carve through the rebellious Mooks as a farmer cleaves wheat from a field. Khaos, the Tripods, and the Mukarian bowmen had turned the tide of the battle and had all but finished off the last fifty of the Mooks. However, casualties had been extensive. Centuries of breeding royal hybrids and Tripods had gone to waste.

The Mooks had been unaccountably vicious. He'd had no idea the docile, little servants could be so savage. As he watched, he saw another Tripod guard swarmed by several Mooks. He made a note to suggest breeding the Mooks for an army when all this ridiculous foolishness was all over, and he was confident it would be over soon.

The rebellion would only be a minor, although inconvenient, blip in the millennia of Atum Khaos's great and peaceful reign. Atum-Khaos, after all, was the only being who had ever defied the one true Father and survived. Once the rebels were brutally tortured and systematically executed, Atum's warships would demolish the insolent kingdoms of this wretched world, and the craterous remains would serve as warnings to others who dared oppose Atum. The warships would then traverse the wormhole, and the Adamah's home world would be enslaved, just like the thousands of other planets in Khaos's empire.

The Mukarian bowmen, who were entranced and controlled by Atum-Khaos, not only picked off the Mooks one by one but also filled the Awumpai with their arrows. Even from a distance, Lahmu saw that the mighty beasts were tiring. He smiled when he saw the Tripods closing ranks around the tiring Awumpai and the remaining Mooks.

Suddenly, Lahmu's smile disappeared, and his jaw fell open in surprise. An Adamah airplane strafed the glass dome in the chamber's ceiling. The dome shattered, and shards of glass and rubble the size of Awumpai fell from the heavily damaged ceiling, causing Atum and the other combatants to scatter.

Once the dust settled, Lahmu heard the whine of the craft's engines and saw the plane line up as though the pilot intended to land right inside the main audience chamber.

Khaos saw this, too, and signaled for a Tripod to throw him its trident.

Lahmu knew that Atum was more than capable of spearing the Adamah pilot from this distance but that Atum would probably wait for a perfect shot.

The Adamah plane dropped over the chamber's farthest wall and was mere feet from touching the ground when Khaos reared back his mighty arm and prepared to launch the trident. Lahmu knew in his heart that Atum would not miss; he was incapable of it. But then a sword suddenly appeared in the center of Atum's chest.

The red-haired Awumpai, Hu-Nan, was still alive. Although bleeding severely from several arrows, he had managed to sneak up behind Khaos and ram a sword through his back. Hu-Nan put his head over Khaos's right shoulder and growled ferociously to let the dark deity know who had stabbed him.

Khaos spun the giant Awumpai off his back. He stumbled around, the sword still sticking through his body, and turned to face Hu-Nan. In a fit of rage, Khaos hurled the trident, which had been intended for the Adamah pilot, at the Awumpai.

Hu-Nan yelped in pain when the trident slammed into his body. He skidded across the floor and landed in a heap. He struggled to get up but fell heavily back to the ground and moved no more.

Lahmu saw the older Awumpai, Fu-Mar, roar wildly when Hu-Nan was hit, but several Tripods used the distraction and swarmed him.

"FILTHY ANIMAL," Khaos hissed as he removed the sword from his back. He spat at the dead Awumpai and turned to deal with the incoming plane.

But the plane was closer than expected. It had lined up right on Khaos and sped toward him with its guns blazing.

Lahmu watched in horror as Khaos's body convulsed violently again and again from the plane's projectiles that blew threw his body. The Adamah's plane touched down and skidded across the palace floor, heading right for his Atum.

Khaos's outstretched arms did little to protect him when the Adamah's plane careened into him and, like a giant carpenter's hammer, smashed his body into the wall.

Lahmu saw that the Mukarian bowmen's eyes no longer glowed, and the Tripods, now leaderless, wandered about confusedly.

Captain Harry Reed quickly climbed out of his plane's cockpit and drew his pistol. He needn't have bothered.

The dark deity wasn't even visible. His body was embedded in the wall behind the plane's crumpled nose. The Tripods kept their distance from Harry, and none of the bowmen fired arrows at him.

He saw Hu-Nan's impaled body on the floor and was about to run to his dead friend's side when he suddenly glimpsed something descending from the ceiling at a gentle rate. It wasn't glass or falling debris.

It was Mac.

Although her hands, face, and hair were scorched, she didn't look the worse for wear. "I thought you were dead!" Harry exclaimed.

"Duh," Mac replied and pointed to her back. "Parachute." She had finally one-upped him in the quip department.

Harry ran over and embraced her in a bear hug that lifted her feet off the floor.

After the embrace, Mac asked him, "Leo and Tae?"

Harry shook his head. "I don't know. I just got here myself." His face turned solemn. "But Hu-Nan didn't make it."

Mac touched his cheeks, which he knew were damp with tears. Fu-Mar had moved to his fallen friend's body and was removing the trident.

"Oh, how sweet," Khaos said sarcastically from inside the wall.

Harry heard the loud sound of metal scraping and turned to see the twelve-foot demigod push the plane backward and free himself. Harry noted that Khaos's massive wounds were healing but at an extremely slow rate. *At least I managed to hurt him*, Harry thought.

"DID YOU THINK YOU STOPPED ME?" the dark deity asked, stepping toward Harry. "YOU HAVE ONLY DELAYED THE INEVITABLE!" Khaos limped, but Harry knew that the dark god still had more than enough power to kill them. Harry decided that he would go down fighting just the same.

"DO YOU THINK I SURVIVED A BATTLE WITH THE ONE TRUE FATHER HIMSELF TO BE SLAIN BY THE LIKES OF YOU?"

Harry pulled Mac behind him, and Fu-Mar and the small handful of remaining Mooks encircled them protectively.

Atum-Khaos turned to his army of Tripods and Mukarian bowmen and commanded, "FINISH THEM!"

As the army closed in, Harry noted that the bowmen's eyes were once again filled with black hate.

—— o ——

Back in the inner sanctum, Leo fought for his life, and he was losing.

Towering over him, Tripod-Stein smashed Leo and his tiny sword down again and again. Near exhaustion, Leo backed into an alcove that contained a large table and chairs. He threw the chairs in front of him, but this did little to slow down the menacing Stein. Ducking a swipe, Leo dodged out of the way of Stein's descending trident, which smashed the heavy table into two parts.

Leo was trapped in the alcove. There was nowhere else to go. In a desperate move that surprised even him, he flipped the short sword around, so he was holding the blade, and flung the sword at Stein's head.

The offensive move surprised Stein, too. He didn't have time to dodge out of the way, and the blade caught his forearm, which he lifted to block his head.

Tripod-Stein dropped his trident and howled in pain. Grimacing, he stumbled backward and attempted to pull the sword out of his arm, but the wound bled too much. His back still to the wall, Leo dove toward Stein's dropped trident. Stein stomped after him while throwing overturned chairs and pieces of broken table out of the way.

Leo started to lift the heavy trident from the floor, but before he could, Stein appeared above him. Stein reared back on his hind legs and lunged forward to trample the young astronaut with his mighty front hoof.

Leo abandoned the trident and rolled out of the way just as Tripod-Stein's hoof slammed down on the weapon, pinning it to the floor. Leo backed away until he was against the wall once more.

Looking for a weapon and finding none, Leo tried to make a run for it. As he did so, Stein impaled him with the recovered trident. The blow lifted him off the floor and pinned him to the wall. While it hurt like hell, only one of the trident's points had pierced Leo's narrow waist. The point had gone through just beneath his ribs and to the right. In a daze, Leo marveled that hadn't been a killing blow and that he wasn't dead yet after all that he'd endured. Stein kept Leo pinned to the wall and moved closer, putting his face right next to Leo's. "Déjà vu," he said.

Leo felt Stein's hot breath on his face.

"Now what does this remind me of?" Stein said, turning his head to the side. "Oh yeah, this was the exact same way your friend Tae looked — just before I sent him to hell."

Although in excruciating pain, Leo noticed that the Mukarian short sword still stuck fast in Stein's forearm. "Then tell Tae I said hello," Leo said through clenched teeth. Ignoring the pain in his stomach, he ripped the blade from Stein's arm and stabbed the Tripod in the throat.

Tripod-Stein dropped Leo and the trident. He stumbled backward, clutching the short sword in his throat, and finally fell over onto his side.

Leo slid down the wall and landed atop of a pile of rubble. With great effort, he removed the trident from his midsection and threw it aside, where it clanged to the floor.

Through slatted eyes, he watched Tripod-Stein in the throes of death. As the darkness began to form a tunnel around Leo's vision, the little girl approached him once more. He blinked the slow blink of someone on the brink of consciousness and saw that she knelt in front of him.

"Wake up, Leo. It's not time to die," she said.

—— o ——

In the audience chamber, Harry, Mac, the Awumpai, and the remaining Mooks somehow still held their own. While Fu-Mar and Atum-Khaos battled it out in a clash of the titans, Harry and Mac kept the Tripods at bay using their .45's and the Mooks.

However, Fu-Mar was tiring against Atum-Khaos, and the Mooks were rapidly falling beneath the archers' arrows. Harry knew that it wouldn't be long before he and Mac were on their own.

As he put another two rounds in a Tripod's eye, Harry ducked behind a fallen pillar for cover and was surprised to see Asha there. "Asha!" he exclaimed. "What are you doing here? I thought you were dead."

Asha looked at him sadly and explained, "I am Harry."

Mac, who reloaded her pistol nearby, asked, "Who are you talking to?" Before he could answer, she had already drawn another bead on a Tripod.

"Harry, you have to go inside the inner sanctum and help Leo," Asha said.

Looking at the bowmen and Tripods around him, Harry said, "Are you kidding me? We'll never make it back there."

"Yes, you will." Asha stood up in the line of fire. Harry was tempted to pull her back down, but he saw an arrow pass through her transparent form.

Asha's spirit form raised high above the battle and became visible to all. Harry saw that the bowmen, though still possessed by Atum, halted their attack when they saw her. Harry didn't speak Asha's language fluently, but he thought he heard her say, "My brethren, Atum-Khaos has blinded you.

But now you are free from his lies. Free to follow him or the SongBird Goddess. You are free to choose, as the one true Father intended all along."

Just then, a Tripod leaped over the group's crude stockade. Mac emptied one in its chest before she was mule-kicked in the ribs, which sent her sprawling. Harry fired his last two rounds at it only to be knocked to floor by the butt-end of a trident. The Tripod reared up to trample Harry underfoot, but twelve well-placed arrows suddenly hit its body.

It seemed that the Mukarian bowmen had made their choice.

Harry looked up and saw Khaos ready to behead a beaten Fu-Mar, execution style, but twenty arrows abruptly pierced the deity's back. It was an annoyance to the demigod more than anything else, but it still gave Fu-Mar time to spring away.

Asha looked back down at Harry. "Free the SongBird Goddess!" she said.

Mac saw the bowmen suddenly change sides, and as Harry helped her to her feet, she asked, "What the hell is going on?"

"An old friend stopped by. C'mon. We've got to find Leo." Harry led Mac and Fu-Mar toward the inner sanctum, and the Mukarian bowmen covered their retreat.

—— o ——

Leo successfully picked up Atum's scepter. He pointed it at the pi-shaped wooden doorframe in the stone wall behind the throne but really didn't expect anything to happen. To his surprise, a beam of light shot out of the scepter and formed a swirling vortex beneath the archway.

Leo heard a sound behind him and turned to see Harry, Mac, and Fu-Mar enter the inner sanctum. Atum-Khaos and an army of Tripods were hot on their heels.

Harry and Fu-Mar barred the heavy doors behind them, but Tripod pikes and axes immediately began hacking at the doors.

"Is there another way out of here?" Harry yelled to Mac.

"I don't see one."

Before Harry could come up with a plan, Fu-Mar ran to one of the pillars that framed the doorway and leaned into it as Samson did at the Coliseum. Within moments, the giant

Awumpai had knocked over the massive pillar and caused the threshold's ceiling to collapse, blocking the advance of Khaos and his army. But they knew it wouldn't hold off the army forever.

Harry and Mac ran up the main aisle to Leo and saw Stein dead on the floor. "You okay, Leo?" Mac asked.

"Yeah, I'm fine."

"Where's Tae?"

Leo shook his head. "He didn't make it."

"What?" The word was strangled and Leo swallowed beneath Mac's stare. He could see her processing the information through her disbelief. He struggled to bury the thought of his friend and focus on the present crisis.

He turned to Harry and he said, "Your friend Asha told me that the SongBird Goddess is through there." He pointed at the molecular whirlpool. "She wants us to free her."

"Yeah, I know; I saw her, too," Harry replied.

Loud crashing noises emanated from the sanctum's entrance as Khaos and his followers worked their way through. Fu-Mar took his place just inside the doors and readied himself for combat.

Mac told Harry, "Go. We'll hold off Khaos as long as we can."

Harry checked to see that his pistols were loaded and took the heavy scepter from Leo. "Okay, I'll be right back," he said. After giving Mac a wink and a smile, and Leo a slap on the back, he dove through the portal.

Seconds later, there was a loud explosion near the doorway. Before the cloud of dust settled, Khaos and his army of Tripods were walking briskly toward them.

Chapter 31

The Europa Moon Temple

CAPTAIN REED'S BODY flew out the portal at a high rate of speed. He tucked and rolled at the last minute, his boots and arms spraying white sand into the air as he came roughly to a stop.

He quickly pushed to his feet and scanned with his pistol. Looking around the circular room with the round pool at its center, he realized he recognized this place.

He had been here before.

Just as he had in his vision, Harry walked over to the circular pit filled with water and looked down. He saw the SongBird Goddess floating beneath the surface and two, six-foot long serpents slithering around her. The goddess looked up at Harry, and he saw her agony. He could just make out the heavy chain that held her beneath the water line.

Hefting the scepter and taking deep breaths, he readied himself to dive in the pool. He didn't see the vortex behind him flash when someone stepped through, but the SongBird Goddess must have, for he saw sudden fear in her eyes. Suddenly, a single shot rang out, and a .45-caliber bullet passed through his lung.

Harry dropped the scepter, and it landed at the pit's edge. He staggered but managed to turn around to face the person who had shot him in the back.

Leo stood there with the pistol in his outstretched hand. His eyes had turned completely black — just like the eyes of the twelve-foot tall being that stepped through the portal to stand beside the young man.

"YOU HAVE DONE WELL," the deity said while placing a fatherly hand on Leo's shoulder.

Harry couldn't stand any longer and collapsed to his knees. He rolled over onto his back, his hand instinctively covering his bloody wound.

"NOW, BRING ME THE SCEPTER OF POWER!" Khaos commanded Leo.

—— o ——

Leo swelled with pride. He had pleased Khaos, and that was all that mattered to him. He moved to the pit's edge and bent down to retrieve his master's scepter.

He heard rapid, shallow breathing nearby. It was Harry. He was still alive. Leo saw blood pooling where the bullet had passed through his friend's chest.

Why did I do that? Some small part of Leo's brain wondered. *Why would I shoot someone like Harry in the back?* He looked down again at Harry, who was dying at his feet, and the voice in his head grew louder. Leo had grown up without a father, so he didn't know what it was like to have one, but if he were to choose a father, it would be someone just like Harry.

And Khaos had made him shoot Harry in the back.

Rather than pick up the scepter, as his master had commanded, Leo knelt down next to Harry. "C'mon, Harry. I'm getting you out of here," he said. There had to be some sort of doctor back at the palace.

"I can't, kid. My legs don't work," Harry replied. A smile flickered at his lips.

The front of Harry's shirt was completely red with his blood. Leo was surprised that Harry was still conscious. He shook his head in remorse. *No! Not Harry, too.*

"It's okay, Leo. You've got to save the SongBird Goddess," Harry said, resting his bloodstained hand on Leo's jacket.

"No, I don't. I have to save you," Leo said matter-of-factly.

Harry no longer seemed to feel the pain, and he smiled up at Leo. "Son, listen to me. Remember that talk we had at the ruins about some things being more important than one's own life?"

Leo wiped his tears away and bobbed his head. "Yes," he said.

"Well, this is one of those times." Harry coughed and clutched his jacket tightly as a spasm of pain racked his body. After it subsided, Harry's lopsided grin crossed his face one last time. "Save her, Leo." His body then went limp and lay lifeless.

Leo covered his face with the palm of his hand. Mac, Tae, Brett, Stein, the Awumpai — they were all dead. He was the only one left. He began to cry.

But then Leo felt anger brewing inside him. *That monster made me destroy the most descent man I ever met in my life.*

Leo spied Khaos's scepter, which lay on the edge of the circular pit.

"HE WAS WEAK," Khaos said. "NOW BRING ME THE SCEPTER."

Leo wiped away his tears on the back of his hand and picked up the fallen scepter. *Funny,* he thought, *I couldn't even touch it before without being shocked, but now I can lift it easily.* He smiled at Atum-Khaos and took one step backward into the watery pool.

The heavy scepter, like an anchor, took him immediately to the bottom of the pit. He knew it wouldn't be long before Khaos dove in the pool after him, so Leo raised the scepter and pointed it at the chain that restrained the beautiful goddess.

As the dragon-headed serpents swam towards him, he heard a loud splash overhead. Khaos had dived in. Leo knew he should have been scared out of his gourd, but one look at the beautiful SongBird Goddess before him gave him a sense of inner peace.

Even as the first serpent's tail encircled his waist and Khaos's massive hand clamped down on the top of his skull, Leo was unafraid. This was his moment. This was his time to accomplish something greater than the needs and wants of his own mortal life.

As the serpent squeezed his waist and Khaos tightened his grip, Leo aimed the scepter at the thick chain and fired. A brilliant light blinded him. His vision returned just in time to see the chain that held the SongBird Goddess fall to the pit's floor.

—— o ——

Outside the pit, it was quiet for a moment, almost serene. If someone had entered the temple at that moment, he or she would have been unaware that a battle for worlds had just taken place in the small circular pit in the center of the room.

And then the contents of the pit erupted from the hole as though someone had thrown twenty grenades into the pool of water, and they had all detonated simultaneously.

The room once again fell silent. Leo, however, heard a loud ringing in his ears as he slowly returned to consciousness. When he opened his eyes, a mouth full of razor-sharp spikes snapped at him.

Instinctively, Leo jerked his head away from the serpent. Its body flailed — a fish out of water. He quickly scooted away and saw that the second serpent lay motionless with its neck at an odd angle.

Rising to his feet, Leo saw that he wasn't the only one who had survived the explosion. Khaos was regaining consciousness near a wall that Leo recognized immediately; it was the same wall that had started it all, the one with the strange symbols.

Khaos spied him and leaped to his feet, and Leo ran to the other side of the pit, searching for an exit. In the time it took him to realize that there was none, Khaos was upon him.

Khaos picked him up by the throat and pinned him against the wall. "Want to know a secret?" he said in an almost mortal voice.

"A secret? That's funny, coming from you," Leo barely managed to choke out. His legs dangled off the floor, and he had both hands wrapped around the deity's wrist, trying desperately to free himself.

Ignoring him, Khaos continued, "Do you know why God loves you insignificant mortals more than what you call 'angels'? Your ignorance. You humans, with your miserable mayfly existence, have only your faith to guide you. Angels cannot have faith because they already know beyond a shadow of a doubt that God exists; they interact with him every day."

Khaos squeezed his fingers around Leo's neck and was rewarded with the sound of cracking bones. "WELL WE DIDN'T ASK TO KNOW!" he shouted.

"RELEASE HIM!" called an ethereal voice.

Khaos fell to his knees and grabbed his stomach. Leo slumped to the sandy ground, his entire world narrowing to the air flooding his lungs.

Gasping from a mortal blow, Khaos asked, "Why? How can this be?"

Leo lifted his gaze and saw that the SongBird Goddess had risen from her tomb, which was now nothing more than a muddy pit. The scepter of power glowed like a radiant beacon in her delicate hand.

Khaos turned, and his eyes opened wide in astonishment when he saw something he had not seen in over a millennium: the SongBird Goddess stood before him in solid form.

She walked over to Atum Khaos and knelt beside him. After gently laying her hand on him, she said, "You have exceeded you timetable, brother." Her aura then began absorbing both his ethereal and physical forms.

Before he faded completely from sight, Khaos cried, "DAMN YOU, SISTER! DAMN YOU TO HELL!"

——— o ———

Commander Mac O'Bryant knew this was her end, though, if anyone had told her it was even possible to die fighting a hoard of three-legged alien centaurs on a distant planet that was controlled by the precursors to Earth's own gods, she would have laughed in their face and assumed they were nuts. Well it was a good thing she had no bet to lose over it because apparently that was exactly how she was going to die — skewered by a hundred Tripod tridents after her co-pilot had been hijacked by a living god.

At her back, a very bloody and worn Fu-Mar growled at their encircling foes. Mac was sure it was his glare alone that was keeping the Tripods at bay. No, she *hoped* it was that; she couldn't stomach the thought of being saved as Khaos's plaything, or worse. She'd already faced that possibility once and once was enough.

Suddenly she wished she'd saved her last bullet. After all this, after losing Tae and Brett, after Joan had risked everything to warn her, she'd still failed to save Earth, save Emma. She'd rather die than watch that failure bear fruit. But then, she realized, it wasn't in her to go down without a fight.

She cast her gaze around for a weapon and found a knife at her feet in the hands of a dead Mook. The creature had died with its eyes open, war paint smeared across its face, completely free in its moment of death. Mac decided there were worse ways to die.

She grabbed the knife and charged the nearest Tripod.

Her Tripod target stiffened in surprise and Mac found a grin on her face. The creature swept with his trident and Mac ducked. She dove between the creature's legs and stabbed the knife into its underbelly. The Tripod screamed and reared. Mac scrambled away as the thing came down in a storm of thrashing limbs, its death knells echoing across the vaulted throne room. The shock rippled through the other Tripods.

Behind her, Fu-Mar roared defiance. The Awumpai surged forward as if a tether had snapped, as if he had been merely awaiting her choice.

Mac found herself another Mook knife and she raced to collect it as the Tripods refocused. Her hand closed over the crude hilt. A ring of tridents descended. She closed her eyes and ... nothing.

She peeked with one eye and then stared in confusion at the Tripods which seemed to have been frozen in time, their arms drawn back for the blow and the deadly points of their tridents perfectly still in the air.

Fu-Mar roared and chopped four creatures in half before he seemed to realize they weren't fighting back. His arm dropped, his massive sword dripping gore from its tip and providing the only sound in the room besides his panting breath and the thudding of Mac's heart in her chest.

"What?..." she asked. As if the word had been the key to a spell, every single Tripod crumpled like a marionette with severed strings.

Mac stood in the center of the carnage, struggling to understand what had just happened. Fu-Mar gazed around the room and then he did something that jolted Mac back to awareness, he tipped his head and began to laugh.

Khaos was dead.

——— o ———

Leo lay against the wall, unable to move his unresponsive body. His labored breathing was the only sound in the room. Mustering all his remaining strength, he was only able to raise an arm toward the SongBird Goddess, and it was a feeble gesture at that.

The goddess knelt by his side. Stroking his hair, she said, "You have freed me."

"What about Khaos's warships?" Leo asked, his voice barely above a whisper. "They're in orbit … They'll head for Earth."

"Shh, shh, it's all right. Do not fear, little one. My brother's forces will never reach Earth."

"What? But how?"

"On my command, they will enter the wormhole, and when they do, it will close around them."

"But how is this possible?"

"Because you and your friends have freed me." The SongBird Goddess smiled. "Now that I am free, I am able to manipulate the cosmos once more. It seems I have been forgiven by the Father, the one True God. Your actions have restored my grace and have restored balance to the universe. And for that, I am truly grateful."

"Then we did it. We saved Earth. We saved them all. My friends, they didn't die for nothing."

"That's right, Leo," she said, smiling once more. "You and Mac will go on to be emissaries of worlds."

Emissaries of worlds, Leo thought, *not bad for a couple of glorified truckers.*

Leo suddenly heard a familiar voice. "Leo!" it called over torrents of wind. Oddly enough, it sounded a lot like his future mother-in-law. Leo turned and watched Mac step through the vortex. The moment she did, it began to shrink closed behind her.

"The doorway — it's closing!" he yelled, but by the time Mac turned around, the vortex had vanished.

Mac helped Leo stumble to his feet. "What about Harry?" she asked, her voice breathless. Her eyes snagged on the pilot lying at the edge of the pit.

Leo shook his head. "He's gone."

"Oh, Harry," Mac breathed, blinking back her tears. "It happened after all. I'd hoped ... I guess it doesn't matter now."

Scanning the room Leo saw the SongBird Goddess had also vanished. He and Mac were the only ones left, alone in the tomb at the bottom of an ocean of an icy moon.

Raising his hands in frustration Leo shouted, "So what the hell do we do now, huh? You just leave us to rot so we can find three corpses in the future instead of just one?"

Mac gently laid a hand on his shoulder. "Stop it, Leo. It's over."

Angry, Leo shook himself free and continued to yell at nothingness. "No! We save her, and the whole damn universe and this is what we get?"

An ethereal voice cut him off. Gently, the SongBird Goddess said, "Oh, Leo. Even after all you have witnessed. Still, you do not believe."

A new burst of wind gusted at his and Mac's hair and after it died down a second voice was heard. A voice neither of them had heard in a very, very long time.

"Mom? Leo? Is that you?"

It was Emma.

As one, they whirled around to see that a second spinning vortex had opened. Mac's daughter was standing on the lush green grass of her college campus holding her books to her chest. "Mom, what's going on, what is this?" Her eyes roved over them and past them to the hieroglyphs on the wall and the carved picture of the Europa Moon pyramid.

"Go to her," the SongBird commanded. "Go to her now for I cannot hold this portal through time and space for long."

Mac stepped forward as if there were not a doubt in her mind but Leo hesitated.

Mac glanced back and quirked an eyebrow, "You gonna sit around here on your ass all day or are we gonna get out of here?"

Leo grinned and decided that maybe he could have faith in something after all. He grabbed her offered hand and together they leapt through the vortex seconds before it winked out and sealed the tomb for another time.

—— o ——

In the tomb, the light faded from the closing vortex, but another softer glow soon replaced it.

The SongBird Goddess returned. She knelt next to Harry, folded his hands on his stomach, and cradled his head in her hands.

Although he couldn't hear her, she said, "Sleep, faithful one. Your wife and daughters are waiting for you in the afterlife. Your long night is over."

The angelic goddess gently laid his head to rest next to the circular grave that had been her tomb. She gently kissed his forehead and bade him farewell.

Captain Harry Christopher Reed was dead.

As an afterthought, the SongBird Goddess removed Harry's journal from his coat pocket. She scribbled something on the last page, her thoughts serving as the ink for an invisible pen. When she finished, she replaced the journal in Harry's right hand and began to fade from the temple and the mortal plane of existence.

Her departure created a fierce wind that opened the journal to the last page, the page on which she had inscribed these final words: *To the reader of this journal, faith is the substance of things hoped for, the evidence of things not yet seen.*

# # #

BEDLAM LOST

The next new novel by Jack Castle

Chapter One

Hank

"PLEASE...PLEASE DON'T KILL ME."

The disembodied voice sobbed in the darkness, begging for his life. The hammer of a heavy-duty revolver drew back...

A tiny light in the distance: a pinprick of light at the end of a long tunnel moved rapidly closer. The growing hot white light, accompanied by a roaring sound, increased in severity, and relentlessness.

CLANG-CLANG-CLANG-CLANG!

Hank McCarthy bolted awake to the sound of a roaring locomotive heaving straight for the car. He flashed open his eyes, squinting from the light and found himself sitting behind the wheel of a crimson red Ford Explorer. He jerked back, but there was no place to go. Far too late to move, he braced for final impact.

As the roaring train ripped past his SUV a scant few yards away, he realized he was idling *parallel* to the railroad tracks. The intense pain of the train's horn still registered in his ears and his body trembled violently for a few seconds while he emerged from his deep slumber. It took him another moment to realize he still wasn't in danger of becoming track paste.

Where am I?

A light touch on his shoulder revealed creamy white, French-manicured fingers. Their owner lovely: almond-shaped eyes, perfect white teeth, and curly nutmeg hair framing a face that would make even a fairy tale princess envious. His wife, Sarah.

"Wow, babe," she laughed nervously. "I knew you were tired but you were really out there." He had been driving for a long time. She gave him a funny look. "You want me to drive the rest of the way?"

Hank's throat was so dry his tongue had swelled two sizes. When he finally managed to talk it was above a hoarse whisper. "Honey, where are we?" He wanted to scream the question at her. The whisper was all he could manage.

"Are we there yet, Daddy?"

A glance in the mirror confirmed what he already knew: five year old Annabelle sat strapped in her car-seat by a five-point retention harness originally designed for fighter pilots. Little Alex shared her mom's good looks, but had inherited *his* limited patience.

"Almost there sweetheart," Sarah answered for him. "We just have to board the train."

"But I'm so-o hungry," Alex complained.

"Have some more Goldfishes, honey," Sarah answered. Without missing a beat the box came over the seat with two quick shakes, and Alex beheld the delicious golden baked treats.

Alex was placated for now. She stared out the window with her mother's hazel eyes as she absentmindedly devoured the helpless fishes in her hand.

One year old Henry snoozed soundly in his car seat beside her. When it came to the looks department, Henry took more after his pop. Dark wavy hair, firm jaw affixed to a kind face. And dark blue eyes, somehow sweet and fierce at the same time.

Hank took this all in, but none of this answered the question that still burned in his aching head: *Where the hell am I?*

He peered through the SUV's open window. A majestic wilderness with snow-capped mountains, stitched with evergreens, sprawled out around them seemingly endless. The overcast skies and down-creeping snowline suggested winter was closing in. *This looks like the Pacific Northwest?* That didn't make sense.

The train tracks emerged from the forest in the distance, miles behind them, and then came up to a rickety but serviceable train station smack down in the middle of nowhere. The station sign read HavenPort, Alaska.

Alaska? When the hell did we decide on Alaska? I must be dreaming. We live in the desert. Two thousand miles away.

"Look Mommy, look!" Annabelle yelled wildly from her car seat. "A moose, Mommy, a moose!"

Hank turned his head and groaned at the stabbing pain in his temples. He rubbed at them mightily: If his hand weren't already there, he'd have thought he'd been stabbed on both sides of his head with an ice pick. *Must've slept wrong while I was snoozing behind the wheel.*

"Oh Hank, she's right." Sarah cooed beside him. "There's a moose in the lake over there."

Just beyond Sarah's window he could make out the moose meandering across a shallow lake.

Hank suppressed the huge urge to punch the windshield. *Why will no one answer me? Where are we?*

Sarah turned towards him. "Do you see him?" Before he could answer, she dug frantically through her mommy purse the size of a saddlebag. "Now where's my camera?" She turned back to the kids, "Alex, honey, do you know where mommy's camera is?"

This doesn't make sense. We live in Wyoming. I don't even remember deciding to come to Alaska, let alone driving here.

"There it is." Sarah took her camera from the center console compartment. Before she could snap a picture ...

WHUMP, WHUMP.

Hank jumped at the sound of a large man pounding the palm of his meaty hand on the hood of the Explorer.

"Hey pretty boy, you're holding up the line," he said in a gruff voice, "We ain't got all day." The big man was dressed in overalls and a baseball cap. His rough, heavily-pockmarked face, oversized bulbous nose, and squinty eyes loomed over Hank. He stepped to the side of the hood and motioned Hank to pull forward. An impatient driver in a rusted Ford-150 behind them laid on his horn.

"C'mon buddy," the driver shouted.

On auto-pilot, Hank shifted into drive and pulled forward. The SUV drove forward up a dirt incline ramp and onto a flatbed train car. They were one of many; all lined up behind an antique locomotive the color of charcoal. Hank put the rig in park and switched off the engine.

"We're on a train!" Alex shouted with glee.

As other cars loaded up onto the freight cars, Hank saw something strange on the train depot platform. It was a comely woman wearing horn-rimmed glasses. Unlike the people wearing layers of warm coats and hats around her, she was only wearing a long physician's lab coat. Not so strange in itself, but the white in her coat was so sharp in color, and such a shocking contrast to the drab filtered daylight, it was as though someone wearing bright colors had stepped into an old black-and-white movie. It actually hurt Hank's eyes to gaze upon it.

The disembarking passengers bustling about didn't seem to notice the strange doctor woman, and she seemed equally disinterested in them. She didn't appear to have anyplace else she needed to be. Instead, she kept staring intently at Hank. She wasn't just looking at the train or at their vehicle, only at him.

What's her problem, why is she staring at me?

He felt his eyes squint and his brow furrow, but before he could ask Sarah if she saw the strange woman, the train jostled into motion. The woman in the lab coat still studied him. Hank looked away, pressed his eyes with the palms of his hands, and then attempted to clear his vision of her by rubbing away the sleep. At this, the doctor, as he thought of her, frowned and wrote notes on her clipboard.

The back of his neck throbbed so bad he stared rigidly forward. The locomotive chugged away, leaving the depot, and the strange doctor lady, behind. The train then negotiated a bend and soon the tracks straightened again. Hank could now see their destination: a dark tunnel opening at the base of an enormous snow-capped mountain. Huge piles of shale flanked the entrance as though they were bones spewed up from those who had dared to enter the gaping mouth before. The impatient driver parked behind them turned up his radio and AC/DC's, '*I'm on the Highway to Hell*', blared over his speakers.

"Mommy, where is the train taking us?" Annabelle must have also noticed the foreboding tunnel opening for she added, "It looks scary."

You got that right.

Sarah barely heard her. She was toggling through her shots of the moose on her camera. She answered, absently, "Remember sweetie? There are no roads into town. The only way in is to load your car on the train. The three mile long tunnel is the only way in or out."

Hank opened his mouth to speak, but the vortex suddenly gobbled up the locomotive engine clanking down the tracks ahead in one enormous bite. The dozen train cars that immediately followed also vanished one-by-one into darkness.

With great effort Hank worked up the will to speak, "Sarah ... I don't want to go in there." Hank shivered uncontrollably. He found both hands clenched on the steering wheel and he could feel his feet pressing into the floorboards. As if that would do any good.

Sarah ignored him. "Look kids, here we go."

Hank glanced at a wooden sign at the tunnel's entrance. The finely crafted sign was supported by two thick tree poles. The sign had seen better days Hank thought, but he could just make out the faded white lettering.

—— o ——

Welcome to HavenPort!
Year Round Population: 492

—— o ——

Before Hank and his family were swallowed by the mouth of the tunnel completely and the darkness closed out the last of the fleeting light, Hank glimpsed a shocking image in the rearview mirror. His children's broken bodies littered the back seat and his blood-spattered wife lay dead in the seat beside him.

—BEDLAM LOST

Jack Castle